Adolessons

fIdGits

a Novel in Three Parts by

gregory r schussele

Book 1

Adolessons

This is Podunk, Illinois through the eyes and ears of the young man with no description, 1969-1976

SchussProse Publishing
Umpqua, Oregon, USA

fIdGits
Book 1
Adolessons

This is Podunk, Illinois through the eyes and ears of the young man with no description, 1969-1976

Copyright © 2011 gregory r schussele

All rights reserved. No part of this book may be used or reproduced by any means, graphic, electronic, or mechanical, including photocopying, recording, taping or by any information retrieval system without the written permission of the publisher, except in the case of brief quotations embodied in critical articles and reviews.

Original cover *January Woods* by Elizabeth Mukerji copyright © 2011. The artist reserves all rights, and any and all means of reproduction are not permitted without the written consent of the artist. Reprinted by the kind permission of Elizabeth Mukerji.
Cover design, graphics and photograph by Richard Harrig.
The author expresses deep gratitude to the monumental contributions of both.

This is a work of fiction. All of the characters, names, incidents, organizations, and dialogue in this novel are either the product of the author's imagination or are used fictitiously.

SchussProse books may be ordered through booksellers or by contacting:

SchussProse Publishing
375 Wolf Valley Dr
Umpqua, OR 97486
schussprose@gmail.com
SchussProsePublishing.yolasite.com

ISBN-13: 978-0615467450
ISBN-10: 0615467458

Printed in the United States of America
Limited First edition

To Jeff, another delayed sacrifice from the Mortgage Derivatives Scam, perpetrated by a relative handful of thieves who stole trillions and caused the near-Depression of 2008. Not a one of these treasonous, slimy scumbags has sacrificed anything for the ruin they have inflicted on millions and it appears less likely, day after day, that any ever will in the US of Apartheid.

Acts

Introduction	i
Act One End of the Sixties	1
Act Two Into the Breach	8
Act Three Staggering Through Last Rites, Part One	16
Act Four Staggering Through Last Rites, Part Two	30
Act Five Is There Life After Your Friends Leave You?	45
Act Six They Call Me the Working Man	60
Act Seven The Herald of Op. Cit and Ibid	77
Act Eight Senator, I Cannot Recall That at This Time	82
Act Nine One More Year and This Too Shall Pass	98
Act Ten Excuse Me While I Bail On Your Sorry Ass	113
Act Eleven The Summer of Irony	138
Act Twelve Welcome to Massively Higher Education	162
Act Thirteen Spring Semester, Spring Break and FLA	190
Act Fourteen Gravity	214
Act Fifteen The Great Depression	233
Act Sixteen Variable(s) Plus Constant Equals Change	260

Introduction

Editors' note: Some months ago we were approached by a distraught woman, who appeared at our offices without an appointment and demanded, or, more appropriately, begged for our help. Her husband had apparently committed suicide a few months before, though it could only be speculated from the evidence left behind; his car was found on a bridge with the engine warm but not running; his wallet with all of its contents and a note suggesting suicidal intent in his handwriting were found inside the car. However, what was missing was his body or any witnesses to what happened. No one came forward having seen the car approach or stop on the bridge, nor did anyone see him get out of the car, leap from the bridge into the frigid water below or walk away from the bridge alive. All of these missing facts pushed this woman out of desperation to ask for our help, since the insurance company refused to pay a death benefit due to a lack of definitive proof of the man's death and the courts would not declare the man to be dead. She was facing financial ruin and had sold everything of value to keep from going under, except for many document files on four separate floppy disks, which is what she brought to show us. She wanted to know if the document files, which seemed to her to be from a novel that her husband had secretly written and which she had just recently discovered and read for the first time, were worth publishing and would we buy them.

We listened to the woman describe her predicament, talk about her husband and her daughters for well over an hour, when she finally handed us the disks. We looked at the files on the disks and immediately saw that the four disks were actually two identical sets, one a copy of the other. The next revelation was that the files were not all from the same word processing program; the files with the highest numbers, which the woman advised were chapter numbers, were created with Word and were easily readable using our version of the program; the other files with the lowest numbers and one that may have been a prologue seemed to have been created with WordPerfect, based on the full filenames and some initial checking of the file makeup. When we tried to open these files with our version of Word Perfect, though, we were prompted for a password. That was why the woman was so distraught; she had no idea what the password was so she had part of a novel that no one could read. Part of a novel that can't be read means no novel, certainly not a novel that can be sold to pay off the mortgage. We liked the challenge, though, and gave her back one set of the disks, promised that we would see what we could do about the password-protected files, and, if we could open those files, read it and let her know. She thanked us for our time, hoped that she would hear from us soon, and left.

We are nothing if not resourceful. We discreetly inquired about computer encryption, seeking anyone who could crack a password-protected document, especially targeting those in and around the local university. Finally, through the proverbial friend of a friend of a friend, we were introduced to a young man who had never attended the university, having built an impressive reputation as a self-taught computer security expert while still in high school. He also had conducted several seminars and lectures at this, and other, universities, but, best of all, he was more than willing to help us. He had been very intrigued with the disappearance of the man and his wife's plight from the very first time he had heard about it and he jumped at the chance to help us.

We copied the protected files and sent him the disk. The next day he called us to let us know he had received the disk and that he was going to run a binary analysis of each file first. Not even two hours later, he called back. "Just a couple things and then I've got a question for you," he said. "First, all the files use the same password. Second, the encryption method the software vendor employs for the password is well-known and not terribly powerful. Third, the vendor also has a back-door routine to retrieve the contents of a document, but it requires the user have a licensed, registered copy of their software and there is a charge for the service; you would have to contact the vendor to proceed with that option. So, here's the question: would you like the password cracked, the document contents dumped, or do you want to proceed with the back-door routine from the vendor?"

He further explained that the vendor option would need to be followed for each and every protected file; he also didn't know of anyone who had ever used the vendor's service, though that was not to imply that the vendor's service was questionable; it only meant that he didn't know of anyone who had needed it. He could dump the contents of each

Introduction

file and retrieve every word in the correct order but he wouldn't be able to save any formatting inside the documents; that would be lost forever. He had already isolated the section of the file that contained the encrypted contents for the password; he could run a program against the encrypted contents until he got a match that would reveal the password, but it would probably take a week. Knowing the password, though, would save each document as it was created and could be used for every one of them. We decided to 'crack' the password, especially because our new security friend really wanted to pursue that option before any of the others.

"I am a human being!" was the excited introduction from the other end of the telephone less than a week later. We initially expressed our agreement that our security friend was, in fact, a human being, but with much less enthusiasm he asserted, "No, no, I just read you the first sentence of the first file in this series, or this book, if you're calling it that. It is the same password for all the files. I've gone through all of them and there doesn't appear to be anything missing, the formatting's consistent. It looks good!"

Thanks to our friend, we now had a beginning. The author's wife —we couldn't call her a widow, yet, since her husband was still legally missing—was ecstatic, and we now had a full manuscript.

After we had read it several times, we decided to publish it with no editing, to let it speak for itself. As for the mysterious title, there was nothing that any of us could discover which revealed the meaning. It appears that only one person knows the significance of these seven letters and we can assure the reader that the password for the first few chapters did not bear any relevance to the title. Unfortunately, the author is not available for comment on the title, but the following is what he left behind under that name. -Eds

I am a human being. The preceding statement is simple enough. It conjures an expectation by the reader that the writer is the same kind of being as the reader, since reading is an activity, at present, limited to one kind of being, a human being. However, reading requires a written language, and the statement above is rendered in English, thus limiting its potential exposure to those human beings capable of reading – and understanding – English, only some fraction of the whole of human beings. Because this statement is now limited to a division of human beings, it is subject to the ignorance, prejudices, misconceptions, and unreasonable, even irrational, expectations of non-English speaking human beings (assuming, of course, that all English-speaking individuals are capable of understanding all English text – a very large assumption, indeed). It wouldn't matter in the slightest what the following pages would reveal; non-English speaking human beings would still be excluded; that statement, and all subsequent statements, would still have no meaning to them. The most interesting part of this argument, to me, is the *translation*, the rendering of the English language into another language, or of any language into any other language. The first sentence in this paragraph, for instance, would be easy. Yet, I have presented the translator with a dilemma concerning the rest of this paragraph: what should be done with the references to "English" as the language used for each and every word? Does the French-speaking translator simply change every "English" to "French", which would make a meaningful connection to the French reader, but would forever change the context, perspective, and position of the English-speaking author? Worse, perhaps, does the French-speaking translator keep the "English" as the language reference, possibly leading to a lack of meaning to a French-speaking reader? Does a compromise consisting of rendering "English" to "Anglais" appeal more? From my perspective as the writer, there is no easy solution to this dilemma. Just in English, there are countless examples of books, documents, paragraphs, even sentences, where the context and meaning are forever subject to debate between two or more English-speaking readers. Ultimately, it is the reader who must be the final arbiter, especially since a motivated writer can use these devices endlessly.

Still, it is not my intention to befuddle, confuse, or place clever literary obstacles throughout this tome that cannot be easily negotiated. Far from it, this is meant to be a re-examination of the past, an honest reckoning of one life, one member of the tribe of human beings. I am reminded of human history when I state that I am a member of the tribe of human beings, since tribe usually denotes a subset of human beings, while the collective whole is often referred to as species. As I write this, however, I have come to the conclusion that when tribes possibly came into existence, it was the next great step in the evolution of human psyche; yet those thousands of years since have failed to accomplish any further evolution. This becomes clear when one accepts the notion that the concept of *tribe* has evolved instead; it can reasonably be applied to national origin, race, creed, gender, age, educational level, political persuasion, income levels, socio-economic status, language, sexual persuasion, employment, family, any division of like-minded, or like-looking, human beings. There really is no end to tribes today and there is no end to recruitment for tribes. One can go anywhere in the world and be recruited to a new tribe. And here's the best thing: no one even thinks of this activity, this human endeavor, as being 'recruited for the tribe'. The *concept* has evolved but human beings have not. I like to think that I have truly evolved, though, because I recognize tribes, and recruiting, everywhere. While it is virtually impossible to disentangle from all tribal affiliations and continue to live and be productive today, it *is* possible to act in the interests of the tribe of human beings, even when it conflicts with the interests of the current tribal affiliation. It's possible. It ain't easy.

While I claim to be a member of the tribe of human beings and am, obviously, a member of the subset of English-speaking human beings – by virtue of having to choose a language, any language, in order to communicate – I can also claim past affiliation with many other tribes. As one reads, these affiliations will be revealed and soon. I have only limited my full meaning, so far, to my language subset; when each affiliation is revealed, I already know I will lose more and more readers, for the same reasons I stated earlier. This observation allows me to state my last position before I start my recollections. The only full meaning that can be conveyed safely to all readers *must be* anonymous and contain no revelations of the writer's tribal affiliations. (As each affiliation is revealed, if the reader is instantly reminded of this diatribe on tribes, at least I will have won a very small victory). The former is impossible in an autobiography (is it possible in *any* treatise?), but I *can* remain anonymous. If I must have a name, I'll take one that is consistent with my perspective. From the universal, collectively, we are insignificant; from the mass of human beings, I am insignificant; and wherever I go, I garner practically no attention. Call me *Non Descript,* for this is the story of one human being that you *do not know.*

There's nothing of useful insight for me to recall prior to my teen years, since so little of it reflects real independent action, reaction or interaction. They may be the formative years but when a human being reaches the teen years, these are the collective moments which will mold that human being forever, with only minor deviations. My teen years also roughly corresponded to the 'seventies', so I have taken a longer view of these molding years and expanded them.

For me, the 1970s largely represent a blur of memories, a few moments of extreme lucidity, black holes where all that *was* now reside in permanent non-existence, and the general impression of disappointment and lack of achievement. When I think of "the seventies", it doesn't begin on January 1, 1970 and it doesn't end on December 31, 1979. It's not so easily linear like that; instead, it's a period of symbolism and so is not subject to the rigid parameters that typically determine a decade.

The 1970s actually began earlier than expected, on a hot, humid day in August, 1969. To be more precise it was the day after Woodstock, which was the symbolic end of "the sixties", the decade of peace and love with its accompanying contradictions of assassinations, undeclared war, horrifying riots and power blackouts and brownouts. After three days of peace and music, there came a long, slow slide downhill; unfortunately, few of us were skiing.

For most, the 1970s mercifully ended shortly after New Year's, 1980, or perhaps after the hostages were released, or when the economy picked up after the recession of 1982. I don't remember it so easily like that. Since "the seventies" symbolize a sort of stumbling about - a kind of collective voice mumbling *"Now* what the hell do we do?" - I can't conscientiously assert that *my* stumbling, mumbling, molding "seventies" were over until 1986, even though that particular year didn't strike me as being much different from the others. Just in the details, but, then, the devil's in...

While I'm now an old, fat fart, I was a shy, smart-aleck thirteen-year-old when it started. A short snort on the under side of five feet, I had wanted to run off to New York for Woodstock, but I had no car and couldn't drive anyway, had no money for other transportation, so the only real option was hitching. Somehow, I determined that, in all likelihood, a short, shy, smart-aleck from Podunk, Illinois might not make it to New York in one piece.

And then "the sixties" ended and with it the summer after seventh grade, and the semi-failed entrepreneurial experiment with a paper route - most of my customers paid their subscriptions by mail but I was notoriously lazy collecting from the others and I had to discount these receivables when I sold the route in June, 1969.

A couple of men had walked on the moon, Richard Nixon was president, the undeclared war raged on in Vietnam, the Beatles had released an all-white album, a nutball in California convinced his deranged self and followers that this all-white album was the spark to start a black insurrection - the blacks just need a little boost from these poor white people - and I had seen Jimi Hendrix on the Tonight Show when Flip Wilson was the guest host for a week. Apparently, there is some disagreement about this appearance, mostly because all the tapes of the shows that week have mysteriously disappeared. Trust me, he was on. I don't remember what songs the group played but it was Jimi and the Experience, no doubt about it.

With Jimi's climax at Woodstock one symbolic period gave way to the next and most were glad to see it go. What did we know? I still had another year in junior high - now called middle school - and there was little that I looked forward to. I was scheduled to have the same teacher for English as last year - nothing to celebrate there - and my Science teacher would be the same man who was renowned for demonstrating sodium's reaction to water by dropping a large chunk of pure sodium in a small aquarium, which promptly exploded. Sweet! Try it sometime. Be sure to remove the little fishes *first*.

    I would need a semester of art. I hated art; I couldn't draw and had no desire. Our music teacher had told me last year that I couldn't sing on key; music would sure be fun, huh? And I was sure to excel in shop class for a semester. I'm being facetious and sarcastic. Get used to it. Facetiousness and sarcasm will permeate this recollection. It's probable that I couldn't live without facetiousness and sarcasm, which, I'm sure, aggravates many acquaintances to no end. You too? In that case, put down this dangerous composition and do something safer, like watch TV.

    My good friend Charlie would help to make it all bearable. He had been the new kid in fifth grade, already sitting in a front-row seat in our home room. I never sat in the front row but there was something about the new kid so I took the seat next to him. Thus began our reign of several years as our class' kings of comedy; actually Charlie was the king and I was the irreverent archdeacon. We were the Marx brothers minus two; sometimes like Martin and Lewis, although neither of us was as goofy and slapstick as Lewis. No we were urbanely witty and stingingly sarcastic like Groucho and Chico. In fact Charlie could do Groucho to perfection when he was into impressions and I was a dead-on Chico; I could do Harpo, too, when I had a horn, though I couldn't whistle like he did. We were the undisputed heavyweight champions with little regard for the challengers: James would occasionally get in some good digs but he was too safe; David thought he was funny but he also thought he was cool and suave and a gift to humanity, he just really never let up; Jim could get up there but he was starting to drift, to mentally go places that few, if any, could follow or want to; J.T. was crude and insecure and, as such, was the class bully and becoming more so; Dallas was content as the athlete, proud, confident, but with no ambition to compete for the throne of humor; and Rick was the scholar, serious and academic, most likely to drive the discussion of English grammar, least likely to utter a pun. You've noticed that no girl's name has been mentioned. That's because in "the sixties" girls were rarely class clowns. Sure, there were a few girls in our class who could be incredibly funny but none could regularly deliver those outbursts that generated raucous laughter from the majority of classmates. Comedic outbursts from girls just didn't happen, except from maybe Carol, whose specialty in humor could be summed up in two words: utter disdain. She had no respect for anyone or anything except for those who also had no respect; sometimes she would resort to simple insults, right in class. For a girl Carol had balls.

    The family had changed a bit although you couldn't really tell by looking at the immediate family. Mom was still the same but after all these years it's not easy for me to talk or write about her; early in "the sixties" she had spent a month of forced hospitalization filled with physical and psychological/psychiatric tests which had most notably resulted in a varying number of prescription drugs - this hospitalization would play a significant role in her medical care in the last months of her life. Dad was making strides in the community earning more and more local prestige and honor; ironically, it would all be forgotten or dismissed barely twenty-five years later. Being a leading independent CPA, he was still the absentee father from January through April every year.

    My older brother, Mike, had graduated from a small college in northern Illinois, having started his collegiate career at West Point; I'll always remember the drive to his graduation, listening to the radio the day after Robert Kennedy was murdered. Mike was already making his mark in the local scene - being sued for libel for stories published in an independent newspaper will do that - little of it positive. While I can't remember when the suit was filed, in my mind I lump it in with the symbolic period of "the sixties". I also was the one "served", not Mike, and this is how it happened. The doorbell rang in the afternoon. I answered the door. A burly, buzz-cut stranger stood on the doorstep with an envelope partially concealed at his side. "Is this the home of Michael Descript?" asked the stranger, who was wearing typical business attire. "Yes," I replied. He thrust the envelope to me and said, "This is for him and consider him served." I took the envelope and the stranger immediately turned and walked away. I asked, "What is this?" Without turning back or slowing, I heard "He'll know what it is." What professionalism. Only in Podunk, Illinois could a court clerk "serve" a court summons to the minor brother of the defendant, but, as it turned out, that very fact would diminish the plaintiff's case somewhat. Jeff, the youngest by two years, was getting fatter and perhaps more obnoxious, if that was possible. With few friends and a personality as a viable explanation, this eleven-year-old was not a happy camper. Sixth grade would put him in the same school that I attended but it was something I would not announce or make known. We would rarely see each other in school and would spend about the same amount of time together out of school.

Introduction

So the change was not in the immediate or, using a term popular then, the nuclear family, and my mother's parents were still living only a mile and a half away, doing fine, Grampa still working as the janitor at Dad's building. The change was on Dad's side. There would be no more trips to Havana, Illinois to visit the grandparents since Granma Descript had passed away during the summer. It was not unexpected as she had been slowly fading for close to a year when her heart finally gave out. Aunts Jeanne and Mary Beth and older cousins had taken turns staying with Dad's parents during those last few months when she laid down on the couch because she was in too much pain to make it to the bedroom and she never woke up again. The funeral was so uneventful I don't remember it much, except that my hair was the longest of any of the males in attendance; this certainly created a large amount of attention, which I handled with grace and poise, though my impeccable manners left the older attendees unexpectedly pleased - long hair on males carried a certain expectation at that time. The four children and the families were so amicable about any estate distribution that there was hardly any discussion, let alone fights about it. The house was sold in a few months with the proceeds deposited for Grampa Descript, who then spent the next four plus years as a human ping-pong ball, spending winters with Aunt Mary Beth in California, then a few weeks with us, after which we would drive to Indiana to meet Aunt Jeanne, who would keep him for the summer, meet us in Indiana in the fall, and a few weeks later we would put him on a plane in St. Louis bound for San Diego. There would be no more Thanksgiving or Christmas dinners and get-togethers, but I really wasn't going to miss that. At thirteen I was getting tired of having to sit at the "children's table", for which destiny would require me to do one more time. I never forgot the "children's table", the lack of status it represented, and I have practically no interaction with any of my relatives on either side, possibly because of it. It especially galled me when I remember the many lavish dinners we would have at Dad's parents' and everyone would sit at the main table; but if any of the other families - who all lived out of state - were there, out came the "children's table". Hey, baby-boomers, try this at the next big family get-together you host: take the worst table and call it the "old people's table" and make all the old family members sit there for meals. And don't forget the rules at the "old people's table": no shouting, no drooling, no complaining, no whining, be thankful for this moment for you could be eating your meal at the hotel. Fuck the "children's table".

On our block, our immediate neighbors were the same, which was nothing to shout about. While the Gannons were welcome - with

Larry Jeff's age, Rich my age, and one-year older Chuck - as always, and good for regular incidents of family drama and comedy, we could do without the Marvins, a middle-aged couple with no children who had moved in a few years before when the elderly, and kindly, Raines' couple had moved and sold their house. They had made no secret of their dislike for children - making their move to a house surrounded on all sides by teenage children unfathomable - and had made continuing efforts to isolate their fortress from all potential trespassers. The deeds in our neighborhood prohibited construction of fences unless the homeowner elected to have the property come under the city's jurisdiction, with all their rules, regulation and property tax assessments. This usually meant an increase in property taxes; I'm sure if there was anything the Marvins disliked more than children it was taxes. So out came bush after bush after bush until our centerfield had disappeared behind an unplayable growth of foliage. But we adapted, choosing a whiffle ball, designating clearly defined foul territory and a home run was hit over the house. Fortunately, the Marvins were home-bodies and not outdoors people so confrontations were few and that was fine with me. Most confrontations involved Jeff, our young rebel without a cause.

   The rest of our neck of West Hickory Dale had also witnessed some change in the last few years before "the seventies" began. Three doors down and across the street, the Sikorskis had replaced a family whose name I cannot recall, bringing a girl about Jeff's age and a young boy. Next door and closer, the Garbers and their three children had replaced the Fabriggias and their three children, the Fabriggias being the franchise owners of the local Coast to Coast Hardware stores. Across the street from Garber were the Olivets and their only child, a boy, who had replaced the Colliers and their three children; the Colliers were good friends of our family, though after they moved we hardly saw or talked to the boys who were the same age as Jeff and me. Four doors down on our side were now the Ivansons and their two boys, the youngest my age - they replaced another elderly couple of whom I remember vaguely and whose back yard was right next to the telephone company's switching office. This office had its entrance off of Hickory Dale Road, the straight access road that connected West Reservoir Drive with Sixth Street, the main drag into or out of town from the interstate highway, which was still more like Route 66 than Interstate 55. Hickory Dale Road was where our back yards ended; the other side of West Hickory Dale was bordered by a finger of the reservoir lake, except at the end, the intersection of West Hickory and Hickory Dale Road; those last two houses on the far side were bordered by woods.

The Greins, who lived at the corner of that intersection on the far side, owned a German Shepard, feared throughout the neighborhood by humans and dogs alike, except our dachshund, Cinderella, or Cindy, as we called her. For her canine courage she earned the loss of a chunk of skin and flesh from the top of her back and a quick trip to the vet; the Greins discovered that the rest of the neighborhood had no appreciation for their dog, which was likely to be shot the next time it was out wandering around. It wasn't that they let the dog loose; the Greins' children were all girls and they loved that dog and liked to take it out for walks but it was simply too much for even the oldest girl to control. After Cindy's injury the German Shepard was never loose again and only the father walked that dog and not often.

Cindy had finally died the year before after twelve years and one escapade where she disappeared for four weeks. One night I sat in the den - which we had converted from an open porch connecting to the garage to an enclosed extension to the house - watching TV when I heard a scratch and a faint whine coming from the door to the garage. When I opened the door, there was our black dachshund, not looking too bad except for the fish hook through her nose. No one remembers seeing her over those four weeks and no one knows how she got a fish hook through her nose, but we were glad she was back. Maybe she was suffering from canine Alzheimer's disease. She died in her sleep shortly after and was soon replaced by two dogs, siblings of a terrier mix, one brown and one black, Coco and Toto, respectively. Toto didn't live very long, never seeing his first birthday. We called Hickory Dale Road the back street, but, because it was an access road, it had its share of traffic, with some vehicles flying down an essentially residential street at sixty or seventy miles an hour. Toto became just one more animal victim of this street's relentless traffic; having been unseen all day, someone told me they thought they saw a dog in the ditch on the other side of the back street. I walked across the street and saw him lying lifeless in the ditch, blood under and from his nose. I picked him up and we buried him in the yard next to Cindy. In the back yard of our old house are buried two dogs, of which I'm certain all subsequent owners of that house are not aware. I would also imagine that this information would not generally be conveyed by the realtor, either, although I can hear it now. "And if you decide to dig in the far eastern corner of the back lot, the previous owners have asked that you remove the two dog skeletons carefully and properly and respectfully re-bury them..." Coco, incidentally, was to live quite a few years, possibly due to the fact that she would never venture into the back street without human company.

The biggest accomplishment completed in our town prior to "the seventies" was the re-dedication of the old statehouse downtown. At the time it was quite controversial, requiring the stone-by-stone dismantling of the entire building, excavation of the entire square down to about forty feet, construction of two underground parking levels, and the re-building, stone-by-original stone, of the statehouse. The north and south streets, Washington and Adams, respectively, were closed and paved with park-style brick for pedestrian congregation to give the area an old-time, square-like feel. It was too little too late for downtown business revitalization, though, as Penney, Woolworth and K-mart had already left the downtown area, never to return.

The Big Prick on the Prairie, the thirty-story, round Ramada, had been completed and was open for business just a block east of the square. The airport was completing its expansion and modernization to make Podunk an easier tourist destination and business travel more convenient. Dad had served on the board and his accounting firm had regularly provided services; several times I was allowed into the control tower. Southeast High School had opened two years prior, replacing Findlay High, which would eventually be retired as an educational building altogether. Southeast was unique with its mound built right up to the building on three sides and windows only on the second, top floor of the classroom area and only on the north side; it also had a sunken basketball court and plans were to add a separate pool at the end of the student parking lot. That's where I would go to school next year.

Being the state capitol Podunk was famous for politicians but less well-known for police and law enforcement agencies. Think I'm kidding about the police? At any time you could conceivably cross the path of officers from any of the following so count these: City of Podunk Police, County Sheriff, Podunk Park Police, Illinois State Troopers, Secretary of State Police, Illinois Department of Conservation Police, U.S. Department of the Interior Police, U.S. Marshals, Federal Bureau of Investigation, Illinois Bureau of Investigation, and the venerable Reservoir Police, whose average age was probably sixty as they consisted almost entirely of retired city and county officers. That's eleven police agencies! The Drug Enforcement Agency had yet to be created or I would have included them, too, as they have officers in Podunk now. I'm sure I've missed one or two or more smaller, perhaps divisional officers with perhaps some small jurisdiction, but any of the former could arrest any citizen under the appropriate circumstances. I don't know what you might be thinking now as you read this but...that's a *lot* of police for a town with a population that didn't even top 100,000.

As for Illinois politicians, they're the stuff of legends. Lincoln, Douglas, Stratton, Dirksen, Adlai Stevenson had all made their mark, but the talk was still loud about Paul Powell and his shoebox filled with hundreds of thousands of dollars in cash. What most people did not realize was the cache of gifts and money discovered in his "permanent" room at the Hotel St. Nick, which topped the shoebox discovery considerably. Ogilvie was now heading a Republican gubernatorial administration, having succeeded Kerner, who would soon chair the national Kerner Commission. Later, he would be the target of a bribery and corruption scandal which would leave him convicted and humiliated; he would never recover, slowly deteriorating until his death in "the eighties", his reputation as a fair, popular and very effective governor tarnished forever. That is unfortunate because he was one of the best governors Illinois ever had, but that's politics in this state. That's a sentence that's rare for me, since I aspire to be completely apolitical; some day, I may cast my write-in votes during a Presidential election on the straight Cartoon Animal ticket, carried by the venerable Heckyl and Jeckyl, crows of a decidedly sarcastic bent; if you remember Heckyl and Jeckyl, you're pushing fifty, bud, so take a moment now to check your prostate if you're a man, your breasts if you're a woman. Go ahead. I'll wait. I'm not going anywhere. That represents my public service announcement for this book and I just checked mine; can you figure out yet what body parts I was just fondling?

That sets the stage. You're stuck in Podunk, Illinois, in August, 1969. I'm thirteen, going on forty-seven. However, I am about to diverge off on another tangent, just to aggravate you. I'd rather write, "and now for something completely different", but the surviving members of Monty Python's Flying Circus would probably sue me for copyright infringement. Oh, wait! Silly me! I just *did* write it. Oh, well, sorry gents. Good luck in trying to "serve" someone as nondescript as me. Besides, I am now "on the lamb". Giddyup, there, my trusty sheep! Yeehaw!

The Tree of Solitary Magnificence

In a small meadow atop the gentle crown in the center, there stood a solitary tree of such magnificence that all who saw it were transfixed by its symmetry, balance, and thick leaf cover. Few had seen it, though, as the meadow was far from the crowds and difficult to reach. Fewer still had seen it during winter, when the starkness of the season left its surroundings lean and barren, yet the tree stood tall, its many branches, twisted and swaying with the breeze, now stripped clean of its summer cover, still conveyed an essence of undying strength. A few months later, the meadow would renew and the tree would sprout its thick leaf cover, and those who stumbled upon the sight would stare in open wonder.

After many years, Rose pushed through the brush and forest and stepped into the clearing and gazed upon the sight for the first time. She had been contemplating a new life, and the scene of the meadow, with its smattering of wildflowers and tall grass, dominated by the single, huge tree, convinced her to make that life in the clearing. Even when she stepped up close to the tree and circled it - noting its large scars, the area where the bark had stripped away and the soft, exposed wood had been forced to harden, the insects that crawled all over it at will, the many branches torn and re-born in garish, awkward angles – she remained undeterred. She built a house way off to one side so that the scene would be as unchanged as possible and loved her moments in the meadow.

Over time she ventured close to the tree less and less while the occasional hiker would meander into the clearing and step closely and carefully to the tree in awe. Eventually, Rose built a fence completely around the meadow and her house to make it more difficult for wanderers to enter the meadow. She succeeded in dissuading others from visiting the meadow but it also had the curious effect of reducing visits from friends and help, leaving her to keep up the meadow herself. She found that the work became more and more tedious and the meadow's appearance seemed to detract, though Rose didn't seem to mind. One day, she decided she needed to get away to visit friends and family, so she left but made no arrangements with anyone to look after the meadow and its magnificent tree. When she returned several months later, the meadow was in great disarray; she was shocked, though, to see that the tree was gone, replaced by a huge hole in the gentle crown of the clearing.

Months passed while Rose sat in her house and dwelled on the loss of her tree. An acquaintance stopped by to check on her and mentioned that there was a tree just like hers that had suddenly appeared in another clearing several miles away. Hearing this, Rose decided to see this new tree herself and at the next opportunity hiked the several miles, following her acquaintance's directions. When she arrived, she was stunned at the similarity of this clearing with what hers used to be, a meadow with flowers dotting the tall grass and a tree of solitary magnificence atop a gentle crown at the center. To one side was a house, too. She stepped to the house and knocked on the door. Garland answered the door and, when Rose explained that she was just visiting her neighbor, he asked her inside, where they talked for hours over coffee and cake. Rose commented on the beauty of the meadow, and its tree, and Garland escorted her out, where she got close to the tree and could tell from its distinctive scars and numerous flaws that it was, indeed, the tree from her meadow. She left disheartened.

Still, she could not resist returning to the meadow where Garland served as its caretaker. She noted with curiosity when he planted beds of flowers throughout the meadow. Surely, this would keep the tree in place, she thought. When he built a fence around the meadow, though, she was alarmed and believed it to be a simple matter of time before the tree would life its roots and transplant itself to yet another, more promising, meadow. After several more trips, during which she would discover the tree still in place, she concluded that it must be the open, unlocked gate in the fence allowing all visitors into the meadow which must be keeping the tree in its settled state. She did notice that a few of the branches had been damaged and were left to dangle and wither, as though care would not be forthcoming except from the tree itself.

A little while later, some friends dropped in on Rose, and during the usual conversation of the news of the day, they told her that the tree in Garland's meadow had disappeared. Shocked and confused, at her earliest opportunity, she ventured to Garland's meadow to see for herself. Once she arrived, she could see the meadow looked more beautiful than ever, with its colorful and varied flora, but the hole on the gentle crown at its center demanded not to be ignored. When Garland answered the knock on his door, he eventually confided to Rose that he had been away for several weeks and the tree was gone upon his return.

"Surely, you put in much time and care in this meadow," Rose assured him. "Its beauty is stunning; and the gate is always unlocked so that all can experience and appreciate it. You must, at least, have many fond memories of sitting under the tree soaking up the calm serenity of this meadow."

"I never really liked to sit under the tree or get close to it," Garland replied. "In all honesty, that tree was very imposing to me. I preferred to view and appreciate its majesty in the whole, from afar, such as looking at it from this window." He glanced out the window, now displaying the hole where the tree had stood just weeks before.

No one has seen the tree since, though there are only a few who could possibly recognize it. The telltale signs of its sudden appearance, though – a tree of solitary magnificence arriving seemingly overnight in some barren meadow on its gentle crown in the center and to the delight of the meadow's caretaker – have never been reported since. Perhaps, the tree returned to its origin and rejoined its fellow trees in a forest where its magnificence would no longer be so solitary. That is what some believe, that the tree was never destined to stand over some place where it could never be truly appreciated, truly accepted, truly cared for. Others, however, believe that more sinister motives are waiting to be discovered. They cite the obvious fact that no one has *ever* seen a tree lift up its roots and move away. Despite these disagreements, there is no one on any side who disputes the one truth: there was a tree of solitary magnificence, which is now gone forever.

Act One
End of the Sixties

Shootin' the tube: the greatest craze in water recreation, preceding water parks (and their sterility, which is not necessarily a bad thing) by many years. It was quite illegal as we were trespassing on city property, posted as such with a gate strung between two posts snuggled up to the edge of the woods and padlocked across the dirt entrance, though the gate was at least fifty yards from Hickory Dale Road. We stepped around the posts or climbed over or under the gate and spent many afternoons that summer and early fall in wet delight; we never worried about discovery since hardly anyone ever checked the place and we couldn't be seen from the road. Dad once discovered us there and threw a huge fit, one I hadn't witnessed in years. I of course had to leave immediately and listen to him plead, cajole, warn and threaten: it was dangerous and unsupervised; anyone could come back there and hurt any or all of us; I'd get the licking of my life if I was ever caught there again; I could break any number of bones or cut myself badly, being completely at the mercy of my 'friends', who, at the very least, would have to run perhaps half a mile just to find someone to call an ambulance; and who knows what kinds of parasites and disease-rendering animals and germs could be thriving in there. That encounter left me quite hesitant to go tubin' for, oh, about a week.

"I'm back."
"Your daddy was pretty pissed."
"Yeah, did your daddy spank you?"
"Can we expect a visit from dear old dad today?"
"Jeff ratted on me but that won't happen again. Cumon, let's ride the wave!"

It was really the last part that made me wonder how safe swimming in the hole was. Maybe something was lurking there, waiting for the right moment, the golden opportunity to strike. Oh, well, no matter, because we spent many days down at the hole, swimming and shootin' the tube and no one ever got sick; we had our share of cuts and bruises, which was to be expected, yet no mysterious ailments. Perhaps we grew up in a dirtier world with many dogs, cats and other pets, with the cornfield across the back street and the woods just yards from our homes, and all of this strengthened our immune systems. I only offer this as an explanation because I certainly don't know; today kids suffer and/or die from disease contracted from swimming holes. Maybe kids have always been suffering and/or dying from disease contracted from swimming holes, but it wasn't making the evening news when we were growing up. I know one thing: we never drank the water. We may have been flirting with untold disaster but we weren't stupid.

To understand what the tube was - and still is, with a great deal more added security - you have to know the local topology, the lay of the land so to speak, and the obstacles to this topology. Many, many years ago as the railroads expanded all over the land, a rail line was proposed, which would run from the south up to Podunk on its east side and eventually merge just north of town with the lines running all the way to Chicago. A few miles from town lay a relatively flat stretch of land with creeks meandering, which was usually dry until an extended period of rain would render the entire area wet and mushy and flooded for miles in any direction. When this happened it could take months for the land to dry out, and it was through this stretch that the proposed rail line would run. To build a rail line that could be out of commission for months at a time was not a practical idea; to avoid running the line through what could be a flooded plain, they simply built a trestle some twelve to fifteen feet high above the rest of the land over a distance of some five or six miles. On this trestle they laid the ties and then the rails over them. Of course, they had to accommodate the natural drainage of the land - or they would permanently flood the land west of the trestle - so in several places they connected huge concrete pipes, three feet in diameter, before covering them by the trestle, which is what they did at the creek near Hickory Dale Road leading to the Illini River, before they built the reservoir. After years of flood water through the pipes, the discharge side had been gouged into a small pond about thirty feet long, twenty feet wide and eight feet deep in the center. This was the swimming hole but shootin' the tube started on the other side of the tracks.

After a good rain a few of the neighbors or some of our friends from Reservoirtown, an unincorporated section about a mile and a half away, would plan to meet at a certain time at 'the hole' for a little tube-shootin'. We'd walk down to the dirt road entrance, check for traffic or spying eyes, and dash to the gate when we felt reasonably unseen and could now meander to 'the hole'. We checked the water for sufficient discharge; if it was too low, we would just swim; if it was roaring, we climbed up the trestle, usually on the north side where the path was well-worn, step over the tracks and shimmy down the opposite side to the banks above the creek on either side. On these banks was plenty of room for as many as ten people to stand comfortably; here we would decide everybody's order, which was easy for everyone to agree on when we first started shootin' the tube. Using this method didn't diminish or improve the experience, since everyone from first to last had more or less the same ride. We were just organizing ourselves. We would jump into the creek, the first would stand before the pipe opening, the second behind him, and so on. When everyone was ready, the first would grasp the top of the pipe and swing feet first into the pipe, laying as flat as possible so the water could carry better, sometimes pushing up from the bottom with his hands and lift his butt up to avoid bumping the first connection. Once the first one cleared the first section, the second would repeat the process until everyone was in; if there were six of us and we were efficient, all six of us could be in the pipe before the first one hit 'the hole'.

    Shootin' the tube for the best ride required knowledge of the pipe sections' various pitches. The first section of pipe is relatively flat; the water is deepest here than anywhere else in the tube and often has little carry so one would typically push off the bottom with one's hands two or three times and lift the butt to clear the first connection. From the second section until the last three sections, the pitch was consistent, perhaps three to five degrees; beginning with the second section, the water would now carry one. Still, the best ride required concentration as one approached the next connection, because one would arch the back crossing the connection or one's butt would bump it. The next two sections - getting near the end now - dropped the pitch even more, so that the last of these two sections was pointing downhill as much as ten degrees; if the water flow was adequate, one was propelled over these connections without any need to arch one's back. The last section was the most appropriate climax, with a pitch easily double that of the previous section; it had to be at least twenty degrees and twenty-five wouldn't surprise me, because when one reached the last section, stopping was not an option; one could be expelled from the tube at twenty miles per hour, easily, and the power of the discharging water behind one would send one to the opposite end of the pond in five seconds or less. Was it a rush? Re-read this last paragraph very carefully and emphasize your visualization powers;

what do you think?

    Necessity is the mother of invention and as the summer progressed it was becoming necessary to devise another method to 'manufacture' a ride besides depending only on nature; hard rains were fewer and the hotter temperatures evaporated the water more quickly. Somebody, one of our Reservoirtown buds as I recall, came up with the idea of using a board to clog the pipe opening to back up the water in the creek; when the water reached the top of the pipe, we would pull the board up and away from the pipe, discarding it on the bank above the creek, and 'manufacture' enough temporary water flow to make a decent ride, especially for the first two people. Soon, there was half of a four-by-eight, three-quarter-inch plywood board resting on the edge above the creek, our invention carried by two guys over a mile and a half. Now, however, order became a contentious matter. Fortunately, democracy would prevail, because once the debate was settled as to who would be first and second on the *first* ride, rotation took precedence; for the *next* ride, third through sixth moved up while first and second moved back. The rotations weren't always consistent but invariably everyone got a ride in first and a ride in last. The ideal number for total shooters was six; after six the ride could be very poor, even dangerous. With six the first and second didn't even touch the board; they stood before the board, one behind the other, ready to swing into the pipe once the board was cleared. Fifth and sixth held onto the board until it could be safely discarded, and third and fourth helped lift the board until it cleared the water, swinging into the pipe once fifth and sixth had secure command of the board. It was teamwork at its finest with nary a mishap; and it was eerie watching the board placed before the opening and the creek rising up along the banks; one passed the minutes watching the creek rise one, two, three feet as far back as its meandering path was visible and trying to imagine how much water - and force - was being held back by three-quarters of an inch of wood.

    Two events remain fresh in my mind. One day, after a hard rain had cleared early in the morning, several of us walked down to 'the hole', having heard a rumor that something had happened to the board. While some of us confirmed that the board was now reduced to a couple of small pieces wedged between the pipe and embankment, another had maneuvered around the pond's edge to lay on the top of the discharge pipe and gaze into it; he thought that the water flow near the end wasn't as smooth as it should be and there was probably debris stuck inside. The water was flowing at a good pace and I volunteered to go in and try to clear the debris or at least discover where it was. There were some sticks in the first section, which I passed back to the others, but I made the mistake of not trying to slow my pace enough by pushing my feet against the wall until I got to the last three sections and spotted the debris. Two seconds later my right leg was pinned under the two large pieces of the board, while my body was pushed forward; I had enough control to twist my leg so that I could bend it at the knee - so I wouldn't break my leg - and I tried to pull the debris loose. I got some of the miscellaneous sticks free but my weight on the boards worked against me, so I struggled until I pulled my leg out and slid head first out the last section and a half into the pond. Limping back to the starting side, I filled Chuck in on the situation; he carefully braked himself by pushing his feet hard against the tube walls until he reached the obstruction, and smashed, pushed and threw it out of the tube. We spent the rest of the afternoon gleefully shootin'.

Others have claimed to be first but they're mistaken. My dog, Coco, was the first to shoot the tube, from beginning to end. And she had the ripped paw pads to prove it. She followed us to 'the hole' one day and climbed up the railroad trestle to the other side. She didn't seem the least bit intimidated by the rush of water or the foreboding dark of the tube; after I had shot through twice and had climbed back to see her tale wagging with excitement, I induced her to get in the water, which she promptly did. I tried to hold her above the concrete bottom of the tube, unsuccessfully, as we slid through the opening and were propelled to the exit. I let her go when we splashed into the pond and she paddled out and danced around me, but she wouldn't climb back to the starting side and I didn't discover why until we were readying to leave. She seemed to be limping so I sat down and urged her to come to me. When I looked at the bottom of her paws, I was shocked to see that most of the pads on her paws were torn away, revealing very tender tissue; they weren't actively bleeding but I knew they must hurt. I carried her back home and we nursed her for about a week until they healed. I never took her through it again, though there was never another chance; she never followed us a second time. Since I don't recall anyone describing the same outcome when anyone bragged about their dog, I'm sure there was not another dog that went first. Most dogs would be able to reach the concrete bottom - Coco, after all, was only about twenty inches tall - and their natural inclination would be to stretch to touch the bottom for control. The speed of those paws passing over the rough surface of the bottom would easily tear the pads of almost any dog that went through.

Summer nearing the end meant back to school, back to Thomas Jefferson Middle School, more precisely, and back to the shit that invariably accompanied such a return. I know what you're thinking; you're remembering how awkward and boring and pointless school seemed, all of it, perhaps. But what *I* mean by *return* is that short period, near the end of summer and beginning of autumn, when I would be subjected to hay fever, an allergic reaction mostly to weed pollen; and that period, from middle of August to the first freeze, was true misery. Medication for it was inadequate, which is a mild way of saying that it had no effect on the worst days. My nose could run ceaselessly. I was embarrassed to carry much tissue to school because I could go thru mountains in short order and I would have to get up from my desk and dump them frequently into the trash - no way I was doing that - so I swallowed it; this would, of course, aggravate my throat and initiate a persistent cough; and if my nose was running full-tilt I frequently would wipe it on my sleeve, which would eventually stain them permanently. Freaked out yet? If you are - and you should if you have *any* imagination - now you have a pretty good idea what it was like to sit in a classroom with me for the first two months of school; and if you reverse your point of view, you might gather a sense of the anguish and personal torment I suffered, above and beyond the physical misery. What an impression I could make on a new kid! And every time I go back to school, it always starts at the end of August; allergic reaction and school are psychologically locked together in my perception. I hated that return, yet I always kicked ass in school. For me, school was not awkward and boring and pointless; it was a challenge I could easily meet. Learning is a process that ends at the moment of death.

Eighth grade was going to be more of the same. We would have Mrs. G again for English and social studies. Oh, joy! She had promised hot and heavy sentence diagramming; it was heavy alright. More science was in store but not with Mr. B - bummer. Art? I couldn't draw worth crap and, worse, I had no motivation to do so. I did produce the masterpiece, *First Church of the Nazarene*, which is still renowned today: a triangle with "First Church of the Nazarene" written at the top of the triangle. Many have asked, is it a real church? Absolutely, and accurately depicted if I say so myself. Good luck finding it, though - you'll need it.

Math would be a piece of cake and it wouldn't matter who was teaching it. Physical education would produce a record volleyball team, with Dave, Louie - a guy from our previous school who was only in our PE classes - and myself forming an unbeatable team; literally, we never lost a game. It was only for the class, though; the school district didn't have organized volleyball then. Last and definitely least: shop class. Who can forget the pure exhilaration that comes from building your very own knick-knack box? I forgot. Charlie and I built it, obviously crooked, but somehow we didn't understand that we each had to turn in a knick-knack box. No matter. Our teacher generously split our grade; it was worth a B, so D for both. Woodworking, we could see, was not going to be a skill worth developing.

That was the study line-up. Is your excitement building? Has it peeked? Or did it fizzle out altogether before it got started. Yeah, me too, then and now, so Charlie and I re-acquired our thrones of comedy and the students forged onward.

Forward we marched, 'trudging through the tundra, mile after mile...until we reached...Saint Alfonso's Pancake Breakfast...where I stole the mar-jur-een...' Thus, triggering a lawsuit from Moon and Dweesil, for whom I provide the following helpful information: please enter at the rear of the line, now forming to your right. Be prepared to secure full asset seizure, now estimated at a whopping thirty-nine cents but falling rapidly.

August fell and September. The first freeze passed in October and with it my allergic susceptibilities, freeing me to be more obnoxious and daring. Time to catch up. We ventured into November, then past Thanksgiving, and into December. Studying became less focused the closer we came to Christmas, 1969, until, finally, the break for Christmas and New Year's was upon us. We scattered, all of us, to our respective home fronts for the holidays and counted the time remaining. We were young and stayed up late the last night of the sixties and when the decade turned we lit off some firecrackers; the end of the sixties was behind us, and no one, not a single person anywhere, could have predicted how ironic the 'hopeful expectation' of the end of the 'turbulent decade' would instead yield the most deadly and tumultuous year ever...

Act Two
Into the Breach

Goodbye to the sixties and good riddance. Goodbye to the injustice, the oppression, the exposed prejudice, and good riddance. There was promise, eagerness to solve the evils exposed, to resolve the dilemmas of the day. Those in power promised to end the war; promised to serve and protect with more tolerance; promised to be more open and democratic; promised to make workers' lives more secure, safe, affordable and wholesome. And, we, the young, promised to live in peace and co-operation. Everyone made promises, for what they were worth. More than thirty years later, you be the judge of their worth.

Out here in the fields we had been slow to adopt change, or, more accurately, slower to experience the depth of the change moving over the country and the world. We had a dress code at the middle school, which stipulated hair length for boys, but at the high school, less than a year away, there would be no such enforcement. We just had to get through the next five months...

And I did, though not necessarily in peace and co-operation. The first month was not yet complete when Mrs. G, our English/social studies teacher, stated that she wouldn't be surprised if the individuals who broke into the school and set the stage curtain on fire over the weekend were students from her class; as she said this she looked only at Charlie and me. We confronted her as to her meaning; she insisted that we knew who she was talking about. Up we stood, announcing that we would protest this condemnation to the principal; we didn't have to sit there and just take it. We expected no satisfaction other than that we would be skipping class with no penalty. Charlie kept at it, though, and the vice principal promised to speak with Mrs. G. It was one promise from that year kept and Mrs. G asked us to stay behind the following day and apologized for any misunderstanding we may have derived from her speech.

At my young age it seemed like a victory, but the accusation had been made in public, the apology in private.

As the boredom of unexciting studies coupled with the relentless cold gray of the typical Midwestern late winter laid its crushing weight upon me, a sudden burst of warmth rolled across the plains for a week. Our science teacher decided to conduct a class outside, after which I refused to return to school, having climbed a tree. Eventually I would receive three 'swats' from a paddle; days later I would call one of the music teachers 'Milo' and receive four more swats, or seven for the week. It was the first and last time I would be so punished, but gone was my cooperation, replaced instead by low-lying reluctance.

Soon after, peace fell, too. JT the bully pushed someone too far, this time Dave, who had become much taller and quicker than JT, though certainly not any bulkier. But Dave quickly put JT to the test, shouting, "Let's go right now, fat boy! Put up or shut up!" All of us being outdoors, Dave clenched his fists and lunged at JT; JT stepped back, declining the challenge. "That's what I thought!" exclaimed Dave, as he scanned the faces of those in the circle. Then he shoved his arm out and pointed his finger at JT, warning, "Your days of pushin' everybody around is OVER. The next time you mess with *any* of us, I'll come an' kick the *shit* outta you!" JT said nothing; he didn't even turn around. He simply stepped backward, reaching for the door handle; when he found it, he opened the door, stepped through it and walked out of our sight. It *was* over. It was in his face - not a smile, not petrification, just lost. Dave never became a bully and for that day, at least, he was the king, but he never became someone you could trust, either. As I think about it, though, all of us have our failings and maybe Dave's were a little too obvious. I suppose all of us have interacted with someone who has found us less than trustworthy in the end. It's that most of us refuse to admit it.

Spring arrived and the days got longer, sometimes gray, sometimes sunny, some days warm, then cold, dry, then wet. March gave way to April and April faded into May. I'm sure I learned knowledge here and there but the intervening years have obscured these educational triumphs - the Kalahari Bushmen stick out, for some reason. The More Academically Able or MAA program was reaching its conclusion, whatever that may be, as it would not be labeled as such for our high school careers.

Girls were definitely becoming an attraction, the topics of our male conversations more often than not. Vickie was fine, as usual, and Ginger had filled out quite nicely. The usual claptrap followed the name of any of the girls; boys boasting of what they could do for her or her or her; how nice it could be if various articles of clothing would just pop off without warning, or, maybe, with a little help. Hormones were beginning to rage when May, 1970 lazily rolled into the present, but less than a week into it, a different kind of rage captured the nation's attention.

At the end of one particular day in May, four lifeless bodies lay scattered in various areas over the grounds of a small college in Ohio, shot to death by members of the state's National Guard. All were students of the college; ironically, one was an active member of the college's Reserve Officers Training Corps, or ROTC. An impromptu protest over the war scared someone enough to call in the state's 'regulated militia' (?), thus setting the wheels of destiny in motion. I guess the protesters forgot to tell each other one of my favorite sayings, "Cheese it! It's the cops!" Rage apparently influenced some of the protesters, because some started throwing rocks at the guardsmen. It was eventually returned by rage from some of the guardsmen, probably mixed with a good dose of fear and paranoia; triggers were pulled on guns, some kids were wounded, four died. These events were then followed by more rage; rage at the guardsmen who fired at unarmed civilians; rage at the protesters who showed such lack of respect for college tradition and property and who threw stones at those entrusted to keep order - let he who is without sin cast the first stone is a mighty powerful entreaty in the bible belt, in case you didn't know. The governor of Ohio and the President of the United States were en-raged; all the well-known 'anti-war activists' were out-raged. The war being fought 10,000 miles away had now claimed casualties of those who never left U.S. soil.

It was a point in our lives - in my life - where the events of the 'real world' were beginning to intersect with our worlds. If one goes to college, one receives a college deferment - they won't draft one still in college. What about after college? One can't stay in school forever. I read about David Harris - at the time married to Joan Baez - who refused induction into the Armed Forces after receiving a draft notice; he also refused to claim 'conscientious objection' - refusal to serve on religious grounds - because it was hypocritical, so he surrendered to the authorities and was sentenced to serve five years in prison. He served his time. He didn't run to Canada and he didn't dodge his responsibility, to himself, his conscience, his principles, even his nation. I decided that the most honorable course of action, if I should be placed in the same predicament, would be to do the same, but for me, not you or anybody else.

Rage against the faceless, virtually non-human contingent in faraway southeast Asia generated a new plan; while spokesmen for the government assured us that 'we will not engage in hostilities in countries neighboring Vietnam', American planes were routinely flying over Cambodia dropping bombs on 'suspected enemy targets'. It was the rage of Henry Kissinger; he may or may not have devised this plan, but he certainly made no effort to halt its enactment. I suppose what galls me the most about this is that the man concealed the truth, yet even today he is considered a respected statesman and diplomat. I wouldn't entrust him with a dollar to bring me back eggs from the grocery, even if I promised to scramble some for him, too. That's *my* rage.

While all this rage was, well, all the rage, a little weasel of a man, one of the secretive analysts employed by the DoD - that's the Department of Defense for those of you who may be acronym-challenged - was busy compiling the most extensive and embarrassing collection of classified government documents ever released to public scrutiny. Eventually reaching more than seven thousand pages in length, the Pentagon Papers nearly landed Daniel Ellsberg in prison for treason - he escaped this fate mainly due to public and judicial empathy - but the papers exposed the policy of 'national security' for the danger that it poses: as a threat, an opposition to democracy based on the principle "of the people, by the people, for the people". If you're an American and you want to know how righteous, honest and concerned for the "general welfare" your government really was during the time of the 'Vietnam conflict' - and by extension, those representatives, and by further extension, those civil servants, all people who work for you – and which also applies to the overlying period of the 'cold war', you should read all seven thousand plus pages. I think they're even available on the internet. But if you don't have the time, that's okay, too, because I'll condense all seven thousand plus pages right here. There was a dual objective: the first, to slow, curtail, interfere, and make as difficult as possible any indigenous people's assertion toward independence, regardless of political persuasion, *as long as the second objective was me;* the continued and growing enrichment and empowerment of the military-industrial complex - just as Eisenhower warned at the dawn of the sixties. How dangerous is this? Consider that more than 58,000 Americans sacrificed their lives, hundreds of thousands sacrificed parts of their bodies and millions more sacrificed their sensibilities, all for this. Yet, it was never presented to any of them like the Pentagon Papers expressed; their sacrifices were "necessary to punish the Communist aggressors, whose only aim is to enslave peoples after peoples. They must be stopped." That was how it was expressed to those called for sacrifice. Now, they're just names on a wall, like Boo-boo. Just like all nicknames, you use them because you love the reaction from the target, but over time you love the target, and Boo-boo was all of that. Today, we could probably call him Boo-boo and he'd smile or laugh, but we'll never really know, because he's been dead for years. It's been a while since I saw his name on the wall and I can't remember which year he died, but I do remember that his family moved away from Hickory shortly after, disappearing into relative oblivion. A cynic might say that the whole 'national security' policy was designed to secure the defense industry, and, by extension, big business, and, by further extension, the national economy. Don't laugh. Most Reagan conservatives consider that very assertion both correct, necessary and an extremely patriotic pursuit. If I could undo some jack-off's millions from some company like Hughes and his family's benefits and all others whose entanglement with the jack-off enriched them, too, *just so I could see Boo-boo as an old man like me*, I would do it in a heartbeat. Fuck those jack-offs and their family and friends. Fuck 'national security'. Fuck it all.

There is a tendency to be upset and uncaring when one feels like a target. "They shot four *students* in Ohio. I'm a *student*." It was really the only topic that could generate any substantial participation; everyone seemed to have a strong opinion about it and, with the school year nearly over, school work didn't seem to carry much concern from students or teachers. In short order, then, this school year mercifully came to an end, with distinction not from an academic standpoint but more from a worldly kind.

After another year of growth, the summer of 1970 was more about change than anything else. Charlie and I spent less time together than before. He would spend less and less time at home, so he could be away from Les and his mom, but also so he could spend more time with his new soulmates. I knew that he and his new buds were doing drugs and that didn't bother me other than I had no real desire for that; yet I could hardly get ahold of him since he was so rarely at his home. On top of that he was also discovering the pleasures of the flesh of the opposite sex; on those occasions where we would be together, we would often scout around to the various hangouts he had already scored. The pickings would always be slim - it was probably me - and chasing girls made me nervous. Yeah, I tried to talk a game but I really had no clue; first base, second base, third base, a home run? You have to be in the league before you can play ball and I wasn't even playing in the sandlot. I liked girls, make no mistake about that; I just didn't know how to make that next step without falling flat on my face, which I seemed to do on a regular basis. I certainly appreciated the physical differences, and not just boy and girl, but the many, varied and sometimes very subtle differences from girl to girl. It was all so safe, too, when limiting my engagements with girls to simple observation - far fewer face falls.

What was easier to achieve was retention of more traditional boy activities. Despite quitting my league baseball team two years before - under the belief that I was the third best pitcher on the team but I would never get the opportunity to show it - I still played baseball or, more likely, adaptations of the game. Often, we would play tennisball with two, three or four of us in the back yard; the pitching mound was set in the middle of the yard and the batter faced the house; there would often be only three bases, not four, with imaginary foul lines between home and each base; there was no called balls and strikes - never a walk - but strikeouts could be recorded; besides a strikeout, outs could be recorded by catching a fly ball, or relaying a ground ball to the pitcher before the batter reached first or to the cover man before the runner reached the next base; for any at-bats that did not reach home and the team had fewer members than bases, we used ghost-runners; and a home run, of course, was a hit that sailed over the house.

We would play at any time of the day, whenever there were enough kids wanting to play. The more we moved into our teens the harder it was to find enough kids who really wanted to play tennis-ball, but it only took two and maybe Jeff would play, or some of the others in the neighborhood, or maybe one or more of the next-door neighbors, Chuck, Rich or Larry. The five of us had done a lot together and separately in many ways, shapes and forms, having lived twenty yards from each other for ten years. Two years before, Chuck had even connived me into spending thirty-five dollars of the fifty dollars it took to buy a moped; I drove it twice before the other two 'partners' tore it apart to try to find out why it was 'acting up'. That was the start of motor mania next door; motorcycles were collecting in their garage and motocross was taking more of Chuck's interest and time; Rich would be joining him this year, Larry the next. Quite often, one or more would be gone most of the day, racing, practicing, hanging with friends from other places. If there had been such a thing as 'the five of us' - and I'm not saying that there ever was - it certainly couldn't be said any more.

For years my dad had a membership to the local country club so he could play golf several times every week, usually Thursday afternoon and every Saturday and Sunday morning. Mom played golf when we were younger but eventually quit. They had a tennis court and a swimming pool, too; when we were young, our parents arranged swimming lessons and for a couple years we swam on the various teams until it became clear that the swimmers who would continue to compete were expected to train at the pool every day. Neither Jeff nor I were that committed so it didn't happen. Then, we started taking golf lessons and signed up for the junior golf program, which really just matched you with another one or two others in your age group for four, nine or eighteen holes on Wednesday. The biggest perks were junior golfers could play any weekday after five or after noon on a weekend, provided there was an open tee time, which was often; the other perk was the tournament at season's end, complete with a banquet and trophy presentation. The worst part turned out to be, in hindsight, the best part; out on the course, unsupervised, the game of honor often reveals one's true character; is one honest, is one arrogant, conceited, is one uncontrollably angry, is one hateful, is one offensive, insulting, or is one just a plain scumbag? Often, on the golf course beyond prying eyes and ears, people tend to behave in the manner in which they are predisposed. Being the outsiders, Jeff and I received plenty of abuse on those links and, when we started several years before and were still attending church, it was ironic that the worst offenders were typically the same juveniles praised for their judicious and thorough renditions and understanding of scripture in 'Sunday school'. Shortly after, we stopped attending church and have never returned, except for weddings and funerals.

The year before 1970, I won the second flight trophy. This year I would finish second in the first flight, among the best in my age group. It was with great satisfaction that I accepted the trophy, knowing that the winner was a year older than me. However, change, sometimes painful, was sweeping the country and I would not fail to conform; this would be the last year I would participate in the club's junior golf program.

Are you ready for some football? I thought I was, so I tried out for the junior football league. It wasn't much of a tryout because they took everybody who stayed after they went over the rules and requirements, even a four foot, ten inch wimp like me. They had no idea where to play me, other than NEVER on offense, so I got flattened on the defensive line, crushed at linebacker, and run over at defensive back. After I participated in a one-on-one exercise - consisting of one person with the ball trying to run through, over or around the other in a three-yard wide space, starting two steps from each other - and Reese, the other participant, slammed his shoulder pad onto my forearm, which promptly swelled to twice its normal size, I contemplated the wisdom of the saying that junior league and high school football was designed to weed out the bleeders and bruisers. Being the four foot, ten inch weed that I was, I decided that this summer would be the last that I attempted to play organized football.

Even more ridiculous, I was giving up on football for an even bigger man's sport: basketball. I practiced dribbling and shooting, day after day, night after night. The old man, many years before, had a contractor repair and level the concrete platform in the back yard, including adding a solid basketball pole, and recently he had the porch enclosed, turning it into a den - which was used mostly for watching TV. What was really cool about the den addition was that the contractor also installed a flood-light at the top of the dormer which provided illumination over the basketball court and about half of the back yard. Now I could play basketball day or night, and I did. One-on-one, I could whip everybody close to my age in the neighborhood and eventually I simply played by myself most of the time; such is the price of competitive success, even when most of your competitors are taller than you playing a tall man's game.

  Then there was chess. Over the years the chess board would occasionally be retrieved by some family member and the games would begin. Oh, yeah, chess pieces would fly - I flew quite a few myself - at the end, but, as time marched on, I became the victor more and more often. I consistently thrashed little bro from the start; I started beating my dad regularly so those matches dwindled; finally, I was beating older bro, beginning the previous year. Mike was more competitive than the others so he would still suggest a game; with no time limit, I would simply see more moves and catch him in a trap. That would be fun; each move would be slow, methodical, on both sides; he would make the move I was waiting for, and, *slam, bam, boom,* we'd trade moves rapidly until, uh-oh, Mike knew the jig was up. Once I had established my advantage that was usually the end of it. If we had a time limit on moves, he could win pretty easily. In fact, that is still my weakness; if I have to play with a time limit for each move, most experienced chess players can beat me. Maybe it's mental, that I don't concentrate as hard under the time pressure. It doesn't bother me much, though, because I insist on playing another, without the time limit, during which I thoroughly smash the enemy. If you piss me off, I'll take every single one of your chess pieces until all you have left is your weak and naked king, which I will systematically chase all over the board, dragging the final checkmate out, refusing to accept your pathetic attempt to concede defeat. Take it like a man you pussy.

  As all this came to a head, the summer of seventy was coming to an end and our freshmen year of high school beckoned. Ummmmm, it was destined to be different. That difference would be readily apparent, almost from the first day of class.

Act Three
Staggering Through Last Rites, Part One

Okay, it's ten o'clock in the morning, time to get up for school. Shocked? I told you high school was going to be different. Due to the baby-booming swell of enrolled students and no money for more schools - the justification for spending was tempered by the fact that ten years later there would be a third fewer students - our school district devised the split shift for high school. Seniors and juniors attended periods one through five from 7:30 to noon; sophomores and freshmen attended periods six through ten from 12:30 to 5. Those students who enrolled for six periods usually attended the period before or after their 'normal' shift.

    The first day was short and chaotic. We had our class schedule and were assigned a homeroom, where we were to report, receive our locker assignments, school rules and procedures. That day would be close to the last that I visited homeroom; if the room was not in use during the half-hour for lunch - not guaranteed - then we could gather in that room before the start of sixth period, but it was not required and I and most of my acquaintances gathered elsewhere in the school.

    Two hours that morning the juniors and seniors had shuffled to their brief classes and we did the same that afternoon. We checked our lockers, deposited the books for those classes that dispersed them that day and our notebooks, pens, pencils and other learning utensils and left. It seems to me now that it was mid-week, possibly a Wednesday, and the following day was the first full day. We survived, even the day after that, assuming it was Friday, which came and went, and we recessed for the weekend.

    The following week would be a full one but the weekend after would be three days long in celebration of Labor Day. I remember this because an event took place that would really make high school different and we hadn't even completed our first full week of attendance. Labor

Day was still in the future when it happened. And if it was Wednesday that we started, then the event took place the following Tuesday, because I also remember that it did *not* take place on the first day after the weekend, Monday.

We all made our way to school that Tuesday just like the other days and gathered in the hall near the music rooms, which was through a doorway from the main hall of the school and down a narrower corridor, which turned right before another set of doors were passed to reach them. We were beginning to establish the music room corridor as our 'staging area' before classes started at 12:30, but this day just felt more apprehensive and tense than the previous days. Instead, we lingered in the hall, sensing that something was going to happen. Only a few minutes had elapsed with the 'regulars' together when the doors to the gymnasium swung open violently and scores of kids rushed into the hall to the front entrance of the school and out those doors. Fear and confusion was evident from most of their expressions and the talk was equal; we soon discerned that there were gangs - plural - of four to eight kids walking around the school leisurely punching out random students, usually those with dissimilar skin pigment.

The 'regulars' now split up, Dallas, Jim, Charlie and I making our way into the gym while the others went their separate directions. We wanted to see what was going on and many kids had said that the latest was happening in the gym and directly outside. We squeezed past the multitude filing through the doors to the hall and we entered the gym. The school's gymnasium was a ring around a sunken basketball court with bleachers that rose to the level of the ring above; scattered on the outer ring were doors leading to locker rooms, weight rooms, storage rooms and offices; opposite the entrance from the hall into the gym were six sets of doors to the outside of the school building and we tried to look around or over the crowd in the gym, most of whom were slowly moving to the outside of the building. We could see that most were gathered at the sets of doors closest to us; instead of moving in that direction, we walked around the ring above the court to the far set of outside doors.

As we stepped outside – where a grass area of 100 feet separated the building from the parking lot fence, intersected by three concrete paths – there were students of all backgrounds meandering aimlessly from the parking lot to the school building in small, unorganized groups, clearly separating themselves from the two large groups to our left, one full of black faces, one of white. Each group contained two to three hundred students, separated by no more than twenty feet and the black vice-principal standing close to the white faces looking toward the black and the white principal standing close to the black faces looking toward the white. We walked slowly around the large groups, giving plenty of leeway, until we were squarely in the middle of the parking lot, safely observing the shouting, feinting, and gesturing.

As I remember this scene from a viewpoint of more than thirty years removed, it's clear to me that who said what and the exact words are irrelevant. It was a moment where several people were of one mind; a moment that one experiences rarely in a lifetime, yet a moment one remembers forever. We all knew what our eventual action would be; the conversation was simply a means to properly justify the inevitable action.

"Well, now we know what we have to do to get the principal and vice-principal out of the office."

"But nobody can say we're not color-coordinated."

"Yeah, black is clearly black and white is clearly white."

"Technically, black and white are the opposite ends of a total lack of color."

"That may be, but this event is definitely a show of color."

"And a show of hostility."

"What it shows me is that education for today is a secondary consideration."

"It could definitely be dangerous attending class today."

"Yeah, you wouldn't want to step out of your classroom and be confronted by a hundred hall monitors of a slightly different color than yours."

"'Where's your hall pass, boy?'"

"I think school is to be held outside the school building today."

"I think I just heard the principal say, 'Today, classes will be held all over the city in recognition of today, which comes but once a year this year.'"

"I just heard the vice-principal say that my house is one of the 'all-city' classrooms," lied Charlie.

"And, that's good enough for me. Let's all attend class at Charlie's house."

"We can't just leave school and go to Charlie's house…can we?"

"No, you're right. We should just stay in school, even though it's the scene of a race riot, where we'll all be safe and sound."

"And if we're lucky, sometime during our shift the gangs'll pull their knives and guns, kids will actually die, and if we survive, we'll get to go home early."

"Getting the picture yet?"

"Got it. So let's get up and go."

Away we went to the only one among our families' homes which should be empty. To avoid arousing the suspicions of the local enforcement contingent, we deviated from the road a block from the school following the railroad tracks. When the tracks intersected with another set, we took the second set to the south. Soon we walked over Stevenson Drive on the railroad bridge, past the small shopping center that was directly behind Charlie's house, and twisted through or climbed over private wire fences to the road where his house was located, a horseshoe-shaped court with two entrances. Emerging from between two houses a couple of doors away, we walked on the road to his driveway and moved along it until we were behind the house. From the 'secret' hiding place, Charlie pulled out a key, inserted it into the lock of the back door, turned it and opened the door. After replacing the key he then stepped inside the house and we followed.

Charlie warned everybody not to move anything other than the chairs at the dining table and our first item for discussion was to decide where we would go from here. Staying all afternoon at Charlie's house was not in our plans. We sat down on the chairs at the table, barely beginning our discussion in earnest, when we heard a car enter the driveway, and saw a green blur pass by the side window.

"Shit, it's Les," Charlie cursed. Quickly, he organized the escape. "Go to the front door, open it when I say so, get out and head for the tracks." Charlie ran to the back door, locked it, turned and ran to the front and said, "Out, now."

Jim opened the door and we ran out, Charlie gingerly pulling the locked door behind him and keeping the screen door from banging. We ran across the yard and hurdled the ditch between the two yards; I fell in the ditch but got right up and scrambled away. Ten seconds later we were already between the two houses we had passed between before, fifteen seconds later we were through the fences, and within a minute we were all crouched or sitting on the ground in a bushy area near the railroad tracks.

None of us were mad; we all recognized the humor in the situation. I was almost laughing when I asked Charlie, "Shit, man, what happened to 'he always comes home at 11:30 for a half-hour then goes back to work'?"

Charlie laughed before he answered, "This day would be the one where he had a busy morning and had to take a later lunch."

"No shit!" Jim agreed and we all laughed.

A few moments later, Dallas uttered the legendary phrase spoken almost everywhere when the best-laid plans go awry. "Now what?"

We decided to lay low until Les left for work, occasionally sending a scout behind the shopping center to see if the car was gone. Finally, Charlie returned from a scouting expedition and announced that the car was gone, so we returned to his house. On came the radio to serve both to entertain and to keep track of time. Out came the cards and we played hearts, spades, poker, whatever.

We had decided not to venture about, such as the bowling alley across the street or the shopping center, because we didn't want to answer why we weren't in school, which we felt would just seem suspicious. Instead we hung out at Charlie's until a little after 3, about twenty minutes to a half-hour before his mother was due home. Before we started back, we pooled some money and had Jim – he was the biggest and looked the oldest – go to the grocery store and pick up some snacks, then meet us at the tracks going around the front of the shopping center while the rest of us started back the way we came. We waited back from the bridge where we would be difficult to spot but where we could see the oncoming traffic from both directions until the traffic from both sides was far away from the bridge; we dashed across the bridge on the tracks, trying to keep ourselves from being spotted not just by the authorities but also by family members. Stevenson Drive was a route that anyone in our families might use at any time. We were taking any and all precautions, not because we were scared of being caught and punished, but because we were determined not to get caught at all, to outsmart the 'system'.

With absolutely no hurry whatsoever, we walked back to school the way we had come, which was another part of our plan. We intended to come out from the tracks as soon as school let out for the day, run back to catch the buses or rides that would be waiting to take us home, making it appear that we had been at school the whole time. We had to sit on the tracks near the school for about forty-five minutes, which we had also planned, since that was the least-used of the two sets of railroad. We found a path through some brush that led to the field across the street from the school that was used by the physical education classes during school and some of the school teams for practice after school. We watched the P.E. class leave the field and knew that school would be out in ten minutes. Patiently we waited, until we heard the bell ring, and we dashed across the field, through the student parking lot – where we had stood and debated leaving – and split up. Each of us saw people we knew, some of whom would ask where we had been or why we were at school now, but we had all agreed not to answer anyone's questions. We were to simply get to our respective transportation vehicles and keep our mouths shut. That's what we did and all of us made it home with no family member or close friend of a family member any wiser.

The next morning came and my preparation began. We had all anticipated that this would be the weakest part; we would have to forge a believable excuse, sign it, and convincingly present it to the attendance officer. Since we had no experience with the attendance office in high school, its policies, expectations and procedures, this part of the plan gave us little to anticipate and, consequently, to devise a counter-strategy. We all agreed, though, that we would not try to trick our parents into signing a blank page nor would we write up an excuse at home, which would create the risk of discovery by family members and blow the whole thing.

I followed the same routine, showered and dressed, caught the bus, and arrived at school a few minutes before noon. The first couple of days of school, I had wandered about looking for the place where I could hang out before school, a place where I could call my own. Everybody looks for that place when one is thrust into a large group of unfamiliar people, the place where one can be comfortable, safe and secure. Charlie had found his place the first day and told me about it: the hall where the music rooms were.

When I arrived at the music hall, I had already heard the rumors of hundreds of kids lined up at the attendance office – a point in our favor. Dallas and Charlie had already received their excused absence cards and assured me that I need not worry about the note; the attendance officer wasn't even reading the notes. Still, I was nervous drafting my note about my stomach-ache; my penmanship was – still is – atrocious, hardly flowing and consistent like my parents'. I kept it short and simple, signed my mother's name, and left for the attendance office.

The rumors were true. The line to receive an absence card extended from the attendance office, through the waiting room, through the short hallway, into the main corridor halfway into the cafeteria, and lengthening every minute. Thirty seconds after I had become the end of the line, ten more kids were behind me. Ten minutes later – an eternity I presented my weak excuse, trying to keep my nervousness from being obvious, to the attendance officer, Mister White, who was black.

"Name?" Mister White demanded.

I responded with my last name.

"Spell that," Mister White further asked.

I spelled it. Mister White scanned several pages stapled together for a few moments, then sounded my first name inquisitively. I responded in the affirmative.

"You were sick yesterday?" Mister White asked matter-of-factly, but looked at me unblinkingly.

"Yes," I answered slowly, formulating a further explanation, when Mister White reached for a stamp, slammed it onto the inkpad, stamped it onto a pink business card, and handed me the card with his free hand. He laid the stamp down on the other side of the inkpad and handed me the note.

"Next!" he shouted, looking past me.

I turned and walked out of the office, looking at the pink business card that was printed with "ABSENCE" and "Date" below it with a line across the card next to "Date". On the line was written the month, the day of the month, and the year in numeric representation and separated by slashes; stamped diagonally on the card was the word "EXCUSED".

We compared our absence cards and discussed our strategy, its results and the conclusions we could reach, all in about five minutes before we had to disperse for our classes. Playing hookey for the first time in high school had netted four excused absences out of four attempts; of course, it helped that out of about a thousand freshmen and sophomores, more than three hundred and fifty were absent from class the previous afternoon. Still, in this world, results speak for themselves and we were batting a thousand. I learned a few things, too. The lessons for group subterfuge are in this story, but I learned an important individual lesson, one that I still sometimes forget: when confronted by an authority figure never, NEVER, offer any more explanation than that which will answer the question simply. Even when you're the innocent party, just answer the question, nothing more. Why? Let me ask a better question: do you think you're the only one in this scenario carrying unnecessary baggage? Here's another one: do you think that an authority figure doesn't have their own shit to deal with? Believe it or not, every authority figure is a human being, too, each with a set of unique faults and flaws; you don't give them the opportunity to misinterpret what you meant when you simply answer the question and *never* volunteer any more information.

We had made it to September; we had survived our first race riot – there were more to come; and we were getting more acclimated to the high school routine. My hair was getting longer and stringier; I was still short and it was nerve-wracking at times because you just never knew what might happen when several fellows with a shade of pigment different from yours had gathered in the corridor near you; and this was the first year in several where most of my male classmates were not in every one of my classes. It was a time for change and we were all changing.

There was a new kid in some of my classes: Eddie. Eddie was in my social studies, physical education and science classes. He was cool and I liked him immediately and he liked me. He was tall, about six foot two, with medium-length brown hair, slightly awkward but in an endearing manner. He had an excellent sense of humor with an appropriate dose of sarcasm – a requirement if you wanted to get close to me. While we rarely would hang together before or after school, we quite often would walk to class together. Maybe it was a sense of security in an insecure arena, or maybe it was just because I liked the guy, enjoyed his company and our conversations.

Charlie was in my social studies class, too, and the three of us would quite often become the terrible trio. Charlie was also in my English and mathematics classes, but something was pushing us apart. It wasn't anything obvious; there was a lot that was new, more difficult, that everyone was learning how to cope with. Our drifting apart wasn't drastic, it was gradual and mutual; we spent less time together away from school, less time talking on the phone. We were finding our own ways.

Then, about halfway through September, we heard the news; Jimi Hendrix was dead. No more Electric Ladyland, although it's still in existence, but without Jimi it was just another music studio. I remembered hearing Jimi's rendition of *The Star-Spangled Banner* from the Woodstock album on a local radio station, WVEM, complete and uncut. What a masterpiece! We figured, like everyone else, that he had partied too much and died from an overdose; only much, much later would we learn that he was probably sick, which caused him to vomit while unconscious, but his body was too fatigued to even react naturally to resist drowning, to clear his air passageway. At the time, we had no idea that his death was just the beginning for some of the biggest rock icons; we just knew that probably the greatest guitarist ever was dead before he had even hit middle age. So with his death, it was time to perform last rites; that weekend as many of us got together as possible to celebrate his life and accomplishments, and, oh, yeah, we cranked his tunes LOUD, man.

We were gathered in our usual spot before school started, the music hall, where only a few people would be, including a few girls like Cheri and Renee. Jim, Charlie, another guy whom I don't remember, and I were chatting away with the girls, telling lies, flirting, and the like. The door separating the long hallway from the school corridor opened and a couple of loud, jive-talking voices could be easily heard. One said, "Heah cum da nigguhs!" Soon, five black boys turned the corner, passed the open double doors and came down the steps before us. Two were tall, as tall as Jim and Charlie, and one was well-built; two were medium height, and the last, and most vocal, was short, even shorter than me. They all walked loudly past us; one stopped while two went into the far music room to see if anyone was in there; nobody was. The other two checked the closer music room; nobody was in there either. One of the medium boys stayed near the end of the hall at the far music room, near the light switches, we noticed. The other four started back toward us, sizing us up, each separating and silently picking a target. When each was near the target, the one at the end of the hall flipped off all the lights. I was standing against the wall and when the lights went off, I slid down the wall, heard a loud crack, a scream right next to me of "AHHH!", followed by other smacks and shouts and screams, boys and girls. I moved to one side, anticipating that the boy in front of me, who had just punched the wall with full force, might want to kick whatever was in front of him. Maybe ten more seconds elapsed, with more smacks and scuffling; the one boy at the end of the hall flipped the lights back on. Jim took a swing in front of him, a trickle of blood dripping from his lip. His combatant looked relatively untouched. Charlie had a bump on the back of his head and his chest was sore but he had bloodied his combatant. The other guy was doubled over and looked like he had the worst of it. The boy in front of me held his right hand gingerly with his left wearing an expression of pain. Just like they had come in, they left, talking loud, boastful, heated, and, again, it was the shortest one that talked the most and the loudest. We took stock of our injuries – none serious, even the other guy – and I took some flack for ducking. It probably sounded lame but I argued that it didn't seem to be the time to fight. If I had to do it over again, I'd do the same thing. The situation didn't appear to unfold as an all-out, gang battle, fight to the death type scenario; my combatant hurt himself, which was deserved, and I didn't start it, he did. The rites of passage to manhood may dictate that you stand up at all times to unprovoked aggression, but I don't see it that way. When I stand up in that manner, it's the last thing to do. I make room for discussion and dialogue, because I'm always hopeful that there's a compromise waiting to be discovered. If it's not, then I fight to kill, and one of us is dying. You can fight for honor or anything else you want. Fuck that. We skipped school that day, too, and repeated the process to receive an excused absence successfully the next day. Fuck that, too.

At this point, we were staggering through the rest of the year, just handling it. It was barely October but it had seemed to be forever. Charlie and I were definitely into music and I have to give Charlie the credit – he was *into* music. One of our favorite performers had already left *Big Brother and the Holding Company* and set off on her own; before the first week of October was complete, Janis Joplin left for good. Being an old fart I can't presume to know what young people think today, but if you're young and you're *into* gritty rock and roll *and* you've *never* listened to any recordings from Janis Joplin, you haven't heard shit. You should get out there and find some of her stuff and *listen to it*, because that's all that's left. Back in my freshman year, though, we were no longer staggering, we were positively floored. We were thinking that these kinds of events come in threes…

One day in my social studies class, as we were all sitting around the room in a circle, I observed a most interesting phenomenon. Directly across the room from me, at a distance of perhaps twenty-five feet, a girl who had been rather sweet on me since the beginning of school sat next to her girlfriends. For the first few minutes of class, she would lean to one of her friends and whisper or one of her friends would lean to her and whisper. Then she would look directly at me and smile; her friends would look directly at me and smile. It was all seeming very conspiratorial when I watched her uncross her legs and her skirt fall just above her knees. She glanced about for any unwelcome observers and apparently seeing none, she slowly opened her legs. With a singular, focused curiosity, I gazed along her white inner thighs between her legs, up to where I expected to see a patch of white – her panties – but instead her white skin was unbroken right to the middle of her crotch, which was revealed to be a patch of black. In an unhurried and smooth manner, she closed her legs and I moved my gaze to her face and watched her smile briefly for me. All I could think of doing was raise my eyebrows with a bemused expression. As the class continued, I would catch her gaze, she would glance about, and, if the coast was clear, spread her legs again and again. She would lean to her friends, her friends would lean to her, and all would smile. I leaned to Charlie and asked if he had seen that; he had no idea what I was talking about. I was convinced that no one had seen it but me. When we all filed out of the room at the end of class, she moved slowly with her friends so that I could catch up; she smiled and said something, but I don't remember what it was. I just responded with "Hi, see you tomorrow."

When I told my friends about it, I heard all the useless suggestions. You know. "She wants you, man." "If a girl shows you her snatch, she's telling you, 'come and get it, boy'." "She could be just a tease, you know; she wants you to look at her body, just don't touch." "Just because a girl lets you see her bush, it doesn't mean she's ready to fuck you. But if you do it right, she certainly won't put up much of a fight. After all, she spread her legs for you once and that's a good indication that she'll do it again."

It was all useless because, in reality, I had no idea how to proceed toward that elusive goal, copulation with a female, a desirable goal for most young, teenage boys. What should I say? How should we meet after school? What should we do? How would I know when to kiss her, fondle her, move my hands to her womanhood, attempt to take her clothes off, and where would I attempt to do this? Indeed, how, when, where?

As it turned out I did nothing. Oh, I was friendly with her but I was friendly with everyone and her attention soon drifted away. I would rationalize it by believing that she really wasn't my type; she wasn't a knockout and she wasn't plain, either, but, in all honesty, she didn't appeal to me in the manner that I had to have her. Granted, if things had been different, had proceeded differently, I definitely would have pursued whatever advantage may have befallen upon me. However, they were not different and that was that.

Norman was a black dude about my height – no advantage there – but even skinnier than me. However, he had a tall, well-built friend who always followed him around. One day that fall I was at my locker switching my books when he and his bigger friend strutted down the hall toward me. Norman was mouthing off, obviously looking for a victim, and at that moment I was it. I looked at the two of them approaching me and when Norman was about ten feet away he shouted at me, "What are you lookin' at, honky?" I glanced into my locker to check that I had everything and avoid looking at him. Norman shouted, "Oh, so, now, I'm not good enough to look at, huh, honky? Maybe I oughtta kick your ass!" He was right next to me when he shoved me into my locker. I leaned against the lockers and looked at him; with my peripheral vision I could see him clenching his fists. He threw a couple of mock punches at me but I didn't flinch. I glanced over at his friend, who took a step toward me. For a moment the three of us stood there unmoving. The big guy said, "Cumon, Norman, he ain't gonna fight. He ain't worth it." Norman shouted in agreement, "Yeah, you ain't worth it! You ain't worth nuthin', honky!" Norman turned and started walking away from me down the hall, still mouthing off with the big guy in tow. Although Norman and his friend had their fair share of scuffles and fights, suspensions and detentions that year, neither one ever fucked with me again. Don't ask me why because I don't know. They just never did.

English class was becoming my favorite, not because I liked English, but because our teacher let Charlie and me go off. It was the one class in our new high school careers where we could continue our class clown traditions with little abatement. Of course, there was another side to it. Renee and Cheri were in that class, too. Little wonder that Charlie and I would gather at the music room before school started. Who do you think would almost always be there at the same time? Did you say, Renee and Cheri? That's a winner!

Charlie was sweet on Renee; I enjoyed flirting with Cheri. Both were very fine and we knew that they liked us, at least for our wit and intelligence, if nothing else. Yet there was always some underlying sexual tension when we were all together and I always found it hard to believe that Cheri had a serious boyfriend, considering some of the topics we would discuss. She was tough, meaning she was far from demure, emotionally and mentally. She didn't let anything slide and was up for any verbal challenge, but I could talk to her about things that were very introspective and revealing and she would expose a softer side that few people ever witnessed. Renee was more the lady, so I imagine Charlie was interested in her for that. The two of them, though, were much more racy in their sexual innuendos than Cheri or I were. Despite how well we all got along, though, there was never a serious attempt to get closer than where school brought us.

One week our teacher, Mrs. K, was sick and our substitute decided to go out on the edge, so to speak. She borrowed a turntable from the audio-visual department and brought a copy of *Tommy* by The Who. I know she meant well, over the next two days, when she played an album each day and attempted to guide a serious discussion of the merits, meaning and influence of the music and lyrics. I may have felt a bit guilty because I hardly said anything as did Charlie. She must have sensed it because the two of us were hardly quiet until those two days. We just wanted to jam. We were also a little surprised, too. This was Podunk, 1970; here hip came in pairs and you could find them just below one's waist.

Eddie made the freshmen basketball team – not a bad feat considering our high school's short but growing legacy. The varsity was sneaking up on people and our junior class was turning into a formidable force; the sophomores and freshmen, representing the junior varsity, would put a hurt on the rest of the conference and some of the junior varsity outside the conference bold enough to play them. If the freshmen had a weakness it was lack of height; at six feet two, Eddie was one of the tallest on the team. His role was the enforcer, guard the basket, rebound, serve as the outlet to move the ball around, but not necessarily score. He relished it, though, and played a lot during the fall. I guess the team was sneaking up on me, too, because I didn't watch any of the games that fall. While I enjoyed playing the game I wasn't really enthused about watching the games; lacking a mode of transportation to and from the games after school was a huge hindrance, too.

That fall also featured one of the Frazier-Ali matches. I could look up on the Net which one took place in 1970 – I think it was the first – but it's not the history of their bouts nor what took place during this particular one that sticks out in my mind. It's Sam and Jimmy, two black dudes in my gym class, every day for a month, doing their Ali and Frazier routine in the locker room before gym, during our games or workouts, and in the locker after gym. Sam was Frazier, slow, deliberate, stuttering like him, and Jimmy was Ali, quick, darting, mouthy. It was great entertainment. Sometimes they would do entire rounds, true to the actual event. Frazier and Ali – and by extension, Sam and Jimmy – hold some of the most engaging memories I have of the last four months of 1970.

As we passed the day of thanks – with my Dad's father in attendance, after which we drove him to St. Louis and put him on the plane to California to stay the winter with Aunt Mary Beth – and moved into December and the holidays, we were all looking for a break. There were a couple more days of absence – even one where I went to the attendance office the next day, only to have the attendance officer tell me that I wasn't absent and couldn't give me an excuse.

"Your name's not on the absence list, young man," Mister White, who was black, said calmly, adding, "No one listed you as absent."

"Huh, maybe I got the days mixed up," I mumbled.

"Maybe. Next!"

I went to all my classes, having been absent the day before, and not one teacher asked me for an excuse. It's not anything I worked hard to achieve, but it can be unnerving for some people how easily I can hide in plain sight. It amazes me, too.

About a year before, *Butch Cassidy and the Sundance Kid* was released in theaters and I thought it was one of the best films ever, until I saw *M.A.S.H.* over that summer. Still, *Butch Cassidy* was an influential movie at my age, so much that my neighbor Larry and I posed for some *Cassidy*-like photos, using a cheap Polaroid my parents had given me, using props like cigarettes and guns. It was a pleasant surprise, then, when our English teacher, Mrs. K, pulled out some copies of a play, adapted from the movie, *Butch Cassidy and the Sundance Kid*. She only had a few copies, not enough for everyone, so only those who would be performing roles would have copies. Then she did something I never expected; she chose Charlie to perform the role of Butch Cassidy and me to perform as the Sundance Kid. I thought Charlie was great, but I messed up a few times, sometimes from laughter, but we were excellent choices; we had the whole room, even the teacher, laughing so many times, that we easily held up our appointments. There were even a couple of times when school personnel heard such a loud, raucous demonstration coming from our room that they knocked on the door to check it out. One teacher even stayed for the rest of the period. For those two days, Charlie and I performed with the approval of all, instead of performing for ourselves only, and I think that everyone enjoyed it. I certainly did.

With the change back to standard time, we would get out of school and it would be dark. I looked forward to the twenty-first day of December. It was the shortest day of the year, but now all the days would slowly get longer, and in two days it would be Christmas break.

Act Four
Staggering Through Last Rites, Part Two

The day before Christmas was hectic and restful, slow to awaken, rush to secure gifts for those not yet found, wrap gifts, eat, and watch TV. There was no real magic tied to this day, however; Santa had long ago abandoned our chimney - probably wise considering the pyromaniac in residence there (another story) – so we weren't expecting any presents from him this year. Still, it was refreshing to know that school and all of its nerve-wracking implications were just distant memories – out of sight and out of mind.

The following day unfolded much like that of most homes in America, as long as most homes didn't pray, give thanks, eat breakfast before opening presents, wait for the grandparents, go to church first, or otherwise do any of the traditional Christian family activities of Christmas *before opening the Christmas presents.* Not us Descripts. As soon as Mom and Dad were up and their coffee was ready, we all went straight to the family room where the tree stood, littered with the many wrapped packages. Jeff and I pushed the agenda, grabbing packages, reading the label identifying to whom the gift was intended, and handing to the recipient. Occasionally, Dad would attempt to slow us down, trying to keep the routine to one package distributed and opened at a time, but at our ages this was a fairly futile endeavor. Once all the packages had been properly inspected and ripped apart, we surveyed the usual booty: clothes, albums, books, games, toys.

The difference this year with previous years was that Christmas was losing its luster and its family bond with the Descripts of Podunk. Mike had driven up to the big city weeks before to spend some time with one of his college buddies and his wife. During the day, we would each split up and go our separate ways; Mom would sit in the bedroom, watch TV while reading magazines, drink wine and smoke cigarettes; Dad would sit in the den, watch TV while reading magazines and smoke cigars; Jeff would head next door and hang with the neighbors; and I would bundle up, hop on my bike and pedal over to Charlie's house and hang with him and his brother Mark. We all gathered together for dinner, ate, and split up again. I watched a little TV and went to my room to listen to music, playing the rock star.

 If I told you that precious little of the conversations, activities and events of these last few days before the new year are available for me to actually remember and recount, would it serve to temper your disappointment some if I reminded you that the past year had produced four students shot to death by national guardsmen and two huge musical counterculture figures dead by lifestyle? That all this came on the heels of Helter Skelter in LA? That the Manson Family was preceded by the murders two years earlier of Martin Luther King, Jr. and Robert Kennedy, which was preceded, in turn, by the murder of President Kennedy in Dallas, which still presents unanswered questions forty years later? All of this taking place before I could even say goodbye to fourteen. Would it matter to you?

 If so, then you can understand the further shock when my mother hands me the newspaper on New Years Day. The previous evening my younger brother and I had spent a relatively quiet night at the ranch with nowhere to go, sneaking out prior to midnight to light off a few firecrackers to ring it in. All of our friends were 'busy' with their own 'things', so we had stayed home and whiled away the countdown together. My mother drew my attention to a short article about three inches in length, asking me if I knew the boy since it read that he attended our high school and was my age. I told her that I knew him and took the section of the paper she held before me so that I could read that Eddie was dead…………..The article stated that he died from an accidental discharge from a shotgun while cleaning it…………..When I returned to school, nobody wanted to talk about Eddie, or, at least, they would quickly attempt to change the subject. I did learn that his girlfriend had broken up with him shortly after Christmas and had spurned him by telling him that she was going out New Year's Eve with another guy…………..Fred, his best friend who was also in my gym class and lived in the same block, told me that he heard the commotion from the family and neighbors, so he snuck over to Eddie's house. He knew that Eddie would mess with his gun in the basement, so he looked through the basement windows until he found him. The right side of his head was missing, the gun was laying next to him with a cloth strip around his right foot and through the trigger guard of the gun. It seemed to me that very few of my peers considered his death accidental.

January, 1971 faded to February, 1971 with scarcely a whimper of protest from anyone, even from my own memory today. The dynamics of all my relationships with anyone and everyone were changing and I simply adopted survival mode, low-key, low profile, an attitude of "you're not even worth my time to consider." It was about this time, though, that the conversation at the dinner table one night revolved around the general discontent and violence in society and schools in particular. I asked my parents what they would think if I went to school one day and there were gangs of kids wandering around school randomly beating up kids and I decided to leave school to get away from all of that crap. Would that be a smart or foolish thing to do? My father then pronounced that he considered that a smart thing to do. But what if I had skipped school because of it and got caught the next day - that I was in big trouble. My dad then said that kids have a responsibility to attend school and schools have a responsibility to provide a safe environment to learn and when schools cannot meet their responsibility, then the kids' responsibilities to the schools become null and void. I have to say that his remarks, with my mother's concurrence, came as a mild surprise, but welcome none the less. It was now good to know that, should those many days of unexcused absence come to the light, the old man would be ready to defend me.

Two vacation days in February – a couple of presidents' birthdays but not Groundhogs' Day, my personal favorite – were breaks much appreciated, but winter's stranglehold was always toughest during this month. February should be renamed National Depression Month. It's, fortunately, the shortest month, a scant four weeks, which is followed by progressively milder weather – although Illinois has a tendency to be overcast and rainy during the early spring and that can be depressing, too. Mike had his birthday in February, his twenty-fourth, and I had mine in March, only a year removed from legal driving age. The previous summer I had commandeered both of my parent's vehicles – at different times of course – and had driven at the highest speed, a hundred and fifteen miles per hour, that I still have yet to eclipse. I also had run a car off the highway that I had not seen coming up in the left lane on the interstate, so I had decided that my sneaky driving days were over and I stuck to that promise. Now I was fifteen and a little closer to manhood, yet, before March, 1971 yielded to April, 1971, a single day's developments would dramatically change everything in my life.

That day started like any other – up late with Mom fixing me breakfast after taking Jeff to school, a shower, collecting my schoolwork, catching the bus, arriving at school, making my way to the music room corridor. It was when I made the turn at the hall leading to the music room corridor that the day began to be different, because Charlie was not where I expected him to be. When I asked where he was, one of the girls matter-of-factly replied that she didn't think Charlie was going to be at school today. Jim added that he hadn't seen Charlie get off his bus and one of the kids on that bus had said that Charlie was not at the stop where he normally caught the bus. As the day moved along, I heard from some people that knew Charlie but usually hung out with his brother, Mark, who was a year younger. They were all saying the same thing: the two had planned from the night before to run away. That information also changed my life dramatically; my best friend and I were certainly doing more and more things separately, but, if it was true that they had run away, his failure to tell me – my having to hear it from friends of his brother – was deeply hurtful. How could you be best friends with someone and never confide such a life-changing plan? I couldn't, so I took the "rumor" as just that, unbelievable, until Charlie's mother called our house and spoke to my mother to ask her if she would ask me if I knew where her sons had gone. It dawned on me that I knew why he hadn't told me anything; he had anticipated his mother's actions and my probable reaction. Since I had a tendency to refuse to lie to cover for somebody else, I would surely have told something, probably everything I knew, so he told me nothing. Still, I expected they would turn up soon, and it would be just like old times. Any day now.

    It was about this time that I played the best basketball game of my life. When we played basketball in my gym class, invariably we split into two games; the jocks and those who would be like them would play at one end of the sunken court and we scrubs would play at the other end. Granted, my idea of the best game ever didn't really include rebounds, assists, steals, even defense, it was baskets made. This day, I made a lot of them, so many that guys on the other team were complaining that I couldn't miss; so many that guys on my team would have a reasonably open ten-footer and pass to me for a wide-open twenty-five-footer (this was before the three-point shot, mind you); so many that the other guys tried double- and triple-teaming me, but I would just dribble around until I shook them, or my guys picked them, or I had one brief moment to spin and throw it up…and in; so many that, despite my enormous ego, even I was amazed. Even so, it was still a contest until the last minute when a teammate snagged the rebound, flipped it out to me and I immediately buried it from twenty-five feet; a few seconds later, I stole a pass, dribbled out to establish possession, twisted and flipped up another twenty-five footer; a few seconds after that, I grabbed the next rebound, dribbled out along the baseline, turned to find no one had followed me, so I buried the baseline jumper. Game over.

With everybody in the scrubs game talking about *my game* in the locker room, apparently some of the jocks heard about it, too. A few days later the jocks are short a player, so Fred, who is a member of the freshman basketball team, asks me if I want to play b-ball with them. Betraying my scrub buds, I agreed to play. What a mistake that was. Maybe I should have known better when Fred turned out to be on the other team – the guy who asked me to play in the first place. Every one on my team ignored me, the play was rough and dirty, Fred being one of the leading instigators. You couldn't breathe on him or it was a foul but he could arm-tackle you around the neck and he would complain about you calling a foul. Even Dave, who played in that game, complained about Fred, and they were teammates on the freshman team. I think I touched the ball twice in forty minutes and that was enough for me. True, I was never asked again but it only served to ensure our mutual understanding, because I was never going to play with those guys ever, at least not in a pickup game. Fred turned out to be a broadcaster, first working for the Podunk station, then making the jump to CNN, then – probably for money – moving to Detroit and falling prey to drugs – almost blowing his career but, hey, that's par for the course nowadays – then, under reprieve, heading back to CNN. I haven't seen Fred on the tube in about ten years, though. Now he's kind of a "whatever happened to" wonder.

Sticking with basketball the varsity team had done well that year but I had not ventured to any of the games. There would be a few graduations, but the seniors weren't carrying the team, it was the underclassmen. They had a winning record and they won a game in the regional tournament, but they lost in the regional finals, keeping intact the history of futility for the school. Of course, this was only the fourth year of the school's existence, the seniors being the first class to spend all their four years at the new school.

Weeks went by and Charlie had not returned. Weeks turned into April and May and I ached for the end of school. I was slowly turning into the last hippie in the freshman class, or so it seemed to me; the other longhairs were dopes, dopeheads, or drinking fools, or so it seemed to me. Hippies – individualistic, reasonably intelligent, skeptical and questioning of all authority – were vanishing, or so it seemed. The music wasn't as compelling anymore, everywhere people were selling out, going for the bucks, avoiding 'rocking the boat', joining the establishment, the status quo, or so it all seemed to me in the spring of 1971. It was a time of disillusionment, disappointment, and when it became deep and penetrating, only the thought of Eddie kept me alive. Mercifully, school ended the first week of June and I boarded the bus for that last ride home and never looked back. My freshman year had come to a close and I would be a sophomore in August – like there was any doubt – but I would have few fond memories of that first year. I would never want to go back.

    I would not be sliding into my summer vacation empty-handed, though, because I had discovered and secured a cache, in the form of a large, heavy leather duffel bag, filled with girlie magazines, dozens and dozens and dozens of them. Being a teenage boy somewhere near a micron shy of clueless about girls, the duffel bag was a welcome bonanza. I had been near the pond, scouting the woods, when I came to a clearing; wandering around scoping the site, I climbed over a log and spotted it partially covered with leaves and sticks, dirt packed up against it. Of course I opened it and was astonished at the sheer number of girlie magazines inside. I pulled out some of them and looked at the many pictures of naked women, feeling a surge of blood swelling my dick. That's enough. Next, I had to decide how I was going to keep this spectacular find. At the time, I determined that it was not wise to try to move the whole bag back to the house, especially since it would be both difficult – the bag full of magazines was very heavy – and the time was not opportune for avoiding detection. Instead, I moved it away from the clearing into a thick set of bushes and brush, scattering leaves and sticks to conceal it. As I walked home I contemplated how to get the entire cache to safekeeping and I knew that I had to do it quick. Some parts of the bag were damp and some of the magazines were starting to mildew and smell. By the time I reached home I had developed a plan and I immediately began looking for the item I would use, a knapsack – called a backpack today – that Mike had abandoned years before when he stopped being a Scout. I didn't waste any time either. I had noticed that very few people were out and about in the neighborhood, most importantly, people who would take any real interest in me or what I was doing. Everybody in the family was gone doing their own things except Mom and she was kind of out of it, so with the knapsack in hand I went right back to the woods. I was nervous as I approached the bag's new hiding place, looking and listening for any suspicious movement or sound, probably because I was about to remove someone else's property and make it my own. Still, I opened the bag with anticipation and lifted magazine after magazine, eventually becoming so unconcerned that I placed less deserving ones back for others. When I had selected ten or twelve, I put them in the knapsack, zipped closed the duffel bag, re-positioned brush, sticks, leaves and dirt to hide the bag again, flipped the knapsack over my right shoulder and walked back home as nonchalantly as possible, emerging from the woods only about a hundred yards from our house. I made it to my bedroom without a single intervention. Confident that my secret was undiscovered, I walked around the bed opposite the door, having closed it, of course, and laid the knapsack down on the floor. I removed each magazine and positioned each separately on the floor under the bed so that they would air out and release their musty smell quicker, then hastily covered them all with an old sheet from my dresser, long unused. Since my mother expected me and my brothers to gather our own laundry and drop them down the chute to the laundry room downstairs, I knew she wouldn't look around my room. I wasn't so sure about my younger brother; he typically didn't snoop around my room as I did not typically snoop around his, but, if he did find them, I figured he would be as intrigued as I was.

    I decided that I had to get the entire cache out of the woods as soon as I could, so I made three more trips over the next week. Before I would leave to go get the next batch, I gathered all the magazines under the bed and hid them in one of my dresser drawers; I followed the same routine, though I didn't enter or exit from the same general area twice. The following weekend I made the last trip, being as careful as possible because I intended to remove the bag on the last trip as well and that would be a much more easily identifiable object of interest. I placed the magazines in the knapsack and slung it over my right shoulder, folded the ends of the bag into the middle, lifted it up and cradled it under my left arm as I turned away and began my walk back to the house. This last time I stayed in the woods all the way to the neighbor's house directly across the street, moving along the side of their yard in the deep gully that drained to the lake. I checked the road for traffic, whether vehicular or pedestrian, and deciding it was safe crossed the road. Traversing the twenty feet of our front lawn, I set both items in one of the window wells around the basement windows at the side of the house, and walked to the opposite side to enter the house to determine if it was safe to bring them in. It was finally safe enough much later that day, but I was not going to be discovered so close to complete success, and my patience was rewarded. Now I had the whole cache in my own room. After a reasonably sufficient amount of time to air out, I stored all the magazines in the duffel bag, although the musty smell never completely vanished.

    For those now imagining that the next section will reveal my epiphany that I was moving down the metaphorical road to eventual mental, spiritual and psychological degradation and destruction, which subsequently led to my disposing of these magazines filled with pictures of naked women, I must post this advisory: *the following prose contains material unsuitable for children, the self-righteous, the intolerant, the indignant, the inconsiderate, and other mental midgets. It contains sexually explicit content, which may be graphic enough that some of the above may find offensive. One may wish to put down this tome, fold away and destroy these loose papers, click to another web site, or close your word processor immediately.*

    Okay, now that *those* people have filed out, what were you imagining would come next? Was it pullin' the pud? Nope. Spanking the monkey? Nope. Yankin' the wanker? Nope, although I've employed that method more than a few times, it's not the one I use most often, and not the one I would use at this time in my life. First, I would scan some magazines to select the pictures or series of pictures I wanted to use; next, I would arrange the opened magazines at the head of the bed, sometimes across and sometimes one on top of the next; last, I would place a pillow just below the magazines, slide in under the sheets, scrunch up the pillow and let *my* imagination run wild. Once I got excited enough, I would push down my pants and underwear (if I was wearing either), concentrate on the fantasy I was harvesting and, finally, shoot my load right into the bottom sheet. After the exhilaration passed, I would reach for the box of tissues and wipe off my stomach, my dick, and the sheet. Sometimes, I would have the tissues in my hand and tilt at the moment of ejaculation and shoot it into the tissues; I would do this to lessen the stain that was growing on the mattress below, more than any other reason. Of course, with all that sperm squirting everywhere, this particular method was messy, to say the least. I would develop a less untidy version later, but I'll leave that for another chapter.

    Besides shootin' my wad, basketball was my obsession. The television networks were showing more pro games and had devoted more coverage to the playoffs instead of just the championship series. This was the year my favorite team – no, not the Bulls, those lovable losers – would take it all, and why not? With Kareem no longer a rookie and trading for the Big O, the yeomen on that team were more than a match for all the others; Greg Smith, McGlockin, Dandridge, Lucius Allen, super-sub, were the class of the league that year and I can still remember their names and their positions easily despite the considerable number of intervening years. Yet, the games they played during the playoffs didn't intrigue me as much as what took place in the Eastern division, because those playoff games yielded the most unlikely contender for the crown, the Baltimore Bullets. Who did they have? Their most celebrated player, Earl the Pearl, was well-known but, really, who else did they have? An under-sized center, at six feet seven inches, who simply out-muscled the competition to lead in rebounding, named Wes Unseld. A forward with chronically bad knees who had career game after career game named Gus Johnson. Another forward better known for the huge birthmarks on his body but with a shooting touch that was velvet from twenty-five feet out named Jack Marin. And a no-name distributor who barely averaged in double figures for the season but who dispatched the competition almost single-handedly with twenty-five, thirty, thirty-five point games now known as the Coach, for some reason. Freddie Carter piqued my curiosity, stoked my imagination. He seemed fearless, a gunner's gunner, when he threw it up from literally anywhere amidst two, three, possibly even four flying, flailing bodies around him. Up and in. It was great. It was a show. It was a spectacle. The Bullets weren't even picked to clear the first round and, at times, all four of his starting mates were sitting out games or large parts of games with nagging and/or new injuries, but nobody picked Freddie to score more than thirty points a game continuously, regularly. To this naïve eye, the guy also seemed to inspire his teammates with his refuse-to-lose attitude; usually a gunner doesn't have that effect since they just heave it with seemingly little regard for the rest of the team, but then Unseld would seal one side, and Freddie's miss would sneak into Johnson's hands, who would muscle enough strength from his weak knees to put it back up and in. It was almost sad that they had to play the Bucks for the championship; it wasn't that they were 'clearly outmatched' as they were clearly outhustled. The Bucks simply had fresher personnel and they also had an answer for Freddie and the Pearl; those two were not going to beat them. In the end Freddie couldn't make enough shots and the others couldn't gather enough strength to counter the running onslaught that was the Bucks that year. BUT, whenever they show any of the Bullets' playoff games from seventy-one on the classics shows, DON'T miss them. They are gems.

  With that for inspiration I spent a lot of time on our basketball court, practicing dribbling, practicing moves, but mostly shooting. Sometimes others would join me and practice or play some games; the games would be spirited, which is an understatement no doubt, but outright fights were not part of the fare. Usually, those disappointed would storm off or walk away, me included. Nevertheless, I would bounce the basketball at any time, day or night. If at night, I would switch on the floodlights and shoot baskets until midnight, sometimes even later than that. The parents would be sleeping at the other end and opposite from the court; Mike's bedroom was in the basement, again at the other end and opposite the court; the closest was Jeff's bedroom, and he could hear the bounce of the basketball in his room, but he was also as likely to be up as I was. The neighbors on either side were far enough away that they wouldn't be able to hear it and there were no houses across the street, so night ball was no burden to anyone. I knew it so I had no qualms when I would suddenly stand up in the den, walk over to the light switch and flip it up, walk to the basketball inevitably lying next to the TV, pick it up, open the door a few feet away, step outside, close the door behind me, bounce the ball on the walk as I moved to the court and heave it to the basket once I cleared the tree next to the court. I would shoot and dribble and make moves for an hour or two hours or more. I was bored, there wasn't anybody I wanted to hang with, and I could play basketball any time I wanted so I did.

Playing night ball alone created a second endeavor that I really stumbled upon: checking out what was going on behind other people's glass, or voyeurism, or window-peeping, call it what you want. It started one night when a shot from the corner caromed to the opposite corner and the ball bounded off the edge of the walk and rolled all the way to the front yard. After I retrieved the ball and was carrying it back I looked over at the neighbor's house, noting the bathroom light was on, when a head of black hair appeared at the window, bobbing around. The head belonged to the neighbor's wife, which got me wondering what she was doing, so I stopped and watched for several minutes. This bathroom was on the second floor so I couldn't see into the room from the ground, but I could make generalizations, and I decided that she was in the bathroom for such a long time because she was preparing a bath or shower or preparing for after the bath or shower to go to bed. I wasn't going to see anything else so I went back to the court and shot around some more, thinking about the next step.

The next step came the next night, as I stayed outside with the basketball, but occasionally checking where the neighbor's wife was in their house. After dinner she had posted herself in the living room reading and that's where she stayed for more than two hours; she got up a few times and I tried to track her but she eventually returned to the living room and her read. Finally, the living room lights were turned off and I ran around to the front yard and down the street to see that her bedroom light was on. I walked back to the court when I saw the bathroom light on. Instead, I raced around the front and side of the house to the TV tower erected in the back yard right next to the house about midway between the ends of the house. I climbed up the tower until I reached the roof, which I stepped onto and walked gingerly to the end of the house facing the neighbor's bathroom. I could see into the bathroom easily as the top of our roof dormer was almost directly across from their bathroom but she was not in view. I had to be at least fifty feet in a direct line from their bathroom, which obviously diminished detail, and I was nervous and afraid of being seen so I lied down on the roof, further restricting a good view. After a long wait I saw her emerge from the right side of the window, where the bathtub was located, and for a brief moment I spied her bare breasts, which she soon covered with a towel. She fiddled around before the sink and mirror on the other side of the bathroom, staying in view for most of it, until she opened the bathroom door ten minutes later and left the bathroom for her bedroom, still wearing the towel.

  Now that I was making progress I started planning the next step. Standing as far away from the bathroom as I could reasonably get, detail was lacking so I had to devise a way to somehow get my vision closer: binoculars! When the opportunity presented itself, I surreptitiously rummaged throughout the house until I found the binoculars Dad stored in its case for use mostly at college football games. Once I had them secured I snuck them outside and hid them in the foliage that wrapped around our house next to the TV tower. That night I played basketball again and waited. Again, the neighbor's wife read in the living room for hours and turned off the lights to go upstairs. When I saw the living room lights go dim I walked quickly to the TV tower, pulled from the foliage the binoculars, drew the strap over my head and put my right arm through the strap and climbed the tower to the roof. The bathroom was dark as I moved to the end of the dormer, but the door was open and I could see the glow of the hall light behind it. Soon, she suddenly entered the bathroom fully clothed. She preened and inspected herself in the mirror for a few minutes, and left the bathroom, leaving the light on, moving to the right where her bedroom was located. A few more minutes passed when she entered the bathroom again wearing just her underwear and closed the door behind her. In short order I watched as she reached behind her back, unhooked the back strap of her bra, slid the shoulder straps down her arms, baring her breasts, letting the bra fall to the floor. A moment later she slipped her fingers under her panties and pushed them to her ankles, stepping out of them with her left foot followed by her right foot. She turned around to do something with the bathtub – probably drawing the water for a bath – and I received an excellent view of her bare ass. Over the next couple of minutes while she inspected herself in the mirror or got her bath organized, she finally turned toward the window so that I could get a good view of her bush, a big black triangle marking the spot where her legs met her abdomen. With the binoculars the detail was greatly improved; I could clearly see the size of her nipples, the crease of her legs just below her bare ass. I stayed on the roof through the whole routine, watched her step into my view from the tub, remove a towel from the tub side – out of view – and wrap it and tie it around her body, spend a few more minutes before the mirror, open the door, turn to her right in the hall while flipping the bathroom light off.

  I should explain that our neighbor's wife was quite the looker; while we were growing up she would often wear a bikini and sunbathe outdoors, which today would elicit a reaction that she was *hot*, though that term was not in use much then – fox was more typical – and I didn't think of her like that. After all, she was the neighbor's wife and part of the older generation, too. Still, at under five feet tall, she was almost a prototype Italian brunette bombshell, due, no doubt, to her Italian-American heritage; she was well-proportioned for her size, sufficiently endowed on top, not skinny but in good shape for a woman in her mid-thirties with only a slight paunch, a well-rounded butt and a complete absence of cellulite. In short, she could hold her own against most any twenty-year-old. Having witnessed the total package unencumbered, I can attest to that; add to that her penchant for constant sunbathing, a deep tan on top of that body was a definite eye-catcher for any man with active blood circulation.

  As the summer progressed I got bolder. It was apparent early that observing from our roof into the neighbor's bathroom provided a limited field of view which binoculars, while magnifying detail, could not improve. History had demonstrated that, due to the flat roof over the neighbors' garage, objects would easily land on the roof and stay there, so we always had our ladder in the back which we could quickly throw up against the outer wall of the garage to climb to its roof and retrieve said objects. Upon return to the ground we would often leave the ladder against the garage wall, so it was not unusual that the ladder would remain there for days, weeks, sometimes months at a time. The garage roof was also strategic in this voyeuristic mission as it extended beyond the bathroom window and ended barely eight feet from it. If I could get to the garage roof surreptitiously during the 'revealing events', I knew my field of view would be greatly enhanced. Surreptitious was the key, though, and I never used the garage roof unless the neighbor's wife was the only one home, although I would be on the roof occasionally when someone would return unexpectedly, which created a total rush to avoid discovery. Despite the obvious risks, the rewards were, well, eye-popping, for a fifteen-year-old boy. Eye-popping events such as a woman steps into the bathroom fully-clothed slowly removing each item of clothing until she stands buck naked before me; she fondles, rubs and squeezes her bare breasts and nipples (more than once); she rubs her hand over her thick bush and crotch for minutes at a time while in the bath; she wraps a towel around her naked body and holds it in place while she opens the door to yell at a family member and friends, re-enters the bathroom, unwraps the towel for placement on the towel rack to stand once again bare-ass naked before me; she bends over the tub for several moments testing the water, her breasts dangling with her nipples defined at the bottom, her bare ass soft, round, inviting. I experienced a considerable number of erections on that roof, but that wasn't the end of it.

On the other side of the neighbor's house was a two-story home with a half-basement and its TV tower was on the side facing the neighbor's house and the neighbor's wife's bedroom. From the bold to the daring and even downright dangerous, I would climb up that tower, binoculars hanging from a the strap around my neck, to witness the woman parade topless around her bedroom, or perform leg lifts with her back to the floor, her bare breasts flattened and spread out over her chest like bean bags, her nipples standing up right in the middle, or propped up in bed reading, her bare breasts becoming visible when she lowered her book. There were even a couple of times when she would parade around the bedroom or lay in the bed completely naked. At times I would venture on this house's roof to widen the field of view, standing on the edge with a twenty-foot drop inches away.

I would venture to other homes, too, such as the house across the street with the college-age daughter. I had noticed that there were two or three young women over there, but the only place where I felt safe enough observing was a small basement window to the side. I looked in it once and one of the girls was doing laundry wearing a T-shirt and panties. A few days later, the light was on again so I crept up to a few feet away; it was the same girl, about twenty with light brown hair, average height, breasts filling the T-shirt she was wearing over her shorts, below which were strong, smooth legs. She was filling the washer when she crossed her arms to grasp the bottom of her shirt and pulled it over her head in one motion to drop the shirt in the washer, revealing two full, milky-white breasts with light brown circles in the middle crowned by similarly colored nipples. I watched until she left the room about five minutes later, hoping that the shorts she was wearing might end up in the washer, too, but that didn't happen. The girls left a few days later.

Things had changed quite a bit in just a few months; it was time for me to make a change in appearance. The long, stringy, greasy hair had to go. I had my Mom take me to a barber for the first time in about a year and a half to lop off the hair that had grown more than four inches below my shirt collar; when we left my hair was above my collar in the back and above my ears on the side. The barber never did know what to expect and I think he was still freaked out when we left. The other change I made was to start parting my hair in the middle instead of the natural part from the left side that I had always had from a young age. That weekend I freaked out my surviving grandparents – my mother's parents – when I came over to mow their lawn. My grandfather tried to tease me mercilessly but I was unfazed. I was getting older and bolder, but in a sneaky way as you have probably surmised, so I freaked them out even more when my grandfather tried to give me the five bucks he always gave for mowing their lawn. I refused the money and instead insisted that he treat my thirst with a beer. They both tried the argument that I wasn't old enough to drink alcohol, but I countered that I was fully physically capable of drinking alcohol, especially since my own father consistently brought home cases of Schlitz for me. I knew that they knew it was true and a few moments later, my grandfather ordered my grandmother to get me a beer. I rode my bike home that afternoon buzzed.

This summer was also the start of earning a driver's license. The first step: attending the screening of accident movies, sponsored by the state police. The idea was if you saw all these graphic results of all these accidents you would drive a vehicle more responsibly. I think it was three separate showings about an hour and a half each, conducted by a representative of the state police. I felt like throwing up one time but after I reached the bathroom at the school and composed myself over ten minutes, I went back and sat until the end. The movies consisted of actors who closely resembled the victims re-enacting what might have taken place just prior and up to the accident based on the evidence available, and showing the scenes of the accident. The only one that I can remember clearly was about three black guys in their late teens or early twenties driving an old bomber; the narrator insisted that a responsible driver should keep the vehicle in good condition, inspecting it frequently, and know the signs of trouble. The three guys had stopped at a gas station and ordered coffee because they had been feeling sleepy, thinking it was the effect of the long trip they were taking, but a broken exhaust pipe can leak carbon monoxide into the cabin of a vehicle, which is what their car suffered from. Miles down the road the driver had lost consciousness from the fumes and the car had run off the road at a high rate of speed.

There was the driver, the camera located at the front of the car on the driver's side, his head embedded around the windshield post of the car. And I mean imbedded into the metal post as it was clearly two to three inches past the part of his face wrapped around it. *Road trip!*

"Did you hear?" my brother Mike asked me. He didn't wait for my response when he added, "They found Jim Morrison dead in his hotel room in Paris today."

I don't remember saying anything. I didn't even know he was in Paris. Were the Doors on tour? Out in Podunk we hadn't even heard their latest release. Looking back it seems that the Doors, and especially Morrison, were deliberately ignored in the latter part of the band's, and Morrison's, lives. Their radio play had continually decreased and the legal trouble that Morrison faced, the scandal concerning whether he whipped out his cock or not, and the ever-growing disappearing act, was already moving the band toward the ignominious fate of a faded memory. Even the rock press and hip people were paying little attention to them. I had heard most of the Doors' music and Mike had given me the album *Strange Days*, but after Mr. Mojorison died, so did their last album. Ironically, it contained perhaps their best rockin' tune, *L. A. Woman*, which eventually became a staple of the Classics radio formats.

Morrison's death didn't affect me as much as Hendrix and Joplin, but I'm sure it didn't hurt Don McLean's *American Pie*. The saying, "sex, drugs, and rock 'n' roll," ignores a term that should always be included, "premature death". It goes with rock 'n' roll, like mashed potatoes and gravy. Morrison's passing was the last of the trifecta and a whole lotta people recognized it for that, but by the summer of 71, I just didn't have much feeling left. I knew it was the end, but life goes on, which is just another beginning. Or maybe I was just dizzy—from standing on roofs leering at a naked female, from people dying around me and far away, from friends disappearing without a word, from traffic accident 'movies' (they don't show these at Halloween, do they?). It could have been a lot of things. Coulda been gas—runs in the family.

Act Five
Is There Life After Your Friends Leave You?

Sometime around Independence Day I got a letter from Charlie during *his* road trip. It came from somewhere out west – I don't really remember where or what he wrote in it other than he added drawings, which was his style, and I used to save his and others' letters but I couldn't begin to tell you where they are now. He was just letting me know that he wasn't dead – he might have written that, or more aptly 'I ain't dead yet' – and that he and Mark had been to many places. That was pretty much all of it, other than the usual ranting against the establishment and pigs (law enforcement authorities) and rednecks and church-types, the usual gang. There was no relating of plans; it was just short, a note that he was thinking of me, which was good since I hadn't heard squat from him in months.

A few weeks later the phone rang. It was Charlie on the other end.

"What the fuck do you want?" I asked.
"Eat shit and die, fuckbubble," he replied.
"Where are you calling from?" I asked.
"I'm at Mom's house," he said. "Let's get together."
"Let's," I said.

Just like that we were back to old times. I rode my bike over to his house, where I found Charlie's Mom and Les cordial, and Charlie being, well, Charlie. Charlie dominated the conversation, per usual, as he talked about what he did and where he went during his time away. He and Mark spent most of the time in Iowa in an attic with a bunch of young people in a house rented by some college age people who, apparently, sold dope for a living. He and Mark eventually made their way through Missouri and Kansas, where they split up. Mark headed further west and was in or near Seattle at one time. Despite all the regaling, the deepest impression I had when we left his house was how completely unapologetic Charlie seemed, and how accepting his Mom and Les seemed. It was eerie.

Cool. My best bud was back, after we both had diverged in different directions, we were now back together again, just like old times. Well, not exactly. While we were usually together every day for the next couple weeks, Charlie, his Mom, and his Dad were negotiating. Those negotiations led to a phone call from Charlie; he just wanted to let me know that he was not attending Southeast High School next month, but instead would be attending school in Champaign. He was going to live with his Dad and he was packing up and leaving that day. He would give me a buzz with his new phone number later. See? Not exactly.

True to his word, Charlie called me a few days later. He asked, "What are you doing Saturday?"

"Nuthin'," I said. "I got nuthin' planned."

"You wanna go sailing with my Dad and me?"

"On what?"

"Dad's got a little fourteen-footer," Charlie explained. "It's fun, relaxing, you'll enjoy it."

"Where?"

"We've got a spot at the marina on Lake Decatur."

I groaned audibly.

"It's not bad," Charlie suggested, adding, for further persuasion, "It's better than Podunk, by far."

I wasn't in the mood to argue the merits of either, so I agreed to go. They were to drive from Champaign, pick me up and drive to Decatur, a total driving distance of about 130 miles before we even get to the boat.

Nevertheless, come Saturday morning, there they are pulling up in my driveway, right on time. Charlie's dad was at the wheel of an old Volvo, smiling and chiding like a maniac. I had known Charlie for five years but this boating trip was the first time I had ever seen his old man. I liked him right away. He had a constant sense of humor and the Irish gift of blarney; I could see which parent was most responsible for many of Charlie's character traits.

We drove straight away to Decatur but detoured south around the city until we reached the lake environs, driving around one of the inlets until we reached the marina. My groan when Charlie and I talked on the phone concerned my memory of Decatur from the few earlier trips there, and as we drove around the city with the car windows down, the reason was olfactory due to the old factory. The plant built on one end of the lake by the same owner who was the founder of the professional football team that eventually became the Chicago Bears simply spewed chemicals from its smokestacks that threw out a noticeable stench for miles downwind. I hated that smell but I have to admit that as the day wore on the stench became less pervasive; one just gets used to it.

After we parked the car we walked to the berth. It was a small sailboat, all wood, with one mast. Never having done much sailing since, you'll have to forgive me for my inability to remember some nautical terms, such as the name of the beam that runs perpendicular to the mast – can't remember it. That beam is where they tie the main sail for storage and Charlie's Dad hopped in to prepare the boat and sail for our little excursion. When it was ready he called for both of us to board, which we did, and I initially sat in the front. Charlie untied the ropes to the dock, pushed off and hopped in the boat; his dad steered the rudder to move the boat parallel to the waterway. Both maneuvered the beam and sail to catch the wind from the correct side and past the docks and out into the open lake we went. We steered clear of the local sailboat race, staying outside the course but watching it with fascination. Charlie's Dad knew many of the sailors and boats in the race, some of whom he obviously admired and some of whom he obviously didn't, with sometimes hilarious comments. This was also where I learned about a spinnaker, the second sail lifted at the bow after a turn to catch more tailwind to go faster. Still, I was left with the second dubious impression: the sheer number of small, dead fish floating on the surface of the lake. There were so many dead fish I wouldn't have wanted to count them all. Even so, we all enjoyed the afternoon and we did it again a couple weeks later.

A few weeks before school started for either of us, Charlie took a bus from Champaign to Podunk to spend the weekend at his Mother's house. He had called me during the week and we made plans to spend Saturday and most of Sunday together. Saturday morning, I called him and we decided that I would ride my bike to his house and we would take the bus into town and walk around. We eventually made our way to a pool hall on Fifth Street and played pool for about an hour and a half. We walked around some more, checked out a bookstore – Charlie bought a couple of magazines, but I just looked around – and walked through the library, went to the last department store left downtown – didn't buy anything – and visited the local 'head shop'. We caught the bus back to Reservoirtown and walked the couple blocks back to his house. His mother wanted him to eat with them so I rode my bike back home and ate with my folks. A little later Charlie's mother drove him to our house and we goofed around for a while outside; we went back inside and played a game of hearts with Mike, pretty much destroying him, played a game of chess, which I lost, and we went to my bedroom to listen to some music and talk.

We jackjawed for a while when Charlie asked, "You think anybody's gonna come in?"

It was after eleven o'clock at night, so I replied, "I don't think so. It's kinda late and the parents are getting ready for bed. Mike and Jeff wouldn't want me for anything, so I wouldn't expect anyone."

Charlie plunges his right hand deep in the front pocket of his jeans and removes a baggie of chopped, green vegetable material. "I got some stuff, here," he said, as he moved to his overnight bag he had brought, "and I thought I should roll one up and we'll go outside and smoke it."

"Cool, man," I replied, with unexpected enthusiasm considering that I had never smoked pot before and hadn't really wanted to.

Charlie removed a little box from his bag that contained a pack of rolling papers and some other items; he flipped the top of the box over, reached into the baggie and pinched some of the green vegetable material – marijuana – and spread it on the box top. Using the lid of the rolling papers he strained the marijuana with the box top tilted so that seeds and larger pieces would slide to the bottom and the smaller, smoother pieces would stay at the top. Once satisfied with the straining, he removed a paper and twirled it around the first three fingers of his left hand; with his right hand he used the lid of the rolling papers to scoop the strained marijuana and dump it in the twirled paper. He leveled the marijuana in the paper, held the paper with a hand at either end and spun it into a cigarette, quickly licking the glued side and running his fingers over the end to secure it. "Let's go," he said, standing up and walking to the door. Outside we went.

We walked to the very back of the yard and Charlie removed a pack of matches, put the cigarette between his lips, tore out a match, struck it and fired up the cigarette. The smell was distinctive, surprisingly sweet and thick; emitting a snorting noise to hold the smoke in his lungs, Charlie raised the smoking cylinder to me and I grasped it, put it to my lips and sucked the smoke into my lungs, immediately coughing. Charlie laughed, trying to control it in spurts, spewing smoke from his nostrils. With his body machinations, I started to laugh in spurts and spew smoke through my nostrils, too. We smoked the cigarette down to a stub, coughing in spurts and spewing smoke from our nostrils and mouths through the whole process. Charlie stamped the cigarette out in the ground, put the stub in his mouth and ate it – waste not, want not.

"Can you feel it?"

"Feel what?"

"Feel that pot reaching your brain cells, the tetrahydracannabinol?"

"Yeah. Whatever."

"No. Tetrahydarcannabinol. THC. The active ingredient in pot that causes pseudo-psychedelic reactions in the brain-"

"No pseudo-psychedelic reactions in my brain-"

"And enhanced sensory synaptic processing-"

"Nor enhanced sensory synaptic processing-"

"And a sense of 'Wow, I can't shut off my brain.'"

There was a brief pause as we both looked at each other. "Oh, yeah," I said, and we both laughed. Once we gained control over our senses of humor, I observed, "I'm looking up at the stars and thinking how far away they are, some billions of light years away, and how some of them may not even exist anymore, having burned up or blown up in huge super-novas. We're simply looking at a past that has no bearing on today or our future."

"With that, consider how many civilizations have invested so much time in studying the stars, constellations, much of which may not have been in existence even back then."

"The past is the future."

"The future is the past."

There was another pause. "What in the fuck are we talking about?"

"What are you asking me for?" protested Charlie. "You started it. I think you're getting' fucked up!"

"I think I *am* fucked up."

Once again we erupted into uncontrollable laughter. With some difficulty, Charlie managed to say, "Did I mention that it also promotes euphoria?"

When I finally got enough control, I added, "More like goofiness."

We laughed a lot that night and we were goofy beyond any acceptable convention. Everything was extremely funny. Thus my introduction to marijuana was sustained, inexplicable, virtually uncontrollable humor. I was now a full-fledged dope fiend. Isn't that funny?

The last full week of August – if you were not of majority and your home happened to be in or near Podunk – meant the beginning of school. '71 was the start of my sophomore year, the last year of split-shift ending at five in the afternoon and the last year of riding a bus for forty-five minutes to an hour after school to get home. Eddie was dead, Charlie was going to school ninety miles away, Cheri and Renee were not going to be in any of my classes, Jim – who at one time in the past was a part of a threesome with Charlie and me – was deep into a disappearing act attributable to considerable drug use, and everyone else was into their own things, whatever they might be, none of which held any interest for me. This year was different; there was no sense of wonder, no sense of innocence, no sense of discovery, no sense of enthusiasm. It was just nonsense. In one year I had abandoned hope for anything of significant value to take place during the rest of my high school career; I had clearly accepted the attitude "let's just get this fuckin' shit over".

Remembering the classes I took this year is difficult. It's like most of the year was sucked down into a black hole and attempting to retrieve those memories could just be the end, since we know that nothing escapes a black hole. I know I had physical education and English because I had those classes every semester throughout high school. I'm sure I had a mathematics class, some kind of social studies or, maybe, world studies and probably a science class. I also took a four week course of driver simulation on the machines in a trailer.

I did make some changes. I made the golf team in the fall, though I never played in a match; Dave thought it was hilarious, because my golf game had deteriorated so badly that he could beat me almost a stroke a hole; two years before that would not have been the case but he didn't know that. I was tremendously disappointed when I learned that I would not even get our class-year numerals for just being on the team; they only give out the numerals for athletic teams you make in your freshmen year. I tried out for the junior varsity basketball team; I had grown eight inches from fall of freshmen year to fall of sophomore year, so I thought "why not?" Let me count the ways: they'll run me but a few minutes short of a massive heart attack; they'll give me less opportunity than none to prove my basketball worth; for my one and only three-on-three match, they'll decide my teammates should be one mentally-challenged and one bow-legged, semi-cripple (after the announcement, the best on the other team, who made the junior varsity that year, tells his teammates he's gonna guard me because I'm the only one who can beat them); they'll have the team well-decided before the try-outs begin. But I tried and I did not get my name on the list at the end of the week. Dave made it, Fred made it, Leo made it; Leo was the guy who complimented me before the three-on-three match, then stuck to me like glue on paper. Participating in the try-outs gave me insight into our junior varsity, which I didn't think was that good; I hoped that they would learn a lot from the varsity, which would be ranked in the Sweet Sixteen the entire year. Unfortunately, you can't substitute for height and the junior varsity didn't have much. Still, I earned some respect from the jock contingent that fall; no one would ever consider me a geek, a dweeb, or a nerd; I may not have possessed the natural talent that others did, but I wasn't a pushover, either. Besides, who had heard of Freddie Carter before the previous spring's playoffs and from what planet, really, did Pistol Pete come from? Surely he must have been the lone survivor of some UFO crash carrying aliens from a planet of basketball phenoms.

With Morrison's passing over the summer, another rock 'n' roll death was overlooked by the mainstream, though it hadn't escaped the faithful. His band was just beginning to garner the recognition and praise it deserved and his slide guitar on *Derek and the Dominoes* was rightfully hailed for the musicianship it represented, but that fall he smashed his motorcycle against a car and that was the end of Duane Allman. Some people think that people who ride motorcycles are just dangerous and irresponsible, but having known two people who died from motorcycle accidents and riding one myself I can attest that the previous belief is not entirely true. What is true is that most people will have an accident while driving and while most of those accidents will be minor or yield minor injuries, a minor accident involving a motorcycle and a car or truck will be minor for the car or truck occupants but will usually be anything *but* minor to the rider(s) on the motorcycle. There's just no protection, especially when you remember that many car and truck drivers just don't pay any attention to motorcycles. They don't care.

Baseball had provided, for me, a grand spectacle that fall. Still a Cardinals fan, even after the debacle of the World Series loss to the Tigers in 1968, and with the exception of the Miracle Mets (who broke my dad's Cub heart), baseball's annual climax yielded little interest to me during the previous year. Please, the Orioles and the Reds? Granted, both were good teams but they lacked any real excitement, pizzazz, for me. Then came the Pirates with a whole cast of colorful kooks led by the quiet Roberto Clemente, a man whose English was weak but whose bat and arm spoke volumes. Watching him run down a line drive along the foul line in right field, twirl on his right leg, push off and fire to third base to throw out the runner stretching from first to third on the fly was absolutely enthralling. His consistently outstanding play pushed his team to the crown, finally earning him the honors and recognition he had deserved for the years of overlooked toil he had experienced as a Pirate. It seemed to be just the first of what could be many more to come and even this Cardinals fan looked forward to it. Long before the following preseason started, though, Nicaragua, Clemente's home country, was the site of a devastating earthquake. Clemente helped raise funds and food for survivors, boarded a plane to help organize the relief and never came back to Earth alive. Such was the life of this baseball man, whose one and only shot at the championship was victorious, whose talk was slight but whose heart was big. I try to think of the outfielders who have come after Clemente and I just can't think of anyone who could do everything that he could at his level. Can you?

In football, the two independent leagues had merged, propelled by the victories in the league championship games in January, 1969 and 1970 by the American Football League. The Cleveland Browns, Pittsburgh Steelers and Baltimore Colts shifted to what was now called the American Football Conference and that year the season led to Super Bowl Six. Remember that one? Don't feel bad; I don't remember it either.

With little fanfare school was dismissed in December, we had our traditionally short gift unwrapping Christmas Day, and we trudged through the last days of the year and brought in 1972. It all seemed quite boring and hardly pointed to what would be a watershed year, but how was I to know.

"For several months now the President, with the assistance of key members of the State Department, has been negotiating normalization of relations with leaders of the Republic of China, and we are pleased to announce that, due to the success of this effort, the President will be visiting China later this year. Dates and details are still being worked out, and once all parties are in agreement, we will provide those dates and details to all." Or words to that effect were used when the talking fedheads proclaimed that Richard Nixon would visit communist China, which he did in February. It was certainly a milestone in world history at the time, but it was something of a shock considering the principal American politician involved. The conservative right-wing could feel somewhat betrayed that 'one of their own' should legitimize a ruthless communist dictatorship. The liberal left probably thought it was some trick; wasn't the current President one of the chief figures who drove the agenda of what would become known as McCarthyism? I viewed it as an attempt to divert attention from Vietnam; *anything* to keep the American people from thinking about *that* debacle. True to the proclamation, Nixon went to China. If I'm not mistaken, he took his best diplomatic bud, Kissinger, too. Well, somebody had to do it. Pretending there is no legitimate representation for one billion people in a world with only five and a half billion is like ignoring the neighbors down the street with their half-dozen elephants hosting the circus every weekend. "No, those aren't really elephants. They're just slightly over-developed, mutant Great Danes." Just don't call, 'Here, Rover,' or your house might get knocked down.

I started looking for the sports section of the local paper every Tuesday when they published the statewide Sweet Sixteen rankings of the high school basketball teams. I wanted to see where the Spartans, our basketball team, stood in relation to the rest of the best teams in the state. They never dropped out of the rankings and that had the whole school excited.

The third week in January was always time for the city basketball tournament. The four major high schools would receive their rankings and begin a round-robin tournament on Thursday, culminating on Saturday night with the expected championship game between the teams ranked one and two. This year the Spartans were expected to dominate and I wanted to be there. I missed the first game Thursday, which we were expected to blow out the Senators and we did.

The game on Friday matched the Spartans against the Cyclones. It was all but over after the first quarter; at halftime, the Spartans were up more than twenty-five points. It could have been truly embarrassing except that the starters hardly played at all in the fourth quarter. The Lions had played their games tough and had managed to win both, so the expected championship match had come to pass.

Attending that game, it was not, in my humble opinion, a match and it wasn't a slaughter, either. At times the Lions got clutch shooting from one player to keep it interesting, but the Spartans had faster players, taller players, stronger players, and more basketball talent. We scored quickly on every fast break, we scored inside, we scored on second chances, we hit from deep, we stole the ball, we blocked shots, and we shut them down whenever we had to. We played more guys and just wore them down; in order to avoid humiliating them, the coach pulled the starters with two minutes left even though the crowd wanted to see three digits for a final score. As it turned out, the Spartans scored ninety-six, whipping the Lions by thirty-two, and it wasn't really that close almost from the start. It was the most lopsided championship game of the tournament in decades. I thoroughly enjoyed it.

The next month featured the Winter Olympics. Yeah, what a feature! Where was it that year? Grenoble? Was this the year for Jean-Claude Killy or was that 68? Hell, I don't remember and why should I? The U.S. participates in the Winter Olympics every four years for those Pyrrhic victories, like, "HEY, we won a BRONZE! Let's tear this place apart!" I think the movie *Downhill Racer* came out that year. That was pure fantasy; the guy who wrote that movie had to be on heroin – a downhill ski champion from America???!!! Sure, and the electric company *never* shuts off the power on poor people during winter, either.

Early one Thursday morning in the middle of February, everyone but Mike had their bags packed, ready to make our way to the airport and a charter plane headed to Nassau, the Bahamas. The old man was now the Potentate – the top dog, for those unfamiliar with the hierarchy of Shrinedom – of the Ansar Shrine, the central Illinois affiliate of the national organization. Local affiliates more or less have free reign, and the old man's reign was going to be travel and party. Hey, we hadn't been on a family vacation for four years, so it was time, except for Mike. The rift between Dad and Mike had been festering for a few years and this was just the latest in the growing feud; even though Mike had been invited, it was no secret that Dad hoped he wouldn't want to go. Dad wasn't disappointed. Oh, well.

Nevertheless, I enthusiastically grabbed each bag and stuffed it in the trunk of the car. I was ready. We were going to leave the frigid chill of the Midwest behind and be in the warm, sunny Carribean in a matter of hours. Let's get the fucking lead out, people! Sunburns and mai-tais are calling! Let's go!!

Finally, we piled into the solar destined vehicle and made it to the airport a half-hour later and the old man quickly took charge. He made sure that the charter flight was on time for departure; he took the travel agent going with us aside to question that the customs arrangements were smooth at the Nassau airport, that all the arrangements were in place at the seaside motel, that the excursions that some had booked were solid, that there wasn't any problems that should be addressed now. Of course, I was not privy to any of these discussions, but everything went very smoothly, because a number of people told me so on the way back.

We boarded the jet, which soon rolled down the taxiway, turned onto the connecting roadway, turned again to point down the runway, and came to a dead stop. A few seconds later, though, the pilot throttled up the engines which responded with a roar and we accelerated down the runway until the front of the plane tilted up and the rear wheels left the pavement. We climbed to the overcast sky and burst through the cloud layer to be drenched by the blinding light of the rising sun. We watched the landscape and clouds beneath change ever so slightly for about two hours, until the landscape disappeared, replaced by endless blue-green water, punctuated with the occasional island way off in the distance in various directions. Another half-hour, we were descending down to the international airport at Nassau, the Bahamas. The jet rolled to a separated area of the airport, away from the main gates, where we could all be checked and cleared by customs as a group, part of their usual routine with charter groups.

We waited together, watching our bags unloaded from the plane before us. Once unloaded, everyone claimed their bags and lined up before the roped customs podium, as it wasn't a desk or counter at all. The customs agent asked the leader of each party a few questions, made some marks on a pre-printed form that looked like it had names on it, then announced, "Thank you and welcome to Nassau." He would repeat that process until all were accounted for. What impressed me the most was that there was no inspection of any bag.

We walked out of the airport into the hot sun and, with no sunglasses, everything seemed to take on a strange, bleached tone. Dad approached a cab and the driver emerged from behind the wheel on the *right* side of the cab and spouted something in a lilting, strangely British accent. Dad asked him if he knew where the motel was, naming it. The cab driver responded with that same lilting, strangely British accent some words that were unintelligible to any of us. Dad started to ask him again and was getting audibly and visibly upset, until a constable stepped up and assured Dad in a less lilting but still strangely British accent that the driver knew where the motel was and would take us right to the lobby entrance. Driving at a good clip but not reckless by any means, the cabbie had us right before the lobby entrance of the motel in about twenty minutes. Dad was certainly pleased and gave him a good tip after he lifted the last of our bags from the trunk and said, "Thank you."

"Ya welcum," he smiled, stepped around to the *right* side of the car, opened the door to sit behind the wheel, started the cab and drove off.

Dad got the keys to our rooms – one for our parents and one for Jeff and me – and asked me to take our bags to the rooms and get Jeff to help while he stayed near the lobby to oversee the rest of the group's check-in. Our task was easy, helped by the fact that we were on the first floor, and we had it done in minutes. Now it was time to change, since it was obviously shorts, T-shirt and bare feet weather.

We hung around our room, where, not long after, Dad and another guy appeared at the door. With them was a cart loaded with beer. Jeff and I were going to lose our bathtub and we were going to have to make some trips to the ice center for buckets of ice with the worst of it all being that we would spend the rest of the vacation with alcohol in our room, an obvious teenage infraction. Poor us. The other guy turned out to be the group lush and he turned to me and said, "Okay, you're in charge of the beer tub, which means you have to keep it iced and let us know when it's getting low. For that, you can have one every once in a while."

I looked at the old man as he nodded his head and I replied, "We can do that, but anybody that wants a beer's gotta show us ID."

Minutes later we were walking on the beach over the surprisingly hot sand and stepping into the Atlantic Ocean. The water was cool but kind to our feet, yet we both knew what we had to do next. A short time later, money in our hands, we were at the small shop at the hotel buying cheap sunglasses and thongs. We were officially island tourists.

The hotel was really a resort, with a considerable beach area, a pier, an outdoor stage and dance floor, and fishing and boat excursions. The tourist company also had arranged many tours, but the four of us never left the resort. Instead, Jeff and I would walk up and down the pier, hang out on the beach, walk in the water, drink beer, listen to the steel drum band play music, and listen to the musicians or the resort employees – all black - as they talked to the tourists or to us about some of the rougher areas in town. Whether the talk was true or not, the parents weren't interested in going to town. Since Jeff and I had no means to even get to town, we weren't going there either, but we didn't care. The weather was great, the scenery was great, we were in relaxation mode, and we weren't in school. What else do you need?

It was like that for four days and three nights. The resort provided all the meals so there was never any need to leave. Some of those that did had some pretty wild stories but we didn't care. Nobody got hurt and everybody had fun. The only disappointment was that we had to leave; the only insult was that we had to go through customs on the way back and most everyone's bags were searched, making it a much longer trip back than when we came.

Cruising along in school, nothing much of interest occurred. Everyone had noticed a change in me, how 'clean-cut' I seemed, how much less I joked around in class. Occasionally, I would smoke some pot with my younger brother or the neighbors or Jim, before or after school; at some of the basketball games, during the intermissions, I'd run into some people – some I knew and some I didn't – who were tokin' up and I'd be offered a hit and I'd take it. Dad still bought me beer when it got low and I'd drink some when I felt like it, not every day and not a lot. All in all, I was reasonably content, but few people really knew what that change at school was all about; it wasn't that I had 'turned a new leaf'; I wanted to get in school quickly, get through my classes with no hassle, and leave school as soon as it was over. Other than the basketball games I attended, few people from school ever saw me outside of school, and that was okay with me.

I went looking for the driver's education teacher about a month from my birthday to get my training scheduled. I had passed the written test for my learner's permit the summer before, had passed the simulator classes, had attended all the state trooper accident movies, so I had all the requirements fulfilled to get my driver's license except driver's ed. When I caught up with the teacher, I soon discovered that the next class he could get me in started well after my birthday and would last four weeks. When I muttered that the class would be over about two months after my birthday, he admonished me that I should have scheduled my training in January, right after school started again. Where were you in December, man?

The basketball team kept winning and when the season was complete, the Spartans were the best team in the conference, which, at the time, still had teams from Peoria and a total of twelve. When the regional pairings and sites were announced, it was obvious that the state tournament administrators were going to make it as difficult as possible for us. We were seeded number two in the Lincoln regional, which was not good as Lincoln was one of a handful of teams that had actually beaten us; if the Spartans were going to win their first-ever regional it looked like they would have to do it on the home court of a team that had already beaten them. Both teams won their respective games easily and would face each other in the championship on Friday. I convinced my accountant father, in the heat of the tax season, to drive up with me to Lincoln and watch the game.

The opposition had the tallest player with the most skill downstate, Norman Cook, who would leave for Kansas University the following year - though personal troubles short-circuited his basketball career - a scrappy, well-regarded forward, and two guards with excellent ball-handling skills who could shoot the ball from downtown. In the first half the Spartans looked nervous and made dumb mistakes, to the delight of the home fans, who enjoyed a sizable double-digit lead as both teams retired to their locker rooms. In the second half, though, the Spartans played inspired defense and their tactic was demonstrated early when they trapped one of the Lincoln guards away from the basket, eased up so he could move to the middle of the court, then our quickest guard would take a quick step to him, slap the ball to the their basket as our forward moved up the lane, picked up the loose ball and threw it to our guard streaking to the basket for two points. They did the same thing, on either side, five or six times, all successful, and when the third quarter horn sounded, the Spartans had better than halved their deficit. Now the game was on. The Spartans used their greatest advantage, speed, to which Lincoln had no answer. Lincoln held on valiantly during the last quarter, but they were rattled and it showed. With less than a minute remaining, the Spartans got the ball inside away from Cook and quickly from six feet away the shot went up that tied the game. Lincoln called a timeout and when play resumed, it appeared they were content to play for the last shot, to win or force overtime, but the Spartans were relentless on the ball and ultimately Lincoln turned the ball over. Now the Spartans called a timeout. They brought the ball up the court quickly and worked it around the defense with seconds left; the pass came into the paint to our star forward, who seemed the likely player to take the last shot, so Lincoln converged on him, only to watch helplessly as he threw it back outside to our tiny guard who knocked down his wide-open shot from twenty-five feet out with a couple ticks left. When Lincoln brought the ball in after their final timeout, they tried to throw it the length of the court, but it was tipped away and bounced around until one of the Lincoln players picked it up and desperately heaved it toward the basket harmlessly. The Southeast Spartans were regional champions, winners of a thrilling game with a final score of sixty-six to sixty-four.

The euphoria was short-lived, though, as the Spartans blew a nineteen-point lead in the fourth quarter and lost in overtime to Decatur Eisenhower, a team they had handily beaten once before. The insult to the injury was the team that won the Springfield sectional by beating Decatur Eisenhower eventually played the state championship game against the team of destiny, Dolton Thornridge. Thornridge had a star player you may have heard before, Quinn Buckner. The team Thornridge beat: Quincy. What was the injury? Quincy was a one-man offense and he was good, but they would never have beaten the Spartans like they beat Eisenhower, with their main man scoring forty-five points. No player scored more than twenty-five against the Spartans all year. Quincy was no match for Thornridge – they lost by more than forty points – and there may not have been a team that was a match for them…except maybe the Spartans. All the starters could carry the team at any time, they had a deep bench, and they had speed. Marcus Haynes was the guard that kept slapping the ball away from the Lincoln players and hit the game-winner; he scored twenty-two points that game and was named MVP of the regional, which is not bad for a guy barely five foot, eight inches tall. Jeff Allen was the other guard, although he played inside a lot; he scored over thirty points against Lanphier and was named city tournament MVP.

Stark Nelson was the shooting forward who passed to Haynes for the game-winner against Lincoln and played four years in college. Herb McMath was the power forward, the enforcer, six foot four and built like a linebacker; he was the top rebounder but not much of a shooter; he was more interested in football and played several seasons for the Oakland Raiders, mostly on special teams. Rick Montooth was the center, the tallest player on the team, but he was thin with little power; he had a good touch, though; he now coaches the Spartans. They had one weakness. They were their own worst enemy; they wouldn't lose a game so much as beat themselves. They lost to Eisenhower because they couldn't find the discipline to slow the game down and run out the clock; the coach even apologized the next day over the intercom. Thornridge may have won the game if the two had played, but they wouldn't have beaten them, the Spartans would have beaten themselves; and, at least, it would have been a game, not a massacre like they committed against Quincy. Quinn Buckner probably wouldn't see it that way and that's his right. Since he went to Indiana to play for Bob Knight, though, I can say this about Buckner: he was good in his element, since he has a national championship, he played on the victorious Olympic team, and he even has a ring from the pros. I have to ask, though, does anybody remember the tremendous contributions Buckner made to the Boston Celtics that year? Do you even remember which year? Perhaps the pros wasn't his element, so I rest my case.

Act Six
They Call Me the Working Man

"Somebody's sweet sixteen," I heard my mother sing out when she heard me stumble from my bedroom late in the morning on the Ides of March. I couldn't help thinking just how sweet it would be…if I had my freakin' driver's license, but, *noooo,* I was looking at several more weeks before I would even begin behind the wheel training. So today would be the same day like all the others before it – take the wonderful school bus with the wonderful school bus driver at the wheel and take the short way to school and the long way completely around the lake back home. How sweet it is!

    We moved into April and celebrated Jeff's birthday. When that became the past, we anticipated the next major event. We were going to London, Jack, for a week with a one-day diversion to Paris. It was going to be cool and I counted the days when we would board another charter and fly away from Podunk.

    That day came in late April and we had our bags packed the night before because we would be leaving even earlier than the trip to Nassau. We would actually be taking off before the sun rose and, again, Mike would be staying at home. Just like last time, when we got to the airport, Dad was the travel organizer, keeping the tour agent honest. After the bags were loaded and the plane was checked, the tour agent announced it was time to board. We all got on the plane in our assigned seats, the plane rolled into position and off we went. Once we pierced the cloud layer, after a few minutes, we watched the sun rise above the horizon. We flew northeast, over Canada and Greenland, and about eight hours later, we set down in England.

Customs in London was more stringent and formal than in Nassau. We all had to get a passport and many of the group's bags were searched, but it was all done very politely, very businesslike. Soon, we were out of the airport, in a taxi, and whisking through the London traffic to our hotel buttressing Buckingham Park and the princess' palace. This time Jeff and I were staying in a room on the seventeenth floor with a third, Keith, who was Jeff's age and lived in the same area of the reservoir. Both sets of parents were initially peeved that their rooms were not on the same floor and the hotel staff was very apologetic, but we convinced the parents, once the hotel confirmed that it would be hours and probably not until the next day when they could put all three rooms on the same floor, that we would be alright. We agreed that we wouldn't leave the hotel without first coming to one of the parents' rooms and they relented. Of course, as soon as we got to our room, it was party time. We're free. Let's party. Before we left England we broke both lamps in the room with a soccer ball. We were very sorry.

We scouted the park and the palace and interacted with the locals, while Keith's parents bought him the infamous soccer ball. We made a day of it by grabbing a cab to take us to a restaurant for lunch, checking out Hyde Park, to dinner and back to the hotel. Most of the group took a tour up north to see castles and buildings, including the one where the architect built the columns two inches short of the ceiling to prove the point that you can design a ceiling structure that's strong enough to hold up without columns every twenty feet. It rained most of the next day, Tuesday, so nobody really did much until the afternoon when everybody in the group was talking about the death of J. Edgar Hoover. Hoover, the icon of federal law enforcement, first and only director of the FBI, keeper of the files, died in his sleep. Some wondered if this was a sign that we would have 'problems' getting back into the country. I wondered which big, important person would die the next time I left the continent. I still haven't left the continent since then, so all you big, important types can rest easy. I'll give you a heads up when I do.

The following day most of us packed into some buses for a drive to the airport and the flight to Paris. Once on the ground, we boarded more buses to take a quick tour of Paris, including a drive through the Arc de Triomphe and Notre Dame, then to a section of Paris where we were to have lunch, exchange money, shop, be tourist-like, as though we weren't already. The late lunch didn't go off as well as the tour company had hoped – the restaurant wasn't prepared and they didn't expect as many, or so we were being led to believe. Dad just told the tour agent that nobody was going anywhere and the tour company needs to fix this little problem. It got fixed.

While the late lunch was being fixed, I set out to scope the neighborhood. Now that Hoover was dead somebody had to pick up the torch and develop their powers of observation. I rounded the corner and halfway up the block, leaning against a building flush to the alley, I spotted her, the Woman in the Light Blue Mini. I walked up to her and by her, glancing at her out of the corners of my eyes, and she smiled, so I smiled back. Quickly, her gaze shot back up the walk and as I turned to look at her, she approached a man in conversation. He stopped briefly, shook his head slightly and walked away. Over the next hour or so I watched her approach other men, move to a different block, chat with some other fine-looking women dressed in a similar skimpy fashion, and walk back and forth down the block. Eventually, I was standing with the old man, occasionally glancing down the walk in front of the restaurant – we had just finished eating our late lunch – when I noticed she had moved to that side. One of the male group members stopped to talk to her, smiled while he shook his head in disbelief and walked back to us. When he got next to Dad, he told Dad to look down the street to the Woman in the Light Blue Mini, because Dad wouldn't believe what she asked him.

"She wanted to take you to her room, right?" I asked.

"Yeah, for a little intercourse, and we're not talking about talking," he finished. Then he looked at me and asked, "Say, how did you know that? Did she proposition you, too?"

"No," I replied, in disbelief that anyone would ask that. "I'm sure she knows I'm too young and don't have any money." I paused and turned around in the other direction, and added, "But she has friends, like that one there against the wall." I pointed to an attractive woman at the other end of the block, leaning against the wall across the street wearing a black dress. "And the one down there in white." I pointed down the walk to the corner where another attractive woman wearing white shorts paraded back and forth. "And there's probably two or three on the other side of the block, too. At one time, there was six of them standing around talking until they split up again."

Dad looked at me incredulously as he asked, "So you've known all along that they were prostitutes?"

"I got eyes. I see things and I love looking at women. When I see a woman hanging around, walking but not going anywhere, greeting every man that walks by, ignoring all the other women when they walk by, what else could she be? She's not sellin' athletic supporters."

Everybody that was in earshot got a good laugh from that one. I walked away listening to some of the guys talking further about the women and me, but I joined up with Jeff and some of the other teenagers and we shot the shit until it was time to go. Back we went to the airport, back we went to London, and back we went to the hotel. The rest of our stay was uneventful, just seeing the sights and portraying the polite tourist.

On the flight back we stopped at the Gateway to the U.S. for all charter flights, Bangor, Maine. If you've been on a charter flying back from Europe, you know what I'm talking about, but for those of you who don't, it truly *is* the gateway. Almost every charter flight to the U.S. from the northern hemisphere crossing the Atlantic is going to stop in Bangor, Maine, for customs inspection. The international airport where the charters land is home to a wing of the U.S. Air Force and is closed to normal, commercial airline flights; it's strictly a military base combined with a customs facility for charters. We waited for an hour in its huge hangar-like building as everyone and everything was inspected. Finally, we were turned loose and we flew back to Podunk without further incident, although it just didn't seem the same with Hoover gone. Who could replace the vacuum cleaner of the Feds, anyway?

When I got back, I could *finally* start my driver's training class. Since there were always at least two trainees, I was paired with Vicki, a short, thin, reasonably attractive blonde with a penchant for excessive conversation. Two days a week for an hour or so before our classes started, we would meet in the gymnasium, walk to the parking lot, one of us would start up the car and we would drive that day's intended 'course'. We drove various roads, streets, highways, and the interstate under as many of the situations as possible in the amount of time given. There was nothing challenging about driving to me and I was pretty comfortable doing it and the instructor said so after the second class; the only act that I didn't have much experience and confidence doing was parallel parking, but I accomplished the task the first time to the instructor's satisfaction. When it was Vicki's turn, we eventually ran out of time, so the instructor advised her to practice for the next class and she would have to try it again. She did and passed. I got my piece of paper proclaiming my satisfactory completion of driver's training and on a Friday my mother drove me to the examination building, where I took my driver's tests, written and driving, passed both, and received my temporary driver's license. In those days, they sent permanent driver's licenses from the state central facility and I would receive mine in four to eight weeks. To celebrate, I called Jim to see if he wanted to go see a movie and I would be driving; he liked the idea, so I drove to his house, picked him up, and we drove downtown to see a movie. I don't remember what movie we saw, but I very distinctly remember what happened next. The parking lot for the theater was all angle-parking; as I backed out of my spot, I cut the wheel too soon and bumped the back of my mother's car against the tail end of the car on my left. We got out and saw that the rear quarter panel on the driver's side had been pushed in over a nine-inch circle. When I got home, I told Mom that someone must have hit the car, because that's what it looked like when we got out of the movie. I also told her that I thought I could fix it. The next day, Saturday, I borrowed a rubber mallet from the neighbors, opened up the trunk, saw that the dent was quite prominent from the trunk, pounded the area for five seconds and it was back to normal. You couldn't tell it had been dented from the outside and there were no scratches or paint scrapes.

At about the same time I got my driver's license – within a few days – a security guard was making his rounds at the Watergate office complex in Washington, D.C., walking through the halls looking for suspicious activity, things out of place, checking doors to the offices. When he tried one door that should have been locked, it opened and when he inspected it, he discovered that the bolt was held inside the door with tape. Discreetly, he called for assistance while staying put and when the reinforcements arrived, they entered the office and arrested two would-be burglars. It would have been just one of thousands of burglaries committed every year and of no special import except for two co-incidences; the office was the Democratic Party's national headquarters and the burglars were not searching for money. Maybe they were looking for directions to another party.

Right before school ended I heard that the grocery store in Reservoirtown was looking for part-time clerks so I drove over to the store after school one day and filled out an application. When I brought it to the office, Leroy, the store manager, took it and looked it over. He asked me a few questions. How old are you? How are you doing in school? Ever been in trouble with the law? (I stretched the truth on that one). Do you have a driver's license? Do you have a car? Can you work late nights?

Then Leroy asked the question that sealed the deal. "Can you work tomorrow night?"

"Yes, sir," I replied, dutifully.

He extended his right hand to me and I grasped it. We shook and he said, "You're hired. You'll work six to eleven. Be here about a quarter 'til. We'll fill out some papers and get you started."

"I'll be here," I said, feeling pretty good at being newly employed.

"Yeah, uh-huh," Leroy said, seemingly absent-minded, adding, "see you then." It wouldn't be long before I realized that the phrase, "yeah, uh-huh', was Leroy's signature utterance.

Tomorrow was Friday and Mom let me borrow the car so I could leave from school and get to my new job on time. I got to the store a little after five-thirty and went straight to the office and asked for Leroy; the woman at the office asked what I wanted Leroy for and I told her my name and that this was my first day on the job. She smiled as she welcomed me to the store, reached for the microphone to the store's loudspeaker and said, "Leroy, come to the office, please."

A minute later I saw Leroy emerge from the stockroom near the dairy case and amble up the aisle past the produce. When he saw me, he smiled and greeted me when he was within conversational distance. He leaned against the office shelf at the window and asked the woman there to retrieve the forms for new employees, which she had readied and handed right to him. Leroy told me to follow him as he turned around and walked through the back room door next to the office and I followed right behind. Within a few steps of the door, to the right, was a table for general employee use, with notices posted on the wall above. Handing me the forms, Leroy picked up an empty, wooden soda case, set it on its long side and told me to sit there. He handed me a pen from his shirt pocket, told me to fill out all the forms but read the instructions first, and if I had any trouble he'd help me finish them. Once I had finished the forms I should go back to the office and the woman would call him, he'd make sure they were all right, and then we could get started.

I had never seen a W-4 form, so I took my time reading the instructions. Since I wasn't married and had no dependents, it was relatively easy to comprehend, make the appropriate entries on the form, sign it and be done with it. The other forms regarded the union rules and dues to be collected, with the notice that part-time employees had virtually no union protection but were subject to dues deductions anyway, and a description of the job and the company, including an explanation of legal rights for employees, including notice of location for the 'official' bulletin board and rights for employee postings on the board, equal opportunity statements and safety and unemployment notices. Most of the notices and legal rights statements were all a direct response to the civil rights movement from just a few years past, so most employers were being very careful. When I finished I took the whole stack of papers and walked out into the store and up to the office, handing them to the woman behind the window. She called for Leroy over the store speakers, handing me the notices as they were mine to keep.

When Leroy reached the back room door he told me to follow him as he ducked into the back room. As we passed the table where I had just sat, he turned to his right and said, "This is the produce area." As he pointed to his left, he said, "That's the produce cooler, where we store fruits and vegetables that must be kept cool." He moved through the produce area, where I noticed on the right against the wall were tables and preparation equipment, then turned right into a short hall that ended with double, swinging doors leading out to the front of the store. "This is where we keep the bulletin board," he said, pointing to a four-by-four, cork-lined board with posters required by employers, adding, "where we post required notices, the employee schedule, and other notices." I looked at him and nodded, looked back at the schedule and saw my name with hours for working that day and the following day, Saturday. I noticed that my name was not at the bottom of the employee list; it was second from the end. The last name on the list belonged to Dave.

"I see I'm working tomorrow," I said.

"Yes, you'll be working tomorrow," Leroy explained, "mostly sacking up front and collecting carts. We're very busy Saturday mornings and early afternoons." He moved closer to the door and reached for one of the aprons hanging from several racks and handed it to me. "Here's where we keep the clean aprons all the clerks wear," he said, "so put this on." He turned around and motioned to a basket at the end of the short hall that we had passed and added, "When you're through tonight, be sure to leave your apron in this hamper."

I pulled the ring of the apron over my head to rest on my neck and fall over my shoulders, then struggled to tie it in back. Leroy offered to tie it for me but I insisted I should do it as I was going to need to learn to do it myself anyway. After a failed attempt or two, I got it and asked him if I was ready.

"Well, you're dressed good," he said, inspecting me. "Nice tie and dress shirt and pants, dress shoes. You might consider steel-toed shoes, but you're ready." He added, "Yeah, uh-huh," and stepped through the double doors and I followed.

For the next half-hour, Leroy stood next to me as I bagged up the groceries in paper sacks, first showing me the sizes of the bags and what would normally fit in them. For purchases with a large number of items, he first demonstrated that heavy items go on the bottom, light items on top. "And, always, use the bag for the size of the items," he advised, adding, "using a bag too big for the items wastes money. Them bags cost money, too, yeah, uh-huh."

I didn't want to waste money, either mine or anybody else's, so a thought immediately crossed my mind. "Where do I get some more bags for a size that I run out of up here?" I asked him.

"Over here," he said, motioning me to step over with him to a small area between the last register and the cart stalls where a bunch of paper-wrapped bundles of various sizes were stacked. "Printed on the wrapping are the sizes of the bags inside, right here." He pointed at the end of one of the bundles, where the number "16" followed by "#" or the number sign were displayed on the top of the bundle. He then turned the bundle over to show me that the same information, which also included manufacturer's name and address, were printed regularly over the wrapping at various intervals.

"Where can I get more bags of the size I need if there are no more up here?"

"Grab some from one of the registers that are not in use," he advised, "and have one of the girls get on the speaker to have me come to the checkout."

Leroy asked me if I thought I could handle it on my own. "Sure," I said, confident that I could get the job done without intervention. After assuring me that he could be summoned if necessary, he told me I was on my own, reminding me to always offer to carry the bags out for every customer. One of the first interactions I had with my new colleagues, one of the checkout girls, came when I asked a customer, a man with one bag, if he wanted me to carry the bag to his car and he looked at me with some amusement before declining.

"I know Leroy wants you guys to ask everyone to help with their bags," she began, "but you don't really need to ask people with one bag, except for the older women."

"It does feel a little strange to ask a man twice my size if he needs my help with his one bag," I replied a little sheepishly.

She smiled and said, "When Leroy's around, you should ask, but we don't mind. We're just trying to help you out."

I followed her advice for most of the night, which seemed to work quite well – far fewer strange looks from men. The night seemed to go quickly, sacking groceries, carrying out orders, picking up carts in the parking lot, running an occasional price check, cleaning up in the back room at Leroy's request, taking a fifteen minute break, bringing up bundles of sacks for the next day, and it was time to go home. I punched out my card and Leroy asked me what time I was expected at the store in the morning. "By nine o'clock, sir," I dutifully replied.

"Good," Leroy responded, adding, "but you don't have to call me 'sir'. 'Leroy' will do."

"Okay, Leroy," I said. "See you in the morning."

"Yeah, uh-huh."

The next day Mom let me borrow her car and I drove to work, making it on time. I punched in, put on a clean apron, stepped out to the registers and went to the first lane that needed a sacker and got busy. After about an hour, one of my old school chums, Dave, walked into the store. Out of common courtesy I greeted him, though Dave and I had long since moved beyond our school chum days and rarely saw each other, or, for that matter, really cared. This was his first day on the job. Dave would be working right next to me as a clerk, too.

I was acquainted with Dave since the start of fourth grade, at that time a total of almost seven years. All of us had changed considerably in that time, but I remembered Dave as the happy-go-lucky Dick Van Dyke type, sometimes funny, rarely silly, good when he had to be, never outrageous. Since his confrontation with J.T., he slowly seemed to lose a relevant sense of humor in that it just seemed more and more irrelevant. On top of that there was a growing sense of deserved detachment, purposeful, as though he perceived himself as above his peers. And the irony is that this was now the second time Dave's employment track intersected with mine, the first that we were both paperboys at the same time. By this time in our lives, Dave was slightly over six feet tall, slim build, good-looking, usually pleasant, courteous and playful, a guy most would probably trust. Having witnessed the change he had undergone over the previous two years, I couldn't.

There we were, Dave and me, working side by side, all day. We were courteous, mannerly, even to each other, engaging in friendly competition over who can sack faster, who can run the most groceries out to customers' cars, who can collect the most shopping carts. We cranked them out and kept the need for the other clerks to help out to an impressive minimum, so that they could work on keeping the shelves stocked. I took my lunch first and Dave took his lunch when I returned and we worked the rest of the day at the front.

I clocked out shortly after six and left satisfied that I had done a pretty good job, though I was a little disappointed that Dave was working with the same employer. Still, Leroy had said to watch the schedule sheet and I had learned already that the names from top to bottom held a special significance – the higher the name on the sheet, the more seniority. Before I left I stopped and looked at the sheet, just to admire the fact that my name was above David's. I would return late the next day, Sunday, to check my schedule for the next week.

The following day, when I walked into the store and stepped through the swinging doors to the back room and gazed up at the schedule sheet, I was shocked, dumbfounded, and my worst fears seemed to be confirmed. Dave's name was still the last on the list but now his name was directly under the last of the regulars; my name wasn't even on the sheet! I went to the office to try to talk with Leroy but he had left for the day hours earlier. I went home not knowing exactly what to do. I knew I had to talk to Leroy about it but I was anxious about why my name was not even on the schedule. Was I not needed or wanted? Did I not measure up and therefore being let go? I didn't want to hear that when all the old-timers were around so I put it off until the end of the week, catching Leroy at night when there were fewer people around.

A strange thing happened when I finally caught Leroy and timidly inquired what my status with the store was, because Leroy turned into an uncharacteristic, stumbling, bumbling buffoon. He simply forgot to put me on the schedule but I would be on it Sunday. He apologized more than once. That Sunday I walked into the store to see what my schedule was, to see if it was true. There was my name back on the sheet again along with Dave's, too, but a not-so-funny thing had happened in those two weeks when both our names had appeared on the sheet. The first time my name was above Dave's; from this week forward, Dave's name would *forever* be above mine. A short time later I would discover that Dave's uncle was one of the managers and that his family had known the owner's family for a long time. Much later I talked about this very development with the store's union representative, one of the checkers who had worked for the store for many years. She told me I should file a grievance and even volunteered to help me but I decided against it. I sucked it up instead. I never considered that I would work at the store for my career, whereas I always had a gut feeling that working for the store and its owner would be Dave's sole career move. If I truly thought I was going to stay, I would have filed the grievance and I would have won, too. I gave Dave a break because I knew he was beyond understanding. Inevitably, I was proven correct.

Of course, with the weather warmer, I had renewed my sneaking around, catching the late night shows through select open windows. Our neighbor was consistently baring it all, so it was always a priority to check on her movements, since I would so often be handsomely rewarded. A few houses away were teenage sisters, Sandy, who was my age, and Susan, who was a year older. Since they were so fine, I really wanted to catch a glimpse of certain sections of their flesh, but they lived in a split-level home with the bedrooms and bathrooms on the upper floor. There was a frustrating lack of a strategic roof or tower, the window of the bathroom they used had privacy glass on one of the panes and had no decent angle of view, Sandy's room had no window, and, while Susan's corner bedroom had large double windows on both outer sides, the window facing the neighbor always had the drapes drawn while the other usually had the drapes drawn but it faced the back road, where there was no object to climb to level the view, except for one night.

As we grew up in the neighborhood, we observed the farmland across the street slowly give way to a growing subdivision. Having built about forty houses in the main part of the subdivision past the end of our front lane where it intersected with the back road, the developers had finally started building houses directly across the street, one at a time, moving one by one farther away from the rest of the subdivision. The newest under construction, still just an open frame, was directly across from Susan's bedroom window, and the second story floor was being laid, with stairs leading to the section already completed. This was crucial, because standing on the second story put me slightly above the level of her window. I had been outside as it was starting to get dark and I could see the light on in her room from my yard, so I discreetly wandered across the street to the house being built, so I could check out the scene through her window and see the layout of the house while there was enough light to determine what was dangerous and what wasn't. I made it up to the second story and mapped the area that yielded the best view into the window, with the drapes uncharacteristically open, periodically glancing to the window for movement. Satisfied that I could make it back up when it got dark, I went back to the first floor, and hid behind some panels where I could still see into her room. After a long wait, she suddenly appeared through the window, though I could only see her blond hair. I carefully made my way up the stairs to the second story and, from that vantage point, I could clearly see her down to her knees, though I can't say for certain that she was wearing nothing but a pair of panties since she could have been wearing socks. Even from my considerable distance, which had to be around eighty to ninety feet, I could see that her bare breasts were full, well-formed and well-rounded, her aureoles were light brown circles centered over her milky white breasts, which contrasted with the rest of her darkly-tanned skin. Her nipples, though, were an undefined feature, not visible from my distance, which is not that unusual as many women have no defined nipples until they're extremely sexually aroused; then the nipples literally pop up out of nowhere. The show lasted not even five minutes, ending when she threw on a T-shirt and eventually turned off the light and left the room. I had wandered over there without retrieving my binoculars from inside because I never expected to see anything; it so surprised me to see her drapes open when I got to the house under construction, that I dared not leave for fear of missing the show. I needed time to scope the house and I expected her to appear at any time, so I figured if I left to get the binoculars, I'd miss the whole display, if there was one, so I stayed at the house. As I waited, it turned out that there was plenty of time to get them. Man, that would have been made a GREAT memory, especially when I'd run into her at school or around town. With considerable satisfaction, I could think, "I remember those honkers." Still, that window with a view for one night almost always had the drapes drawn, and after a week the house across the street could no longer be used as an observation tower, so I don't truly understand why such a smart, careful girl would parade around half-naked with her drapes open. Oh well, her pain is my gain.

After that initial awkwardness of my name disappearing from the store schedule, things kept getting better and better at work. I was getting along with everybody, sometimes joking with fellow employees about Dave, the go-getter. The owner or one or more of his four sons would be in the store at any time, but after the first moments of quiet respect and courtesy, they all saw that I was both competent and was great with the customers, so they started having me do more and more stocking, and unloading of trucks, more work of the typical stock clerk. They liked my response when the cashiers called for a sacker and we would be in the back unloading a truck or 'moving dairy'; I would say, "I'll get it. This is important but the customer pays the bill." That summer also brought something that hasn't really been duplicated since: the meat shortage. We actually had bare meat shelves at times and it wasn't because "sales were busting out all over;" grocery stores just couldn't buy enough meat because there wasn't enough supply. JoJo Gunne, a rock band of the times, even recorded a song called *Red Meat* as a strange sort of pseudo-honor; my favorite line was "Due to the shortage, I keep mine in storage." I got up to working three or four days a week and, in a month, I had enough money to buy a lime-green, ten-speed bike, which I rode to work most of the time, even when I got off late.

One of my best buds from the old baseball team that I had quit four years before moved into the neighborhood with his family, into a new house that had been built on an empty lot that had previously been thick brush and trees for years between the two existing houses. I don't know the specifics, but I do remember that one of the houses had an older couple and the wife had just recently died after a long illness; later that year that house went up for sale and was snagged pretty quickly so the husband moved away, too. The short amount of time until the house was sold was not unusual for the neighborhood; it was normal for houses in our neighborhood to sell within a month.

After I quit the baseball team, I hardly ever saw Mike, since he attended the Catholic schools. Shortly after he moved in, though, we would get together once in a while, smoke some dope, tell some tall tales, and just goof off, maybe drive around, whatever. Before the summer ended, I convinced him to apply at the store, so he did and they hired him. Hey, it wasn't ALL benevolence; the more new guys, the farther I moved up the seniority chain.

With the summer drawing to a close, my attention turned to the pending Summer Olympics. The last one, in '68, was way cool, with plenty of drama and excitement: the brothers raising their black gloves on the medals stand and Bob Beamon demolishing the long-jump record by a foot and a half, among the most memorable highlights. The pomp and ceremony of opening day was interesting, watching the U.S. team march in wearing their snappy uniforms. Let the games begin! Soon there was lots of swimming, since those events last almost the entire Olympics, and the U.S. was doing okay, but at the end of the first day, politics reared its ugly head with the day's medals count, the American broadcasters consciously keeping count of the U.S., Soviet and eastern-bloc nations like East Germany. Swimming was alright but I wanted to see track and field, cycling, wrestling, boxing, weightlifting and basketball. Water polo? I could miss it. After a few days, though, more politics came to the forefront of the Munich Olympics. Kidnappers and murderers took over a section of the dormitories and held ten members of the Israeli wrestling team, after killing one of the team members during the initial minutes of the takeover. Claiming to be motivated by Israeli occupation of Palestine and threatening to kill all the hostages, they negotiated for safe passage to the airport and out of the country, presumably giving up the hostages right before takeoff. Twenty-four hours later all the hostages were dead from grenades unleashed as the authorities tried to overtake the terrorists. The Israelis, in recognition of their part, secretly tracked the surviving kidnappers and murderers and killed all but one over the intervening years. All I can fathom from the senselessness, after more than thirty years, is this: while Soviets and Americans played at politics for decades, you gotta hand it to the Jews and Arabs. They've been living and dying at politics for millennia. *That is serious politics.*

The following day all the events were cancelled and a debate began about canceling the Olympics altogether, yet it was really a half-hearted debate – no one wanted to bow to a handful of butchers. Still, one can imagine, then, that once the games continued, it was almost anticlimactic. I remember Steve Prefontaine giving his all to get caught from behind. The U.S. basketball team lost for the first time ever. There were victories, to be sure, and some surprises – Nadia the gymnast being perhaps the biggest – but it didn't seem to hold my level of interest as in years past. While the coverage of the Olympics has consistently grown and gotten better every time around, the once every four-year event never appealed to me as much after the Munich version.

The final summer entertainment venues were the political party conventions, peculiar traditions where delegates and other 'party representatives' would meet to nominate the party's respective Presidential candidate. After the fiasco also known as the 1968 Democratic convention, both political parties were determined to avoid a similar disaster and keep the order, both at the convention site and the general city environs where the conventions would be held. I had started a subscription with *Rolling Stone*, which provided the best entertainment of all the coverage of the political process in 1972. Hunter Thompson's extremely twisted, paranoid, ramblings combined with Ralph Steadman's stark, dark, unflattering illustrations were perfect for my totally cynical psyche. The Democrats chose McGovern, a decent man, and the Republicans would stay the course with the incumbent, Richard Nixon. The most unforgettable image of that summer was the sight of conservatives jumping up and down at the Republican convention and the most unforgettable sound was thousands screaming, "Four more years!" That wail would prove to be enormously ironic.

Before the summer concluded, it was back to school, but this time in the morning and by noon, I would be free for the rest of the day. There wasn't much of note in the classes I took my junior year, but I remember having the basketball coach for Algebra. Coach G was cool, and gave his students considerable freedom to express their thoughts, however nutty or irreverent. Every once in a while we run into each other and he still remembers me, which is very gratifying to me.

Mom let me borrow her car to get to school and if I didn't go to work, then I stayed at home most of the time. Work was improving and they were letting me do more and more. I could even ask off for some days or times, and I would ask off on Saturday mornings and afternoons so that Dad and I and others could drive to Champaign and watch an Illinois home football game. Dad had been contributing for years to the University of Illinois grants-in-aid program and as a reward he had been able to get season tickets to football games; over the years, his seats had improved to the point where we now sat between the forty-five and fifty yard lines, barely twenty rows from the field. They were great seats, despite the fact that Illinois' football team consistently sucked during the seventies; they were still playing in the Big Ten and teams like Michigan and Ohio State would still have to come to Champaign to play. After a few times asking off on Saturday, Leroy just stopped scheduling me for Saturday until after the football season ended and I told him I wouldn't need Saturday off anymore.

"Yeah, uh-huh," Leroy replied.

Charlie's dad had taken a new job over the summer and the two had moved to Massachusetts, north of Boston. Occasionally we would talk over the phone during the weekend; we also exchanged letters. My letters were always longer and always grammar-based; Charlie's letters were always surreal and punctuated with laughable cartoons. We started making plans early for me to visit the next summer.

Because I had worked and earned money the entire summer, I had accumulated a stash of disposable income. My dad had advised me to open a savings account and I put a lot of my earnings in it, but I still kept a bit around and started buying albums that I had never heard, mostly from reviews from *Rolling Stone* and *Rock* magazines. I listened more and more to *hard* rock – precursor to heavy metal – from bands Blue Oyster Cult and New York Dolls. Mike and I would talk about music at work and when we heard that Blue Oyster Cult was scheduled to play in Decatur, about forty miles away, we bought tickets and made plans to go see them together. The day of the concert finally came one day in October and Mike picked me up and we drove to Decatur. They were playing at the Decatur Armory, a big rectangular building with a raised platform in the middle at the back. Of course it had no acoustic qualities to speak of; echo and deafening, indistinguishable noise ruled the night and we loved it. We smoked a lot of pot, some that I had rolled in preparation and some that Mike rolled while we were there. He had told me that he had scored some acid, too, on the drive there, but we waited until we got to the concert before we ate a spot each. It was a good time; we rocked, even got to the front of the stage, where I was struck by how short the guys in the band really were. Mike had even found some friends who had brought some beer and he had a couple but I didn't feel like drinking. Even so, when it was time to leave, I was really tired and kept closing my eyes and resting, despite Mike's continually furtive pleas to help him drive because he was so wasted. I can report from first-hand knowledge that his driving was alright; we both made it home unscathed. I think, since we never went out together after that night, that Mike was probably mad at me for not staying awake to help him. It's just conjecture on my part possibly derived from the fact that Mike reminded me every single time we saw each other for the next two weeks that I had fallen asleep on him.

At work, we were doing more and more stocking, and I was noticing the ever-increasing prices of the dairy items. When I started stocking the dairy items, a half-gallon of whole milk was twenty-three cents; before the year ended I remember stamping half-gallons with the latest price change, now fifty-three cents. The price on just one dairy item had more than doubled in just a few months. There was a lot of bitching from customers but they bought it anyway. What could they do?

What we used to stamp the prices was called a 'garvey', though I don't know why. Every time I thought about its name, I always thought of Steve Garvey, the baseball player. It was a sign of moving up when you got to strap on the holster and slide the garvey into the holder. It consisted of a stamp pad in the middle, a series of rubber dials that you pushed around to set the numbers or symbols, like the cents and dollar signs and a period, and a heavy-duty spring that held the dialed end in the pad until you pressed the apparatus against an object; the dialed end, freshly inked from the pad, would flip around and stamp the dialed numbers and symbols onto the object. If you worked hard on it, you could stamp the prices on an opened box of twelve cans in less than two seconds and not have a smudge or a miss. The other tool we always carried was a box-cutter, the kind that held a single-edged razor blade with a slide cover, the kind of box-cutters that the hijackers reportedly used in 2001.

That fall the American Broadcasting Company decided to try to cash in on the baby-boom generation demographic and started broadcasting pre-recorded live concerts from various rock bands of the time on Saturday nights after the local news. I missed the first broadcast but I knew who was appearing the following week, the Allman Brothers Band, so I made sure I didn't miss it. It was an excellent show, even though the sound was hampered by the lack of acoustic quality typical of television speaker(s), and it was long, easily an hour and a half. The show was well-produced and the band performed well, despite the cameras and production people ever present. I got to see all the band members, those that carried on after Duane Allman's death, including bass player Berry Oakley. Two weeks later, though, Berry would die in a crash, riding his motorcycle barely a couple blocks from where Duane died and almost a year to the day when he died. That concert, recorded and televised by ABC, was the last live appearance by Berry Oakley, but the band carried on after that, too. Rock 'n' roll is like a long road, with crashed vehicles and bodies cast off to the sides every once in a while; if you want to drive down that road, don't look left or right, stay between the ditches, and keep looking forward down the long road ahead, or you and your vehicle might end up as one more roadside marker. Even if it's a particularly gruesome accident, though, there generally will be a lack of privacy violating pictures to prove it. After all this is only rock n roll and the paparazzi usually don't waste the time chasing rock n roll musicians. They chase former princesses and the party girls regularly featured on *Entertainment Tonight*. Those pictures sell the tabloids at the checkout stands in the grocery, the kind of "news" rags that the Moms in their flattering "pajamas" buy as they wait to pay for their CoCo Puffs and Dad's six pack. They'll be listening to country and western as they drive home with the pit bull in the bed of the rusting pickup truck.

Act Seven
The Herald of Op. Cit and Ibid

HEARYE! HEARYE! HUZZAH! HOORAY! O! HALLELUJAH! Our sitting commander-in-chief is re-elected. God save the President! It was a nail-biter of an election and our Chief Executive could only deliver forty-nine states out of fifty, a real squeaker. In thanks, let's all shout the cheer of the day. Come on! Don't be shy! Here we go. "Four more years! Four more years! Four more years! Four more years!"

The first Tuesday in November, 1972, Richard Nixon was re-elected President of the United States. The plan had worked beyond all expectations: try to manipulate the Democrats' process for choosing their candidate so that the Democrats' choice would be the easiest to defeat in the election. That had been accomplished with stunning efficiency. They only made one mistake. They delegated 'research' and 'investigations' to a couple of egomaniacal ex-CIA operatives who hired other ex-CIA operatives who then bumbled their way to an arrest for 'breaking and entering' and attempted burglary of the Democratic national headquarters. Despite that obvious fiasco, there probably would have been nothing of substance come of it except for the work of two persistent, junior reporters working for the Washington Post, who couldn't shake the story even after five months.

Grampa was back. Ol' Henry was still hanging in there, having flown into St. Louis from the west coast. I had grown a few more inches the last time he was with us and I was as tall as he was and he mentioned it. That felt good because Grampa was always, in my young view, a cranky old codger. He wasn't that way anymore but he was slowly drifting away at the same time. He stayed through Thanksgiving and that weekend I drove him to Crawfordsville, Indiana, about halfway between our house and Aunt Jeanne's house in Ohio to meet Aunt Jeanne and Uncle Ben and transfer him. Off they drove toward the east and we drove back, westward to Illinois. We didn't spend much time with them – Dad and I – because I sensed that his sister, Aunt Jeanne, might start some political discussion, which she did. Dad was polite but firm in his opinion about Nixon, his administration, and the Republican 'mandate' in general. Undeserving, untrustworthy and mostly talk and little action were pretty much how he summed it up. To be honest, I didn't hear or listen to much of it; at that age, if you wanted me to go away you just started talking politics. "Bye!" Still true today. Some things never change.

On the way back, driving Dad's Buick Electra, I continued using the cruise control, which I've always loved. I loved setting my speed, ensuring it was set, and kicking up my feet, in a figurative sense, of course. The traffic was light on the interstate, but it only ran halfway home to Champaign; the rest of the drive was whichever way we wanted: state highways all the way, state highways to some back roads shortcuts to another state highway, or back roads all the way. This trip back we took a state highway to a county road to another county road to a state highway back into town. When we got home we put the cruise control back on, all the way to the end of the year.

Cruise control also included cruising through the duffel bag for the next appropriate images to use in the psychological adventure I called 'exploding the sausage'. With the volume of magazines and pictures I had from which to choose, there were almost limitless combinations, but even so there were some pictures of naked women that were developing into favorites. Some that I would reject frequently were obvious: the woman in the picture was a skank or the picture wasn't revealing enough or the pose didn't lend itself to some reasonable fantasy which I could contrive. Many of the pictures that didn't suffer from the above would be used over and over again. Unfortunately, I noticed that the mattress under the sheets was developing a bigger stain. Maybe next time, I had better do something about it.

I kept the cruise control on into December, past the thirty-first remembrance of Pearl Harbor Day, through the second week of the month and on to the winter solstice. A couple of days later school was dismissed for the holidays so, other than work, cruising was done strictly at home. Christmas celebration was the usual: waiting for everyone to get up out of bed, the parents making coffee and filling their cups, moving to the living room where the tree and gifts were located, passing gifts to the recipients and tearing them open, saying "thank you" to the giver when present, and cleaning up the mess about forty-five minutes later. Everyone would soon go their separate ways to do their separate things, until the day came to a close.

The rest of the last week of 1972 was spent pretty much the same day after day; I would get up late, eat, read, watch TV, eat, listen to music, read, goof off, watch TV, eat, go to bed. I worked a few days that week, no biggie. New Years Eve came and went. I watched football most of New Years Day with the old man when they had the four Big Bowl games: Rose, Cotton, Sugar and Orange. All the other bowls were lightweights with the also-rans of the conferences and they were all played before New Years day. The Rose Bowl was the game I was most interested in watching because it was the Big Ten winner against the Pacific 8 winner. Of course, it was somewhat disappointing that the Big ten winner throughout my adolescence into manhood was always either Michigan or Ohio State, but I always pulled for the Big Ten. Still, I have no recollection of the Rose Bowl game played in 1973, but I imagine it was probably Michigan and they probably lost. After one more day of rest, recuperation, and mostly doing nothing, it was back to school.

Back at school the English teacher assigned the term paper that she had promised we would have to write. We had only a handful of choices, although she did conduct a discussion of possible topics and added a couple of those suggestions. The paper was to be between ten and fifteen pages and we had to follow the standards of research papers with proper reference citations. My topic was an examination of the history and evolution of black American authors and their works. The next step was to gather research material, but I wouldn't have to do it right away. Hey, I had five weeks. No sweat.

At the store we had a new sacker. I was acquainted with Kerry from previous gym classes together and remembered him as a fairly easy-going, affable type. After working with him over the next couple weeks, that earlier impression proved to be correct in this new situation, also. Only later would I realize how much this event would evolve into the catalyst that it would eventually become. Before that realization, I soon learned how much his family knew my family and the reverse. Kerry was cool and we liked each other and started looking for the other at school, too.

Oil was dominating the scene and the dollar. The days of gas wars and twenty-five cents a gallon were over. The fledgling Organization of Petroleum Exporting Countries was flexing its newfound muscles by cooperating on limiting oil production; while the participating countries did not represent a majority of the world's total production, their cooperation sent oil, and consequently gasoline, prices soaring. Long before school would let out for summer the price of gas in Podunk would see seventy-five cents a gallon. Our social studies teacher invited the owner of the station at the Fifth Street curve – one of the discounters that had been springing up over the last few years – who simply confirmed what most of us suspected; of the forty-six cents a gallon raise in his price in the last two months, forty-three went to the oil company, two to the state and he got one. The most impressive demonstration was his 'subsidiary chart' of one of the major oil companies, which was writing about a quarter-inch in height spread over a roll of paper that stretched over fifty feet in length. The list of foreign companies, especially those based in OPEC nations, was especially damning. The previous year, food – most prominently meat and dairy products – prices had nearly doubled and now gas prices were already tripling. The rich get richer, the poor get poorer, and the emerging middle class in America, legacy of World War II, is squeezed hard. Can you say "Fuck the little guy?"

My English teacher had a couple of books that I could borrow for research on my paper; I asked for them and she gave them to me but I could keep them only for two days, even though my paper was the only one that would be submitted under the topic covered by her books. As things turned out, the books were compilations of various stories concerning different subjects and I didn't have enough time to go over them and take notes with the proper citations. Before I turned them in, though, I went to the city library and found three or four books, and two of them had the same stories from the same authors but in different compilations. I kept the notes I already had but changed the citations to agree with the new books so I could keep everything consistent. I could keep these books for two weeks and renew for another two weeks if I wished. It was a better deal for me but a fateful decision nevertheless.

I was behind in getting started and moving through the term paper – it was the first extensive term paper I had had to write in my educational career – but the last two weeks I worked hard on it every night. The hardest part was actually putting together a theme to hold the paper together in order to reach a conclusion that satisfied me, but I did it, leading the reader to understand that the price for outspokenness as a black person in America in the mid-twentieth century, by being published, was an early death or exile, self-imposed or otherwise. The second hardest part was drafting the citations, ibids and opcits according to the writing guidelines and fitting them at the end of every page where they appeared. I never completed a rough draft; instead, I would write sections or paragraphs in longhand. When I was ready to commit a section to the typewriter, I would start up, sometimes making changes on the fly, but typing until the section was complete. I followed that pattern all the way to the last day and finished it that night. I was very pleased with it and was quite confident of the outcome.

Grades would not be returned for two weeks so that the teacher would have enough time to read each submission and properly contemplate each student's accomplishments or lack thereof. We moved on and forgot all about it. The day finally came, though, when she carried in the stack of graded papers and passed them out. It was then I learned how that fateful decision had come back to haunt me. My teacher had written a big "D" on the front of my paper and in a paragraph composed in red ink accused me of plagiarism and improper reference citations, because I had clearly copied references from her books but they were not listed in my citations. It didn't matter that the authors cited were the same; the references were *not* from *her* books, so I must have improperly copied them.

There's a lesson to be learned from this and I think I know what it is: don't borrow shit from your teachers. If a teacher offers you something, politely ask, "Is this mine to keep?" If the answer is a negative one, politely hand it back and politely, but firmly, state, "I can get my own. Thank you." It's a lesson you may apply in any situation in life. Don't let anyone set unreasonable expectations simply because they're "doing you a favor." Decline the favor politely, but firmly, by telling them to fuck off. Be sure to be polite, though. You wouldn't want anyone to mistakenly think you're an ungrateful shit, now would you?

Act Eight
Senator, I Cannot Recall That at This Time

There wasn't any shock to get over with the 'D' on my first term paper. No, it was anger, pure and simple. I was angry with my English teacher, with the fact that she wouldn't even bother checking my cited references to determine without a doubt whether they were accurate or not. But I got on with my life, didn't let it hold me back, still joked around with everybody, except in English class. There, I just withdrew, meeting my obligations but no more. That's how I usually deal with that sort of thing. Fuck me over and you're on your own, forever. See ya! (Despite the 'D' I still moved 'up' in the English 'track', as they called them, for the next year. That's how my experience in English went in high school; freshmen year was the second highest, sophomore year was the highest, junior year was the second highest, and senior year was the highest.)

Winter was slowly receding, February yielded to March and my birthday approached. When the weather cooperated, I experimented with kite-flying. I hate the kites that are available today. I just want a diamond-shaped kite, paper or plastic doesn't really matter to me, and two sticks to cross in the back. I'll tie them together where they cross, punch a small hole where they cross to attach the kite string and tie a strip of cloth to the stick at the bottom of the kite and add or subtract cloth depending on the wind and other conditions that affect stability. Once I have that complete, that kite's going up easy, even in a very light breeze. As I would wind out the string off of its roll to the end, I'd tie more string and wind that out and repeat the process until I was satisfied in the length or concerned about how long it would take me to wind it back in. One Saturday afternoon during this year I had a kite with three rolls of string attached and wound on a stick – a stick being easier to wind and unwind – and put the kite up with all the string unwound. It easily stretched from the barren field across the street, over our house, over the houses across the front street and probably dangling above the little pond area of the lake behind those houses. I was sure I had close to nine hundred feet of string unwound. The wind seemed steady and so did the kite, so I shoved the stick deep into the ground and let the kite fly itself. I checked it every once in a while until dark and decided to leave it up. I got out of bed the next morning, threw on some clothes, socks and shoes and went out the door to the backyard and across the street. Once I got into the field I could see the string stretching into the air and there was the kite, still pitching back and forth, like it was saying, "Hey, man, sleep well?" My brother and some of the neighbors saw me pulling the kite in and wondered why I had gotten up so early to fly a kite.

"Hell, man," I said, "I'm pulling it in after I let it fly all night!"

"No shit!" they said.

Yeah, no shit. Have you ever done that? A few weeks later, after I continually would unwind the kite and let it fly itself while I played basketball or baseball or some other thing, some body cut the string and put the kite in a tree in one of the yards way across the front street. I chalked it up to jealousy, which is a condition you can't fight, because everybody knew that kite-flying for me was a piece of cake. I can just go out and get another kite, put all my customizations on it, have it in the air with ease and soon be kicking your would-be kite-flyin' ass in no time.

I ran into Kerry in the gym as we were both heading to the parking lot after school. We shot the shit as we walked together to the gym doors and out into the yard between the gym and parking lot. Kerry stopped, turned toward me, and asked in a low tone, "You smoke pot?"

Smiling as I looked him straight in the eyes, I responded, "Thought you'd never ask."

He started walking again, quickly admonishing me, "Come on."

As we passed cars in the lot another guy started walking toward us from a row beyond and I thought I heard him say, "What the hell took you so long?"

Kerry shouted to him, "You just can't wait for anything, can you?"

The guy said, "It's bad enough I have to come here every day. When that bell rings, I'm outta here."

Kerry laughed – that was a tendency of his – and when we got close to the other guy, Kerry introduced us and that was the first time I met Kent. We walked to Kerry's car, got in with me in the back, and we left school. We drove out around the lake and Kent pulled down the glove compartment and retrieved a couple joints. We smoked one as we drove, talking about anything that came into our minds, though as the tetrahydracannabinol hit my brain I became more quiet. When we reached Center Park, Kerry pulled into the drive and we tooled around the park, firing up the second joint. While we cruised Kent expressed the desire to get a job – every teenager needs money – and I told him that the store was looking for more stock clerks and he should apply. Kerry agreed that it was a good idea and Kent ought to do it. A week later he went into the store, filled out an application, interviewed with Leroy, and started working at the store with us.

Let me explain a little about Kent. It wasn't the first time I had seen him. We had been going to the same school since seventh grade; we had never been in the same class before and we had only exchanged the usual "Hey" and "How's it going?" That's not unusual when you go to a school with many hundreds or even thousands of kids in attendance.

A couple weeks later, Kerry and I are outside after school chatting when Kent strolls up. In a conspiratorial tone, he confides, "I heard from two different people, so it's on. Tomorrow is senior skip day."

"I heard the same thing," Kerry agreed.

"I didn't hear shit," I added.

Kent looked over to me, smiled, and said, "Nobody's gonna tell you 'cause you'll turn 'em in."

"That's bullshit and you know it!" I protested.

"Gotcha," Kent and Kerry both said at the exact same time.

"Alright, alright," I said, calming down and smiling with them. I added, "So let's make a plan. What are we gonna do tomorrow?"

Kerry spoke up. "We should all meet in the parking lot before school, ask what's goin' on, where the parties are, and decide where we want to go. How's that sound?"

Kent had been looking back at the gym doors when he suddenly said, "There's Jeff."

Kerry and I glanced at the doors and spotted Jeff strolling toward us; we looked back to each other. "We should come to school first," I agreed, adding, "That's the smart thing to do. We'll be sure that it's still on and we'll get the latest on where things are cookin'."

"Yeah," Kerry said, "that's what I was thinkin'."

When Jeff was close enough to talk in a plain voice, without regard to the many who could overhear, he asked, "So, are we skippin' school with the seniors tomorrow?"

Kent chuckled, I lifted my eyebrows, and Kerry shushed him. Jeff stepped up to us and dismissed Kerry's concerns with a slightly lower tone, saying, "Like, people are going to be surprised that we're not in school tomorrow." Jeff was another of the old buds with Kerry and

Kent and the three of them had befriended me and accepted me in a relatively short time. Now we were all going to skip school and party. We agreed to meet in the school parking lot the next morning and finalize our plans based on what we could find out from other kids.

The following morning the four of us gathered in the lot and exchanged what information we had managed to gather. We discussed our options and decided to drive out to the lake to East Cotton Hill Park, where we had heard from more than one source the seniors were going to meet for the big senior skip day bash. We slipped into Kent's big blue bomber of an Impala and drove out to the lake and our eventual destination. Minutes out of the parking lot, Jeff pulled out some stash and rolling papers and rolled a joint. He fired it up and passed it to Kerry in the front seat and we all were getting high before we even got to the lake. As we started driving the winding road around the lake, we noticed a few cars that acquaintances at school drove. They sure looked familiar. When we drove the long straight next to the golf course, a huge line of cars came around the turn heading toward us, many of them honking their horns and we recognized a lot of the cars and their occupants. Something's up.

The cars kept coming at us as we reached the turn into Center Park and noticed that some of the cars were turning into the park, so we turned into the park and pulled up next to some of the stopped cars with kids gathered around talking. While we were driving and schoolkids' cars passed us, we thought we heard them say that the cops had busted the park and to turn around. A friend of Jeff's came over – none of us even got out of the car – and confirmed it.

"What the hell's goin' on?" Jeff asked him.

"Man, you should've seen it," Jeff's friend said, excitedly, as he leaned into Kent's car and continually glanced from one of us to the next. "There's a couple hundred of us out there already. We got beer and pot and more and we're all partyin' an' all of a sudden about six cop cars from the state police come from one direction and about six cop cars from the county come from the other direction and pull into the park and block it off and start arresting everybody they can get ahold of. They didn't even have their sirens on, they just roared right in, and when I saw them scream into the park I just took off across the park and ran into the woods, climbed some fences, got out on the road and flagged those guys down." He pointed back to the car he had walked from. "Told 'em, 'You cats better turn this mother around unless you're bent on runnin' into some pigs.' They let me bum a ride here after they turned around." He slapped his right hand on the door through the window opening and added, "Shoulda been there, man, it was like precision. The pigs knew what was goin' on and had it all planned."

Kent spotted another guy that he knew, shouted out his name and asked what happened. The guy walked over and told us that he and his friends had been at the park when the police busted the party but they had been allowed to leave, along with most everybody else. They searched all the cars and were looking mostly for drugs but confiscated any alcohol and arrested anybody who resisted or had drugs, including pot. The police took their beer but they had ditched their pot when they saw the police cars. When we asked him how many got arrested he said he thought it was about ten but the cops hadn't finished searching all the cars and kids when they left. He asked if we had any pot since they had to dump theirs and Kerry put enough for a joint in the plastic wrapper of a cigarette pack and handed it to him.

The four of us began discussing our options, what we should do and where we should go. What we should do was easy; we were going to party and if we did anything else that was fine but partying was topmost. We soon agreed that hanging out at a public park was unwise; the police seemed to know that it was senior skip day and it occurred to us that they would probably be more interested than normal when they spotted any group of young people. I suggested that I knew where we could go and never be seen, where we would have privacy to drink beer and smoke pot; all we needed was the beer.

"Don't worry about the beer," Kent volunteered, "I've got that covered."

Kent started up the bomber and we pulled away from the rest of the group, saying our goodbyes but not revealing where we were headed. We passed through the rest of Center Park, exiting the west end near the beach house, crossing the Vachel Lindsay bridge, passing a city police car coming the other direction. The officer looked at us suspiciously but we ignored him and Kent drove slowly around the lake while we watched behind us for the cop but he obviously decided not to chase us. We got back to Reservoirtown and to Stevenson Drive and Kent pulled into the small parking lot of an even smaller liquor store. In he walked and two minutes later he emerged carrying two six-packs of Busch beer (the beer companies did not package twelve-packs yet and, in fact, they only delivered cases consisting of four six-packs, with each can of a six-pack connected inside a plastic ring and each can with a removable tab). We wondered how we would keep the beer cold – it was a nice warm day for March – but we weren't too concerned.

We drove to the party spot, of all places, the little pond where we used to 'shoot the tube'. Kent drove the bomber all the way in and turned it into the grass and bush where it couldn't be seen from the road. Out we all climbed from the car, around the pond, up the path to the railroad tracks, and down the path to the stream on the other side. Kerry and Jeff tested the water and deemed it chilly enough to keep the beer cold, so we all grabbed a beer, popped off the top and dropped them inside the beer —people supposedly swallowed the tops when putting them inside the beer can and that's why the tops are not removable now—then put the rest of the beer in the water of the stream about ten feet away from the drain opening where the stream turned ninety degrees and the current was light. We smoked a few joints over the next several hours, drank all the beer, talked and laughed and wandered around the 'Tub' and just passed the time away without a care.

That was our skip day, or more appropriately, skip morning. When it got to noon, we climbed back into the bomber, drove back to school, and went our separate ways for lunch. Later that day we met again at Center Park and played catch, drank a little more—with great care to leave the beer cans out of sight since the cops patrolled the park regularly—smoked some pot, flirted with girls, and just enjoyed ourselves. We were young, irresponsible, none of us were scheduled for work, and we could do that. Still, it would have been a buzz to watch all those cop cars roaring into the park.

Dad bought a boat. Actually, he bought the boat a couple years before, from a client in Virden who was a boat and marine engine dealer. It was a fourteen-foot basic pleasure boat with a fixed bench seat across the boat at the front, and dual seats that could be lifted up for additional storage on either side for a total of seven passengers, all driven by a thirty-five horsepower Mercury outboard. When we first got it, we spent a lot of time during that summer out on the lake, mostly skiing, and I had gotten good enough that I could not only ski slalom—that's using only one ski—but I could actually get out of the water with one ski. When you can do that, you're a pretty good water skier.

State water law held that you had to be fourteen or older to operate a boat on your own, so most of the time Dad or Mike would tow the boat to the ramp next to the Lindsay bridge; we would back it in and release it from the trailer, Mike or Dad would pull into a parking space and we would unhook the trailer so Mike or Dad could drive off without having to bother backing the trailer at the house and we could take off on the lake by ourselves. Some times we would have to be back at the ramp by a certain time; other times we could drive the boat behind the house – only when the lake was real high – up to the bank which was the back yard of the houses across the street and walk to the house to request pickup service. Rarely would any of the adults go with us, though.

Last year, I had gotten my driver's license, so I did most of the driving and backing up, both at the ramp and when we got back home. I had impressed Mike and my parents enough that they let me do it on my own a few times at the end of the year. Now I had the green light to take it any time I wanted, so when the weather cooperated, the guys from the store or school, with the girlfriends sometimes, would drop by and we'd go out on the lake and cruise around. We thought about fishing and did some fishing at times, but we didn't catch much. We tried a lot of places all over the lake to fish, but we knew, just by listening to some of the old-timers, that the best place to fish was in the cove where the discharge from the power plant was located. The problem was that it was illegal to take your boat back there, and you could be fined if caught in the discharge cove. We did try it a few times and had some success, but we were pretty cautious about it and didn't make it a habit. Mostly, we just got off joyriding.

With the school year winding down, I had my eye on a motorcycle. The neighbors had always been into motorcycles and now all three were racing motocross, frequently driving down to a park for motorcycle enthusiasts, with a campground, a motocross track and lots of trails for riding motorcycles. The park was near St. Louis on the Illinois side very close to the Mississippi River. I definitely liked riding motorcycles on the dirt, but I wanted a bike that I could ride on the street, too. I had noticed the signs on the interstates about what type of vehicles were banned and one of them were motorcycles with engines of 150cc or less, so I was going to buy one bigger than that. I checked some magazines for recommendations and decided I wanted a Honda, so I went to the Honda dealership and checked out what they had. They had an orange 175cc that I really liked, so I got a price on it and talked to Chuck, the oldest of the neighbor kids. I told him about the bike, what it had, and how much they wanted.

"That sounds like a good bike," Chuck said, "but what I'd do is when they tell me it's two fifty, I'd tell them for two twenty-five I'll buy it right now. If they won't go for that, then I'd pull out two hundred and fifty dollars outta my pocket and say, 'Throw in the title and tax and I'll take it right now.'" He paused and looked at me. "Be prepared to walk, though," he warned, "because you can get a good street bike in that size for two fifty."

"What about the license?" I asked.

"They can't make you buy the license for that size bike if you tell them you're only gonna ride it in the dirt. Besides, they like to charge extra for that. You can go over to Motor Vehicle Services with the bill of sale and pay for your license any time you're ready."

"If I do that," I said, thinking ahead, "I'll have to haul it back. I won't be able to ride it off the lot."

"We can take my truck," Chuck offered. "Just let me know ahead of time when you want to get it so I'll be around. I get to ride it when we get back."

"Thanks, Chuck."

We went to get it the next weekend and I paid two hundred and fifty dollars even. We walked it out the showroom and up the ramp into the truck and used tie straps on the front rods to position and hold the bike upright. We drove it home, unloaded it, put gas in it, checked the oil and looked it over. I got on it, kickstarted it and rode it around the neighborhood. I let Chuck get on it and he started popping wheelies and other tricks and rode it around the neighborhood, too. When he got back, he shut it off and pronounced it a good bike and fun to ride.

With the neighbors and my brother, Jeff, we went down to the motorcycle park for the weekend twice. The second trip they let me bring down my bike and we all went tooling around on the trails. Everybody else brought their motocross-style bikes, which are great for quick acceleration and handling, but are dogs going uphill. It was exhilarating for me to get blown away and watch them get way ahead of me on the straight in the valley only to blow by them on the big hill going up to the camp. After I did that a few times everybody wanted to ride my bike, but I kept that to a minimum by insisting that I ride theirs, too. That didn't seem so appealing.

The second day, Sunday, was all about the races, and there were lots of them, in lots of divisions, and experience, and age groups. All three of the neighbors were registered for separate races. Chuck did well in his race, finishing in the top three; Rich did alright in his race; he finished. Larry was not so fortunate. A key aspect of the motocross race is the general mayhem at the start, when everyone is spread out in single file, only to typically be squeezed into a width of about a third of the start line about fifty yards into the race. This creates congestion, bumping, pushing, dumping, crashing, and, often, separating of the winners from the losers long before the first lap is completed. Just surviving this chaos can be a matter of luck, and in Larry's race his luck ran out right at the start. When the rope dropped to start the race, Larry got caught behind two bikes that slowly squeezed him in the middle while he tried to catch up and clear them at the first turn. The guy ahead of him on his left veered to his right and Larry couldn't react fast enough to avoid hitting the guy's back tire with his front, which threw the front of his bike way up in the air and threw him off. Unfortunately, he fell in the path of a bike behind him, whose spiked foot peg caught him on the left side of his back. Doubling his misfortune was the fact that this was the race when he forgot to wear his kidney belt, a leather wrap that ran around the waist, right where that foot peg caught him. Ouch. That meant the end of his racing for quite a while. The ambulance rushed him to a hospital, where he spent the night while the doctors tested and checked him to ensure they controlled any internal damage. The gash in his back, though, was about two inches by three inches. As a footnote, this happened to be the first summer after the tragedy of his best friend's death, who died when the two were playing around with a loaded shotgun, which discharged while Larry was holding it, pointed at his friend.

Mom and Dad left with Larry while we stayed with Chuck and Rich. Chuck had a second race for the top finishers, but he kept having problems with his bike, swapping parts from other bikes. He finally got it under control and raced to second place and won some money. After Larry's crash, though, our exuberance was a bit muted. We packed up immediately after the finish of that race and drove home.

Before the summer ended, I had my first 'accident' riding the motorcycle on the street. The city had been improving the road system in the northwest end of town, so I was cruising the new pavement of North Grand from Bruns Lane, both recently completed. I was also looking for dirt roads off the main roads that I could explore, as that was the best part of owning my bike; I could ride on the street, but immediately take off up any dirt road I wanted. I spotted a promising one to my left at the bottom of two hills. The road had been widened to four lanes but none of the lanes had been striped, including the stripe between the lanes designating opposite directions. It was a very bright day and I slowed down and flipped my left turn signal on. I had to wait for two cars to clear before I could turn and when the second passed I started my turn. Suddenly, an old, brown station wagon was on my left, attempting to pass me while I was making a left turn! I turned the handlebars quickly to the right, we scraped against each other, but the force of the station wagon's momentum pushed me and the bike to the pavement. I got scraped up a little, my left foot peg and the gear shift both got bent a little, and I lifted the bike back up and tried to bend both back when the driver, a middle-aged, balding, bespectacled imbecile came up, having stopped his station wagon about fifty feet away.

"Are you okay?" he asked, sounding a bit apprehensive.

"Yeah," was all I could muster, being both severely pissed that my bike was now injured as was I.

Then the guy, apprehension suddenly gone, said the words that really pissed me off. "Well, I guess it was your fault for turning from the wrong lane."

"What?" I screamed.

"Well, I thought you were having problems with your bike, since you were in the right lane," he insisted.

I could feel my jaw drop. I also glanced at his car and noticed two young boys in baseball uniforms, one straining against the rolled-down window in the back passenger seat. Less loudly, I asked, "Didn't you see my turn signal?"

Very calmly, he stated, "Well, that's the problem, boy. You just weren't doing anything to let me know you were turning left."

The boy at the window yelled, "Dad, what's the matter?"

"The matter is your old man fucked up and ran me down, boy," I informed the boy, and, without a pause, added, "You're lucky it's nothing I can't fix, but if you don't get outta my sight *right now*, I'm gonna kick your fuckin' ass right in front of your boys." For further effect, I dropped my kickstand, rested the bike against it, and started to get off the bike.

The old man scurried back to the driver's door of his station wagon, opened it up, got in and took off. I yelled a few more choice words, but I was really pissed. Eventually, I realized that it was probably true that he didn't see my turn signals or really pay any attention to me. Drivers in cars don't really look at any motorcycles seriously, as evidenced by the fact that two people with whom I was acquainted as a kid are dead, having been smacked full force by cars whose drivers admitted that they didn't see them. It makes the fact that I had to take the driving test for my motorcycle license twice because I couldn't resist the impulse to put my foot down while I turned a little less glaring.

One morning in the middle of July I found myself boarding a prop plane destined for Chicago's O'Hare airport, where I would transfer to another plane destined for Boston. Charlie and his father would meet me at the Boston airport and we would all drive back to their house in Ipswich, about thirty miles north. When I arrived at O'Hare I faced the task of determining which terminal would hold the gate for my departing flight. I wandered about the central area of the airport until I found the right one, carefully dodging the Hare Krishnas scattered everywhere. I had plenty of time, which was good, because O'Hare airport was huge compared to the airports I had been previously. Still, in the years since, the airport has only gotten bigger, to the point where there really is no central point; instead, it's more like a haphazard connection of buildings and walkways stretching in this direction or that direction or both directions. Anyway, I waited an hour at the gate for departure, boarded, we took off, and a couple hours later landed at Logan Airport.

I filed off the plane, through the ramp and gate and looked for Charlie. I looked for the sign to the baggage area, found it and started walking in the posted direction. I walked to the end of the terminal, scanning the faces as I encountered them, looking for Charlie's face. As I turned to follow the sign to the baggage area, I heard a familiar voice shout, "Hey jerkoff!"

I turned in the direction of the voice and saw Charlie, smiling, with his father behind him smiling, too. "Hey butthead!" I said, smiling back.

I waited as they stepped through the mob and Charlie's dad asked me how the flight was and I told him it was alright. When he asked how many bags I had I told him that I brought one. Charlie and I made small talk, with our usual dose of good-natured insulting, until we got to the baggage carousel. Finally, my bag emerged from the belly of the beast, I moved up to an opening at the carousel, pulled it off, secured it in my right hand and we walked to the short term lot. Less than an hour later we pulled into the lane leading to their small brick house.

I never bothered unpacking. I just laid the bag on the floor at the foot of the bed that I was to sleep in and pulled out the clothes I wanted to wear when I was ready. I kept my dirty clothes in a sack that Charlie provided and packed them into the bag the day I was to fly back to Podunk.

The first day, after we got back and I placed my bag in the bedroom, Charlie took me hiking around the neighborhood, which was surprisingly sparsely housed for a New England address. We hiked back and his dad fixed us dinner, and we listened to music, and stepped outside for a little smoke.

We hiked into town a few days, hiked through woods and rough and hills to look out over the tiny cove that ran up near the town, a cove off of Ipswich Bay, took the train into Boston to goof off for a day, went sailing one day, smoked a good deal of Charlie's stash, and generally enjoyed ourselves. We talked about our current lives and loves, listened to a lot of music, and Charlie showed off his reel-to-reel tape deck. I remember Charlie introducing me to one of the first heavy metal bands, Slade, complete with long hair, glitter, and six-inch heels. Big heels and bell-bottom or wide flare pants were the style of the day and both of us had them in plenty. Corduroys were in, too, especially those with unique patterns or colors. We had those, too.

"You know who lives in Ipswich?" Charlie asked me.

"Who?"

"John Updike, the writer," Charlie answered, adding, "He and his wife just got separated. Ask me how I know that."

I went for the bait. "How do you know that?" I asked.

"Because she wanted to hang out with my dad," Charlie laughed, adding, "Yeah, she comes over here every once in a while and spends the night. What a trip."

I didn't think it was that amusing. It wasn't that I was a prude or infatuated with the institution of marriage, I just wasn't that celebrity-impressed. "You know something, Charlie," I responded, using my best bland and unimpressed tone, "that would mean an enormous amount to me *if* I had ever read any of Updike's work but I *haven't*." Still haven't. Someone should expel me immediately from Club Literati. Oh, wait, I just remembered. I was never a member.

Soon, the week was over, it was time to re-pack and fly back to the flatlands. Though I hadn't missed the state of conservative backwardness, I knew I couldn't stay. Charlie's dad, as cool and funny as he was, could wear on you after a while. Besides, if I stayed in Ipswich I'd probably run into John Updike at some point and might have to admit that I wasn't as cultured and as well-read as I should be. Of course, to save some pride, I'd then have to tell him that, though I wasn't well-off financially, at least I hadn't lost my wife to a red-haired obnoxious mick.

Throughout the summer, between me, Kent, Kerry and Jeff, two or more of us would take a couple of hours in the midday to go hang at the beach house at Center Park. Why? Three reasons: Sandy, the girl that I had been trying to see through her window, Michelle and Susan, the latter two being a year younger and of whom we knew by reputation but had not been able to see regularly at school because they attended during the later shift. We didn't know what job they had at the beach house except that it wasn't as lifeguards, but they were there every week day, adorned in skimpy bathing suits covering their considerably well-rounded assets. We were there almost every day, too. We had the time, we didn't have to pay to stand on the balcony overlooking the beach, and the scenery was great. One day Sandy was on the balcony, sitting in a chair with her feet resting on an opposite chair, knees bent and her legs spread, eating an ice-cream sundae, while Kent and I flirted with her. At the same time we noticed pubic hairs sticking out from her bikini bottom. When we left we started laughing about it, though Kent thought it was kind of sick. I thought it was great. I told him if she were to suddenly pull her bikini bottoms off and reveal her entire bush of pubic hair, are you going to be repulsed? I think not.

I was regularly working Sunday night on Mr. B's shift; it was his responsibility to fill the hard liquor shelves. The hard liquor was stored in a room in the middle of the back of the store, secured not just by a lock but also with a thick steel bar which rested on a pair of steel supports and held in place by a swivel strap locked with a Masterlock. For months Mr. B would make out the list for replacements, throw me the keys, and I would unlock the liquor room and fill the cart with liquor on the list. I'd wheel it out and tell Mr. B what wasn't in the room from the list and he would re-stock the shelves. It was against store policy, which was that no one under twenty-one was to be in that room, but everyone knew what was going on, including all the managers and even the owner. Still, if Mr. B didn't work on a Sunday when I did, the manager on duty would do all the work, and that was fine with me, too. No big deal.

I also helped out at checking, if one of the girls was on break and a manager wasn't readily available. I only did it when the lines were long but there were a lot of people with just a few items; I'd crank 'em out and get 'em out the door pronto. I even checked out liquor and carded some people on occasion, something that is now against the law. There were a few times when I checked for hours, but those times were few. With all of it, I was just trying to help out, to keep the wheels of the store rolling along and make myself useful.

The store owned an old trailer that, for some reason, was parked for a long time, years maybe, across the street in the parking lot considered part of the bowling alley there. After I started working at the store, I discovered what purpose the trailer served; as the cardboard boxes were unloaded, they would be torn down, carried out to the trailer, and thrown in until the trailer was full. It would be hooked up to a semi and be taken to a recycling center and returned the same day. However, it wasn't being cleaned out well and the stock clerks started talking about rats living in the trailer. Kent and I took some cardboard out there one day that summer and when we flung open the trailer, we saw four rats, one of which had to be a foot and a half long. The bowling alley must have gotten wind of it, because a few weeks later, the trailer was moved to the small parking lot behind the store. Kent and I even took the long knives the produce guys used once, determined to kill what rats we could hack; they were in there and we could hear them, but neither one of us had the nerve to get in there and shuffle the cardboard to expose them. Soon after that, I was in the front of the store, when I heard a commotion. Wanda, one of our more rotund checkers, came barreling out of the stockroom as white as a ghost, even though she was supposed to have most of her lunch hour left. Kerry was in the back at the time, saw what happened, and told me later. It seems that Wanda, who was of considerable girth, was sitting on an upended wooden soda case – there were no chairs in the stock room – with her feet comfortably spread for stability, eating her sandwich. A rat darted out from along the wall behind her and scooted right between her feet across the room and disappeared. When Wanda saw that rat come out from between her feet, she screamed, stood up and ran right out of the stock room. Apparently, this was the incident that convinced management to take the problem seriously; they had baited traps laid all over the store, accounts of rat sightings diminished considerably, and they had the trailer hauled away permanently a few months later.

I figured out how to get rid of the growing stain on the mattress. I took off all the sheets and turned it over. I also developed a new method to avoid the stain; I held a handful of tissues and at the moment of fire, I turned slightly and blew the load in the tissues. This, then, seems an appropriate introduction for: the Watergate hearings.

It may be naïve to write it but I'll recklessly proceed anyway. The boneheads in the Nixon administration had their part, Woodward and Bernstein had their part – although the argument could be made that Deep Throat was motivated and would have found someone else – and the prosecutors and judges had their parts, too, but the single most important catalyst for sealing the fate of the Nixon administration was the Watergate hearings, but *not* for the reason you might think. The reason it was *the most important catalyst was the timing* of the hearings. The vast majority of the testimony during the hearings took place during the summer, when school was out, and every student, regardless of age, could see and hear their highest civil servants explain the inexplicable, refuse to testify on the grounds of personal incrimination, or provide the most popular response of them all, "Senator, I cannot recall…at this time." Why was it so important that the hearings take place so that any student could watch and listen at any time? Because in 1973, a huge percentage of citizens of the United States were under twenty-five, the vast majority of these citizens were students, they were already swaying public opinion, and this event, leading to the end of Nixon's presidency, was going to be determined by public opinion. Every student that watched any part of these hearings came to the same conclusion: these people not only had no respect for the laws of the land that governed *all* of us, they truly believed that, due to their station in life, they were *above* the law. In living rooms and dens and bedrooms all across the country, all the students had to say to convince their parents were two words, "Watch this." When the hearings concluded, the court of public opinion cast their collective judgment and Nixon was done. Only he and his loyal minions were too blind to see it and too ignorant to know it.

The images are still fresh. There's Fred Thompson, future senator and Hollywood actor, at the time counsel for the Republican side and looking like the owner of the gas station down the street, grilling the witnesses relentlessly and with ever-growing incredulity. There's Howard Baker, ranking Republican on the committee, whose demeanor over the months of hearings visibly and audibly changed from defensive to caution to eventual disbelief, exasperation, and one moment of very vocal disappointment and admonishment. There's Sam Dash, crafty counsel for the Democrats and the ultimate set-up man; he'd set the witness up and the other committee members would knock 'em down. There's the adorably corpulent committee chairman, Senator Sam Ervin, a master of deceptive simplicity and congeniality, whose diatribes starting with, "I'm just an ole country lawyer, but I've read the Constitution many times and I can tell you without hesitation that the Constitution says nothing of the kind, sir…" Senator Sam took great delight in reminding the witnesses, and, by extension due to the presence of cameras, the American people, that the United States of America was founded as a nation of laws. Its founding document, the Constitution, established three separate but equal branches but only *one* of those branches is charged with drafting the laws and it isn't the judicial branch, judges nominated by the president, and it isn't the executive branch, departments directed by the president. Congress makes the laws and you, as American citizens, abide by those laws or we no longer have a nation of laws as it was founded.

As for the witnesses, there was John Dean, with his wife, Maureen, directly behind him and wearing her blond hair in a schoolteacher-like bun, telling the committee who knew what and when; to summarize his testimony, he knew that then, Jeb Magruder knew that then, John Ehrlichman knew that then, John Mitchell knew that then, Bud Haldeman knew that then, and the President knew that then; as for the wife, no schoolteacher I ever had looked like Maureen Dean. There was combative John Ehrlichman, trying to intimidate the committee with his sneer and beady eyes, only to become the object of satire and ridicule for his mostly asinine statements. There was Bud Haldeman, the second most powerful man in America, whose complete and thorough memory loss was either the most spectacular administrative tactic or confirmation of suspected malfeasance and misguided incompetence; since he was later convicted of criminal misconduct, probably the latter fits. There was likable Jeb Magruder, who, unfortunately, was caught in so many brazen lies before the end of his testimony, you knew he was going down. Perhaps the star of the entire proceedings was a virtual unknown prior to his appearance before the committee, a techno slog serving in the bowels of the White House, unseen by anyone. When Alexander Butterfield told the committee and the world that every conference room, including the Oval Office, was installed with voice-activated microphones tied to tape recorders through and through, the stage was now set for the battle to bring down the administration. The tapes, first limited by transcripts of selected conversations as insisted by the administration, were eventually turned over to the prosecution shortly after the secretary's eighteen and a half minute gaffe, er, I mean, gap. When Butterfield told everyone that the systems could not be disabled unless the microphones were completely removed – and they never were removed – you could envision the Nixon administration as a ship like the Titanic, majestic and powerful, but with a fatal flaw which would eventually lead to its unavoidable sinking. The Watergate hearings, as a whole and as they took place, was mind-boggling for its discovery of the degree of deception, arrogance, and malice that lay at the very heart of the Nixon presidency. If you could still defend them after that, you stood on the slippery slope of rejecting a democratic process properly uncovering an unlawful conspiracy, all while pretending to be a champion of democracy. That's why the cold-war hardliners were thrashed so thoroughly in the mid-seventies. Their hypocrisy was so large and broad that it was impossible to ignore, or defend.

There was one character conspicuously absent in all this. Spiro Agnew, the former vice president or president of vice—take your pick—had invented the term 'pusillanimous pussyfooter', but had already resigned and now faced prosecutorial peril from plentiful plucking of pesos and power—bribery and corruption—and was on the downward spiral. One down, one to go.

Charlie had introduced me to Slade and also had played for me Johnny Winter And's live album, which is an excellent rock n roll offering, more impressive when you consider that it was recorded in 1966. I bought a copy as soon as I got home. We both had the latest release from Yes, with *Roundabout* and *Starship Trooper*, among other songs. Also released was Steve Miller's latest, *The Joker*. When the title song received extensive airplay, some people called me Maurice. Actually, no one called me Maurice, but some people called me shithead. "I mean it in a nice, friendly sort of way…Shithead!"

Act Nine
One More Year and This Too Shall Pass

Before school started for my senior year, Kerry had already left the store, working on an internship arranged by his father and uncle, no doubt. His dad was a state government bureaucrat and his uncle was a prominent attorney. Kent and I used to joke about that between ourselves, about how little Kerry seemed to belong in his own family. We'd ask each other if it was likely that Kerry would turn out to be an attorney and we'd answer in unison, "No!" We'd ask each other if it was likely that Kerry would turn out to be a government bureaucrat and we'd answer in unison, "No!" We both agreed, though, that Kerry was the most likely of the four of us to get married first. As Kent so ably put it, "It ain't gonna be me, cuz I can get pussy anytime. It ain't gonna be Jeff, cuz he just wants to live with 'em; when they start talkin' about marriage, he'll pack up and leave. It ain't gonna be you, cuz you don't even have a girlfriend. But Kerry and Patti fuck like rabbits. If it doesn't happen cuz they *want to*, it'll happen soon cuz they *have to*." I think Kent was alluding to some Catholic thing involving Patti and *possible* subsequent events that may or may not include a shotgun, or three.

Kent and I were hanging out together a lot. Kerry would join us frequently, when obligations did not interfere. Jeff always did his own thing; even if he said he would do something, it never surprised any of the three of us if he didn't do it. That was Jeff.

Kent and I had smoked some pot and were riding in the blue bomber, Kent at the wheel. As we casually cruised down Stevenson Drive, reaching the end of the houses that bordered the street, a squirrel darted a few feet into the street in our lane. On impulse I said, "Get him." Kent swerved, we heard a crunch, and as we looked back we could see the squirrel in the street, unmoving. We laughed most of the way to my house, the kind of laugh where the humor had worn off but you couldn't stop because the other person couldn't stop. When we talked about it later, we always agreed it was pretty sick; it really was the drugs doing it. Sound familiar?

Kent, Mike and I were talking in the parking lot at work when we decided to drive to Iles Park and smoke some stuff. Since each of us had a car, we – really Kent and Mike – decided to race. The park was about three miles away and the roads were city with speed limits of forty miles per hour down to thirty miles per hour at the park. We jockeyed back and forth on Stevenson, where the traffic was greatest, but as soon as we got to Sixth Street, Kent and Mike really went at it, at one time reaching a speed of eighty-five miles per hour. Mike pulled onto the street behind the park first, Kent right behind, while I mosied up with no real speedy desire. I get there when I get there. We congratulated Mike on his victory, told him he was crazy – I thought they were both crazy – and voted him most likely to be pulled from a smashed automobile.

Mercifully, the end of August, 1973, marked the start of the final year, the senior year, of high school with: more math, more science, more gym, more social studies – civic studies, or government, for the first semester – and more English, this time with Mrs. K again, ready for round two. It had seemed a long ride, with bumps and bruises of setbacks and depression laced with satisfaction and reasonable accomplishment, but the journey had an end in sight. I had earned a composite score of 29 on the ACT and my enrollment at the University of Illinois was already assured. It almost seemed like the year might simply require 'going though the motions'.

One Friday night shortly after school had started, Mike and I were working the late shift as the only clerks in the store after ten o'clock. I was working from six to eleven and Mike would be closing the store at twelve with the manager, Marvin. Marvin had transferred several months before and had the proverbial burr up his ass for me ever since he had arrived. He was short at about five feet and two inches and he wasn't muscular but he wasn't fat, either; he just fancied himself the equivalent of a grocery store drill sergeant, but for what reason I have no clue. I don't think he was in the military. At his height, what branch would want him? What was so irritating about him in my case was his propensity to bark orders at me to perform some duty that I had just completed or was in the process of fulfilling. I suppose what irritated him about me was that I told him that it was already done or that I was doing it instead of just saying some inane, mindless, pointless, automatic answer like "Yessir!" It wasn't just me who found him irritating since most everybody in the store complained about him; he had a very bad habit, as a manager, to berate you in public and praise you, if ever, in private. Ever had one of those managers? Take my advice and work with your fellow employees to get that kind of manager fired, laid-off or transferred, or you need to find another job. The worthy managers praise in public and criticize in private; the managers that do the reverse will sink a company faster than the Titanic.

  The night was pretty normal. It wasn't especially busy and it wasn't dead, either. Mike and I kept everything under control along with the others, although I was senior man when I walked in at six. I flirted with some girls from school who were from the junior class that was just starting the early shift and that I hadn't seen at school in a couple years – and were filling out quite nicely, I should say – and who also were friends with Cindy, one of the new checkers that had started a few months ago and was the sister of Rick, who was the number two man in produce and had worked at the store for several years. It was just a normal night, no big deal. When eleven o'clock rolled around, I punched out along with one of the other checkers. I walked toward the exit doors at the front but looked down the dairy aisle and decided to wait for Mike to come out of the cooler with his load of dairy; when he pushed the dolly carrying the crates of products and reached the aisle, I shouted to him that I would see him the next time, and I walked to the exit door, stepped through the automatic door after it opened, and glanced both ways but didn't notice anyone or anything as I moved to my mom's car in the back row. I unlocked the driver door, opened it, started the engine, looked behind me, backed from the parking space until I was clear, shifted the transmission to drive, and drove home through Reservoirtown. Ten minutes after I left the store, all those employees who may have had any problem with Marvin no longer had such, because Marvin got shot.

  It was a robbery that didn't quite go as planned for the robbers, in this case, at least two. First, the phone in the office rang and Marvin answered it. While the voice on the other end told him that a man wearing a ski mask would approach the office, in walked the man in the ski mask, and he proceeded right to the office window. The voice on the phone advised Marvin that he should take the money out of the safe, put it in a bag, come out of the office and give the ski mask man the bag and no one will get hurt. The voice also advised Marvin that the ski mask man was carrying a gun and was prepared to use it if he didn't follow the voice's advice. With the ski mask man watching, Marvin took the money out of the safe, put it in a bag and told the ski mask man that he was coming out of the office. He opened the office door and the ski mask man stepped away from the window, the gun now visible in his hand, so he could watch Marvin come out of the office. Marvin stepped carefully to the ski mask man until he motioned with the gun that he was close enough and hand him the money. Marvin stretched his right arm forward, handing the bag to the ski mask man, but in a moment of insane bravado, Marvin lunged forward and grabbed the gun, trying to wrest it from the ski mask man's grip. For a few seconds they wrestled for control of the gun until the ski mask man simply pointed it at Marvin's left leg and pulled the trigger. Marvin fell in a bleeding heap, the ski mask man ran out of the store waving the gun at anyone he spotted, carrying the bag of money like a football in his left arm, and the three or four other people still in the store just freaked. Mike had to get the office keys from Marvin so he could get to the phone and call the police while one of the checkers wrapped his leg with a towel to try to control the bleeding.

The owner spent every day the next week at the store reminding everyone what they should do during a robbery. "Please, just do what they tell you and give them the money. Don't try to be a hero." Later, when it was just the two of us, I reminded the owner that Marvin was Mr. GungHo, so the whole event didn't surprise me. The owner confided, "The robbers got away with about twenty-five hundred dollars. My insurance carries a two thousand dollar deductible, so, in an attempt to save me two thousand dollars in deductibles, I'll now have to spend tens of thousands for medical bills." He didn't sound very happy.

I met D'Ann in my civics class, although I had been acquainted with her for years. There was a spirited discussion during one class, to which I contributed mightily, and she liked my position and approached me as we left the room. We chatted for a few minutes on the way to our next class and continued the pattern for the next week or so. I thought she was interested in me and I asked her out and she acquiesced. We went to see the movie *The Life and Times of Judge Roy Bean* with Paul Newman in the lead role. I liked it, she said she liked it, and, being the nervous neophyte that I was, I asked what she wanted to do next. She was a little tight and tense – at least that was what I sensed – but she asked if I wanted to take her home, come inside and meet her family. I had been wondering why a girl like D'Ann - who was just as tall as I was, well-endowed upstairs, thin waist, great butt, attractive face with dimples in her cheeks when she smiled, nicely styled brunette hair but nothing fancy – didn't have guys after her much and didn't seem to have any close girlfriends. When we got to her house and I met her father, that's when I figured it out. Her dad was like Marvin on speed and twice as loud, but almost exactly the same size. Being in her family, or just being close to them, would be like a permanent boot camp. She escorted me to the porch and I awkwardly kissed her and left about a half-hour after I got there. That was our first and last date.

I came out to Mom's car after school one day, started it up, backed up and turned, then shifted it to the Drive position and started limping out of the parking lot. I tried the other positions of the automatic transmission, and had some success in acceleration, but I still limped all the way back home. I told Mom about it and we called Les' service station – Les used to live next door to my mother's parents so he did a lot of car service for us for many years – and they came to tow it to the shop and repair it. When my brother got home from school, he wondered where the car was. Somehow, from this point to some point after Dad got home, my brother admitted that he knew what happened to the car. He was getting to school long before his classes started, while I was still in class. He would bring the extra set of keys and, usually, he, Roger, and maybe some others, would get in the car and go joyriding. While he was driving the car, Jeff would play 'racedriver' and shift to Low and Low2 and then to Drive and back and forth like a stupid idiot. He was always careful, though, to park the car in the exact same spot where I had originally parked it so that I would never know it had been driven. I don't know the exact sequence of events that led to Jeff's confession, but I suspect that Dad asked Les what was wrong with the car and how it could have gotten like that and Les told him it was the transmission and the most likely activity for that kind of damage was constant shifting. I think that because the first thing Dad asked me when he got home was if I shifted the transmission while I was driving. I said, "No. Why would I do that? It's an automatic. You put it in Drive and drive." He said, "That's what I thought." When Jeff admitted to me the little devious activity that he had been pursuing for months, I asked, "Just for the record, can we depend on you to be a stupid idiot or do you have even worse surprises in store for us?" As for his buddy, Roger, stay tuned, you'll read more about him later.

I had known Dana for about six years. Her brother had been in the Most Academically Able class a year ahead of me and she had been in the one behind me. She was always nice – and I mean that in the sense that she was not wild and crazy – but I never had much interaction with her as we were going through school. That was due more to our being of different ages than anything else, although if she had extracurricular activities, I didn't know about them and I certainly was not that interested in her to discover what they were.

She started coming into the store, ostensibly to visit her friend, Cindy. She also was friends with Kim, the girl in Dana's class that I liked to call, the Amazon. Kim was tall, blond, muscular, athletic, the daughter of a former major league baseball player. Kim was also somewhat rebellious, since all the rest of her family went to the Catholic schools, but she refused and attended Southeast High School. Kim and I had seen each other around for quite a while and she always treated me with respect; we liked to joke around and flirt harmlessly, and she actually laughed at my jokes. All three, it seems, were long-time friends, so it didn't surprise me when they would show up at the store and chat and laugh and flirt and try to embarrass each other and me. As things progressed, I began feeling attracted to Dana. She had a good sense of humor, both giving and taking, she was naturally attractive as she didn't overdo the makeup, and she was making a conscious effort to touch me more and more. All other things being equal, when a girl or woman consciously touches a man frequently, she likes and is attracted to that man. At least in my experience I have found this to be a true observation.

We would all meet at the park frequently, play softball, throw the Frisbee (which was just starting to get popular and decently made), just generally have fun. To be discreet, the guys would go off and smoke pot away from the girls, but we were pretty sure they knew what was going on. Dana and I never really went on a date but we did a lot of things together, even going to her house with her parents gone so we could neck. That night was fun – I got my first French kiss – but since I didn't have the experience or confidence, I didn't feel comfortable moving from kissing to fondling to removing clothes to fucking. Okay, I feared rejection. Are you happy?

Many times in the fall the guys would meet during the weekend at a school or park that was relatively deserted and play softball or football, usually football, but somebody would always be prepared for either. When we played football it was strictly tackle with no equipment. Once, one of the guys broke his leg. There were a lot of rotating guys that would play every now and then but the regulars were Kent, Kerry, Terry and his younger brother, Gary, Jeff and me. My brother, Jeff, was into other things; I think I only asked him once and he declined that time. The games were tough, guys would get bloodied, but it was fun. Kent always complained that I couldn't catch the perfect passes, but the wobbly dogs that he would heave at me would never touch the ground. "What's wrong with you, man?' he would ask me. A few years later I figured out why. The perfect passes were thrown while I was in full stride and when I touched the ball my next step would often jar the ball from my grip and I would drop it. To counter the jarring of my own stride I consciously jumped when the ball arrived, giving me just enough time to secure the ball under my arm before my next step hit the ground. It worked well, but it was too late for these games.

As for softball, most of the games we played were with few players, so there was a lot of ghost runners and areas that were automatic outs. Sometimes we played softball and other times we played with a baseball. If there was nothing going on, often Kent and I, sometimes Kerry, would play tennis ball out in the street near Kent's house with the church in the outfield. Hitting it onto the church roof was a home run; hitting it over the roof was usually a lost ball.

Grampa's short visit to our house during the spring turned out to be his last. He passed away at my Aunt Jeanne's residence the fall of 1973. Since it was common knowledge between my father and his siblings that Grampa wished to be buried next to his wife in the Easton cemetery, they shipped his body to a funeral home in Havana. The funeral was held on a Saturday and we drove the hour and a half to Havana and stopped at the house of a friend of the family, an older couple that had known Dad's parents for decades and their children as well. They were nice folks and complimentary, as older folks tend to be when they meet children of children they've known for years. They also tend to tell stories about those children, most of which the younger children have never heard before, and some of which are less than flattering. Uncle Jim, Aunt Eddie and Don, their son on leave from the Air Force but in full uniform, dropped by and some of the conversation turned to Uncle Don, who died in World War II. I think some of it was due to my cousin, Don, and his Air Force career, as Uncle Don died when he was shot down in his fighter plane in the Pacific; Dad had always left me with the impression that he disapproved of Don's enlistment choice from the moment he heard of it. He didn't use these words, but I always thought that Dad considered his brother's decision to be a flyboy as foolhardy and glory-seeking. Aunt Jeanne called and said the girls, Aunt Jeanne and Aunt Mary Beth, and their families would all meet us at the funeral home. After the funeral and burial, we would all meet again in the basement of a church for lunch.

The funeral was short as funerals go. The longest speaker was Uncle Jim, who had lobbied earlier to deliver the eulogy, not knowing that his siblings never really intended to challenge him since he was the oldest. That was how Dad's family worked things out, easily, logically, traditionally. When Granma died in '69, all the belongings that Grampa had no need for were chosen and dispersed in hours, all amicably. It was refreshing and I thought that's how it usually went. I was to learn years later when my mother's parents passed on that it depends almost entirely on the principle benefactors involved and their histories.

Once the speeches and the benediction and the prayers concluded, we all filed slowly from the meeting room and congregated in the lobby of the funeral home as we waited for the attendants to ready the casket for transport to the cemetery. Once the hearse was ready, we all got in our cars and comprised a procession of about twenty vehicles, moving like one snake through the streets of Havana, east on Route 10 for about fifteen miles to a road one mile west of Easton and another mile to the cemetery. Dad, Uncle Jim, cousin Don and three other men wheeled the casket from the hearse and carried it to the platform set above the burial plot. The preacher spouted a few more words, and I stood stiff and tight-muscled because it was cold and windy, but I looked around and noticed the attractive blonde eyeing me, the same girl who had her arm broken when a horse bit it. I had hair down to my shoulders – the longest of any of the men – and I had just started parting it in the middle and I knew I looked good, but, as attractive as she was, she was still my cousin. I discovered later that she was adopted, along with her younger brother, by my dad's cousin when he was stationed in Germany while serving in the Armed Forces, and I could have dated her, even married her. If I did, though, I would always be known as the Jerry Lee Lewis in the family and that was enough incentive to keep the hormones in check.

We drove back to the church in Havana and proceeded to the basement, where a virtual feast had been assembled. There was a large contingent of church members and local residents who did not attend the funeral because they felt they didn't know the family well enough but wanted to help in any way they could to show their support. The food was good and there was plenty of it, and the best thing was that everyone treated me like an adult. My courtesy and manners was on obvious display and that certainly made it easier to accept me, with my long hair so prominent. After a few more hours we all said our goodbyes and everybody went their separate ways.

A few weeks later President Nixon fired three of his top-level employees, including the Special Prosecutor for the Watergate investigation, Archibald Cox, in the move immediately labeled the Saturday Night Massacre. It all stemmed from the tapes. Nixon wasn't going to give them to the prosecution and the prosecution wasn't going to settle for transcripts, which could be anybody's interpretation. I can hear Nixon in his office discussing it with his cronies, saying, "Why do they think they can demand *my* tapes? They're *my fucking tapes!*" Oh, yeah, he'd be using that word – fuck – or a derivative of it. If you've listened to the unabridged and unedited version of the tapes, you'd know the Quaker president said 'fuck' a lot so get over it.

The court of public opinion had already influenced changes in the laws since the seventies started. One was a change in the minimum age to vote – one that still holds today – from twenty-one to eighteen years of age. Another was a change in the minimum age to legally drink in Illinois, from twenty-one to nineteen years of age. The latter change was of benefit to us, or more to Kent than any of us, because he looked like he was nineteen years of age, so we were drinking quite a bit on the weekends. Near the Thanksgiving holiday, Kent, Jeff and I decided to try to get into the Lake Club, which we had been hearing from friends was a hopping place with plenty of chicks. We knew they would card us and none of us had a fake ID, but Kent thought that Terry, our football buddy, might have one or lend us his so we drove over to his house and caught him lounging with his girlfriend and his family. Kent convinced him to come outside and we gave him the scoop. It took some gentle persuasion – all by Kent mostly appealing to Terry's sense of brotherhood and helping out a brother – but Terry had just renewed his driver's license and had forgotten to turn the old one in, which he still had. He wouldn't just give it to us so we bought it for five bucks and a promise that if we got arrested we would tell the cops that we found it and we don't know the guy whose name was on it. Deal.

We had to come up with a plan and this was it: Kent would go in first; once inside, he would order a drink and wait at least ten minutes – no sooner than half the drink had to be drunk – then come back out and give the ID to Jeff; Jeff would try to get past the bouncers; once inside, he would order a drink and follow the same process, while Kent would follow a few minutes later; Jeff would come out and give me the ID and I would try to get past the bouncers; once inside, Jeff would follow a few minutes later and we would be home free. Kent got in and we waited, Jeff a little less patiently than me. Kent finally came back to the car, handed Jeff the ID and told him to go and he would watch. Soon, Kent signaled me that Jeff got in and a few minutes later, he disappeared into the nightclub. After an interminable length of time that tried my patience and my body heat – it was November, after all – Jeff walked back to the car and gave me the ID and the touching advice, "Don't be nervous and don't fuck up!" Thanks, Jeff. I walked up to the entrance, opened the door to a small entryway with two bouncers wearing police-like uniforms, the one closest to the door sitting on a stool holding a flashlight while the other stood a few feet behind with his arms folded. I walked up to the guy on the stool and mumbled "Hey," and paused for a second before attempting to move past him. He barked, "ID! Need to see your ID." I stopped and pulled my wallet from my back pants pocket, opened the wallet and flipped it to the ID, where I normally had my driver's license, which was now in my front pants pocket. He took the wallet, shined the flashlight on it, shined the flashlight on my face, shined the flashlight back on the wallet, handed it back to me, and said, "OK." Either he didn't notice or he didn't care that the driver's license I showed him listed my height as six feet and three inches, my eyes were blue and my hair was blond, when, in reality, I was five feet, eight inches tall with brown hair and eyes.

The entryway was very dark – which may explain the first bouncer's mistake – so I didn't see the small table with the girl behind it, but as soon as I got to it, she said something I couldn't hear over the din from the band. The second bouncer grabbed my right arm and for a moment I thought I was busted until he leaned to me and said, "The cover's three dollars to get in." I pulled out my wallet for a second time and handed the girl a five dollar bill, and she dropped it into a small box on the table, retrieved two bills and handed them to me. As I put the bills in my wallet and started to walk away while sticking it back in my pocket, the door opened and I turned to see Jeff, who looked at me and turned to look at the first bouncer. I walked down the hall and could see the band playing in front of me and the bar with stools occupied by a lot of people, some sitting, others milling around. I found an opening to the bar and moved into it, trying to get the attention of the bartender. Eventually, I caught the eye of one of the three bartenders, ordered a beer and paid for it when the bartender set it on the bar. When my change returned I turned around and saw Jeff standing before the seating area, which was also packed, and walked over to him while catching a glimpse of Kent sitting at one of the tables. Jeff and I squeezed our way through the pack and sat down at the table. I started to give Kent the ID and told him so but he said loudly, "No!" and I stopped. He leaned over and shouted in my ear, "We'll go to the john later and you'll give it to me then." I nodded and we drank our beers and congratulated ourselves.

That was the highlight of my night. I approached two girls and asked them to dance but both declined. Kent and Jeff danced and talked freely with several girls and it was somewhat disheartening for me, but in the end the three of us went home together after midnight with no other company. We had a few beers before we went to the nightclub and we were quite wasted when we left. Still, it was something of an accomplishment; we had gained entry into a world forbidden to us, with invalid identification. I even made it into the nightclub, a young man who could easily be mistaken for fourteen years of age, hardly nineteen. It was to be the last time I would attempt to enter a drinking establishment under age and just a few weeks later the others would abandon further attempts, too. Kent, Kerry and Jeff tried to get in the same nightclub using the same fake ID, but Kerry's attempt met with bouncer resistance and he eventually admitted to the bouncer that it wasn't his. The bouncer gave it back to him and told him never to come back until he was truly nineteen and the other guys left after they finished their drinks. It took a while for Kerry to live that one down. Kent and Jeff would remind him that even I had gotten in with no problem and I looked younger than Kerry. Kent soon burned Terry's driver's license and that was the end of it.

As a pure coincidence – or maybe not – my shifts at work were overlapping Cindy's shifts frequently and the closer we got to the Christmas holiday, we seemed to work together even more. We would talk a lot when we got the chance and many times we would check with each other so that we could take our breaks together in the back room. When she started that summer, shortly after she turned sixteen, the minimum age to work at the store, she had confided that she had a boyfriend, but we still semi-flirted with each other. When I started seeing Dana, she would often tell me what Dana had told her, encouraging me to call Dana, stuff that I thought girlfriends didn't normally tell boyfriends because it was kinda secret. Through it all we still would flirt with each other; it just seemed harmless.

It all changed one night when we were sitting in the back on our breaks and I asked Cindy how she and her boyfriend were getting along, especially since I had never seen him in all the time that she had worked at the store. Her demeanor switched from carefree and comfortable to anger and tension; she didn't want to talk about him, she was still mad at him after a week. I asked her what had happened but all she would tell me was that he had shown her 'his true colors,' as she put it, and they were through. When I casually asked Dana what happened to Cindy, I was informed that it was none of my business and why did I want to know? Unperturbed, I discreetly asked everybody that knew her and finally discovered what had occurred. Apparently, her boyfriend had been continually pushing her to 'give it up', so to speak. They had been a couple for more than a year and he thought that was long enough that they should be having sex, but Cindy was a good, Catholic girl and she wasn't going to have sex while she was still in high school and undecided about her future. One of her friends told me that she even said, "It's not that I'm committed to never having sex until I'm married, but not while I'm still in high school." The reason she was mad the night I had talked to her, though, was not because of the sex issue; she was mad because they hadn't officially broken up – she had simply told him she wasn't having sex when he had pressured yet again – and four days later was dating another girl. That's why she was mad. Still, she wasn't mad at me, she told me, and she squeezed my arm as she left to go back to the checkout.

I liked Cindy from the moment I first saw her, which was quite a while before because she would sometimes come into the store to see her brother, Rick. I liked that she was a blond with long, straight hair; I've known quite a few girls in my time and most were not blonds, but I have to admit it, I was a sucker for blonds then. Her face had a smooth even complexion, round cheeks with a soft chin, round, delicious lips, and large, round, soft green eyes, with an easy smile full of perfect teeth. She was about five feet four inches tall with an almost stocky build, but she was far from fat, because it was all muscle due to her athletic, almost tom-boy nature. On that body were generous proportions of female anatomy; her breasts were full, not huge, but considerable and occasionally she would wear shirts that revealed the outlines of her nipples underneath her bra; her waist was streamlined to her body and provided a proper accent to her hips, which fit well with the rest of her body; her legs were thick, smooth and attractively muscular; but her butt was her most attractive feature, besides her face, with its round, soft, smooth appearance. My second admission about women is that I love women's butts; it may be superficial, but the woman I'm romantically attached to at any time has a good butt, one that's round, smooth and soft. She may have everything else, but if that butt is flat or way too big for that body, I can't feel any romantic interest at all. The more time Cindy and I spent together talking and interacting, the more I liked her and the more I knew she liked me. During the days leading up to the Christmas break from school, I was losing interest with Dana while my interest in Cindy was growing. Dana wasn't 'available', she didn't return my calls, and we were never really going 'steady', anyway. Cindy knew that but she also knew other things, too, though she didn't tell me herself; Dana was dating some other guy and that's why she was never available. I suspected it but would have it confirmed on New Year's Eve. Cindy and I started talking about going out, possibly to a movie. Two days before Christmas, the day school let out early to start the Christmas break, we both worked at the store on early shifts. After all the talk, Cindy looked at me while we were taking yet another break together, and said, "Okay, let's go see a movie tonight after work."

Snow was already falling when she said that, and it kept falling, heavier and heavier and heavier. When my shift was done, there was already six inches of snow on the ground and more on the way. Reluctantly, we both agreed that driving downtown to the theaters was not a real good idea, so we decided to postpone the date. Timing is everything and in 1973 there were no multiplexes in malls in Podunk; now there's one in a mall barely a mile from where the store was located and that would have made the difference, except it didn't exist then. I left the store thinking about Cindy even as I drove to Dana's house to leave her my Chritsmas gift and almost ran off the road slowing down for a turn to her house. I stopped in the middle of the street – there was absolutely no traffic - and ran up to her house, dark and empty. Knocking on the door produced no response, so I left the gift in the mailbox attached to the house on the porch. I drove home with considerable care and packed my bag. That night was the last night that I would be in Podunk until New Year's Eve; the family was going to Arizona for a week.

"Let's go! Everybody up! We've got a long drive ahead of us!" Dad bellowed this throughout the house, expecting to rouse all in attendance. It worked. Within minutes, closed doors opened and sleepy souls stumbled about the halls, bathrooms, dining room, kitchen. Mom and Dad were the only ones who took a shower before we left; the three boys settled for the showers or baths from the previous night and a scrub of the face and hands. In thirty minutes the car was packed and we were on our way to St. Louis through the foot-deep snow from the last twelve hours, which had finally relented. Dad drove the entire way to the airport, leaving at five in the morning, on a trip that would normally take two hours at the most, but this morning would take all of four hours and leave us a scant thirty-five minutes before our flight took off. We made it and checked all the bags at curbside while Dad parked the car and met us in the airport; we all rushed to our departure gate, remarking about how many cars were stuck in the snow along the interstate – easily a car every mile – and how nice and warm it was going to be in just a few hours. In those days getting to a medium-sized airport like Lambert in St. Louis with only a half-hour before departure was no big deal and Dad was never worried that we would miss our flight and he was right, although I still don't understand why we flew to El Paso instead of Tucson and drove the rest of the way. Maybe I just don't remember. Two hours after we left St. Louis we had our luggage smashed into a rental, along with our winter coats stuffed in the truck, and Dad drove out of the airport complex, merged onto the local interstate system and headed for Arizona.

After a short time – that's what it seemed to me – Dad pulled into a rest area and everybody got out for a stretch and to go to the restroom.

When I got out from the back seat opposite the driver side, Dad was waiting for me as I came around the front and he tossed me the keys, and said, "You're driving, unless you don't want to."

"Got it covered," I replied nonchalantly, but I was really excited to be driving the whole family on a stretch of road none of us had ridden before.

When everybody meandered back, we all piled in with me behind the wheel. I fired up the rental, backed out of the parking space and pointed it in the direction out of the rest area, pulled the steering column transmission lever down to the drive position, pushed my foot down on the accelerator and drove off. I drove through New Mexico for four hours until we finally stopped for dinner. Mike took over and got us to Arizona, where we stopped once again. Dad took over and by early evening we drove into the secured community of houses in and around Tucson National Golf Course, which is where Dad's old friend, Jack and his family had their winter home.

Of course the old man played golf almost every day, considering that he brought his clubs and had been out visiting Jack to play golf many times before. Sometimes he played with Jack, who wasn't home the whole time since he had his Caterpilar dealership in Denver to run, and sometimes the old man played with some friends who lived in the same community. Mom played once, when Sally, Jack's wife, played and Jeff and I played twice with Billy and Dave, the sons who were about the same age as Jeff and me, Dave being the oldest. It was pretty slick playing golf there. You called for a tee time, hopped in one of the three golf carts Jack owned, and drove to the clubhouse about five minutes away. It was strange playing golf on that course, though, because grass that stays green has to be constantly watered during the winter and watering golf courses is not allowed except for short periods, which is not enough. So what do they do to keep the grass green? They paint it green. That was the only time I ever played on a golf course with painted fairways.

During one of the days while we were there we went out sightseeing and checked out the Sonoran Desert facility west of Tucson. It was pretty neat. That's where I learned about peccaries. Another cool view is the balcony off of the facility, which is up into the hills a little, so you can look south way into Mexico. Hey! Are those specks in the distance illegal aliens crossing into America or just a mirage? Oh, they're too far away to be sure.

After a week we said our goodbyes to our able hosts, packed up the rental and drove to the airport. A few hours later we were back in Podunk. Most of the snow had left, too. I guess everything needs a vacation, now and then. It needed to skip town before the New Year, just two days left.

Act Ten
Excuse Me While I Bail on Your Sorry Ass

The day after the family returned from Arizona was New Years Eve. There was no school, no work, no play as everybody was doing their own thing and preparing for the night, so, what the hell, let's party. When Kent called me and said his folks were gone for most of the day and why don't I come over, I said, "Well, fuck, ya don't need to ask me twice."

I asked Mom if I could borrow her car for the day and she had no objection and I told my parents I would be at Kent's house. Five minutes later I was sucking down a beer and eyeing Kent's sister and her burgeoning bodily attractions, much to the chagrin of my host.

"What?" I asked.

"That *is* my sister, you know," Kent protested.

"Damn near every woman is somebody's sister," I argued, "so, if I shouldn't look at a woman because she's somebody's sister, there aren't very many I can look at."

"Still, man, it's not cool in my house," he persuaded.

"Okay," I said and glanced up to gaze at Stacey's butt as she walked by to sit down and watch TV a few feet away. "Stacey, your brother says I need to stop looking at you," I announced, and guzzled another sip of beer.

Kent leaned toward me with his fist clenched and said, "I oughta punch you right now."

"That would be an accomplishment, layin' me out," I laughed.

Stacey laughed, too, and said, "Kent's just being protective because you're checking me out, and you are, aren't you?"

"Can't help it," I said. "Kent thinks you should wear a bag."

"Yeah, he should talk," she admonished. "He can't keep his eyes off *any* girl!"

"Alright, you guys are pissin' me off," Kent said, a little peeved.

"Relax, dude," I assured him. I stood up as I swigged the last of my beer. "Another?"

"Sure," Kent said, much calmer.

It was really all show. Stacey was two years younger and she was becoming a hot little chick and Kent knew it. He was proud of her, even when his friends were ogling her. He was her big brother, though, and that meant he *should* protect her. When the three of us were together with no one else around, it was a lot like that, a little sexual innuendo, a little gawking, a little smile, a little flirt, and Kent displaying mock anger and resentment.

The phone rang and Kent answered it. Kerry was on the other end wanting to know what Kent was doing. Since we were just sitting around talking and drinking beer, Kerry said he'd be right over. About two minutes later, we heard a knock on the door and Kent shouted, "Come in."

Kerry opened the door, stepped inside, and immediately smiled and laughed, "What's up?" We all slapped hands and Kent advised him that he knew where the beer was, and Kerry stepped to the frig, opened it and pulled out a beer and closed the frig. Popping it open he asked, "So what's on the scope tonight?"

"You mean you're not hangin' with Patti?" Kent teased him.

Kerry laughed and said, "No, she's going to a party with some of her girlfriends from school and it's kinda run by the parents and the school. You know, no alcohol, no drugs, no excitement."

"Well, we've got alcohol, thanks to Kent," I said, and lifted my beer to toast the host, adding, "and speaking of drugs…"

"Well, I just happen to have," Kerry started, shifting in his chair and plunging his right hand into his pants pocket, "a little bit of this weed, here." With that small fanfare, and Kent telling him to "spin one", Kerry pulled out a good size bag, opened it and pinched a finger full of the crushed leaf and spread it on the kitchen table. From another pocket he retrieved a pack of rolling papers and yanked one of the papers from the pack. He took the cover and scooped up some leaf and poured it onto the paper. He scooped the rest after removing any larger pieces or stems and poured that onto the paper, too. He spread the leaf evenly as he lifted the end and flipped it over the leaf, spun it quickly against the table to the glue end, lifted it to his lips and licked it like an envelope. He ran his fingers over it and showed it to us.

"Let's go," Kent said and stood up, moving to the back door. He opened it and the three of us went outside.

It was cold, even in the afternoon, barely into the twenties. Over the week that I was away it had never really gotten above freezing and many of the less-used roads had the snow cover beaten down to ice, which, of course, is a much worse driving condition than snow. Keeping all this in mind, we discussed what we would do or go that night while we smoked the joint. One of us – I can't remember which of us – thought that Tim, a guy from school that we were all familiar with but didn't really hang out with, was having a party at his house somewhere around the lake. Since he was more associated with the jocks and rich kids, we figured there would probably be lots of girls, alcohol, and guys throwing up. Perfect. Let's go there. How do we find it? We know, sort of, where it is, but if there's really a party, there's going to be a lot of cars parked everywhere. Let's crash it.

"How are we going to get in, in case somebody gives a hassle about it?" I asked, fairly naïve about these sorts of things.

Kent had it all figured out. "We'll just tell them Sandy invited us," he said, showing a rather devious smile, adding, "or, actually, Sandy invited you, and you invited us."

"I see how this works," I said, feigning disappointment, while Kerry laughed.

With that exchange, the plot was hatched. We would find Tim's party, we would park at Tim's party, we would gain entry through any devious method imaginable, and we would party at Tim's party. We would also try to find Jeff to tell him about our plot, but that would eventually fail; despite Kent and Kerry's efforts to contact some of his friends and acquaintances, nobody knew where Jeff could be found and all messages we left to contact us were ignored.

We spent the rest of the afternoon at Kent's house drinking, smoking, watching his sister prepare for her night out, get picked up and leave for the night. Kerry and I also left soon after to have dinner with our families and Kent fixed something for himself, but both of us were back at Kent's house in short order. Killing time we watched TV and drank more beer and smoked another 'doobie'. At about ten that night, we piled in Mom's car and drove out to the lake to find Tim's party.

We drove out West Reservoir Drive, through Center Park, on to East Reservoir Drive and heading for Pawnee Road. Kerry thought Tim's house was in one of the little subdivisions opposite the lake, so we decided to pull into each one until we found a lot of cars parked in front of houses. The first one we pulled into had a number of cars parked around a corner at the second, and last, road intersecting the road we turned onto. We slowed down and turned on the road and saw some young people milling before the second house on the right. Kerry recognized some of the kids and figured this was it, so I parked the car in an opening on the right.

We sat in the car for a few minutes watching the action and Kent and Kerry both fired up a cigarette. Kent didn't like the idea of hanging out with rich, smart people – one of his phobias – and Kerry and I spent the time convincing him that it would be fun. "Think of it, Kent," Kerry tried to convince him, "we're going to crash a rich kid's New Years Eve party where we were definitely not invited. What could be cooler than that?" They finished their cigarettes and I opened the driver door and stepped out and told them to "Come on." They got out and followed me.

Before I even got up to the door, several acquaintances from school saw me, and greeted me by the nickname many kids had adopted for me, which was a shorter version of my surname. There were other kids outside smoking cigarettes or just chatting with others smoking cigarettes, but as we got closer, it seemed like everybody told me to go inside, there was plenty to drink. I told them I brought a couple of friends, but I didn't have to introduce anybody since just about everybody knew everybody else, at least by name. Nobody ever said we were not invited, not one single challenge, and we went right in. Kent and Kerry went to find the beer, which consisted of three kegs stashed in a back bedroom with thirty or more people crowded around them. They were charging for cups but somehow both got cups for free and filled them with no problem; meanwhile, I made the rounds of the house, chatting and jiving with kids from school, most of them significantly drunk or stoned already. I had decided before we left that I wasn't going to drink alcohol, so when I stumbled into the kitchen I found some soft drinks in the refrigerator and settled for a ginger ale.

I found a spot to stand relatively out of the way in a little den area and Kent sauntered up a few minutes later, asking if I wanted a beer but I declined. "Can you believe all the girls here?" Kent asked, somewhat amazed at the sight.

"Doesn't it blow your mind how being rich and showing it off attracts so much pussy?" I yelled back because the music was deafeningly loud.

Kent just looked at me with a blank stare. "No, I'm not amazed," was all he said.

Kerry pushed his way to us and immediately started laughing. "You shoulda seen it!" he yelled and laughed some more. "Some guy was trying to get to the bathroom, but he didn't make it and ralphed right next to me, just creamed some girl." He had to stop again he was laughing so hard. "And the girl started freaking, screamin' an' everything, and some guy, I guess it was her boyfriend, was going to punch the guy who ralphed, but I stopped him, and the guy was passed out about two minutes later, without even cleanin' himself up, what a fuckin' trip!"

"Think he drove here?" I yelled to both.

"Think he's drivin' home?" yelled Kent.

"No fuckin' way!" Kerry yelled.

Dana passed by holding hands with some guy. We caught each other's gaze, but I turned away, and yelled at Kent, "That's the girl I was seeing for a while."

"Doesn't look like you'll be seeing her any more," he replied.

I turned to Kerry and yelled, "You guys got your beer. Let's go outside and smoke one o' them doobs you rolled." Kerry nodded and started to move through the room and I turned to yell at Kent, "Come on."

"Where are you goin'?" Kent yelled back.

"Time for the lieutenant," I yelled in response, using the code I came up with to refer to marijuana while in mixed company. I took it from a popular TV show at the time, *Columbo*, whose main character was Lieutenant Columbo.

Kent reached for Kerry and stopped him. "Finish your beer and I'll get us a couple more." Kerry gulped the rest of the beer in his cup and handed it to Kent, who veered off to the left while we headed to the right and out the front door.

Kerry didn't waste any time once we were outside and pulled out the joints that he had rolled at Kent's house before we left. I knew he couldn't wait to fire up a joint at a rich person's house out at the lake. He selected one, put the rest back in his pocket, fired it, drew a long inhale, and passed it to me. I drew the smoke deep into my lungs until they were full and held it, coughing lightly. I could hear somebody say that we shouldn't smoke that here, but the guy standing next to me asked if he could have a hit. I looked at Kerry and he nodded so I handed it to the guy and he inhaled off of it. He passed it back to me and I passed it to Kerry and we started the next round. Another guy asked if he could have a hit and he would roll one and share with us, so Kerry passed it to him, and around and around it went. When it was drawn for the last time, Kerry took the stub and put it in with the other joints.

Kent finally made it outside bearing the two cups of beer and immediately became pissed because we had smoked a joint without him. The second guy finished rolling one, fired it up and started passing it around. That pacified Kent a little. The dope wasn't as good as Kerry's and pretty rough, but as soon as that one was gone, the other guys left to go back inside. Kent whispered something to Kerry and Kerry pulled out another joint and just the three of us smoked. When we went back inside I asked Kerry what Kent whispered to him.

"He said that guy's dope sucked and he wanted me to light up some good stuff, one of mine," Kerry replied.

"And what did you say?" I asked Kerry.

Kerry laughed and said, "I told him, next time, stick with us or get your own."

We took breaks like that a couple more times before midnight. Kent came back after another beer run and told me that the guy who had been holding hands with Dana had thrown up all over himself. "Your girlfriend was pretty shook up about it, because now she didn't have a ride home," he added.

"She's not my girlfriend," I protested.

"Whatever you say, little man," Kent teased.

"And fuck you, too," I replied and Kent and Kerry laughed.

When midnight struck, Kent kissed the girl that he had had been talking with for the last five minutes. A couple girls kissed me, saying, "Happy New Year." Even Kerry got kissed, but that was the highlight of the evening. There were very few people at the party who still had any kind of 'light' in their eyes; most were dull and drunk and some were downright sickly. Slowly, people started to file out and by one that morning we decided to hit the road.

Mom's car, however, had very bald back tires and the road in front of Tim's house was almost solid ice. When we tried to leave, I managed to get onto the road from the parking space, but I couldn't get any traction to make it up the slight hill in front of us. I tried backing away from the hill but managed to stop the car before hitting any of the parked cars when I realized that I was not going to make the turn without some serious driving maneuvers. We now blocked any access past us and some people were starting to get loud and pissy about it. One of the guys I knew from gym class came out and told me that I needed to move my car. I told him that I couldn't get up the hill so he offered to push me up the hill with his car. He pulled up behind me slowly until the bumpers touched, and as he pushed Mom's car with his, I gave the car enough gas without spinning the tires. We made it up near the top of the hill and the tires on Mom's car finally caught and pulled away from the car pushing us. As I started to slow to thank him, Kent told me to just keep going so we don't get stuck again. We made it back to Kent's house without further incident, laughing about all the strange things that had happened, and I dropped them off and drove home. The next morning, I told Mom we really needed to get her some new tires.

Back at work the following day, I had the misfortune to be teamed with Manager Pompador. Pompy was the managerial replacement for Marvin, transferring from one of the smaller stores a few months before, and what a replacement he was. In a single move we went from gung-ho to ass-ho. Granted, he was smarter and had more marketing sense than Marvin, but he was also blatantly egotistical and arrogant, too. You had to do it his way or no way. He started riding me the first day we met and rarely let up. His biggest peeve was not having the store 'properly faced'; facing, in retail, is moving product on the shelves to the front and stacking so that a cursory, superficial glance down an aisle gives the appearance of fully-stocked shelves. In Pompy's mind, facing was more important for me to do than keeping the dairy case stocked – just face it – or sacking to keep lines moving, helping a customer with the bags to the car, or rounding up the carts when they got low. Face it, just face it. I hope you're not drawing the impression that I considered Pompy very superficial. He had substance, and what little he had was stacked and faced every half-hour. I'm almost sure of it.

This day was just more of the same. He assigned an aisle for me to do and when it wasn't done as fast as he expected or spots weren't filled the way he wanted it, it was public reaming and I needed to take my break right now and think about it. Later, in the back he would walk in and softly plead his case, but he would not let me go until I 'agreed' with him. The biggest bitch I had with his methods was his insistence that we fill *all* spaces, even where we were out of stock, with stock that was next to it. I thought that was stupid. Customers got pissed off because they expected that the stock that was really non-existent was simply behind the 'faced' stock, so they'd spend precious time looking for something that was nowhere in the store and then raise holy hell. No argument here. The night crew would get pissed off because they would have to move all of the 'faced' stock *before* they could even fill the previously out-of-stock items; if they had to grab milk crates to haul away the excess 'faced' stock, you did not want to be the first clerk in the store that morning. I didn't mind it, though. "You're preachin' to the choir, guys," I'd say, adding, "and your bitchin' is misplaced. But, you guys *know* who you need to bitch at." That was always as far as it would go.

Pompy also caught on to Mr. B's deal with me on Sundays so he started scheduling himself on Sunday nights just so he could assign me aisles to face while he filled the liquor section all by himself. I wasn't having much fun at work anymore, nor did I really sense that anyone else was having any of that either, except Dave, but his nose was brown, so what could he smell? I smelled a rat, even though they had finally gotten rid of the real ones. I had no real expectation that this would have any kind of happy ending; I was holding back my temper, keeping the explosion under wraps, but the clock was tick-tick-ticking. When would I finally be completely and totally ticked off?

Back at school two days later, the talk – never to your face because this is high school, mind you – was about Tim's party and the consensus was two-fold. First, the three of us showing up out of 'nowhere' brought a much-needed sense of cool that was somehow missing from the entire proceeding. Some people who had been there most of the night sensed that things were getting a little out of control, that some of the guys and even some of the girls were getting too rowdy, almost begging for a fight. We showed up and, for some inexplicable reason, that stuff diminished. Sure, kids got drunk and stupid and sick, but there were no fights and Tim's house remained mysteriously intact. Second, everybody was now convinced that I was a stoner; they may have thought it before, but now it was certifiable. 'Hey, man, you're actually hangin' out with Kent and Kerry and we *know* those guys are stoners." That was incredibly easy for me to deflect. Who could argue with the fact that I could drink half a case of beer, smoke a quarter-ounce of pot, and I would still be smarter, more rational and reasonable than ninety-nine percent of the stuck-up snobs in school at any time in their lives? Okay, it's a stretch, but it was impressive back then, because they all knew I *was* smarter, more rational and reasonable, and had *earned* more respect from more of my fellow students than they had, all without compromising my dignity or kissing anyone's ass to be with them. In high school, you almost *have to* compromise your dignity or kiss someone's ass just to get to graduation day.

After the first week of school and work had slipped into the past in this new year, it became obvious to me that both Cindy and Dana were deliberately avoiding me. From comments and rumor, I could safely draw the picture that both of them thought they could do better than me, that they had 'played me' for the fool that they thought I was. By that time, even though it had only been a couple weeks, I had lost all interest in both. It was now time to bail on them and I did; there was never anything other than a cursory nod or greeting whenever I saw them again. As a matter of confusing curiosity, Kim never dodged me, avoided me, or acted like I was some kind of pariah; she consistently greeted me with pleasantry and maintained her wonderful sense of humor.

What the hell is this shit? I thought as our English teacher explained her 'point system' for grading our work for class for the second and final semester. Points would be awarded for homework, more points for book reports, points for quizzes, more points for tests. Every week she would list the points needed for each grade and it would grow each and every week. "It's what I think is a fair system, you'll know what you can get for anything you do, so it's not swayed by judgment on my part," she explained. Once the first week passed and she posted the minimum points needed for each grade from A to D and I had fewer points than the minimum for a D, a story in the Bible came to me in a vision. I could see the handwriting on the wall – or blackboard, in this case – and the expected outcome was not going to be good.

At least I had accomplished one thing for the final semester. I only had to take four classes to complete my college requirements and graduate from high school, but the automatic scheduling system from the school district put me in gym class the first hour, followed by an open period, which I would have to spend in the lunch room for 'study hall', and the last three classes. When I got my schedule I went to the counselor's office and asked the counselor if I had to accept this schedule as it was or could I change it.

"It's too late to change the classes, now," said the counselor, adding, "but what did you have in mind?"

"Well, I don't want to change the last three classes," I began my argument, "but this gym class at first hour is the problem. There's a gym class every hour, so why can't I switch my gym class to the second hour and come to school then?" I looked at him when I added, "Let's face it, study hall is not a class."

The counselor looked at me for a moment in silence. "You got a point. I don't see any reason why you can't switch gym class to second hour and skip study hall altogether. But," he paused, and I waited for the catch, "you have to clear it with the phys. ed. teachers from first and second hour."

So there was no catch. "I'll have it cleared with both in ten minutes. Thanks," I said, relieved that I had dispatched the black hole of study hall so easily. Ten minutes later I caught Mr G, the teacher assigned to first hour, in the gymnasium above the basketball floor, showed him my schedule, laid out my proposal and listened as he told me that he had no problem with it but I needed to check with Mr. M to ensure that he had room for me. Slam dunk, game over. Mr. M always had liked me since my sophomore year when he was my gym teacher and he always greeted me by name whenever he saw me in school and we would often joke around. Mr. G told me that Mr. M was in the office in the locker room, so I quickly walked into the locker room and up to the office. I knocked on the door and opened it and announced, "Mr. M?"

He sat at a desk with his back to the door and didn't flinch when he said, "Yes."

I said my name and that I wanted to ask him a question. He rolled his chair back and swiveled to face me; he used my nickname when he asked what he could do for me.

"They set my schedule next semester for gym first hour, then study hall," I began, spelling it out quickly because Mr. M liked to get to the point, "so I asked Mr. G if I could switch gym to second hour for your class. Whaddaya think?"

"See ya Monday," and he swiveled back and rolled forward to his desk and continued with what I had so briefly interrupted. That was it. So far as I knew, I was the only student in second semester whose regular attendance started an hour later than normal; I liked it because I could sleep later. I never was one to regularly get up early and I still don't.

Two weeks into the second semester, the point levels for each grade were posted for English class, and I was farther from a D than the previous week. Despite it being February, a warm front had moved in to heat up the area, and Sandy, my neighbor and classmate in English, had worn a white halter top while I sat in the seat behind her, so I could see her globes through the space between her halter top and her side when she moved or posed a certain way. You could also see her nipples leaving a dark bump on the front of her halter top. She would wear halter tops three or four more times that semester and each one of them was quite revealing.

Pompador was unrelenting. Of course, Kent had left almost as soon as Pompy started at the store last fall, and there just wasn't anybody left at the store who was fun to work with. Mike was still there but he was drifting somewhere I didn't want to go, so we didn't hang out at all or say much to each other at work. This particular Friday night, Pompy was especially aggravating. Finally, he pushed me to the point where I had had enough.

"You want me outta here? Is that your goal, your objective? Is that what you want, for me to leave? Consider this my two-week notice." Pompy smiled and walked away. Leroy made sure that we didn't work together those last two weeks, but he didn't say a word. There was some type of power struggle going on at the store that I could see and feel, but could not understand because I was not in a position of confidence. In just these last few months, a lot had changed. The stock clerks that worked at night were both gone, Mr B was gone, a number of the checkers had quit; when I left I had the second highest seniority of the stockers – the highest if you recall that Dave actually started the day *after* I started. I worked my last Saturday and walked out for good. The next week at school, Dave made a point of catching me walking through the halls so he could ask me if I knew that anyone who worked for two consecutive years at the store would automatically earn full-time wages. I said that I did not know that.

"Too bad," Dave said, "and you only had three months to go, too."

What a guy! A prince among men, baron of the wine and cheese bazaar, Dave the great. When I heard him say that, I saw the money I was losing for *one summer* and that was it. The owners had no stores or co-operation with any other owner where I was going to college, so I wasn't losing much. It also revealed to me the aim of the power struggle and the motive behind Pompy; his riding me wasn't due to my incompetence or that he didn't like me for some reason; it was all about the money. Still, the most important fact was that I was free; I had bailed again and there was no looking back, except for now. Even though this can be considered looking back, I have absolutely no regrets.

We were into the tail end of winter, freezing temperatures were mostly items to ignore until next winter, so, what the hey, let's shuffle the Cutlass up to the boat, strap her on the hitch and roll her out to the launch ramp. We had a Saturday afternoon with nothing to do, so why not go cruising on the lake. Sure, it's cold and windy and cloudy, just not a pretty day at all – in short, a great day to wind her up because nobody's going to be on the lake today. Kent, Kerry, my brother, Jeff, Gary, a friend that all of us had known for many years, and I got everything ready, loaded the boat and away we went to the boat launch. Despite the cold we were all feeling frisky and goofy to boot.

When we got to the ramp, I swung the car around so that I could back the trailer straight into the water between the docks and stopped. Everybody piled out and we unhooked the snaps holding the back of the boat to the trailer and one of the guys grabbed the rope attached to the front of the boat and walked with it as I backed into the water the first try. I unhooked the boat from the trailer and we pushed it the rest of the way into the water and I pulled the trailer out and parked the car. We all climbed in the boat as I walked over the dock and jumped in while two of us held on to the dock. After priming the engine, I crawled over the seatback to sit on the bench behind the steering wheel next to the controls and plugged the key into the ignition switch, turned it and the motor turned and fired up the first try, even after sitting all winter. We pushed away from the dock while I put it in reverse and slowly backed away from the dock. When I had more than enough room to turn it out to the lake, I shifted to neutral, then to forward, pushed the throttle stick slowly and accelerated away from the dock. I kept giving it a little more gas until I opened it up and we were bouncing over the wind waves at thirty-five miles per hour on a lake with absolutely no boat traffic at all.

    I took her out to the first island and cruised around it and let Kerry take a turn. He headed around the second island and then veered for the bridge across the interstate and went under it, slowing down a little but not by much and I advised him to watch it in case there were any cops around. Kerry gave way to Jeff and he ventured close to the Chatham shore, brought it back under the bridge and all the way past the boat launch and under the Lindsay bridge. Gary wanted to take a turn next so he got behind the wheel and gunned it; Jeff and Kent, who were in the back, were caught a little off-guard and fell onto their respective benches. After a minute or two, Kerry, sitting next to Gary while I sat farthest from the driver, started playing with Gary, punching him, slapping him, pulling at his arm, just giving him a lot of grief. He kept at it and Gary kept trying to swat him away, keeping his right hand on the wheel. Kent got up in a crouch as if he was trying to sneak up on Gary, who was keeping his attention to the water ahead of him. Gary was wearing a sweatshirt with a hood, which he had flipped to the back, but I watched Kent slowly pull Gary's hood open and flip it over Gary's head and face while Kerry stepped up his punching and hitting. I knew what was going to happen next as Gary unsuccessfully struggled with his left hand to put down the assault and lift his hood from his face; he lifted his right hand from the steering wheel so he could effectively lift his hood, but as soon as he let go of the steering wheel, the wheel *and* the boat both immediately spun to the right. Fighting the centrifugal force pushing me away from the right side of the boat, I grabbed the steering wheel, stopping its spin. I knew that was going to happen because our boat had simple cable steering and since the wheel was located on the right side of the boat, there was less cable on that side, so that when the boat was moving and the steering wheel was released, the shorter amount of cable on the right side would spin the wheel to the right. After I grabbed the wheel, in only a matter of two or three seconds, I glanced at each of the occupants and noted their faces – all wearing virtually the same helpless, hopeless expression of deep fear and imminent demise. Jeff was almost falling into the water and Kent was desperately trying to hold onto the seatback to keep from falling since he had been standing. I told Kerry to help me pull the steering wheel back to the left and he soon grabbed it with both hands and we spun it a couple of times so that Kent and Jeff could finally settle onto the bench beside each other. I yelled over the roar of the engine to Gary to pull back the throttle. He did, all the way back and we came to a stop in the water.

"Okay, now that we almost had a boat accident and nearly drowned," I announced, "what else do you want to do?"

The four other voices mumbled instructions like go back to the dock or the boat launch, mostly directions like that, so we did. I pulled the car around and backed the trailer down into the water under the boat and the others gingerly pushed it up the trailer so that I could secure it to the trailer. I pulled it out of the water, jumped out and attached the snaps and we left.

I chalked up another week of school for the record books, falling yet another several hundred points farther from a D in English. Hopes were dim and getting dimmer. Where does the time go when you're not having fun? Ah, but, then you can walk into class one day, having an especially fun and inspiring morning, complete with bountiful and timely levity and wisecracks, only to have your English teacher suggest to all your classmates that this type of behavior is what you can expect for the rest of your life when *you smoke pot.*

"So let me get this stttrrrrraight, teach, you think I'm high on pot right now?"

"Unfortunately, there are far too many students in this school who sneak out the doors to smoke pot, and, yes, I'm certain you're one of them."

"So, ya think I stepped out the door and fired up a reefer with my stoner buds so I would be sufficiently wasted for your English class, is that it?"

"Exactly. It's no secret."

"And you know this because you can smell it?"

"No, I can't smell it."

"Then, on the basis of my behavior, you have drawn this conclusion?"

"Yes, you're obviously high."

"Well, I *must* defer to the resident drug expert among us, due to that doctorate you completed in pharmacology, which was awarded to you, when was that? Last December?"

"Very funny. You'll be happy to know that today we will be spending the entire class writing a paper about our lives, what concerns us, where we see ourselves and our futures. It is open-ended but you will have to formulate some reasonable expression of thought, for which you will earn points, something some of us need quite badly."

"Ha, ha, ha. I have *just* the topic in mind."

Whipping out my number two pencil, delicately wrapping my entire left fist – I'm right-handed, by the way – around it, I proceeded to draft an exposition – in appalling penmanship with letters an inch tall - decrying uninformed value judgments, shlock psychiatry, conclusions based on superficial and lazy research, opinions formed solely from hearsay, a resignation from healthy skepticism, blind refusal to question any accepted wisdom for its appropriate justification, and presuming someone fits a pattern based on appearance alone, the worst offense of all. What was *my* paper's conclusion? All of these – and others that escaped me – human failures represented the most dangerous threat to the survival of the human species, since they generated incalculable and undeserved harm to billions because the vast majority of human beings committed one or more of these failures *daily*, as a matter of course, of simple daily life.

The following day we all received our papers back. I received the most points possible with the absolute worst appearance imaginable – such is the power of reason. I also received a brief, but well-intentioned, apology in front of the class, and I never received that type of simple judgment from my English teacher again.

With the weather getting warmer, we would frequently hang out at Center Park, almost nightly. We could easily drink beer, we could play softball if one of the diamonds was open and not reserved, we could throw the Frisbee, or we could just sit around and talk, maybe even smoke a joint as inconspicuously as possible. Kerry would sometimes be there and Patti would sometimes stop by to check up on him; Jeff would be there when it suited him; Kent would be there almost every time with his girlfriend, Cheryl. Occasionally, there would be other groups of acquaintances from school, too, like Rick, who lived in Glen Aire and I had known for years, and Richard, who was good friends with Rick, and had been in the same school with me since fourth grade. Steve, who I met when I worked at the store and still worked there, would sometimes be at the park, too. It was sometimes a difficult juggling act, since the individuals from each camp were essentially mutually cynical and distrusting, but Steve and Rick helped on that side and Kerry helped on the other side, and I just simply dismissed the jaded opinions from members of either side. "Maybe you don't know him that well and maybe he only acts that way when *you're* around. You know, nobody acts the same with *ev'ry single human being*. Maybe he's afraid of you or, *maybe, you're afraid of him*." That would usually bring a laugh and a scoff, but it also got them all thinking, and that was the goal. Cheryl seemed to get it right away; she always backed me up, and that helped. It was the same with black people, since all of the people in these camps were white. When the inevitable degrading, insulting, offensive comments started, I just said I didn't want to hear that. "I would bet money that somewhere in town there's a group of black kids saying the exact same words, except for one difference; they're using the word 'white' and we're using the word 'black'." Black people, white people, red people, yellow people, they're all people, human beings. And there's a reason for the term human beings; it's easy to classify hue-man beings, since color is impossible to hide, unless your audience is blind. It sometimes amazes me how little the sighted can see compared to how much the blind can.

Cheryl, on the other hand, never backed me up during my objections over comments about people of another color. Some character traits are deep-seated, fostered by fear of the unknown; most white people don't know many black people and vice versa. Despite that, I liked Cheryl. She was friendly but sassy, spoke her mind, and liked to party. When I first met her, her dark brown hair was long and straight, hanging to the middle of her back, but she had since cut it short to her shoulders, with a soft, layered look, parted on her left side. She was well-endowed and liked to show it, though Kent didn't seem to mind, but, even with her very womanly features, she often acted just like one of the boys. Cheryl tended to keep Kent's testosterone in check.

In early April I had to fill out some papers. For some inexplicable reason, I had qualified for the National Honor Society without being in the top fifteen percent of my graduating class – I was two positions outside the cut-off, ranked sixty-eighth of a class size of 444. When I started high school, our class size was 666 – ooooh, the sign of the beast – so a full third of my classmates had dropped out, transferred, or failed to earn enough credits to graduate on time. The papers were for acceptance of the certificate and whether I would attend the dinner for all of this year's members from all the city's high schools. I decided to attend – what the hell. When my classmates found out that I was accepted into the Society, we all discussed how I could have made it, since we all knew where the cut-off was and my rank in class. A few stated that the teachers of all the eligible and near-eligible students received a questionnaire with room to add comments and rate whether, based on the qualities for membership, the student was deserving of membership, and why or why not. Thomas, a classmate of mine since freshmen year, was ranked forty-fifth, but they declined him membership. The person ranked sixty-seventh didn't make it either, so I had basically taken Thomas' spot. I kidded with him one day while we were both loitering in the gymnasium, telling him that I had taken his spot and he concurred.

"I can't believe these fuckin' asshole teachers," he complained. "How could they trash me but praise you?"

"I can't answer that one, Tom," I said. "Maybe it's because you seem to be angry and pissed off all the time. Are you pissed off at me?"

"Fuck no!" he emphatically replied. "You didn't have anything to do with it."

Ah, but I did, because, as I saw it, Thomas consistently challenged and commented derogatorily to the teachers and their attempted command of the classrooms in those classes we shared together; I, on the other hand, delivered sarcasm targeted at the subject or satire pointed to anybody or anything that deserved it. I wasn't interested in challenging teachers or demonstrating their possible incompetence to the rest of the class, because I already knew that and believed – still do – that it's an individual's responsibility to discover things like that themselves. Besides, I had a higher calling; I kept it all loose; I was the tension-breaker, to the delight of everyone, including the teachers. In Thomas' case, he was the opposite, often *adding* tension to an already tense circumstance. A high school classroom may not be a session of the United Nations, but it's a mini proving ground; when diverse people gather to accomplish some common goal, they're going to be more successful when everyone's more comfortable and loose than when everyone's uncomfortable and tense. However, Thomas is probably a successful businessman now because businesses are organized under an aristocratic model rather than a democratic one.

The National Honor Society banquet featured rather forgettable food, forgettable speakers, announcement of all the members' names, when each would stand for a brief moment, and a little chit-chat with some of the members. The highlight – really an embarrassment at the time – for me was having one of the volunteer organizers returning my high school ring which I had left in the bathroom after washing my hands. When I ordered the ring the year before I didn't pay attention to the ring company brochure, which advised to order the ring in your current ring size; I ordered a size bigger and it never fit. I lost it permanently a years or so later.

Kent and I, and, occasionally, Kerry, would often take the boat out to the boat launch after school and pull into the tiny bay where the discharge from the power plant entered the lake. It was the ideal fishing spot of the lake and as such was also off-limits to boats at all times. Kent insisted that it had been made off-limits through the efforts of the *real* fishermen of the area lobbying the city council years ago so that they would have the area more to themselves; *real* fishermen, according to Kent, didn't care whether an area was off-limits or not, only if it was a good fishing spot. The discharge bay was such a spot, even during a very hot afternoon. We caught a lot of perch, which we usually threw back because they were a poor eating fish, but we also caught a good number of lake bass, striped bass, channel and flathead catfish. Finally, though, we got caught by the Lake Police in the off-limits area. They pulled in, advising us to stay where we were over their speaker. We had finished a joint about fifteen minutes before, so we were a bit stoned and a little paranoid; we reeled in our lines, since we usually had two each, while the cops pulled up to us. The two cops were yelling something at us that we couldn't understand, but I noticed that one of the cops was Dana's brother, Curt.

"Kent," I said softly to my fishing buddy, "the guy on the left is Dana's brother."

"You mean that's your ex-girlfriend's brother?" Kent teased me.

"She was never my girlfriend," I protested.

"So the one with blond hair hanging over the side of the boat is Dana's, your ex-girlfriend's, brother?"

"No, she was not my girlfriend, ever."

"So, what you're saying, is that's *not* your ex-girlfriend's brother."

"No, that's not what I'm saying. What I'm saying-"

Meanwhile, the cops have continued to yell unintelligible instructions to us – or maybe we weren't paying enough attention due to our stoned condition – until their boat rammed our boat, knocking us to the floor of our boat and almost dumping Dana's brother, Curt, right into the drink. Apparently, what they had been yelling at us was to grab their boat as they got close to keep them from colliding. When the other cop told me that, I looked at him in disbelief and asked, "You don't know how to pull up *next* to another boat?"

Curt, who recognized me but never let on, smiled at my valid point and looked over to his partner. Figuring that we would be fined when we first spotted the police boat, instead they gave us a mild tongue-lashing, a warning, told us we had to get out of the off-limits area and they would stay until we did – all because they were noticeably embarrassed with how they pulled up to our boat. We motored out past the off-limits marker, dropped the anchor and fiddled around with our poles, all the time watching them as they motored out of the bay and headed back in the direction of the boat launch, away from the dam - where they could disappear for a few minutes, then re-appear after reaching the dam end of the lake, heading to the other end. Fiddling with our poles was just for show; we had pulled up our catch and hidden it, not knowing what was going to happen. Due to their ramming us and their reaction from that, they didn't ask for licenses, board our boat, search us, or anything, so we decided that they wouldn't be back to our end of the lake for an hour or more, and we went back in to continue our excellent fishing fortune. We spent another half-hour or so and caught a few more keepers, packed up and pulled up the anchor and left.

Kent and I had fished in the discharge bay quite a few times that spring and that was the first time we had been caught. We had fished there so many times we had started contests like how many fish one could catch during one trip; once, I caught over seventy in a two-hour period, though Kent did about the same three or four times. Another contest was for how many fish we could catch with a single worm; I once caught a dozen with one worm, which was not so difficult since we never put an entire worm on a hook but usually tore them into thirds or less; I'm sure Kent caught as many with one worm, too, because he was the better fishermen between us. Now, though, after our brush with the law, we had to decide on a better course of strategy and that course was to fish in the early morning, from daybreak to nine o'clock, because at nine-thirty in the morning, the police fired up the boat and scoured the lake for the first time in the day. We started going out on Saturday mornings and found the fishing much better. The big boys seemed to be out foraging for food more in the morning than the afternoon and our take-home catch was filling both our freezers. After a couple expeditions in the morning, we decided never to fish in the discharge bay at any other time but early in the morning; afternoon fishing was a thing of the past. Soon we were throwing back anything less than a pound or under nine inches and all perch; we had grown very tired of eating perch.

In late April I was running an errand after school and driving down the street that runs by the school, eventually heading downtown. As I got close to the street where I would turn right to go downtown, where the street was four lanes, two lanes in either direction, I was driving in the right lane and approaching three cars in the left lane, the first waiting for the opposing traffic to clear in order to make a left turn. You probably are anticipating what's going to happen next and you're going to be right, because the middle car got tired of waiting and, apparently not seeing me approaching, pulled into the right lane to go around the turning car. It happened so quickly that I couldn't even thing of honking the horn; I just tried to brake as quickly as possible without panicking since there were cars right behind me and get over as far to the right as possible. None of it mattered; the woman driving that brown, middle car kept moving until she hit me as I passed her and came to a stop. The car in the left lane finally made its turn and cars slowly passed us on the left, but, before either of us could get out of our cars, a state police car with its lights on pulled up right behind me. He checked on us both to see if we were hurt; no one was hurt. He got back in his car after telling us to stay put while he parked in the lot on the left side of the street; he then would step back out into the street and stop the traffic and we should then pull into the parking lot. In a few more minutes both of our cars were safely in the parking lot and the street was back to normal.

The state trooper came up to me as I sat behind the wheel and asked for my driver's license and vehicle registration. I handed both to him and he bent over the front of the car and wrote something in one of those little pocket notebooks while he kept glancing at the papers. He handed both back to me and told me he was going over to the other driver to get her story and to wait until he came back. After ten minutes he returned and handed me a piece of paper.

"That's the other driver's name, address, phone number and insurance information." The officer said. I looked at the paper and noticed the surname of the woman and felt a sense of dread starting to overtake me; that name was a common one for city police officers and some bureaucrats and other workers for the city and county as well. *This is not good*, I thought.

The officer continued to tell me that he had been driving a few cars behind me and had seen the entire event as it happened and had seen that I had tried to avoid the accident without creating a bigger mess, and he praised me for that! He had gone to the woman to get her story first and she admitted hitting me and that it was all her fault. He concluded with the advice that he had to complete an accident report, that I should have my parents contact our insurance company with the other driver's insurance information and that I was free to go. I had just suffered my first accident as a driver *right in the view of an Illinois state trooper and that trooper had just praised me for my reactions*. I was just thinking, *hey, at least I wasn't involved in a bloody mess where I'd be throwing up or something.*

Charlie called me every once in a while or I'd call him and we'd talk. Sometimes, we'd send wildly ridiculous letters to each other. Charlie had graduated from high school and immediately landed a job working for a printing press. He liked it because he had already gotten so good at it that he worked with no supervision. The printing press was closing down for a week in June due to a slowdown in business and to upgrade some equipment, so he wouldn't be working and he was planning on flying out to Illinois for the week and goof around. I told him to bring it on.

Into the first week in May and I was still falling farther and farther behind the minimum points for a D in English. Still, I would show up for class and contribute – always attempting to sit behind Sandy for the free display – but I had resigned myself to the fate that I was never going to catch up. I knew I was going to have to live with the consequences – so be it.

The rest of my classes were settled. No matter what I did the rest of the year, my grades were set once I reached the middle of May. Class work was winding down, all the tests had been taken and there were no finals scheduled for any of my classes. We were seniors, there was less than two full weeks of class left and nobody wanted to spoil the party.

Party is what we decided to do and for those last few days of school, attendance in class was the exception not the rule. I still drove to school, I just never attended class. I would walk around the school during intermission and we'd head out to the parking lot and drive off. One day the four of us showed up in street clothes at Mr. M's softball game during second hour and we played softball with all the other kids. Mr. M didn't care that Kent, Kerry and Jeff weren't in my gym class or that I was wearing jeans and not the gym clothes that all the other guys were wearing; he had us play on the team that he picked and we, of course, killed the other team. Mr. M even asked me why I never went out for baseball after I made a fairly spectacular play at second base.

"Why don't you ask that about Kent?" I asked back.

Mr. M laughed hard at that. "I *know* why Kent didn't play," Mr. M replied, between laughs, "he wanted to smoke dope instead, but you could've played baseball for me, makin' plays like that, hitting the ball like you do. You would've had a spot on *my* team."

We all had fun that game, except maybe Kent. For the rest of the game, we always referred to him as 'dopehead'.

"Good hit, dopehead!"

"Nice catch, dopehead!"

"Hey, dopehead, you're up!"

Even Mr. M got into it, when Kent threatened to punch one of us after he had called Kent 'dopehead' once again. "Now, let's not have any of that talk during my game," Mr. M admonished him, adding, "dopehead."

We didn't really have a skip day in our senior year, at least not that I remember. The last two weeks were pretty much all skip days. The only classes I attended were those where some paper or important homework had to be turned in. Most of the time, I was absent from class and never bothered to get an absence or any kind of pass. Nobody hassled me, nobody questioned me, even if I hadn't been in class for days and just walked in. If I was asked where I had been, I would turn it around. "Oh, I *shouldn't* be here? Maybe I should leave?" That would be the end of it.

Kerry had been bugging me for about two months to help him out by taking Patti's girlfriend, Jean, to their school's prom. He was relentless and Kent and Jeff didn't help matters, either. If I was with Kent or Jeff or both and Kerry showed up, immediately I'd hear from one or both in a sing-songy voice, "So, you taking Jean to the prom?" Thanks, dickheads.

Finally, I just gave up under the pressure. He would even bring Patti and Jean out to the park or wherever the guys were at, knowing that I would be uncomfortable trying to just ignore her and them. Of course, Kent and Jeff would take great pains to greet Patti and Jean and include them in the conversation and ask how they were doing and, generally, making my life a living hell. I relented when Kerry said he had to make a decision on his tuxedo, the girls had to decide on their dresses, and he had to know *now*. We settled on a gray tuxedo. Kerry even paid for a night out with all four of us to a drive-in theater.

Jean was a nice girl, under five-feet tall, with short, brown hair, and a nice body. She was very shy and quiet and I really had little idea what she was like or what her interests were. She so rarely talked about anything except to Patti, and when the two of them got going it was incessant girl talk.

The weekend before the official end of school was Sacred Heart's prom, held that Saturday. Kerry picked me up early in the afternoon and handed me a beer as soon as I sat down in the passenger seat. I welcomed it and drank it pretty damn fast. We went over to Patti's house, where the girls were going to get ready, mostly, I think, to reassure them that I *was* going to take Jean to the prom, or, more exactly, Kerry was going to take all four of us to the prom. We chatted for a short time and Kerry asked Patti if they should start getting ready since we were going out to dinner first and Patti agreed. Kerry and I left and when we got to the car, Kerry joked about how that took forever, but we had to do it and *now* we could get back to drinking beer, smoking joints and getting prepared for tonight.

He had rented a room at a motel not far away and that's where we went, after making a quick stop for a few bags of ice. Once there we hauled the bags of ice upstairs and set them in the bathtub; we went back down to the car and I carried one of the cases of beer while Kerry carried the other two. He set the drain plug in the bathtub and we removed each beer from the plastic holders and laid them in the tub, opened the bags of ice, one at a time, and poured the ice over the beer. I stepped out of the bathroom, turned on the TV and sat in one of the chairs to kick back. Kerry came out of the bathroom after emptying his bladder; he stepped over to the cooler he had brought up with the ice, bent over and opened it, removed two beers and tossed me one. I suggested we smoke a joint as Kerry settled on one of the beds; he pulled his stash and rolled one. We were a little paranoid about smoking it in the motel room, so we stuffed towels into the cracks at the bottom of the outside door and the door adjoining the next room. We talked about the plans for the evening and he said that some of the other guys attending the same prom had other rooms in the motel and another guy was supposed to deliver a pony keg to leave in our room. There was going to be a small party in our room after the prom, with people coming and going from all the rooms scattered over the motel.

A couple of the guys came by later and we all drank some beer and I listened to everybody's tall tales. The guy bringing the pony keg showed up and we set it in the far corner of the room. The rest of the time we had guys and girls stop in and we walked around once to check in on some of the arrangements. We were accommodating with our beer with these people – only a few with whom I was acquainted and Kerry was familiar with them from Patti, mostly – but shared the pot only with those that produced some first.

About four-thirty, we started putting on our gear. The tuxedoes came with separate buttons and cufflinks and we were having too good a time putting it all together – neither of us had ever worn a tuxedo with all the trimmings before. There was one concession, though, and that was the bowtie, which came already tied with an elastic, adjustable strap; that was good, because there was a time as we walked around the motel seeing how the other guys were doing that we discovered we had our cummerbunds on backwards. I have to admit that I felt slick wearing the tuxedo gear, even without the jacket. Cool! Let's have another one.

We picked up the girls at Patti's house, posing for the several obligatory parents' photos of their kids on prom night. We went to dinner at a restaurant I can't remember, probably because I was pretty loaded by then, but I was a good drunk until I tried to talk, so I kept talking to a minimum. The food helped and, of course, we were too young to drink legally, so we could only have water or soft drinks. By the time we left the restaurant I was fairly sober, but we did take the time to have one more beer and smoke a couple of joints before we walked into the prom.

    What was the prom theme, you ask? Come on, this is 1974, what do you think? Can you say Led Zeppelin? Yep, that was the theme, along with about ten thousand other proms that year. We danced, we talked, we stepped out for a while to suck down another beer and smoke another joint, we stood in line for the usual couple's picture, they crowned prom king and queen, and it was all as it should be. The band was okay but nothing spectacular, loud but not deafening. It was a nice affair, Kerry and I were sometimes loud but we were gentlemen, there were no fights or skirmishes, everyone was reasonably well-behaved, somebody tried to spike the punch, and a couple of guys brought flasks of liquor that we shared. After that it was back to the motel, where we drank and smoked, kids came and went, some kids got sick, we stepped over to some of the other rooms and basically tried to keep things pleasant and not too loud. We all got so loaded that by two or three in the morning, all four of us were laying on the beds, each couple to a bed, with our prom clothes still on and the beds still made.

    Kerry woke up about seven and woke up Patti, who woke up Jean, who woke up me, and the three of them left soon after so Kerry could get the girls home before any of the parents started getting concerned. I struggled to conquer my still drunk condition but managed to empty the bathtub of beer by putting them in the cooler. I changed out of the tuxedo and back to normal clothes when Kerry returned. We gathered up the rental clothes and Kerry discovered that he was missing the cufflinks; we never did find them. We carried the stuff down to the car in two trips and Kerry drove me home, where I immediately went right to bed. Kerry did the same but later returned the pony keg and the rental clothes. He also tried to keep Jean and me together, though not nearly as aggressively as he recruited me for the prom; after a few weeks he gave up trying. I think he realized that neither of us was that interested in the other.

    The following Tuesday was the next to last day of school. Kent and I had already fried up some fish at the park for friends a couple weeks earlier, so we decided to have a fish fry for anybody from school that night at the park. We went to school and told as many of our acquaintances as we could find that we had plenty of fish for a fish fry that night, there would be beer and you were invited. It was a crappy day in the morning and afternoon, but it only sprinkled so it wasn't wet enough to call the party. We spent the entire day getting everything prepared and had grabbed the best spot in the park to fry up the fish next to plenty of tables. We got started about six at night and all our closest friends appeared; I even brought my brother, Jeff. When Cheryl arrived with one of her friends, she told us that Sandy, my neighbor and English classmate, had been telling everyone at school that we had canceled our party because of the weather. She didn't think anybody else was coming and she turned out to be right. Everybody that did turn up got plenty of good fish and other food, but we packed it up at nine and crashed Sandy's recommended party. Actually, we didn't crash that party, except to walk around it to discover there was no alcohol – it was hosted by the parents – and no dope, but it was only a block from Kerry's house and two blocks from Kent's house, so we started walking around outside with beers and joints. In fifteen minutes most of the people at the party were outside the house with us. Now, *that's* a masterful method of crashing a party. Eventually, the party spilled out over the entire neighborhood, so that even the police stopped by to join the festivities. The parents had to explain that it was some other kids that were responsible, but 'those other kids' were over at Kerry's house by then, so the final outcome was: party over.

Thursday was the graduation ceremony, which Kerry and Jeff attended, but Kent and I declined. The ceremony never appealed to me and I had decided long before that I was not renting a cap and gown nor attending in any manner. Graduation from high school just didn't mean much to me, not to celebrate it like that. Moreover, the school was planning a deviation from the traditional speeches from valedictorian and salutatorian; instead, they wanted shorter speeches from all of the top ten graduates, which was going to be interesting considering that Edward, the tenth-ranked student, was, also, not attending the graduation ceremony. They had to settle for the top nine.

Kent and I spent most of the day together, just goofing around, smoking dope and drinking and having a good time. After dinner with our respective families, Kent picked me up in the blue bomber and we went out to the park. We played catch and batted the ball to each other, would take a break every thirty minutes or so to sit in the car and drink a beer and maybe smoke a joint, and just pass the time. Around nine, kids who had been to the ceremony arrived at the park and soon Kerry, Jeff, Cheryl, and some of the other camps arrived; some wanted to tell us about the ceremony but neither Kent nor I wanted to hear about it, so they stopped. Before the park closed, a few of us went to Kent's house for another beer or two and Kent drove me home before midnight.

Having bailed from high school two weeks early, I still graduated and received a diploma, anyway. I know that, because I went to the school Friday, June 2, 1974, to the counselor's office and picked it up. A couple weeks later I received my final grades; to my surprise, I received a D- in English. Somehow, I had received enough points in the last two weeks to avoid flunking English. I know, it's a mystery to me to this day, too.

Act Eleven
The Summer of Irony

I'm free [short musical interlude courtesy of the Who's *Tommy*] I'm free! Yet the questions remained: free to do *what*? Free to *be* what? Free to work 9 to 5 under the immediate direction – whim? – of an insecure power maniac who's been promoted one level beyond incompetence? Fuck that! Free to be unleashed and tethered to no one or no thing with no responsibility to anyone or anything, but with little access to funds and no real method of keeping up such a lifestyle? Fuck that, too! Free to pursue investigation of a higher education, in liberal arts studying sociology, to see if there really *is* a branch of human learning that can capture my imagination, my desires, my dreams? Perhaps. Or free to drink, do drugs, get wasted, goof off, sleep late, stay out late, and generally harm no one but maybe myself? Yeah, well, you got me there. I wanted to be that kind of free, at least for the next three months, and that's what I did. My first full day of newfound freedom, Saturday, after picking up my diploma Friday, started late, almost noon. I could put a check next to 'sleep late'.

We got a baseball game organized for the afternoon on the field of my first elementary school, which we decided would be best because the park would have more people on the weekend and it would be less likely to be visited by the police, an excellent place to surreptitiously drink beer, smoke pot, and play ball. Twelve of us gathered at the old ball field where I threw my first pitch over the backstop when I was seven, and we sided up and warmed up and got started. We played 'pitcher's hand', meaning that the team in the field did not provide a first basemen; instead, a ground ball to an infielder was thrown to the pitcher; if the batter did not reach first base before the ball reached the pitcher, the batter was out. Each team in the field had a pitcher, two infielders and three outfielders. Several balls were hit over the street for home runs and one we never did find. We took a judicious number of 'beer breaks' and 'smoke breaks', some of the 'smoke breaks' were for those who smoked tobacco and some were for those who smoked leaf, and generally enjoyed a hassle-free afternoon. When we got tired of playing baseball, some of the guys left almost immediately, while the rest of us sat around drinking and smoking and telling jokes and the usual tall tales. We were looking forward to the rest of the summer, since none of the core guys, Kent, Kerry, Jeff and myself, had full-time jobs or other similar obligations, not did we expect any of the like. We were going to have a good time for as long as we could.

Sunday, I drove over to Kent's house and we called Kerry but he already had other plans that he couldn't break. We drank some beers, played tennis ball out in the street in front of the church, filled a pipe I had bought a couple times and smoked some weed, and made plans for our next fishing endeavor. We were looking forward to fishing in the discharge bay of the power plant on a weekday, since there had usually been several boats and fishermen there in the morning on weekends. Kent had heard that Tuesday through Thursday were the mornings that had the least fishing activity so we decided to hit it on Tuesday. We also drove out to the beach house to check on the bikini bodies for a little eye candy and maybe some innocent or not so innocent flirting. I drove back home at dinner time and stayed home the rest of the night.

We took it easy the next day, planning to go to bed early so we could get up easier. Since Kent and Kerry were best of friends for many years, I expected Kerry to be at Kent's house if I came over or call Kent or Kent call Kerry while I was there. The unexpected event this day, though, was Kerry calling Kent early in the morning to say that he would be starting a full-time job with the state later in the week. Even though it was a temporary job until the end of the fiscal year, which was the end of June, Kerry expected that he would be moved to a permanent job once his temporary job was completed. In just two days, we had gone from four unemployed but free goof-offs to three. "Shit," I told Kent upon hearing the news, "maturity is calling us. We must resist, *resist*, I tell you." I said this with a mock expression of intense mania. Kent just looked at me with a mock expression of disgust and said, "No more pot for you."

Up at four in the morning, I threw on my clothes, walked out the door to Mom's car, started it up and drove to Kent's house a mile away. I knocked hard on the door and woke him up. He immediately came to the door and let me in while he went back to his room to put on his clothes. His tackle box and poles were waiting neatly at the front door and two minutes later he emerged from the hall to the front room. I grabbed the tackle box, opened the door and stepped out to the car with Kent right behind me carrying his poles. Back to my house we went and I backed up the car with Kent guiding me to the boat trailer. We pushed the trailer the few inches to the hitch and wound it down on top of the hitch, locked it, plugged the cable connectors and connected the safety cables to the hitch assembly. By twenty minutes after four we were on the way to the boat launch, about a twenty minute ride. I whipped the car and trailer around for a straight shot into the water and launched it down the ramp on the first attempt. After disengaging the boat from the trailer, I pulled the car and trailer out of the water and parked it in the first space; there were no other parked vehicles in the entire lot. With everything set and Kent holding the boat next to the dock, I ran to the boat, jumped in to the back and set the gas tank on, primed the engine, jumped over the front bench behind the wheel, inserted the key and the motor fired up the first time. Everything was going smoothly so far. We pushed the boat down to the end of the dock while the engine warmed up, we pushed away from the dock, I put it in reverse and idled farther from the dock, put it in forward and gave a little gas until we cleared the Vachel Lindsay bridge, then threw it open all the way to the discharge bay five minutes later. It was already light out when we dropped the anchor about twenty yards from another boat with a single fisherman, who we nodded at when we idled in and who had nodded back. The sun would rise over the horizon in fifteen minutes and we wanted to catch a fish before the sun rose, so we got out the worms from the night before, speared them on the hook and threw the line in the water, then repeated the process for our second poles. Kent did it, reeling in a pound's worth of striped bass. We both glanced over at the fisherman and he nodded his acknowledgment. Over the next couple hours we caught a few keepers, a couple bass and three channel catfish, but the fisherman was consistently pulling in bass up to two feet long. Each time any of us caught a fish that was a keeper, the other party would nod in acknowledgment, but as time passed it was becoming clear to Kent and I that we were clearly outclassed.

  Kent had another bite on one of his poles and when he yanked the pole he felt the hook sink in and the fish resist. Per custom, I grabbed his other pole and moved it to the other side of the boat and slowly reeled it in to ensure that the line was out of the way while he fought his fish and reeled it in. My poles were already out of the way on the other side so I left my lines in but I watched him pull the fish in and listened as he said he thought it was a good size fish but it wasn't giving much of a fight. Finally, he pulled his pole back and we got a glimpse of the fish as it reached the surface; it was a huge flathead catfish. I had the net ready and Kent reeled in the slack and steered the fish to me and I swooped the net under the fish and pulled it out of the water. As I held the fish in the net and swung it into the boat, we started laughing and glanced over at the fisherman, who knew we had caught another fish, so he briefly glanced over at us while I held the fish, looked back at his poles, but immediately swung his head back, craned his neck and stood up from his seat. He smiled and gave us a thumbs up. It was clearly the biggest fish any of us had pulled out yet.

Not long after the fisherman reeled in all his poles, got his boat in order, started up his engine, pulled up his anchor and gave us a courteously wide berth as he trolled out of the bay. As soon as he was out of sight, we fired up a doobie and talked about the events of the morning; we had to laugh when we discussed what the fisherman was thinking when Kent pulled that monster catfish out of the water. Once the fisherman left we didn't catch any more bass, though we did catch a few more catfish that we kept. In all, we caught more than a dozen fish worth keeping, so it was well worth the effort of getting up that early. We left a little after nine and watched the lake police boat pass by while we were readying the boat over the trailer. When we got back to my house and prepared the table in the back to gut and scale the bass and skin the catfish, I had grabbed a tape measure so we could see how long that catfish really was. It measured thirty-eight inches and probably weighed between five and six pounds. Kent thought we should take a picture, too, so I hunted around the house and finally found the Polaroid camera and I took a picture of Kent holding it by the gills, its mouth level with his shoulder and its tail extending to a few inches above his knees. When Kent showed the picture to anyone for the first time, they had the same reaction as the fisherman.

We celebrated the rest of the morning and early afternoon, drinking beer at Kent's house, after we finished preparing the fish and putting them in our freezers. We smoked the rest of our doobies that we had rolled but didn't have a chance to smoke while we were fishing and Kerry stopped by for a smoke and a drink, too. We were pretty wasted by dinner time, so I went home, ate a quick meal with the folks, and crashed in my room. I woke up late that night and Dad was already in bed. I went out to the den and popped a beer and watched TV with my Mom for a little while until she went to bed. I drank a couple more beers and watched TV until about two in the morning.

The next week Charlie flew into town and we immediately got together. Suddenly I was at his mother's house for the first time in three years, and it was a completely different place. Charlie had a full-time job and it must have made an impact on his mother and Les, his stepfather, because they both treated him – and me by extension – like real adults, equals in fact. We had real conversations under properly reserved and respectful proceedings; just four years before, we were kids, juveniles, persons virtually unable to make any informed, valuable or thoughtful decision. The transformation of our respective positions in our families was not lost on Charlie; he was as amazed as I was, considering that we truly couldn't identify what had changed in ourselves other than a modest increase in age. To further reflect on this odd change in family life, we went to my house and cracked open a few beers and fired up some reefers.

Charlie was in town for the week but we didn't see each other every day. He hooked up with some of his other friends that were still in the area and I respected that; he made it easier by calling me early every day to either see what I had planned or tell me what he had planned. We went out to the park a few times to toss the Frisbee and he showed me some different throws, such as the two-finger toss, thrown with the first two fingers of your hand under the Frisbee and the middle finger providing most of the control; the reverse sweep, which is thrown with the hand over the Frisbee and the thumb under it, in a sweeping, stiff-armed motion from back to forward; and my personal favorite, the thumb toss, which is thrown with the thumb under the Frisbee and the fingers holding the edge tightly, with a slight tilt downward on the outer edge and a flick of the wrist and thumb. Over the years I've practiced the thumb toss so much that I can throw it with little effort, with great accuracy and with so much spin over all the other tosses that most people misjudge it and drop it or have it hit them with surprising force. We even spent an afternoon and evening with the rest of the new gang and everyone was on their best behavior but for most of the week Charlie and the new gang remained apart.

Charlie and I talked about the Vietnam war, in the context now of possibly being drafted and having to serve or make some other decision. We were both eighteen and legally required to register for the draft, so we decided to go to the local office of the Selective Service and register. It was painless, official, and took only a few minutes, but we were now legal; they couldn't come after us for failing to register. We would have to wait a few months to see what else would happen. Before most states created lotteries, there was a national lottery for the draft, which assigned a number to each birth date of the year; the lower the number for your birth date, the more likely you would be drafted – not as good as winning one hundred million dollars, is it? When the lottery numbers were finally announced months later, my number was 352. I figured if *I got drafted*, everybody was going. At the time no one knew what would happen in Vietnam; the conflict had dragged on for so long, the United States military and the corrupt officials from the south had hung on for so many years, it could go like that for six months or five years. Who knew?

Since we were already downtown after registering, we played pool at the billiards room on the second floor of a seedy building with very dim lighting. After that, we walked about six blocks to the adult theater, the only one in town that would be at the same place for about thirty years, and saw some X-rated films of little renown, but they did show just about everything: red, spongy vaginas, tits galore, round, soft, spankable butts, schlongs aplenty, fucking in lots of positions, and cocksucking and pussy-eating, too. There were only a couple of other guys in the theater and they both were wearing long coats in the middle of June; how did we get in wearing only T-shirts and jeans? Charlie even bought a magazine in the adjoining sex shop, but I thought they wanted too much money for all these accessories. Obviously, that's where they made their money, but I had a big bag full of help at home to get past those horny moments.

Speaking of horns, many times I would spend the evening hours with other now former schoolmates or by myself while Kent and Cheryl spent the night together, Kerry and Patti spent the night together, or Jeff and some girl spent the night together. That's the price you pay for being slow to grasp the romance game and being shy at the same time. On those occasions when Kent and Cheryl or Kerri and Patti were together while I was around, I did get to interact with the other gender, and I considered that interaction valuable. Both Kent and Kerry had sisters, and I concluded that was why they had such an easier time talking to girls than I did, since I had only brothers as siblings. A second predicament was finding girls that liked to party; it seemed to me there were more that didn't than did.

Because we liked to party, Kerry decided that we should party an entire weekend, so he called Kent to see if he thought it was a good idea. Having twisted Kent's arm to the near- breaking point, Kent abandoned all his objections and gave in to partying. They tried to contact Jeff by phone at his last known address – his mother's house – but he was not home and no one knew where he was, which was Jeff's way of leaving the message that he had partied himself all the way to incognito, but purely on an indefinite basis. They called me and I knew immediately that the arm twisting was surely coming so I broke down without a fight, having absolutely no defense against partying. They called Ed, one of our impromptu baseball and football players, who set a record for how quickly he caved. Kerry called his father to tell him who would be at the farmhouse near Chandlerville for the weekend and to ensure it was alright, to which he received the blessing, and the party was on.

Kerry left work early and met Kent and Ed at his house; after he packed up for the weekend, they drove out to my house in his father's Ford truck. I was waiting in the driveway and I threw my bag in the back of the truck and climbed in the truck and Kent stepped in behind me; all four of us sat on the one seat of the truck, a little cramped but we were gonna party. We made a stop at our favorite watering hole and snagged six cases of Bud and a bag of ice, including one that was cold, which we put in the cab, filled a cooler that Kent had brought, and put the rest in the back of the truck, along with the cooler. Out of town we went, heading west to Virginia, about forty minutes away, depending on the traffic, which was two-lane once we left Podunk. When we got to Virginia, we stopped again to pick up some food for dinner that night and breakfast and lunch the next day. We got back on the road and Kerry almost forgot to take the turn at the stop sign just past Virginia, but Kent reminded him and down the next road we went. Kerry and Kent debated the next turn, which was about twenty minutes later, but Kerry was just giving us a hard time; he knew which turn to make all along. Another twenty minutes through back roads, past a few farmhouses and lots of farm fields, some creeks, grass hills and some wooded areas, and Kerry pulled up into the short drive to a large farmhouse with a big barn, some sheds, and a small lake in the back.

Kerry took the food and went into the house first to see who was there and found one of the co-owners and some of his family; there were nine co-owners of the farmhouse and the surrounding property, including Kerry's father and uncle. The co-owner knew we were coming so he welcomed us in and then stayed out of our way, as we stayed out of his, too. We grabbed the beer and our belongings and made ourselves at home, letting Kerry decide which rooms we could have. We could only have part of the refrigerator with enough room for two cases of beer, so we all agreed that whoever took the last beer from the front case had to replace it by putting the warm case in the back and moving the cold one in the back to the front. The cooler was to provide cold beer while the beer in the refrigerator cooled; we were already down to one six-pack left from the cold case.

We brought fishing poles but in our haste had forgotten to get bait. After a brief discussion, we decided to blow off fishing that night and we could get bait in the morning if we wanted. Instead, we grabbed our baseball gloves, a bat and ball and took turns batting the ball and throwing it around, trying not to kick over anyone's beer. Kerry went inside after a while to get another beer but didn't return until ten minutes later.

"What took you so long?" Kent asked Kerry when he finally returned.

"Check this out, Kent," was all Kerry said as he walked right past us to the barn. Kent followed him and they disappeared into the barn. Shortly, Ed and I heard a motor rumble and we looked at each other, wondering what was going on. One of the big doors of the barn swung open and Kerry emerged from the barn, grinning, on the back of a little Honda 70cc motorcycle. He rode it around in the dirt and rocks of the drive, trying to spin out and throw dirt and rocks, and pop wheelies, finally pulling up next to the three of us, as Kent had emerged from the barn, grinning, too. Kerry turned it off and put the kickstand down and got off the bike, smiling.

"Whose bike is this?" I asked.

"It belongs to the farm," Kerry explained. He added that the co-owner inside had mentioned that they had just purchased a small motorcycle from the general expenses of the farm and that he and his friends were welcome to ride it, as long as we were careful. The co-owner retrieved the key from a key rack next to the kitchen and gave it to Kerry.

"Cool," was Ed's only comment.

"Lemme ride it, Kerry," Kent demanded.

Kerry put his right hand up like a stop sign. "First, we need to check the gas tank," he advised, twisting open the top on the tank. He looked inside and swiveled the bike back and forth, and announced, "I'm gonna take it around to the pump and fill it up." He twisted the top closed, plopped down on the bike, kicked the engine on, gunned the throttle twice, put it in gear, let out the clutch and sprayed dirt and rocks as he gunned it around the side of the barn and disappeared. We could hear the engine die, followed by a few minutes of silence until we heard the engine start up again, but Kerry, instead, went around the far side of the barn through the farmhouse back yard and came around the opposite side of the house. He waved with a big laugh as he gunned it going past us, down the drive, into the road and away from the farm until we couldn't even hear the engine any more.

Kent was pissed. "Dammit!" he spewed. "It's supposed to be my turn and that fucker's gonna be gone forever!"

I started laughing and Ed joined me. Kent turned to me with a scowl, until I said, "Relax, Kent. Kerry's gonna have some fun and take a long ride. So what? Then, it'll be your turn, and you'll have some fun with a long ride. Then, hell, Ed can take a turn and I'll go last." I stepped up to Kent and slapped his right shoulder, adding, "We've got beer. We've got dope. Let's smoke a bowl while he's gone."

"Alright," Kent said, "but first, I need another beer."

Ed said, "Me too."

"Me three," I said, "and I'll go get my smoke."

"I'll get the beer, Ed," Kent said, and Kent and I turned and walked to the door of the house.

"Will you take my empty can?" Ed asked.

"Throw it," I replied and turned, walking backwards. Ed threw it past me and I turned, swooped it off the ground and threw it into the trash can inside. After retrieving my smoke from the downstairs room I occupied, I met the other two outside and took a beer offered from Kent. We walked away from the house to some trees for a little cover from those inside. I filled the pipe, lit it, filled my lungs and coughed a little, and passed the pipe to Kent. Kent inhaled and offered the pipe to Ed, which he declined. Ed didn't like to smoke marijuana. Just as we finished the last of the pot, we could hear the distant rumble of the motorcycle coming up the road. Soon, Kerry tore into the drive and skidded to a stop just in front of the lawn, clicked the shifter into neutral and left it running as he whipped his leg around the bike, laughing enthusiastically.

Kent got on the bike and Kerry tried to tell him how to work it, but Kent insisted that he knew what he was doing. He pushed the shift lever down into first gear, let out the clutch, the motorcycle lurched and died. Now everybody laughed, except Kent.

"You gotta give it some gas as you let out the clutch, man" Kerry laughed.

"I know that!" Kent snapped back.

I was on the right side of the bike, so I stepped over and twisted the kick pedal out. Kent told me to get away, but I just laughed and told him I was getting the kick pedal ready. Kerry told Kent to hold the clutch in, but the first kicks resulted in the engine firing, the bike lurching and dying, and Kent cursing. Kerry was almost going to take it away from him, when Kent held the clutch in, kicked it and it fired up, and he slowly let the clutch out while revving the throttle. When the clutch engaged the bike lifted up and Kent almost freaked, but he lowered the throttle, turned the bike, and slowly headed down the drive and out to the road. We were yelling at him to shift gears and we could hear the engine slow, and gear changing missing, then hitting, and finally we didn't hear the engine at all.

"Think he'll be riding or pushing it back?" I asked rhetorically.

"Well, I hope so," laughed Kerry, "because I'm thinking we might have to go out to find him and carry him back."

We all chuckled at the thought of that. "Here, Kent got you a beer," I told Kerry, picking up an unopened beer in the lawn and handing it to Kerry. "Let's go over by those trees and smoke some lieutenant."

"Let's go," agreed Kerry, and we went, Ed bringing up the rear. We smoked another pipe full of pot, walked back to the drive and waited about another five minutes and Kent returned, still riding the bike. Kerry came over and squeezed the clutch when Kent seemed to have a little trouble putting it in neutral; after Kent dismounted, Kerry clicked the shift lever into neutral and held it for Ed to get on. Ed listened to Kerry's advice, put it in gear and slowly eased away, until he had turned to the road, when he twisted the throttle for more gas, shifted, hit the road and the sound of the motorcycle rumbling faded away.

After Ed returned, it was my turn. Ed didn't try to put it in neutral, so I squeezed the clutch as I mounted the bike. Kerry started to tell me about it, but I rattled off all the items, one by one, pointing to each one as I said the name, then I finished with, "That's the front tire and that's the back tire. Think I should check the air pressure?"

"Get out of here," Kerry said, smiling as he walked away.

I spun the tires as I turned the bike in a complete circle, went around the house and around a tree about ten feet from the water, up the yard, across the front lawn, out of the drive and into the road, hitting fifth gear and flying across the pavement. I pulled off the road down some dirt paths between fields, taking them down to the dead end or when I felt I was getting too close to another house, and then back out to the road. About fifteen minutes later I returned to the farmhouse and turned the key to shut off the motor.

We took a break from the motorcycle to prepare dinner. Kerry had already started the grill, so we took out the ground beef and made hamburger patties. There were ears of corn all over the enclosed porch and we wrapped them in foil and put them on the grill; the others had eaten about an hour before and they invited us to all the pork and beans and green beans that were left, which was quite a bit. Kerry took a short spin on the bike around the house before he put the patties on the grill. We all took short turns on the bike and checked what else needed to be done for dinner: Kerry and Kent set the table, put the potato chips on the table, got some more beers, and checked the beans. When Kerry finished the cheeseburgers, we put up the bike for the night, ate dinner, laughed and talked and sat at the table for a while. We cleared the table, Kerry rinsed the dishes and put them in the dishwasher and started it up. We played cards, watched a little TV, snuck outside to smoke some more pot, drank a lot more beer, and separated to our rooms by two in the morning.

The sound of growing activity in the house woke me up by nine, so I put on some clothes and went upstairs. Kerry was sitting at the table drinking coffee, and, after our greetings, he offered to get me a cup. I accepted. I sat down at the table and Kerry returned promptly with a steaming cup.

As he sat down Kerry lifted his eyebrows and shook his head with a half-smile on his face. "Woo, we drank a lot of beer yesterday," he said.

"No shit," I agreed.

"There's barely three cases left and that's supposed to last 'til tomorrow afternoon."

"No way that's gonna happen," I said.

"We'll have to get some more," Kerry said, looking out the window,

Kent straggled up the stairs and stepped slowly into the dining room. He and Kerry exchanged 'heys' as he continued into the kitchen. "We got any juice?" he yelled from the kitchen.

"There's orange juice," Kerry replied. "We're gonna need to get more beer."

Kent came back to the dining room carrying a glass of juice and sat down. "I know that," Kent said. Immediately changing the subject, he added, "Let's go to that bar in Bath tonight. If it's like last time, there should be some pussy there."

"We can go there," Kerry said, "but I was thinking of going to Chandlerville first. We can eat there, drink some draft for a while, get some cases to go, then, if it's not too late, we can drive to Bath." Kerry took a sip of coffee and turned to Kent. "Waddaya think of that?"

"Sounds like a plan," Kent replied.

Kerry turned to me. "You're the driver," I replied. "I'm just the cargo."

"We may have to dump extra cargo for extra beer," Kent remarked.

"That's so unlike you, man," I said. "Did you crack your skull riding that motorbike yesterday?"

Kerry had gotten up from the table for more coffee and we heard him laugh in the kitchen. Kent just said quietly, "Fuck you."

Ed appeared in the dining room, rubbing his forehead and look-

ing a bit groggy. "I think I drank too much beer," he said.
"Are you hung over?" Kent asked.
"Worse, I think," Ed replied.
Kerry stepped back into the dining room. Seeing Ed, he cheerfully asked, "Ed, how's your head?"
"Don't ask," Ed moaned, asking, "Is that coffee?"
"Yeah," Kerry affirmed. "Want some?"

When Ed replied that he did, Kerry went back to the kitchen and fetched Ed a cup. As we all sat at the table, the conversation revolved around hangovers and possible remedies, but Ed decided to just bear it. We discussed breakfast and decided to fix some scrambled eggs for everybody and omelets for Kerry, Kent and myself. We also fixed hash browns and ate breakfast forty-five minutes later, cleaned up and went outside, down to the lake to check out the surroundings and contemplate. Kent brought a beer with the explanation that it would help his headache, but the rest of us decided to wait.

Kent and Kerry showed us where the duck blinds had been built and pointed to some areas of the lake that had proven to be the best fishing spots. We discussed what we should do for the day, and talk eventually settled on the motorbike. We all liked riding it and I suggested that we could design a course and ride against time using my watch. Everybody thought that was a good idea and we plotted the course around the house and around the tree that I had gone around the night before.

Some of the hired help drove up, intending to harvest all the chickens, about two dozen, and prepare them for storage in the freezer. Right after the help arrived, another co-owner's family arrived, including an attractive girl about sixteen years of age. When Kent saw her, his immediate comment was "Jailbait"; but Kerry didn't pay any attention to the newcomers; instead when he saw what the two very fat women were doing with the chickens – running around in the pen trying to grab them by hand and twist their necks off – he suggested a better idea and ran into the house. In seconds he was in front of the chicken pen with a .22 rifle and ammo box and the women were out. He loaded the gun and took aim, as the women reminded him to shoot them in the head, and began picking them off one after the other, right in the head. He only missed once, which was a clear miss of everything, and even let Kent pick off a couple. In ten minutes, it was over and the two women picked up the chickens and got to pluckin'.

"That calls for a beer!" Kent exclaimed, once the carnage was complete.

"Draw two!" Kerry chimed in.

"Ed?" I asked, looking in his direction.

"Ah, what the fuck," was his reply.

"Make that a full round, bartender!" I shouted to Kent.

In practically no time, Kent returned with four beers and tossed a beer to each of us. Normally, none of us liked to open a beer that was shaken, but this time we just laughed as we popped our beers and the foam ran up and over the cans.

"Heads up!" Ed said.

"I could go for some head right now," Kent snickered.

"Cheers, bro," I said, and lifted my can to Kent, who banged his against mine. Then we all banged each other's cans and drank heftily. That first beer went down easy and quick and in minutes we were all working on another. Kerry wondered aloud if it was time to do some biking. "Let's do it!" we all cried out and walked down to the drive between the house and the barn. Kerry got the key from inside, went to the barn, kicked it over and rode it around the house.

We all took turns going around the house for practice. Finally, we started our race; after a few laps with everyone completing at least one, it was clear that it could be run in under a minute. We used my watch, the timer would shout "Go!" when the second hand was at twelve and the rider would try to beat the best time. Kerry and I started out with the best times, but Kent started getting better and challenging us. Ed, though, was not doing as well, and we started to give him a hard time because his best was ten seconds off the best time.

On his turn, he vowed that he was going to run his best time, yet. He took off and disappeared around the house. Once on the other side of the house, the rumble from the bike couldn't be heard, so I looked at my watch. Thirty seconds…thirty-five seconds…forty seconds…forty-five seconds and still no bike rumble. Something's wrong. At that moment Jailbait came out the front door and announced, "Your friend took a tumble."

We ran around the house to the back yard to see Ed lying on the ground on his back next to the tree by the lake. The bike was on its side still running in first gear with the rear tire spinning slowly in the air. As we approached, asking what happened, Ed slowly got up from the ground and simply said he wasn't going to race anymore. We looked him over, noting the scratch on the side of his forehead and the torn jeans over his left knee that appeared to be bleeding. He limped into the house, declining any help, and attended to his wounds. Jailbait told us later that she was looking out the picture window and watched as Ed lost control of the bike as he maneuvered between two trees, swiveling left and right, until he hit a stump that threw him off the bike, which caused his injuries. Once he stopped rolling he looked up to see that the bike was still upright and headed directly into the lake. He jumped up and ran as fast as he could, caught the bike just feet before the lake and sat it on its side with the rear tire off the ground, exactly where we found it.

The three of us raced for another hour while Ed stayed in the house, nursing his pride more than his injuries. Kerry and I got the record to about forty-two seconds around the house and we decided to take a break. We fixed some sandwiches and chips, drank more beer and retired to a room downstairs to play cards. Ed said he was tired and wanted to rest, so he retired to his room.

After cards we wandered around the house, checked what was on the television – we all agreed that nothing was on television – and we tried to think of things to do as we sauntered outdoors. Kerry suddenly said he wanted to show us something and we walked to the bike parked in the drive; he kickstarted it and Kent slipped on the back and they disappeared down the road. About twenty minutes later Kerry returned and I climbed on the back and he took off into the road. About a half-mile away, he turned left onto a dirt road; after a couple stops where he explained who the property owners were, including a break in the corn where he pointed out the farmhouse of a former shortstop of the St. Louis Cardinals in the fifties, he reached the end of the road where Kent was waiting. The dirt road actually cut through a gully and proceeded on the other side of a line of trees that started where the current road ended, but that was the property line that Kerry didn't want to cross.

Kerry pulled a joint out of his cigarette pack and lit it and passed it to Kent and around it went between the three of us. While we were smoking, we wondered how long it would take to go to the farmhouse and back to where we were standing on the motorbike. Kerry proposed a race from the spot where we were standing to the back of his truck at the house and back to this spot. To ensure that each rider went to Kerry's truck, the first rider would carry a beer can and leave it on the back of the truck; the next rider would have to pick it up and bring it back, and we would just keep repeating the cycle. Kent suggested that we would need to have some beer out here and Kerry said he would take care of that right now. He hopped on the bike, started it and took off.

Ten minutes later he came back up the dirt road with his cooler strapped to the back, filled with beer cans and a little ice. Kent flattened one of our empty beer cans and told Kerry to use this one; Kerry pulled out a pocket knife and scratched the "B" off the name on the can, "just so there's no mistake about it." He was looking at Kent when he said that.

"Come on," Kent said to Kerry, "you go first."

I took off my watch and when the second hand reached twelve, I said, "Go!" Off Kerry went, positioning the can under his leg. He got back about a minute and a half later, and that was about the time it took every trip. Kent cheated once on a trip where he left the can at the truck; on my trip, expecting the can sitting on the door turned down at the back of the truck, Kent had thrown it into the bed of the truck, and I had to get off the bike and jump into the bed of the truck to get the can. We all remembered there was a large stump next to the drive between the house and the barn, so that became the place where we left the can at the house. It was competitive and a slow time from one generated ridicule from the other two, but we were passing the time, having fun, drinking beer, and, shit, what the hell is Ed doing? It was a little after five in the afternoon; time to head back to the house, get cleaned up, and have a night out in the sticks.

Ed was up and around and feeling better when we got back; he had even taken a shower and was ready for a night out; out of sympathy, we didn't razz him much about his misadventure. We all took showers, got ready – including blow dryers for our hair since it *was* the seventies – and we crammed into the Ford truck and drove to Chandlerville.

We parked on the street and walked the half-block to Butch's Tavern. Even on a Saturday night, we saddled up to the bar and took our seats on four consecutive stools; a rather crusty, old codger, friendly nevertheless, stepped over to us from behind the bar and Kerry ordered our drafts and asked what was good on the menu. We heard a few of the items but we all quickly settled on breaded and fried catfish on a bun, served with potato salad and green beans. Kerry and Kent, mostly, made small talk with the locals, generally older men in jeans or overalls, some wearing ball caps, and some particularly soused. We were well into our second round when the crusty old codger and a woman wearing an apron brought our plates and Kerry paid for the meals, although we all gave him money to cover it. We dug in and the meal was good.

After we finished eating, we played some darts and threw some money into the pinball machine they had in the back. Of course, we drank plenty more beer, and Kent tried to introduce himself to any reasonably attractive young woman that wandered inside, which, according to my count, was strictly two. We drank eight to ten beers while we were at Butch's, but when ten at night came and went, Kent lobbied more and more to drive to Bath and Kerry finally agreed. Ed was looking pretty wasted, but he mumbled his agreement, too. Kerry ordered two cases of beer, paid for it, we took the cases as they were handed to us from behind the counter, carried them to the truck, placed them in the bed, and took off down some incredibly dark and twisting back roads, over one rickety bridge, and into Bath some twenty minutes later.

To my surprise, as tiny a town as Bath was, this place was hopping. We could hear the jukebox music long before we got to the door; inside, the patrons were considerably younger compared to the tavern, there were more of them, and the atmosphere was more like a party, something with which we were quite familiar. Room at the bar was tight, but Kerry squeezed in and got some beers and we stepped around the place, smiling at any girl who looked our way. We managed to secure a table after a few minutes – establishing base camp – and planned our mode of operations. They had a dance floor and Kent was up and circulating in no time, dancing and flirting and cavorting; eventually, some girls sat down at our table and we talked, and danced. Ed stopped drinking altogether; he was bombed and knew it. We had a good time but by two in the morning, even Kent was looking wasted, so Kerry decided it was time to go; I was obviously inebriated, too, but for some strange reason, I wasn't surprised when Kerry asked for a beer and I popped one open for him and handed it to him. He finished that beer before we got back to the farmhouse without incident, to my amazement.

Up by nine-thirty, one of the co-owners invited me to help myself to coffee in the pot on the kitchen counter. He also advised that I should make another pot with the extra pot next to it, which I did. Both were the old style with a strainer where you poured the coffee grounds that sat in the self-contained pot; you would plug it in and it would propel the water at the bottom through the strainer for a few minutes, you would remove the strainer and have coffee. While the second pot was brewing, Kerry appeared in the kitchen.

"There's just enough for one more cup, but that other pot's brewing, so go for it," I said.

Kerry grabbed a cup from the cupboard and filled it. He fixed up the now empty pot for another brew and plugged it in. "I need to go outside to drink this," he announced, and walked outside, while I followed. His intention was to smoke a cigarette, which he refrained from doing in the house when possible. He lit one up and said, "Well, what did you think of Bath? The place was jumpin' last night, huh?"

"I was amazed at how much pussy was in such a small town, that's for sure," I commented.

"Kent and I go there almost every time we're down on the farm."

"I had fun last night," I said. "We sure drank a lotta beer, too. How you feeling today?"

"I feel alright, no problems. You?"

"I feel great. Tell ya what, though, I was a little concerned with you driving back last night, drinkin' that beer, and you almost missed that turn. It was really dark."

"To be honest," Kerry chuckled, "I fuckin' forgot about that turn, but we made it. I was glad you stayed up with me, unlike some other people." We both cracked up on that one, since both Kent and Ed were sound asleep as soon as they got in the truck.

We were so wasted and tired when we got back the night before that we had left the three cases of beer – we picked up another at the bar in Bath - in the bed of the truck. When Kerry finished his cigarette, he suggested we take the beer inside, which we did.

Kerry and I sat on the tailgate of his truck, enjoying our second cup of coffee, when Kent staggered out to us, looking bleary-eyed and tired. Kerry immediately laughed at the site and Kent told him to shut up. Eventually, he confessed that he was so hung over he had to get up out of bed to throw up and he still felt like throwing up. It took him a couple hours and about three beers to feel 'normal', as he put it.

As bad as Kent was feeling, it was practically nothing to Ed's feeling. He not only threw up the previous night's lingering consumption, he also threw up breakfast *and* lunch. In fact, there was a time when we could say the word 'beer' and watch Ed wince with pain.

The rest of our time at the farmhouse was spent lounging, drinking beer and smoking pot. We played cards, too, but it was really just Kerry and I lapping it up, Kent trying to catch up and rid himself of the pain in his head, and Ed finally coming around. When we left the farm about five in the afternoon, we barely had one case of beer left, and we drank most of that on the way back and for a short stay at Kent's house.

I don't know if this weekend convinced Ed that a change in the course of his life was in order. I do know that after this weekend Ed gradually faded out of our lives; in my experience, there were two or three more impromptu baseball games during which both Ed and I participated, but once the current year yielded to the next, I never saw or talked with Ed again. In any case, the following weekend was the Fourth of July celebration, which marked the end of my first month of freedom. Kerry was working full-time, Jeff was working most of the time – or so we were led to believe – and rarely made appearances, so it was just me and Kent holding up the cause of freedom.

In a surprise development, Jeff called Kent Friday before the Fourth weekend and wanted to get with all of us and make plans for the weekend. Saturday, we decided to take the boat out on the lake for the afternoon. It was really crowded but we found some space to ski and cruise and, of course, we brought plenty of beer. Jeff apologized for being difficult to reach; he had apparently gotten involved with an older woman, who had her own entanglements to disentangle, and he had just finished moving in with her. However, he had spent so much time with her over the last month, he needed a break from her for the weekend. Of course, Kerry and Kent lit into him, in mock anger, for using us as a 'crutch', as nothing more than a break from his dreary life of domestication.

"Why aren't you giving me grief, too?" Jeff asked me.

"Because you've been around so little," I explained, "that I'm not so sure you'd take it as a joke or haul off and punch me."

"I get the point," Jeff apologized.

Sunday I was invited to one of the private clubs on the lake to watch the guys and their slow pitch softball team play in a tournament. That was the day I was introduced to the term 'ringer', which is slang for a person who is good at a particular sport and who becomes a member of a team for a short time, such as during a tournament with prize money, but is not a regular member of the team. It was used a lot by members of the guys' team, because they were getting beat with home runs by ringers they had never seen in league play and who were playing on teams they knew from league play. In softball tournaments during the summer, the ringers would typically be college baseball players on scholarship who were friends with someone on the team.

I guess I wasn't sympathetic enough. "Is there a rule in this tournament prohibiting guys from playing on a team if they're not regular members of the team?" I asked Kent and Kerry and Jeff.

"Well, no, not technically," was the response.

"So, if there's no rule against who can play, then you're getting' beat fair and square, so what are you whinin' about?" I asked further.

"You'd feel different if you were playing and it was your money."

"But I'm not playing because you guys never asked if I wanted to play on your team, so I don't have anything to do with it."

"We're new to this team and we couldn't bring you along. Anyway, you don't seriously think you could make a difference, do you?"

"We'll never know, will we? And, maybe, your new team sucks."

It should have been a clue for me, but I was, apparently, extremely dense about the guys' softball team and their collective opinion about my ability to contribute to their team. Still, even when I was hanging around, not playing, I was drinking beer for free. After a while, though, that 'buddy' sitting on your shoulder named Pride, providing that 'unbiased voice of reason' buzzing in your ear, starts to make more and more sense.

They didn't do very well in the tournament, but we did drink plenty of beer. Later, we drove out to the park, where there were plenty of girls, more beer, and a place where we could smoke some pot. I couldn't resist a final dig. "At least we can smoke some dope here. Maybe that was your problem: no pot!"

"Fuck you!" was the unanimous response.

After a long afternoon and evening of heavy-duty partying, we all split for our own digs to recover, to sleep, to dream, to waste away. But not too far away – there were whole packs of firecrackers, cherry bombs, smoke bombs, bottle rockets, and m-80s to blow up. We all descended upon Kent's house before noon and immediately started blasting off, both with explosive items, and beer and pot. We drove around to several parks and blasted away, driving off long before the authorities could arrive. We threw explosive devices out the window of moving vehicles; we blew things up; we threw lit devices at each other. We reveled in the sheer lunacy of it all and when we blew up everything we had, we drove out to a party that Jeff knew was going on out near New City. There, we drank and ate and smoked into the wee hours of the morning. Kerry and Jeff went to work hung over the next morning while Kent and I got up late, as usual; Kent and I, it seemed, were the only two left that were truly free. At least, that's what we told ourselves.

Kent and I went fishing in the early morning later in the week, hauling in a fairly usual catch of medium flathead and channel catfish and some smaller bass. We'd get with Kerry when he was not with Patti; we'd try to reach Jeff, with little success; and we'd drink beer and smoke pot as much as we wanted. We always smoked a joint when the sun started coming up while we were fishing; it was almost a religious experience. We definitely enjoyed it, in a somber, silent way.

The following weekend after the Fourth of July produced more softball practice, where I watched and drank and shot the shit with some of the other guys on the team. We'd hang out at the park until it closed. Sunday, Kent and I packed it in early; we were fishing in the morning.

Monday morning was difficult for me to get up on time, so I was a half-hour late as I drove to Kent's house. I knocked on the door for a long time – very unusual – until his sister, Stacie, opened the door with a face still half asleep. She simply said that Kent was gone; his uncle had come by and the two were driving to Davenport, Iowa, to work on a construction job. Now, I was the only one free. Now what?

I rode my bicycle and my motorcycle. I shot the basketball. I called Rick at his home in Glen Aire and we hung out together for an afternoon. We didn't drink any beer, but we smoked a lot of pot and threw the Frisbee and goofed off. I drank a few beers and listened to music at home at night.

I got a call from Kent about 8 on Friday. He had just got back from Iowa and wanted to get together and party. First, though, he wanted to slam me for being late on Monday. If I had been on time, we would have left his house before his uncle got there; his uncle would have found someone else to help on the construction job because he didn't have the time to wait for Kent to get back from fishing; and we would have partied like always through the rest of the week. But, no, I wasn't on time; Kent was now committed to working the job for the next two or three months, driving to Iowa early Monday morning and driving back Friday afternoon; and it was all my fault.

"Sorry," I said.

"Is that all you can say?" Kent demanded, adding, "You owe me more than that!"

"I'll spin from my lieutenant."

"Is it that punk weed shit you had before?"

"No, redbud, from Kerry's stash."

"Okay."

I drove over to Kent's house where we partied until late into the night. He told me about his job – laying bathroom tile in a new apartment complex – and his dismay at the lack of quality he believed was being consciously, purposefully, followed. The apartment complex was part of a national chain of apartment complexes under a name everyone would recognize. What really bothered Kent, and me, too, as I thought more about it, is that, despite all the sub-standard materials and practices in use, all of it was done with the approval of the local inspectors and code enforcers. It's all about the money, I suppose.

The four of us managed to gather the next day and we even had a fish barbecue dinner at the park for a few of our friends, some of whom brought their own dishes to round out the meal. Cheryl was there and she confided to me that she didn't like the idea of Kent being away for days at a time. Patti was there, quiet and shy as always. Jeff brought some girl none of us had ever met before, but we all drank and ate and smoked and had a good time.

Soon, though, Monday rolled around too quickly and my freedom meant alone, a lot. It was like that through the end of July, doing whatever I wanted during the week and getting with the guys during the weekend. Kent was making good money, more than any of us, and he shared it without reservation, too. He also spun some tales about the nightlife in Davenport, which was wild by our experience, where strip clubs and all-night bars down on the river were hopping and crazy, and like that every night.

I read an ad in the paper during the first days of August that the state fair needed laborers at two dollars an hour, which was slightly more than the minimum wage at the time. It would only be for a couple days before the fair and through the fair and I thought it would be a good way to earn some more money before school started, so I went to the fair and found the building to fill out the application. Once I completed it, I gave it to one of the men sitting behind the portable tables they had set up; he asked me a few questions and told me to report to work at the maintenance building at the east end of the fairgrounds by three-thirty in the afternoon on Wednesday before the fair started. I drove out to it to make sure I knew where it was; it was a big, quonset hut and I spied some parking spots and had the plan.

I showed up on time and reported to the man in charge and was given a time card to punch – which I did immediately – and a green jump suit that I had to wear during my entire shift. There were a lot of men, young and old, there, some issued green jump suits like mine – the laborers – and some issued red jump suits – the garbagemen. The reds seemed cooler and had a better job – they drove around the fairgrounds with a modified lawn tractor towing one or two carts behind it emptying garbage cans – and they were definitely more cocky and talkative. The garbagemen got better pay, too, but those jobs were all taken early – you usually had to know somebody to get one. The laborers were farmed out to some of the vendors, for the most part, and my first day was spent helping set up booths and carrying boxes and gear. It wasn't too demanding and once the fair started, I figured I could have some fun, too, because I chose the best shift - from four in the afternoon until midnight - when most of the partying and good times would be taking place.

The next day started a little slower, as I waited around the maintenance building with the other laborers waiting for an assignment. One of the laborers came out of the building and said that he heard that one of the garbage details had just had an accident and they were headed back; one of the guys in the detail was hurt bad enough that an ambulance had been called. A few minutes later, one of the tractors pulled into the lot and up to the building. One of the guys in the detail was laying on his back with a bloody shirt wrapped around his head and two others limped out of the cart they were sitting in when it came to a stop. The managers helped the guy with the bleeding head out of the cart and checked his wound, applying some stuff from a first aid kit including a bandage, until the ambulance arrived.

The crew chief – a young man a year or two older than me with brown hair to his shoulders and a mustache – initially looked a little flustered, but after he talked to his manager, he looked around at the milling laborers with an intense, more business-like appearance. I had noticed the three guys who got hurt from the day before – they had impressed me as a group of hicks just off the farm or some carnies, guys who worked at carnivals, trying to pick up a few extra bucks. I had wondered at the time how they got the good jobs and we were the laborers. A few more minutes went by and one of the managers approached the crew chief, and the chief's appearance turned to anger briefly; he walked over to one of the trio, said something, and the guy, still rubbing his head, shook his head and the chief walked toward us. The manager shouted that they needed three guys for a garbage detail – with pay at three fifty an hour – and those who wanted the job were to gather around the tractor. I walked over to the tractor with about ten others and heard the manager tell the chief to pick his replacements. Immediately, the chief pointed right to me and said, "I want that guy right there." He pointed to two more guys and the new crew was set.

"Okay, you three go back inside and find a red jump suit," the manager said. "I'll get your new time cards and write in the start time so you'll get the pay as garbagemen for the full day. Let's go!"

When we got back we all introduced ourselves. There was the crew chief, Kenny, the lone remaining crew member, a fit and funny black guy who called himself, Johnny, the Hispanic wise guy, Jose, but we all called him Joe just to needle him, another black guy calling himself, Sammy, who was quick witted and quick tongued and fancied himself a singer and babe magnet, and myself. Next, the three new crew members wanted to know what really happened.

Kenny said, "Well, that's why we're going to go over the rules of operation, so that it doesn't happen again." The rules of operation were all common sense stuff, but the one wrinkle concerned driving the tractor with the carts in tow uphill. Since the tractors didn't provide enough traction on their own, one or two of the detail had to stand on the fenders above the wheels to provide the necessary traction, which was obviously not recommended by the manufacturer due to the danger involved. The three guys had been goofing off and one of them had his foot slip off the fender, catch between the wheel and the fender, which threw the tractor's front end straight up into the air, threw off both of the guys on the fender, and the third one got banged around in the lead cart. We asked Johnny why he didn't get hurt.

"I was in the back cart, expecting it to happen," he calmly explained, with noticeable disgust. "I stayed away from those morons."

Kenny hopped on the tractor, the rest of us piled into the lead cart, and out of the parking lot we sped, at a blazing three miles per hour. Kenny kept up his tough act for about a half-hour, while we stopped to empty garbage cans and put new linings in them, throwing the bags in the cart. After we made it up our first hill with Johnny and me standing on the fender and without incident, we were all laughing and carrying on, Kenny included, but sticking to business when we needed to. We took our lunch break down on the midway, flirting with the girls, and struttin' our stuff wearing our genuine, red jump suits, looking like escaped convicts begging to be re-arrested. Kenny had confessed that he was pissed off because the other two guys, who weren't hurt badly at all, didn't want to work anymore, so he was going to have to train almost an entire new crew the day before the fair started. At the end of our shift, I had Kenny agreeing that, not only was his new crew better, we also had more fun, too. I couldn't believe that I was tooling around behind a lawn tractor, telling jokes with the guys, flirting with girls as we drove past, and getting paid for doing it, too.

Kenny and I clicked right from the beginning. "When I saw you the first day, I wished you were on my crew," he said, "because, at least, I'd have somebody in the back I could depend on."

"Sometimes, things happen for a reason," I replied.

Kenny introduced me to one of the other garbage crews, two guys who happened to play keyboards and guitar in the same rock band with Kenny, who played sax, some keyboards and sang. Those guys were cool like all of us; when we had a chance, we would smoke a joint. We did our jobs, though, with no problems.

After the fair started, that's when it really got fun. We could drive right behind a group of girls and beep at them, not really to pass them but to let them know we knew they were there. On Sunday, Ed McMahon was in town for a show, but when we saw him walking down the main drag of the fair, I just lit into him, saying nobody wanted to see him, he was a hack, and on and on, for about three minutes. Amazingly, with as many state troopers and police officers as there are at the fair every year, nobody busted me or even challenged me. The guys thought I was crazy; Kenny thought it was surreal. It was misplaced anger directed at a symbol of the status quo, of power and money, unworthy of trust from the masses. Whether or not that was true, today it's just embarrassing. What a putz.

There was no partying with friends while I was working at the fair, though I did see some acquaintances from various and previous endeavors of my life. A couple times, Kenny and I, with Joe once, went to a bar outside the fair after work and drank some beers and talked. Once, we got some beer during our lunch break and got it inside the fair and drank it after our shift in the privacy of the back of a band mate's van.

One night, we were at the hog barns, checking and emptying the cans just outside the buildings. A hog demonstrator had set a chair next to the door leading to one of the barns and had placed a small television on the chair. As I stepped up to check the garbage can a few feet away, I could see the face of President Nixon on the screen, his lips moving but I couldn't hear the sound. Three or four people were standing around, talking in low tones, or looking about, and back to the TV.

"Nixon's resigning the presidency," one of them said.

Watergate and its aftermath had finally caught up with Nixon. In an irony befitting the whole sordid affair, there was a picture of Nixon making his resignation speech just outside the hog barn at the state fair. Another irony was that free did not mean "without consequences". Free meant we *could* drink and smoke all day, but only while we had money. To get money, you had to work for it, so no more drinking and smoking all day. The lesson of Watergate was *not* about the actions of the burglars, or the campaign and its dirty tricks, but the *lies* which followed in the hope that none of it would be discovered. However, the biggest irony of all, after all these decades since, is that it's a lesson that regularly needs to be reinforced. Apparently, it just doesn't seem to sink in with many people.

Act Twelve
Welcome to Massively Higher Education

My venture as a garbageman at the state fair was mostly a worthwhile one, despite two nights of rain and drizzle, an impromptu Ed McMahon bashing, and the unexpected television appearance of soon-to-be-ex-President Richard Nixon at the hog barn. One of our perks was running down to the stage at the grandstand to pick up the afternoon's garbage there. That gave us the opportunity to see the night's entertainment close-up. Unfortunately, the entertainment lineup for 1974's state fair was unspectacular. Herbie Mann was good and we watched most of his set standing in the equipment booth directly to stage right. We also caught the ill-fated solo act performed by the former lead singer from a certain rock band from the Peoria area, who came to his senses a few months later and re-joined the band.

Kenny and I had gotten comfortable and trusting of the other over the short time we worked together, so, once the last night's work was complete and we picked up our checks at the maintenance building's office, we were still wired and contemplating what we could do to wind down. We decided to pick up a couple six-packs of beer and drive to Center Park and drink and talk, which is exactly what we did. Despite the fact that the park was 'closed', we parked our cars in the spaces at the east end of the park, grabbed our beers and walked down to the water's edge, which was at the bottom of the hill, where we could not be seen from the road or the parking area. For the next two to three hours, we talked and laughed, and quaffed the beers, careful to walk up to the can to deposit the empties when finished, enjoyed the company, wound down and sucked down every beer and had thrown away every can, just as the fearless lake police discovered us in the park after 'closing'. Since we didn't appear to be drunk, though they could smell the beer on our breaths, they made no real attempt to detain or arrest us. Kenny did most of the talking for us and in a few minutes we were ushered to our cars and left to go home while the police followed us for a while, veering off after we left the lake area behind. It was four in the morning when I quietly entered the house, walked to my room and laid out for sleep.

The week after the fair, I was due to move my necessities to Champaign-Urbana and start my higher-education life, with a supposed expectation to setting a career path. The day before I was to drive Mom's car with my stuff to my assigned dormitory on campus, Kenny called and invited me to the band's rehearsal that evening. I had already met some of the guys earlier, but this night I got to hear what they could do together with music. What I heard was exceptionally good, considering that most of the guys were born and raised in central Illinois, not an especially appealing stop on a music lover's journey to discover musical roots. There was Jimmy on drums and Charlie (who preferred Chas) on bass, making up the band's strong – and true – rhythm section. Jonny played several guitars and sang backup, and Paul played keyboards and sang lead and backup. For some arrangements, there could be a horn section of five, consisting of Peter on trombone, Mike on trumpet, Edward on clarinet or sax, Kenny on sax, flute or clarinet, and David on sax, trumpet, clarinet or flute. All the members in the horn section would also contribute to percussion and could sing, and most could play each other's instruments and often shared them; they even had an oboe and a French horn. They looked like a band similar to Chicago or Blood, Sweat and Tears, and they played some of those types of songs, but they also performed songs like *Roundabout* from Yes and *The Bitch is Back* from Elton John. They were both good and versatile and I was very impressed with the rehearsal. They called themselves The Joint Session.

Bobby, who was working the mixing board at the rehearsal and also operated the lights during their live appearances, was the real reason that I was invited to the rehearsal. He introduced himself with the question, "So, you're the guy Kenny thinks can replace me, huh?" Bobby had some more pressing things that he either wanted or needed to do, having already expressed that sentiment to the band's members, and, even though he was an old school mate of many of the guys, he wasn't going to be able to make the rehearsals and appearances regularly. He showed me the board with the channels taped for the various pieces of equipment and who they were tied to in the band. Like most small, local bands, their mixing board did not include all the musical items; while it would vary between bands, the Joint Session had all the microphones plugged to the board but only the tiny Farfisa-style organ; the electric bass, the electric guitar, and Paul's stacked keyboard ensemble all ran from their own, separate amplifiers. Of course, no local band mikes the drums and the Joint Session was no different. With Jimmy's hard, pounding, clean style, though, only the biggest places would need them and your small, local band wouldn't be playing at those places.

The rehearsal broke up in a haphazard fashion, which I would later understand was almost typical of small-time ensembles. Kenny and David wanted to work on some more arrangements; Paul, Jonny and Jimmy were ready to party with some smoke, after which Jimmy had to go; Peter and Mike and Bobby were ready to go, while Edward and Chas just wanted to jam. Three left within a few minutes and somebody revealed some beers and I had one. I played around with the board while some of the guys jammed, checking the mikes while in use so I could notice the differences. Paul and Jonny came back from outside and took up their instruments and the remaining musicians jammed for another hour.

The next day I filled up Mom's car, said my goodbyes to the family and drove the ninety some miles to the big U. Even though I had never been to Oglesby Hall, my dormitory, I was familiar with the campus towns and knew it was directly east of the football stadium. An hour and a half later I pulled into the drive in front of the entrance and parked as close as I could, which was about fifty yards away. Following the orientation papers sent to me, I walked into the dormitory and immediately spotted the registration tables in the middle and got in line, something I was going to be doing several times that week. I produced my papers and identification, received my room assignment and key, signed some papers, walked back out to retrieve my suitcase, walked to the elevators with a ton of other students and their families, and took what seemed an incredibly long time to get to the twelfth and top floor. My room, 1224, was on the south side of the building, about halfway down the hallway. The door was locked so I opened it with the key and observed an empty room; Matt, my roommate for the semester who was a classmate from Southeast, had not appeared, yet, so I picked one of the closets and slid my suitcase in it. I scoped the room, which was about ten feet by ten feet, with three feet square on either side of the room right at the door wall devoted to closet space up to the ceiling. There was one desk with two chairs in the far right corner, a shelf above it, and two beds, one along the left wall and the other along the far wall. It was quite basic.

"Hello, fellow grunt," I heard from behind me, uttered with a decidedly Chicago-style accent. I had left the door open, so when I turned I gazed upon a short, squat, almost elfish young man with brown hair not quite to his shoulders, a full beard, sporting gym shorts and a white T-shirt, smiling at me.

"Grunt?" I said, not fully comprehending his meaning.

"You never heard of a 'grunt'? You know, like, 'you're in the Army, now'," he said, continuing to smile but shaking his head slightly and raising his left eyebrow.

"Oh, yeah, grunt," I said, smiling back. I turned my head from side to side, looking around the room, as I added, "It *is* like a barracks. They had *real* barracks here, after the war. My Dad stayed in them until he graduated from here in forty-nine. Won't be any drill sergeants, though."

"True," said the little guy. He said his name and stuck out his right arm; I wrapped my fingers around his hand and we shook as I stated my name.

The little guy's name was Pete and he was from Schaumburg, one of the many subdivisions that were exploding in population with the exodus of WASP-type people from the city limits of Chicago. At the time I had no concern for where it was located; in my world, you were from the Chicago area or you were from anywhere else in the state, which was more or less how those from the Chicago area thought, too. Later, having business in the area, I would learn that Schaumburg was a city southwest of Chicago.

"You musta left pretty damn early to be already moved in before I got here," I stated.

"We left before six this morning," he said, "which *is* pretty damn early, I'll admit."

"Too early for me," I commented. "Well, if you don't mind, I gotta bring the rest of my stuff up and get settled in." I moved out the door and Pete stepped back to let me through. As I started walking down the hallway, I turned around, still walking, and asked, "By the way, what have you got planned for the rest of the day? Any?"

Pete stopped and turned around, and replied, "I was thinking of braving the Assembly Hall multitude and see if I can get registered for classes. They advise that the earlier you register, the better your chances of getting the classes you want."

"Well, if you haven't left when I finish hauling crap, I'll go with you," I offered, and I turned around and walked to the elevators. I heard Pete say, "Okay," and I threw up my right arm with my thumb pointed up.

After four more trips, which took an interminable length of time simply because I had to go to the top floor and back again every trip, I finally had the car unloaded and its contents placed in my closet. Matt had finally made it and I told him that I had already ordered the phone service in both our names and had paid the deposit; I showed him the paper and the phone, which I had already plugged in, and told him that they advised the service would be turned on next week, probably Monday. We decided on the beds – mine would be the one along the left wall – and Matt advised that he was bringing his snakes. That didn't surprise me, since he had been working at the zoo in Podunk for a couple years, and, for the summer now concluded, had worked exclusively in their herpetology exhibit. Once I had everything upstairs, I knew I had to move the car, so I had no intention of unpacking and I figured I might as well move the car and go down to registration instead of coming back upstairs.

I walked down to Pete's room to see if he was ready to register. In his room were a bunch of guys shooting the breeze, including Barry, Pete's roommate and friend since childhood, Jeff the motorcycle enthusiast whose room was next door to Pete's room, and Bruce, a large but mild-mannered fellow with a love for the banjo. I announced that I needed to move my car so others could park close for unloading and I was going to register after I parked the car. Pete suggested that we could all *ride* in my car to registration and I could park the car *when we returned*.

"So, you're the guy on our floor who's always on the lookout for the easiest thing to do that will take the least amount of work," I stated, adding, "I was wondering who that would be."

"I'm just saying if you're gonna park the car anyway," Pete protested, among the laughs all around, "it would be useful for everybody to ride to the hall first."

"I've got a funny feeling that walking is a foreign concept to Pete," I said. Before anyone else could interject, I added, "But if we're all ridin', let's go." I turned and started down the hallway to the elevators. Suddenly, everyone in the room scrambled, with shouts of "Hold up! I'm coming." I checked with Matt but he wasn't ready to go register, yet, though he was done bringing his stuff up to the room. "Okay," I said. *Whatever,* I thought.

I waited at the elevator until everybody appeared, Pete, Barry, Jeff and Bruce. We went down to the car, piled in, and I drove to the Assembly Hall parking lot, where we climbed out and walked into a mob of thousands, with signs for virtually everything. I found my starting spot, waited in line for a half-hour, but got the classes I wanted: rhetoric, algebra, sociology, philosophy and Spanish. When everybody had their classes registered – some took longer than others because their desired classes were full and they had to choose other classes – and we all were at the designated meeting point, we discussed what to do next. I had planned to get some lunch at one of the restaurants nearer the main campus, but I had planned to walk since parking was extremely limited there. Everyone else, except Barry, thought it was a good idea; Barry wanted to walk back to the dormitory, since he had some food there, until Pete offered to buy him lunch. We managed to find a decent parking space, found a restaurant we all liked, and had some lunch. When we were finished I drove us all back to the main parking lot at the dormitory.

We all just hung around, checking out the later-arriving students, sometimes heading downstairs – mostly to watch the girls arrive, since the dormitory consisted of twin, twelve-story buildings connected by a common lobby and basement, one side for the boys and the other for the girls. We discussed the adverse consequences of our generation, school overcrowding, and our particular manifestation – the fact that we had no student lounge, since there would be four students living in the lounge for an indefinite period. Because of the overabundance of students – a consequence of the baby boom's second wave, which would dissipate in ten years – there was both fierce competition for openings and rules to make it more difficult to move from one college of study to another. None of us really knew any of that, yet, but we would all realize its implications eventually, me particularly.

Mark, a huge hulk of a young man, had finally arrived from Arlington Heights and had settled into the room next door to mine. He had laid the block that allowed his high school football team to win their state championship, but any football dream had ended that day for him; a business degree from the University of Illinois was more accessible and desirable as far as he could conceive for his future. His roommate, Harold, who suffered from epilepsy, had also arrived and both were busy unpacking and readying themselves for their college careers. Harold was a bit reserved, probably due to his malady, but Mark was instantly outgoing, jovial, funny, and I liked him immediately.

I had to return Mom's car the next day but I could have driven it home that night, since we all sought our separate dinner choices, mostly on foot. The next morning, I awoke, fixed a cup of coffee and drank it, used the shower facilities to clean up, and advised anyone who cared that I was driving home to drop off the car and riding back on my motorcycle. Most liked the idea of having a motorcycle handy, until I further advised that nobody was riding my motorcycle without a valid motorcycle license, thus eliminating everyone but Jeff. Off I went to the elevators, out to the parking lot across the street, started up the Cutlass and drove for home.

I pulled into the driveway at home about one in the afternoon and immediately went inside and handed the keys to Mom and fixed some lunch. Mom dutifully asked if everything went okay and I quickly replied that it did indeed.

"No problems?"

"No."

"Did you get all the classes you wanted?"

"Yes."

"What's the dormitory like?"

"Twin, twelve stories, one for girls and one for boys, more like rats packed in a cage. Our student lounge is sleeping four."

"There's students in your lounge?"

"Yep."

"Don't they have the room?"

"Nope."

"How long is that gonna last?"

"'Til enough kids drop out or are expelled. Gotta go."

I went into my room and retrieved two of the three keys for my motorcycle. I quickly checked the duffel bag under my bed; it appeared undisturbed. I didn't feel comfortable having it at the school so it would remain under my bed at home, ready to serve when called upon. I found Mom in her bedroom reading and kissed her goodbye, assuring her that I would be alright. Pulling the motorcycle out from its resting area next to the wall, I turned it facing the street, inserted the key and set it on and kicked it over, after which it promptly fired up for me. I checked the tank, which was nearly full, and, with my helmet on, I pulled the clutch in, tapped the gear lever down to first, pulled the throttle back and eased the clutch out and took off. The ride was uneventful as I kept to the back roads the entire way, stopping about halfway to fill up for about two bucks. When I got back to the dormitory I parked it with the other motorcycles next to a big bike rack and ran the chain through the back tire and the mid-assembly to discourage theft.

Back on the twelfth floor the gang was getting settled. An unofficial tally of the residents had the freshmen outnumbering all the upperclassmen by almost two to one. The door to Mark's room was open and inside were Mark, Pete, Barry, Bruce and Jeff watching TV.

I walked in and announced, "Greetings, fellow grogs."

"Did you smash into anything?" Mark asked, smiling.

"That's why I wear a helmet," I replied, holding up the helmet and smiling back.

Jeff got up and said, "Let's see this puppy." Everybody else got up and followed Jeff and me downstairs. As we all congregated around the bike, some touching it or sitting on it, all wanting to ride it while I rejected that idea for the time being, I eased up to Pete. I was curious what kind of a crowd was forming around me and I whispered to him, since I thought Pete was the most likely candidate, "Think anybody smokes pot around here?"

Pete laughed loudly and looked at Mark as he remarked, "Country boy just asked me if anybody smokes pot around here."

"We should throw him in the pokey right now," Mark replied, looking at me with mock severity.

Jeff turned to me while sitting on the bike and said, "I don't, but you missed several sitdowns with those guys already today." He smiled and added, "You shoulda invested in a trailer and brought your bike with you yesterday. That way, you wouldn't have missed it."

"Snooze, you lose," Barry proclaimed.

"Can't lose when you've got your own stash," I advised.

"That settles it," Pete announced. "You've twisted my arm so much I can't resist." He looked over to Mark and suggested, "Shall we have a taste of country boy's weed?"

"We shall," Mark replied and we all made our way back up to the top floor; and we did.

Finally, classes were starting and the cafeteria was open. I went downstairs with some of the guys to check out the morning's offerings and that's when I saw her: The Brunette. She was average height, sleek, ample curvature upstairs, an attractive, smoothly round butt covered by her tight jeans, long, light brown hair, and a face of such smooth and clear complexion, combined with her very attractive eyes, nose, lips and mouth, she could cause a car crash just strolling down the city street. That was just the surface but it wasn't what really attracted me; it was how she moved, her attitude, the way she projected herself: demure, quiet, almost shy but, conversely, very poised, even confident. She had every reason to be poised and confident; she was, after all, one of the very few exceptions at the U of I, a beautiful woman with intelligence. Of course, all the guys noticed her right away, too. I kept glancing at her while she sat at her table with the other, more talkative girls, and the guys chatted incessantly about her and the other girls at her table. Once, she looked over at me while I was looking at her and I managed to form a weak smile and watched as her mouth formed an almost identically weak smile. I remember thinking, *no way! A girl with almost the same attitude and carriage as me? No way!*

Spanish was up first, at 8 AM every Monday through Thursday.

Liberal Arts required four hours of foreign language; otherwise, I would never have been caught dead in such a classroom. Can I roll my r's? No. Can I put together a sentence? No. Am I a complete failure in Spanish? No. If you happen to be with me in some Spanish speaking dominion and we're both thirsty and we can find a bar, never fear! We'll saddle up to the bar and I'll do the ordering. Dos cervezas, por favor. True, I won't know how much they cost and I won't know, even if we get back change, whether we got ripped off or not, but, hey! We won't be thirsty.

The rest of that semester's schedule was whacked. The only classes which were back to back were Spanish and Algebra at 9 AM, but only on Mondays and Wednesdays. All the other classes were scattered around the day and week; add to that the fifteen minute walk just to get to the class and there was a lot of wasted time in that first semester. Welcome to higher education, at the very height of the freakin' baby boom. I even had philosophy at four in the afternoon every Monday, Wednesday and Friday; I'm telling you, a class at four on a Friday afternoon should be automatic grounds for authorized absence. The other two classes were rhetoric and my introductory sociology class, er, lecture, to be more precise. Three hundred kids in an auditorium to listen to a PhD ramble on was simple and pure joy. The same three hundred kids would file into the same auditorium and take the same tests together concerning the 'covered' material. That was even more joy. And, please, don't get me started about books and their cost and trying to find them in the bookstore and how 'easy' it is to return them for credit at the end of the semester. What a scam! Can I just get a book without all the useless 'eye candy' or heavy duty binding, like it belongs on our bookshelf for five hundred years, that has all the words and course coverage I need for less than thirty dollars, please? No? Figures.

The first week I dutifully attended all the classes and completed all assignments. The second week started a pattern; we watched football in Mark's room Monday night, we watched Happy Days Tuesday night in Mark's room, and I skipped classes intermittently. That was not good, skipping classes, I mean, but it didn't have any immediate deleterious effect, so I left the pattern intact.

Bruce had a roommate, Jeff the guitarist. Yep, Jeff played acoustic guitar and he was good. He could sing, too. Better yet, Bruce played banjo and harmonica and he was good, too. Better still, Jeff had a girlfriend, Linda, and she played acoustic guitar and sang and she was good, too. The best part was they played songs I knew like *MTA* and *Rocky Mountain Breakdown*, and they could pick up songs just by listening to records. The bad part was that I had an electric bass guitar at home and the worst part was that I told them about it.

"You should bring it up here," Jeff said.

"Yeah, man," Bruce said, smiling, "and, then, we can all start jammin'."

"It would be great to have some thumping underneath," Linda said, nodding her head. "Well, you know what I mean," she added, looking a little embarrassed at Jeff.

"The band I run the sound and lights for has a gig this weekend, so I was heading home Friday," I explained. "I'll grab the car for the week and haul that bad boy up here." Thus, my fate was sealed. Now, everyone would know how much my musical ability sucked.

Friday came pretty quickly and I hopped on my bike, strapped on my helmet and headed down the back roads toward home. I thought I'd give Kent a buzz to see if he had gotten back from his weekly paid excursion to Davenport and when the phone was answered it was Kent on that end.

"What are you doin'?" I asked.

"Drinkin' a beer," Kent replied. "You?"

"Not drinkin' a beer."

"College must be rubbin' off on you."

"Not that much. Got one for me?"

"More than one."

"I'll be right over," I advised.

"I'll call Kerry now," Kent said, "and see if we can make it a threesome."

Kerry was already at Kent's house drinking a beer when I arrived. Soon, we were smoking a joint, laughing about anything except college life – which they obviously did not want to hear – and were planning to drive out to Center Park with an appropriate stash. We stayed there until fairly late, drinking beer and watching for the cops; Kent told some wild tales about the bars and nude clubs – all nude was just that – and how he had met some woman that was now hanging out with him where he was staying.

When he heard about the other woman, Kerry shook his head and his usual smiling expression changed to seriousness. "Better hope Cheryl never finds out about that, man," he cautioned Kent.

"She'll never find out," Kent replied confidently, "unless, somehow, she hears about it from somebody who knows." He glanced severely at Kerry.

"Hey," Kerry protested, "she won't hear it from me."

"It's not you I was thinking about," Kent said. "It's your wife is what I meant." Kent was referring to Patti, Kerry's girlfriend, and, no, they were not married, yet. Might as well have been, though.

"I'm just saying, Kent," Kerry said, "if Cheryl finds out, you know she'll dump you in a heartbeat."

"She'll never find out," Kent insisted.

"She'll find out," Kerry equally insisted.

"One of you is wrong," I said.

"Shut up," they both said. Kerry smiled and Kent added, "Drink another beer to keep your mouth busy." He handed me another beer with the one in my hand still half full; with two beers in my hands, I gulped the first and threw the empty can in Kent's car in the back.

The following night was the Joint Session gig at Podunk High for their Homecoming Dance. It would be sort of a homecoming for most of the band mates, since all but a couple attended and graduated from Podunk High. There was always a kind of attitude about Podunk High people versus everybody else in the city; maybe they had the best teachers, maybe they had the best educational facilities and extravagances, maybe they had the most money, maybe they got the most attention. Maybe, but I never started the conversations that would lead to this type of discussion. I always ended it, though. You can end most any conversation that accomplishes nothing but chest puffing. You say, 'Blow me!' You start to walk away and add, 'Which reminds me, I think I'll have another beer. I'll get you one, too, if you shut the fuck up. Otherwise, I'll drink alone.' It works wonders. Try it some time.

This would be the last hurrah for the old roadie; he would be boogeying down the road of doin' somethin' else after this gig and the band mates all expected me to pick up the slack. The lights were the only issue; I wasn't really sure what the band expected so I needed to see just exactly what the old roadie would do with them. Running the mixing board was a piece of cake; the problem with all small-time bands and mixing boards is that not everything is run through them. Let me count the items that are *not*: oh, guitar, bass, keyboards, drums. Since those musical instruments are under the direct control of certain band mates, it can easily become a nightmare to keep everything in the same decibel ballpark. Um, did I mention that even small-time musicians have HUGE, BIG-TIME egos to boot? I didn't? Slipped my mind, sorry.

Despite any seemingly insurmountable complexity, the gig went well. I was very impressed with their rendition of *Roundabout* by Yes; it was both true to the original but different enough to accommodate the various instruments not found on the original. You have to understand, in order to appreciate it, that in 1974, finding a local band of musicians confident and good enough to play something as long, complex and unique as *Roundabout* in as musically devoid a place as Podunk, Illinois is a fairly impossible task. Add to that fact the unlikelihood that I would meet these guys through recruitment to a garbage crew at the state fair and the light begins to shine bright on the coincidental absurdity of human existence. Not to mention that attractive, little girls were running around untethered all night; there was plenty of smoke for all; and, generally, we all had a fun time, despite some obstructioning from school administrative types, and one can see that this wouldn't be such a bad life to live. After the gig, we all proceeded to one of the band mates' domicile to regroup, examine how things went, plan for the next gig and get high and drunk, not in any particular order for anyone. What was agreed by all is that I had a pretty good handle on things and the next gig, a college fraternity party in Macomb, would be my launch.

The parents had discussed my request and borrowing Mom's car for a week was not practical. Instead, Dad would play golf in the morning, as was his custom every Sunday when weather permitted, and would help me load the bass and amp, ride up to Champaign with me as driver, help me unload both, have dinner, since the cafeteria was closed Sunday afternoons, and drive back home that night. That was exactly what occurred and by four in the afternoon, there was a new musical instrument on the twelfth floor of the dormitory. Too bad the musician playing it had so little ability or so I thought; the rationalization I could live with was that this was just jamming with friends and nothing more. It was something to pass the time and not get busted for some illegal activity which was legal a few months before, although that may be mere exaggeration. That exercise I'll leave to you.

Back in the rhythm of school, I would constantly be looking for The Brunette down at the cafeteria or in the central commons and even just around campus. When I saw her I can honestly say that it brightened my day and occasionally I'd catch her looking at me before she quickly glanced away. I never put much stock in it because it seemed so natural, the way she looked away. On the other hand, she *was* looking at me somewhat frequently and I thought it wasn't all bad.

As I would walk to the quad for my classes I always passed this particular dormitory where somebody had hung a big picture of Lou Brock and taped a running number of his stolen bases for the season. Brock set the record for stolen bases in 1974 at 118, which has since been eclipsed by Rickey Henderson. The more interesting aspect of this second-story dorm room was that, quite often, the window would be open and one could hear rock music played inside the room at a considerably LOUD volume. Often it would be a tune with which I wasn't familiar, the same tune over and over as I would walk by. It was a cranking tune, recorded live, but I didn't find out until later that it was *Do You Feel Like We Do* by Peter Frampton. When I *did* find out, I bought the album at my first opportunity. As a further irony, I also discovered that I had the studio version on an album that I had purchased more than a year before and had filed away as a so-so musical endeavor and hadn't listened to it for quite a while. That was one of those moments when one realizes that quality is a highly subjective matter, subject to the merest of whims, moods, attitudes and, perhaps, even egos. If you hear anyone say, 'I know quality when I see, hear, taste, smell or touch it,' just call them a liar. You'll be right and they'll be wrong, because they're saying they're never wrong, that they're perfect. There is no such thing as perfection in this world but there *is* such a thing as suffering from delusions of perfection.

My roommate, Matt, had brought his boa constrictor to our room and soon everybody was calling him *Snakes*, an appellation Pete hung on him. I never called Matt by that name, but he soon purchased a second boa constrictor, this time a Florida king coral. It was almost golden, about two feet in length, and mean as shit. Here's how I could tell. I could put my hand against the glass of the terrarium and, without fail, that snake would smack its head against the glass trying to bite me. Matt eventually had to insist that no one touch the glass or his snake might have a permanent headache. Apparently, Florida king coral boa constrictors are mean *and* stupid. I felt sorry for the other snake as it obviously wanted to keep its distance, preferably anywhere *outside* the terrarium, which is where I found it one day after returning from class under some scattered newspapers on my bed. Matt was nowhere in sight and I was somewhat mad that there were newspapers scattered on my bed by no one else but him when I lifted one and there was the snake, calmly chilling out. *Shit*, I thought. *I hope this fucker doesn't slither off the bed and onto the floor. I'm gonna be really pissed then.* A few moments later Matt appeared and gathered up his snake and returned it to the terrarium. "Sorry," was all he said. "Not on my bed, please," was all I said.

Over the next few weeks I jammed with Bruce, Jeff and Linda, tossed the football with Mark and others from our floor, selectively attended and skipped class, kept an eye out for The Brunette, carefully smoked various flavors and cuts of 'the lieutenant', drank beer when we could get somebody to buy it for us, watched the growing crowd of entertainment seekers who would stop in for the weekly snake feeding by Matt, and tried to stay on top of course assignments with limited success.

True to their words, Bruce, Jeff and Linda were very encouraging as I started jamming, first listening to the song over and over, then plucking various notes to find the key, hearing in my head the bass licks to complement the song. I can't read music at all but I can follow it. I can even 'write' songs, lyrics and all, but the musical parts would have to be played by me, whether singing or through some other instrument; it will never be 'written' on a music sheet by me. I introduced them to a couple of songs, too. *Beauty in the River* by Ozark Mountain Daredevils was one where I would sing and the others picked up their parts from the record; I discarded the bass since I couldn't sing and play at the same time. The other was *Old Man* by Neil Young, but Jeff said he never could get the chord structure right so we never tried to play it; I wasn't sure if he just didn't like the song or really couldn't get the chords, but I'll always give Jeff the benefit of the doubt, since he was a genuinely compatible and unpretentious sort. He also could play tennis, too. After I played him I put up my racket for good, since he was the first opponent that had a real serve and it was disheartening to line up on his serve and hear bam, bam, bam, bam, to be followed by my turn with my serve returned bam, bam, bam, bam. Bruce, however, was the most accomplished harmonica player I had ever heard; it was fun listening to him trash Bob Dylan's harmonica prowess and pick up his and just wail! His banjo picking and his explanation of its intricacies was a treat, too. Linda, for all her desires to remain in the background, was a welcome complement to anything Jeff or Bruce played or sang. She could easily find the appropriate harmonic accompaniment to any melody.

    Mark and I spent a lot of our free time tossing the football or running routes for practice. He was skeptical at first about any athleticism I might possess; after all, I was just a short, skinny nothing. After the first time we tossed the football, it was clear to Mark that the only other guy on our floor with comparable football skills to his own was me. I could throw a spiral as tight as his, but he had better accuracy; on the flip side, I had the better hands for catching than he did. We got pretty confident with our abilities and it would come into play in a pickup game later.

    I was getting a little too cocky about class, or more accurately, skipping class. If memory serves, it would be fair to say that I attended on average two out of three classes or maybe three out of four. I would usually skip a class in every course once a week. That was not exactly the route to success and prosperity, but that would be the job for me. 'Okay, guys and gals, every third day you're on your own. However, you can reach me by phone in an emergency, as long as I don't have it unplugged or turned off.' Man, I could get a LOT of writing done then and

I'll bet the company and the world would survive. You may disagree – rightly so if you think about it – but two-thirds effort from me is more than adequate in most jobs I've had and usually produces better results than most can muster with one hundred percent effort; it won't advance a career but I've never had one. What's it like?

Through persistent observation I had figured out The Brunette's schedule and, when possible, always 'appeared' at the cafeteria at the same time that she would. She very rarely wore a skirt or a blouse or shirt that was revealing and that was alright with me; the more I thought about her, the more I came to the conclusion that she was the female equivalent of me. I always wore what was comfortable, never anything too tight or revealing; I was shy and reserved but still confident and poised. I just needed an opportunity to talk with her. I just want one shot, okay?

Earlier, my brother Jeff had driven up to pick me up from school with Mom supervising his driving. This was so I could retrieve my bike and have some wheels to get around. The approaching weekend was the gig in Macomb, so I skipped the Friday edition of philosophy, donned my helmet, swung my right leg over the bike, turned the key to the on position and kicked it on. I took off though town and out to the back roads and made it home in less than two hours later without incident. After sitting down to dinner with the folks, I cruised out to the lake, hoping to catch the guys, but a half-hour later with no one present that I knew or wanted to hang with I cruised back home. I popped a few cans of beer while I watched TV in the den with the old man and finally retired to my room. The call of the duffel bag was loud so – what the hell – I exploded the sausage and flipped over on my back for beddy bye, relieved.

I called Kent at his home the next morning but he already had made plans with Cheryl and he knew Kerry and Patti were busy, too. There was something about the way Kent talked about his plans which made me wonder that he might be having some trouble with Cheryl. His weekly job excursion to Davenport was putting a strain on their relationship and I sensed that neither was dealing with it well. Add to that Kent's continual refrain that it was *my* fault that he was stuck with the Davenport job and I always felt somewhat responsible. When he got frustrated, Kent would start it up again.

"If you only had been on time for our fishing trip," he would complain, "then I wouldn't be in this mess in the first place."

"You could have told him it would just be for this week," I would counter.

"This is my uncle, numb nuts," Kent would argue. "He's not going to get somebody else and have to train them when he's already spent a week on me."

"Well, even if I was on time," I would argue further, "he would have come to get you the following week and you would have been stuck anyway. After all, you're family."

"Family doesn't come before business with my uncle," Kent would conclude. "He wouldn't want to train me and he would be loyal to the guy who he finally got. Family wouldn't matter to him and I would be out of it."

I was never going to win this argument. Instead, I was going to spend the rest of my years in a Kent purgatory for oversleeping one time. Occasionally, a nasty thought would nag me and I would attempt to dispatch it as quickly as it formed; this wouldn't be the last purgatory to which I would be consigned for a lapse of performance or judgment.

Later that afternoon I hopped on the bike and rode to Jimmy's place where everybody was to gather and pack up for the drive to Macomb. It was a quick job and three vehicles, including the main van, took off for the gig. I rode in the van. After an excruciating two and a half hours of travel on the thinnest of paved roads from this nowhere to that nowhere, we finally arrived in Macomb, which was more of a congregation of apartment buildings with a smattering of large structures than a college town. We followed directions and found the fraternity house and unpacked and setup the gear.

Except for the Joint Session, it was what one would expect at a fraternity party. There was excessive drinking, occasional displays of stomach contents dispersal, drunken male looks of virtually uncontrollable desire, drunken female looks of virtually uncontrollable seduction, and loud, virtually uncontrollable debauchery. Did I mention that there was more than enough alcohol? The band played with a singularity of focus while I had to run the board standing right next to the horn section and couldn't get out at all to hear the levels; it was a mess waiting to flower into a full garbage dump, and one fat, obnoxious drunken fraternity member ended it all when he finally, after screaming nearly incessantly from five feet away, fell into the microphones and against a couple of the band mates. After some tense minutes of discussion with the fraternity members controlling the purse strings for the gig, the band got their money and we all quickly packed up and drove as fast as we could out of town.

In October a new concept emerged: midterms. Oh, joy! One midterm for every course was on each course' syllabus, but, before I could take even one, Harold, Mark's roommate, had an episode one afternoon. Matt was in Harold's room as I walked by returning from class, so I dropped off my class materials in my room and stepped in to chat. Almost immediately, Matt picked up and strolled out of Harold's room, civilly of course – it hadn't taken long for a guy who wanted to room with me to get tired of me – and Harold and I chatted about nothing in particular. About fifteen minutes later, as he continued to lie on his bottom bunk bed propped on his elbow, he suddenly laid himself flat, his eyes rolled back in his head and his body started to shake, slowly at first and then more pronounced. I shouted to Matt that I thought Harold was having a seizure, but, instinctively, I knew that I shouldn't leave him. As Harold continued to convulse, Matt ran into the room and sat down on the edge of the bed at the head and advised that we should keep him from rolling off the bed and watch his mouth and face for signs that he may have swallowed his tongue. I sat down on the edge of the bed at the foot and we patiently waited about ten minutes and it passed. For a few moments Harold looked dazed and spent, but when we told him that he had a seizure he immediately turned sheepish and apologized. We assured him that he needn't apologize and Matt soon returned to the room. I stayed with Harold and we chatted some more, trying to keep the event from taking on any ominous import. He volunteered some of his history and what touched me most was his frank assessment of his high school peers' attitude concerning his malady, the assessment being mostly disdain and disgust. I let him go on until he reached a lengthy pause when I switched the conversation to midterms and class and prognosis of either. After a considerable time of chatting, Harold noticed the clock and announced that he needed to go to the library before dinner.

"Well," I said, "tell the books I'll come and visit them soon." I hesitated a moment before I left his room.

"And take care of myself," Harold added, smiling, and I stopped.

"I wasn't going to say that," I insisted.

"But you were thinking it," Harold countered, still smiling.

"But I was thinking it," I capitulated.

"Thanks," Harold said softly, looking down at the floor.

As I walked out of the room, I said, "I'll pass it on to Matt. He knew what to do. See you at dinner."

Once midterms got under way we twelfth floor denizens noticed that people would do some of the strangest things to relieve tension. One of the guys from the other side of the floor came over on our side and said that there was a 'moon war' going on. Some of the freshman girls residing on the floor opposite ours were just as wild, maybe wilder, than we were so a battle of 'mooning', or the dropping of one's pants and other articles of clothing and bending over to display one's naked butt, had ensued. The battle went like this: one side would gather the participants for the next round, turn the lights off in the student lounge, the participants would move to the window and drop their clothes, and the lights would be flipped on to reveal a row of naked butts aimed at the other side. Repeat until caught or bored or surrendered. The battle would escalate and the winner was the side that could put the most participants in a single row. We did eight this night, myself included, and won the battle. The fun would be the following morning when we would listen to the girls and boys talk about the battle the night before. 'Did you see that butt third from the left on their second turn?' 'That was my butt.' 'No, it wasn't, that was *my* butt.' As I mentioned, though, there were some wild ones on the other side and the girls would eventually claim the most naked butts in a row, which was fourteen. One guy had binoculars but I never got to use them. Sometimes there is no justice.

With midterms behind us and one less student residing in our lounge, the twelfth floor denizens decided it was time to have our own floor party. We convinced the remaining three lounge residents to relinquish their room for this Saturday night and we prepared for the appropriate festivities, which would be mostly alcohol with some 'lieutenant' thrown in with the necessary discretion. Some of the floors had previously printed signs for their upcoming party and had received the expected and unwanted attention of the campus authorities, so we simply passed the word around verbally. We setup the tunes and voted on the selections and several put together a punch, which introduced me to 'Everclear', 200 proof alcohol, or as we liked to call it, 'nothing but buzz'. There was a bucket filled with ice and a pony keg that we snuck in masterfully and several coolers of various beers. We were ready. Unfortunately, few of our fellow campus residents were as ready, so the party started very slowly, or maybe we started a little too early. After ten, though, the elevator got to working as we were filling the immediate air waves with cranking tunes and folks just had to check it out. I think I had a good time but I don't remember anything after we had been going at it for a while; I can remember flirting with girls around midnight, but that's as far as my memory will allow. The Everclear had caught up to me with a sneak attack and had wiped the brain clean, certainly destroying multiple brain cells in the process. Amazingly, it wasn't until about nine-thirty the following morning that it wreaked havoc upon my intake and exhaust systems and sent me scrambling to the bathroom; I made it and left my calling card in the stool and discovered just how juvenile my fellow twelfth-floor denizens were, since most of the toilets were clogged with all manner of objects, including the expected human excrement, some inside the stool and some not. Even more amazing was that this discovery did not cause me to heave even more.

Practically nobody got up in time for Sunday breakfast and I definitely had no intention of eating for quite a while. As each stumbled out of a room, we gathered ourselves and started the clean up, persuaded by the persistent pleas of the lounge students, whose 'room' could have been designated a federal disaster area. Cans, cups, and other assorted trash was everywhere in the lounge, but we had it under control in a half-hour. Someone even grabbed a bucket and mop and we unclogged the toilets and mopped up the entire bathroom. I think we were motivated by the fact that we had escaped the attention of the campus authorities *so far*, and we liked the idea of keeping it that way.

Settling together with the usual cohorts, Pete started calling me Johnny the Wad, for John Holmes, a porn star. All the other guys thought it was funny and it fit; I thought they were making fun of the endowment, or lack of, of the appendage connected midway down my body. After the fifth or sixth such reference to 'the Wad', I had had enough and confronted Pete about it.

"Why are you callin' me that, man?" I asked, not so politely. "It's pissin' me off."

Pete looked at me dumbfounded. As I scanned the other faces, they looked back at me dumbfounded, too. Finally, Pete asked me incredulously, "You don't remember?"

"Remember what?" I asked back just as incredulously.

"The Brunette?" Pete asked even more incredulously.

"She was at the party?" I asked as the incredulity rose to an all-time high.

Immediate, deafening laughter erupted from the entire contingent. I could hear comments like, 'He doesn't remember!', and 'Where was he last night?', and 'He's so smooth, his memory doesn't stick!'. Finally, with great chagrin, I confessed. "I was so fucked up last night from that Everclear punch, I can't remember anything after about midnight."

"That would explain why he can't remember, Pete!" Barry shouted and a second, deafening laughter eruption ensued.

Starting to get it, I looked at Pete and asked, softly, "She came to the party, didn't she?"

Laughing, Pete looked about him as he asked, "Should I tell him?"

"No!" came the unanimous response.

Pete looked at me with a wicked smile and said, "Sorry, Holmes. The penis gallery has spoken."

Mark said, "Pete came up to me this morning and said he was going to call you Johnny the Wad from now on after what happened last night. I thought it was a good name because it fits, country boy."

"I take it I talked to her last night," I sputtered.

"Better than that," Jeff, motorcycle man, commented.

"Let me tell him, Pete!" Barry said, smiling.

"Why not?" Pete asked, laughing. "I want to see what he's gonna do with this since he can't remember a damn thing."

"Okay, here's the scoop, Wad," Barry said, squirming to a position of readiness. "The Brunette showed up after midnight with a couple of her friends and made it into the lounge. You were somewhere else. Anyway, she wouldn't talk to anybody and she refused any drinks and she looked out of place and fairly uncomfortable; we were trying to work with her friends to get her to loosen up. All of a sudden, you walked in, smiled at her, and the two of you started talking. You got another drink from the punch bowl, and the two of you stepped out of the lounge, went down near your room, sat down on the floor in the hall and talked and laughed and, apparently, had a good time with each other for about an hour. We would look out the hall from the lounge and there the two of you were, just going at it."

"So, Holmes," Pete said, "we were all extremely impressed with what you did last night. Hell, she wouldn't talk to anybody but you!"

"Of course, it's even better now that you know I can't remember that she was here," I stated, nodding my head with graven stupidity.

"The best!" Mark exclaimed and everyone laughed.

Pete asked, "So, tell us, Johnny, whatcha got planned?"

I shook my head slowly and mumbled, "I don't even know her name."

More laughter erupted and I could hear Jeff, motorcycle man, shout, "That'll impress her."

Pete declared, "It's clear, gentlemen, that the task before Holmes here is whether he can rescue his meeting the best-looking freshman girl in the dorm from the black hole where that meeting now resides. Holmes?"

"Fuck," was all I could say in frustration.

I would like to write that everything turned out fan-fucking-tastic with The Brunette, but that's not what happened. Looking back over thirty years, I can think of many choices that I could have taken which may have yielded far better results than the choice I eventually took. You never have thirty years of hindsight to contemplate a situation so that you can return and make the right choice; you simply have to make the choice at the time, even if you choose to do nothing, and live with the consequences. I did nothing, except to make feeble attempts to avoid looking at her. I got my shot with her and turned the gun on myself and blew a black hole in my own over-imaginative brain. Over the rest of the school year, I watched as she settled on some upper class man, but she didn't seem to display any truly sincere interest. When the school year completed in May, I never saw her again. I hope she's had a nice life, though. Maybe it's that hindsight again but I always think of her as one woman whose comportment was so special she deserved a nice life. If so, it's quite probable that I sealed it, since I was pretty fucked up back then; hanging with me could have been an excursion into hell. I'm just being honest.

One weekend soon after the party, we looked out the window and noticed some of the eleventh floor denizens practicing football in the field next to the parking lot. They didn't seem to have enough for a real game so we thought we'd go down there and try to scrounge up a scrum. Mark, Bruce, Kevin the sophomore, Barry, and I headed across the street to the field and struck up a friendly conversation with them. We didn't like any of these guys but we wanted to play football in the hopes of beating the crap out of them and shutting them up for an afternoon. They were anxious to play a game and immediately liked the idea of teaming by floor, but they had more guys than we did so a couple of their guys had to play on our team. One of them, who we called Whitey because of his stark white hair, insisted on playing quarterback and we decided to let him; Mark and I stole a glance at each other, revealing our mutual expectation of impending disaster.

They kicked off to us and the runback was short. Whitey was constantly harassed, even though Bruce and Mark blocked well; the other team knew he would only look for the two guys from his floor so they were never open and I always was. After throwing some errant passes and being tackled for a loss, we punted.

Their quarterback was Mope, six feet three inches of former lineman stature who had forfeited his athletic scholarship because the responsibilities as a member of a perpetually losing college football team hampered his student responsibilities. Their first play was a quarterback sweep to the right side, pulling blockers from the middle and the end as lead blocker; with our guys scattered all over the ground in front of him, Mope practically danced into the end zone. They congratulated each other and derided us profusely; demoralized somewhat, Mark and I looked at each other confirming what we had previously expected.

Displaying more ineptitude, our eleventh floor teammates fumbled the ball on the kickoff and our runback was worse than the first. Whitey would run around back and forth trying to find someone open, only to eventually throw the ball into the ground harmlessly away from anyone. On more than one occasion, he and I made eye contact but he wouldn't throw me the ball. Going backwards, yet again, we had to punt; the ball sailed a short distance, and the recipient gathered it and took off, bumped and snagged, only to wriggle free and sneak into the end zone for a score. Now we were down two touchdowns and all was gloom and doom.

Our runback this time was considerably better but the prospect of continued futility created a crisis of confidence in our huddle. Whitey's fellow floor residents were unhappy with his lack of quarterback success, so he announced that he didn't want to play quarterback anymore. *Finally,* I thought, *now we can have a real quarterback.* Not one to waste this opportunity, I nominated Mark for the job. Once all the usual comments about needing him to block subsided, I simply stated that, since their big guy, Mope, wanted to play in the backfield, it was going to take two of their rushers to tackle him. We *are* playing tackle, boys. Besides, Mark has the arm and experience. Initially reluctant, even Whitey understood the compelling logic of the argument, and Mark was the new quarterback. Whitey said the quarterback calls the plays. Immediately, Mark looked at me and called for me to line up on the far right side, do a down and slant in after ten yards. He called the other plays but we both pretty much knew what was coming.

Lining up across from Mope, standing about five yards from me, I couldn't help but smile to myself. The ball was snapped back to Mark and I took off fast, sailing past Mope like he was standing still; before he could recover, I slanted across the field, looked back to Mark seeing me wide open, and he threw the ball in my direction. The pass was thrown behind me, so I had to slow and turn back to catch it. When I did, I saw Mope bearing down on me at full speed; I juked in the direction of my momentum, and dodged in the other as I felt his ham hock of an arm slap me, causing me to spin, lose my balance and tumble to the ground. Being the short, skinny nothing that I am, everyone got on Mope about trying to kill me; while he argued that this was tackle, after all, I popped up, flicked the ball to the center of the field and said I was alright, let's play football. In the huddle, Mark looked at me and apologized for the pass being behind. I said the next one will be better. He called the same plays and to the line we went. Again, Mope lined up across me, five yards back. At the snap, I sailed past him, cut the slant, looked back to Mark and watched his perfect throw right into my outstretched hands as I leapt up to gather it under my arm so that the jarring of my steps wouldn't keep me from controlling the ball. Continuing the motion with fluid precision, I came back to the ground without breaking stride and ran untouched into the end zone, looking back at Mope who was gaining on me, thankful that it was only a hundred yards, because the big fella was pretty fast once he got it going.

Down only a touchdown, their side suddenly was in confusion and constant argument as we prepared to kick off; being the acknowledged ringleader, Mope was rarely subject to criticism from his floor mates, but they got on him pretty good. Their runback was unspectacular, but we had to figure out a way to stop their sweep. Mark had a hunch that they would run it to their right side consistently, so he pulled me aside and laid out his plan. On a sweep, the end gives it away; he starts up the field, stops and tries to lay a block to the inside to open the outside for the runner. My job is to spot that hesitation, come up the field to the outside and force the runner to the inside, hopefully occupying the end so that he can't block anyone else. Mark would line up to the inside, prepared to rush if it's a pass; if he sees the quarterback move to the right like a sweep, he'll come up and take the quarterback. Mark's hunch was correct; they did exactly as he predicted, but this time I suckered the end for his hapless block, which I dodged effortlessly, and came up the field to close the outside. Mope, surprised to see me cutting off his outside hopes and with no blockers in front, cut to the inside, when Mark slammed him to the ground for a loss. Mark got up looking at Mope as he struggled to his feet and said with an obvious lack of respect, "Bring it, big boy." I smiled widely as I approached Mark, who put out his hand and I slapped it and said, "Nice, *very* nice."

Momentum in sports, as in any group endeavor, is a factor of collective consciousness; which side has the most members who believe that things are going their way? At this point in our game, that was definitely our side, and we never gave that belief back. We finally forced them to punt and took it right down the field to even the score. We scored three more times to their one and Mark and I never connected on a pass, again, but we didn't need it. The damage had been done and they consistently double-teamed the short, skinny nothing, so Mark just picked them clean by hitting the open receiver. When it was over, we had managed to do more than we had hoped; the eleventh floor denizens, usually boastful and loud whenever they saw us in the dorm, were quiet and respectful for the next week. We really had shut them up.

It was getting colder and less likely that I would ride my bike so I called to ensure that I had a ride back to school; Dad promised to ride with me and drive back on that Sunday, so I rode the bike back the preceding Friday, ready to store it in the garage for the winter. As soon as I got home I called Kent. He was already back from Davenport but he didn't sound too good. He invited me over for beers and smoke, though.

Kerry was there when I arrived and for a few moments it was like old times. Kent, however, was a bit surly, much more than usual, which was more an act than reality. When I inquired as to why he was so sullen, he lit into me about being late, again. Kerry volunteered the information I sought. Cheryl had found out about his girlfriend in Davenport and broke up with Kent for good. She was already seeing another guy and Kent was continually pissed. The three of us just drank beers and smoked pot and tried to keep Kent from thinking about it, with some success. We all got together, even Jeff, the next day and Kent was getting back to his usual self by the time we all split apart. Kent without a woman was a frightening experience nevertheless.

Our little bluegrass band was getting pretty good, so Linda, Jeff's girlfriend, arranged for us to play a session at this basement coffee house just off campus. As a show of good faith, we all went over there one night before our appearance was scheduled. All the acts appeared without compensation; some that night were pretty good and others stank. After that night we thought we stacked up well against the competition.

Change was afoot, though. When we started out in August, everyone seemed to be adamant against fraternities, but someone had met this fraternity member from Kappa Sigma and most of us had already been over to their house. It was more like dropping in on an endless dope-smoking binge, with plenty of loud rock and roll and beers every now and then. I never thought that I was being recruited, not even after I met Julie, the sorority sister who was a junior. She was quite the looker, though not a knockout, and as sweet and pleasant as you can expect from a woman. At first, she would hang with the fraternity guys and us. Later, she would come over to our dorm, which was closer to her sorority house than the fraternity house, and hang with any one of us. Something happened along the way, and she started asking about me if I wasn't with any of the other guys from our floor at the dorm or the frat house.

Julie was all of five feet four inches, with a deliciously curvy body, a delectable rear (a requirement), great legs, clear, smooth facial complexion combined with an easy, attractive smile (another requirement), soft brown shoulder length hair parted in the middle, and a pair of small but round breasts, certainly not big by any standard (and *not* a requirement) but pleasing to the eye anyway. Her personality was outstanding since her smile or even laughter was so effortlessly generated by almost anything I said or did that the boost to my inherently fragile ego was so compelling I couldn't keep away from her. That said, I truly didn't expect her to slink into a basement coffee house and listen to our amateur musical performance when I invited her.

Imagine my surprise and resulting nervousness when we were on the stage preparing our set and I heard a sexy female voice call out my name from the front of the stage. There she was, looking incredibly good and very out of place, wishing me well and pointing to a corner where a couple of her sorority sisters sat, bored and probably annoyed. I thanked her for coming and thought, *nothing like pressure.* Linda hadn't paid any attention and still wasn't, but when I looked over at Bruce and Jeff, Bruce just looked down to the stage floor. Jeff, however, smiled in his little devious way to signal that we were about to slip into amusing strangeness and asked if I was ready.

I couldn't think of anything else to say except to make light of whatever absurdity may be stalking us. "I don't know about fraternities, but if I grow my hair longer and wear falsies, do you think they'll let me join their sorority?" I asked to no one in particular and loud enough that most in the front row heard it. Apparently, it was just enough to calm our jitters and we launched into our set without any concern. We made our share of mistakes, me included, but we worked past them and the set, condensed to twenty minutes, was better than most expected. The manager of the coffee house came over to congratulate us and offered us a return trip if we wanted it.

Julie came up to the stage as we started breaking down, which was really just my equipment, and congratulated us. Immediately, she apologized to me that she had to leave with her friends, who were standing anxiously at the door and probably still annoyed, but asked when I would be at the fraternity house again.

"I don't know," I replied. "Cap'n Jack is temporarily tapped out." Captain Jack was the purveyor of smoke at the frat house, by the way.

"I heard he might be refreshed Friday," Julie said, smiling.

"Maybe Friday I'll have to drop in on the good Cap'n," I said. "Course, I'll be around the dorm all week, too, and you can see us there."

"This week's kinda hectic for me," she advised.

I smiled as I replied, "I could come over to *your* house, but I'll bet you've got rules against that, huh?"

Julie smiled widely as she softly answered, "Yes, we've got rules against that."

Knowing that my eyes were twinkling, I asked, "Wonder what would happen to me if I broke that rule? Any of you girls packin'?"

Julie laughed as she commented, "You're so funny."

"Humor's all I've got," I stated.

"That's not true," Julie replied, her smile fading, replaced with a look of admonishment.

In all seriousness, I looked in her eyes and said, "Thanks for coming." She congratulated us again, turned to her frowning sisters and walked out the door.

As the semester progressed, a 'ritual' commenced. All the freshmen, one at a time, were to be snagged from their rooms, hauled to the showers with their clothes on, and shoved under the running water for 'initiation'. Since we knew that the students in the lounge were on our floor on borrowed time, we picked on them first. Up to Thanksgiving, we had come close to getting half of the freshmen, including one of the resident big boys, Bruce. I wondered when my turn would come up. It was going to be interesting, because I was always in on every one of them, even though I didn't participate in each; when it did come to my turn, it was obviously going to take a lot of silence on everyone's part. Since I always brought it up about who we would get next, I certainly enjoyed the 'cat and mouse' aspect of it.

Kevin the sophomore acted more like a freshman than he did an upper class man. He hung out regularly with us more than the others and we accepted him for the most part. Somebody, and it occurs to me that it was probably Mark, brought some fireworks from the last trip home, including bottle rockets. Somebody else, quite possibly me, suggested how cool it would be if we shot one of those rockets down the hall to see if we could put it under the door and have it explode right in the room. Oh, and that room would be Kevin's? Perfect. We placed the rocket on the floor, lit it, watched it sail down the hall, under the door and heard it explode louder than we expected since it was clearly behind the door. As we all laughed uncontrollably, Kevin threw open his door, standing in his underwear, and proceeded to curse us loudly. Mark advised him to shut up and go back to bed or we would do it again. Dejected, Kevin turned around, muttering to himself about something we couldn't hear, and walked back into his room, slamming the door behind him. Another round of uncontrollable laughter ensued, but we never shot another rocket inside the dorm again, mostly due to individual conversations each of us had with our floor counselor over the next few days.

One of the upper class men on the other side of our floor, Roger, had a sister attending her first year at the big U. Her name was Sandy and the most imaginative description I can use for her would be 'Amazon woman'. No, she wasn't belligerent, kick-ass, mean-spirited, anti-man, or any of those other adjectives, but she was tall, taller than me. Because her older brother resided on our floor, it wasn't unusual to see her on our floor at any time; coincidentally, she resided on the opposite twelfth floor and even admitted that she participated in some of our mutual 'moon wars'. Since she frequently wore snug fitting jeans revealing a finely curved posterior, sometimes I would wonder aloud during a 'moon war', "Which one do you think is Sandy's butt? You'd think hers would be easy to spot, as tall as she is…"

I liked Sandy. Her personality was both wicked and experimental; she took crap from no one and challenged everyone, even me, which usually elicited the response, "What did I do?" She had a clear complexion usually unencumbered by powders and the like, perhaps rendering her somewhat plain, though it had no effect on her sassiness. She had long, blond hair parted right down the middle flowing halfway down her back, and she possessed ample breasts, too, assuming, of course, that she used no 'enhancements', which I personally thought was outside her profile. Moreover, in a bizarre twist certainly meant to upset the careful order of the universe – why is it tall women love me? I contend that I somehow trigger this primordial maternal instinct, possibly due to my unconscious projection of eternal helplessness – Sandy liked me.

"What the hell," I said, "let's go out on a date."

"Okay," Sandy said, "and do what?"

"Well, we both like music," I proposed. "I could get tickets to the Average White Band concert. They're pretty good. Whaddaya think?"

"I like AWB," Sandy said. "Let's make it a date, then."

The concert with AWB was good, although as a historical note, one of the more influential band members was to die of a heroin overdose a few months later and AWB became effectively a non-musical entity afterwards. I can't remember the front band, but I do remember dancing frequently with Sandy, especially watching her shake that fine body. We walked back to the dorm late in the evening and I clumsily kissed her and she not-so-clumsily kissed me back and I walked her to the entrance of her dorm and watched her disappear inside the forbidden city. That was it, though. We never went out on a date, again. It may have been that we cooled to each other, but from my perspective it was more due to Roger, who suddenly took a more active interest in my activities and whereabouts. Roger was genuinely a decent guy, but his appearance reminded me of a Marine reservist. Since my uncle was a Marine, my other uncle was a former Marine and his son was also a Marine, I really had more than enough Marines in the family. No more Marines meant chilling with Sandy, though that wouldn't be the last of our mutual escapades.

Thanksgiving week prompted an exodus of epic proportions on campus. Since I had a class quiz in Spanish for Wednesday before Thanksgiving, it was like walking through a deserted city after Armageddon while going to class. Thankfully, and isn't that what Thanksgiving is all about, my ride back home was on time to whisk me mercifully out of the environs of the pending apocalypse. I kid you not, because when I left there were two guys left on our floor; everyone else had already left for some place else.

Returning to campus after Thanksgiving week represented the culmination and climax of the semester. It was time to buckle down to studies, pull those all-nighters, salvage what little we could of a previously damaged course experience. We all took it seriously, since some courses placed two-thirds or more of the final grade on a test on the last day of class and the final taken during finals week. The chaos that would appear during finals week is legendary; some students would complete all their finals in the first two or three days and be off the campus by Tuesday evening. Others would have their finals schedule scattered throughout the week, with some poor, unlucky bastards having to take their last final on that Saturday afternoon. My finals were scattered, with the last on Friday afternoon. I pulled several all-nighters, though I had mixed feelings as to their effectiveness. Not to worry, though; my chariot taking me out of the learning center awaited. Despite the frantic, nerve wracking nature of finals week, there was a considerable advantage to the college experience. When would we resume school, studies, class attendance? More than a month from now? Cool! That easily beat the high school experience. But there was the issue of receiving grades in the mail. Oh, yeah, forgot about grades, those nasty little items residing in what is commonly called 'transcripts' and having an enormous bearing on one's future employment prospects. Hmmm, grades.

Act Thirteen
Spring Semester, Spring Break and FLA

Back at the homestead I spent as little time inside the home as possible. You would think that, after spending the better part of four months with Matt as my roommate, we would get together. The truth was that Matt and I never hung out before and we weren't going to start now. Before we all left the campus, Matt, Mark, Harold and I had agreed to swap roommates and I would be bunking with Mark in his room.

Kent was more like his usual self. He had met some women, and was even seeing one frequently; he was getting his rocks off on a regular basis, which kept him reasonably happy. His job in Davenport was through, but his report about the workmanship of the construction was dismal, to say the least. The work was for a national chain of rental apartments, the name of which would be quite familiar. There was one right in Podunk. I vowed that I would never live in one of those places.

Kerry, Kent, sometimes Jeff, and I would gather at Kent's house to watch football all weekend. We would often throw the football out at the old grade school and even managed to hold a couple games. It was harder to keep any of the peripheral people in the picture. No one had seen Ed, the guy who went with us to the farm in Chandlerville, in months. Terry was planning a wedding; Kerry was planning a wedding; Terry's brother was finishing high school and planning his college endeavors. Everyone had their own agenda, everyone, it seemed, except me. I had a gut feeling that the idea about being a sociology graduate and working with juvenile delinquents, gangs, and the like was never going to be. Maybe I knew it all along, since I never told anyone about it. That wasn't so unusual, though. There were a lot of things nobody knew about me and never would know.

Soon, Christmas was upon us and I rushed out to get a modest gift for all the family members. The big day arrived, we all opened our presents, said our thank yous, and went on our merry ways. That was the spirit.

College football bowl games were not as prevalent then as they are now or I could have spent every day watching football. Instead, it was a challenge to discover things to do, though it was mostly playing music and watching television; the news on the boob tube featured the inevitable demise of South Vietnam. That debacle would soon come to an end without a negotiated settlement which Kissinger had been desperately trying to achieve. Now that I think about it, you never hear him talk about that finest hour, do you? On a personal note, they had released the order for birthdays during the fall semester, which would determine who they would call first if they re-instituted the draft; my number was 352, fourteen away from the end. I figured if they did bring back the draft and they called me, everybody was going. Jeff the motorcycle man, however, was in the top one hundred and had to fill out a form that Selective Service sent him to detail his current residence, phone number, main squeeze, whether he believed in UFOs, if he was planning a trip to Canada soon, and the like. I told him to carbon Henry Kissinger as it might be the key to end the deadlock in the Paris negotiations. Of course, if I got bored and horny, there was always the duffel bag; I wondered if they would let me substitute my duffel bag for their duffel bag if I was 'in the Army now'. You know morale would be high in *my* unit. "Outstanding, lieutenant! Your unit is consistently the highest in morale of any on the base. How do you do it?" "Sir, it's not me, sir. It's that short, skinny private over there, sir. He's a natural born leader!" True.

The band had a gig at a club on the shore of the reservoir the Saturday night before New Years. This meant that there would not be the usual assortment of young people with a strong desire for rock music. There would still be the usual assortment of drunken people, a bit older perhaps, but I personally expected fewer people high on marijuana, acid or heroin. I was right, of course, since my crusade to discover heroin at the club yielded zero results. Imagine that!

The gig went off without a hitch, though it was constantly a challenge to satisfy both sides of the noise debate; club member after club member would step up to me and politely ask to turn it down some while the band mates would politely ask to turn it up some. I quickly figured out the best reaction for both: fiddle with the volume knob on one of the unused channels followed by a quick 'thumbs up'. It worked every time. After the gig, it took a long time to get back to the staging house, so everybody broke ranks and headed for home, twenty dollars richer. We were making a killing in the music business.

The last day of 1974 featured a college football game and firecrackers from my brother Jeff's stash, my stash and the neighbors' stash. We didn't venture into the strange act of shooting loaded pistols in the air, though the neighbors had plenty of those. I never understood the rationale behind the desire to shoot loaded pistols in the air on New Years Eve; Newton had determined that everything that goes up must come down. Logic should tell you that sooner or later one of those bullets shot in the air is going to go up and come down right through the brain of some poor, unsuspecting, innocent reveler. Apparently, logic suffers when mixed with alcohol and guns.

The first day of 1975 featured more college football games, at a time when they still played those games on New Years Day and not after. Yes, kids, after New Years Day, there would be no more college football games until autumn, except for the various senior or All-American games.

When it snowed, the neighbors and I thought it would be cool to break out the bikes and tool around the neighborhood slipping and sliding. This was mostly Chuck's idea. His motocross ambitions, eventually replaced with Enduro ambitions, were slowly giving way to the more practical realities of adult life, such as working for a living. Chuck was spending less time riding motorcycles and more time running the family's many farms with his father. Chuck was a real farmer, but today we were all crazy motorcycle enthusiasts, creating irritating noise pollution for our neighbors on the other side, and hapless, disbelieving stares from any motorist who would dare to drive down our back road while we darted in front, in back, and around any such vehicle. Go ahead. Call the police. "What motorcycle, officer? It's freezing cold outside and there's snow on the ground. Do you think we're crazy?" If you don't act obviously crazy, when you ask that question to police officers they usually give you the benefit of the doubt. Been there, done that.

A small letter with small lettering addressed to me from University of Illinois at Urbana-Champaign came in the mail the second week in January. I opened it to discover a small letter folded once; when I unfolded it, inside were my grades. The B in rhetoric, A in algebra, B in philosophy, and C in sociology were all expected; the D in Spanish was somewhat of a surprise, since I half-expected to be anywhere from a C to flunking. My father, though, provided the real surprise. He told me that a C in my major was not good. "It indicates you're just average in that study, son," he said. I should seriously consider finding another avenue of study, he further advised. In other words, we're in the age of specialization and, if you're just average in your specialty, well, then, you're not very special, are you? I remembered the many times our sociology PhD would remind her students during a lecture how her college degree was worth three times more than ours would be, simply because only six percent of those her age received degrees compared to seventeen percent of those our age. Now that my introductory semester of college was concluded, there was something in this experience that bothered me ceaselessly, but I couldn't identify what that something was, yet.

To avoid thinking about it, or anything for that matter, I just cranked the rock tunes on my little stereo, smoked a little lieutenant, drank some beer, perused through my collection in the duffel bag to select the appropriate pictures for an exploding sausage event, and met up with the boys to pass the time, shoot the shit and do anything but be productive citizens. It worked pretty well.

Kenny called me and said there was a meeting with the band and I should be there. We would be meeting at Dave's parents' house at such and such a time in the evening. Be there! So, I was. Some of the band mates knew people in the entertainment business and tapes of the band's material had floated around, managing to land on the desk of an entertainment manager at Disneyland. Those people really liked the band's sound and style and material and had made a preliminary offer of two thousand dollars a week to play several hours in the park every day. Thus began the end of the Joint Session. Kenny, Dave and a couple others were excited about the offer, coupled with the fact that it would put them square in the middle of a major musical center, Los Angeles, California and the immediate vicinity, even if the gig was an hour away from Los Angeles. Jimmy and some others were not impressed with the offer; it was too little money for such a major move and the concomitant upheaval. There was even some discussion about my role and whether I should be paid or even be a part of it. I stayed out of the whole mess and didn't say a word other than to reply that I'd go in a heartbeat, but only if everybody else did. Half a band was no band, in my opinion, but I knew the outcome, already. In any artistic journey, the requirement for success is total commitment, and even that is no guarantee for success. Still, nobody 'lucks' into artistic success; it doesn't happen that way, kids. In any event, the loss of Jimmy's full-time job would have reduced his income by three-quarters and that was unacceptable to him. The others who hesitated were pretty much in the same boat. Before I left to resume the collegiate career, the band disbanded.

Back on campus, the procedure was well understood by then. Over to the hall to sign up for classes as soon as possible and make do until classes and the cafeteria started up. I recall statistics, psychology,

COBOL computer programming, mythology and an elective in sociology, possibly about juvenile delinquency, as the classes I took for spring semester. The more important step everyone wanted to take was planning for spring break, which would come at the end of March. Talk before we left for Christmas vacation was to drive to Florida for the week. Jeff, motorcycle man, had a van that could carry quite a few, so we quickly went from idle talk to active planning. We decided who was going based on who could afford it and who wanted to go and where we would go. A couple of girls, including Sandy, wanted to go, but would break off and stay with some family members near Orlando. The rest of us decided to fill out the itinerary on both sides of the state but actually stay on the gulf side and we settled on Clearwater as the ultimate destination. I found some literature about motel accommodations in Clearwater, including a reasonably priced motel only a few blocks from the beach. I called the motel, got prices for our expected length of stay, the amount for a deposit to reserve the rooms for everybody, and sent them a personal check in that amount. I called back a few weeks later and confirmed our reservations. We were set on that front.

Statistics was a very interesting class, an eye-opening experience into how numbers can be accumulated into compilations which can be manipulated in any manner to reach any conclusion. Of course, one needs to use mathematics to understand statistics; it's the little 'details' which create the possibility of manipulation. Just how easy it is to take the same numbers from the same samples and twist them to come to two entirely incompatible 'conclusions' simply by manipulating the 'details' is disturbing. All one needs to do is bury the 'details' and the heralds of doom and gloom or status quo and blind providence trumpet the 'findings' with cacophonous glee. Whenever a study's statistical findings are reported, I never consider it valid until I see how the study was conducted and can examine those nasty little 'details'. Fortunately, there are a whole lot of people who do the same thing for the same reason; unfortunately, their voices are rarely 'broadcast' as loud as the heralds' voices and never with the same authority. The best defense I have developed over the years is question everything, even that from trusted sources. Consistent questioning has a tendency to destroy the flimsy evidence of a shaky conclusion. Watch it tumble; it's great.

I met Cindy, the how, when, where, and what happened that first meeting forever lost in a shallow, unmarked grave that used to be an active region of brain cells which have since been mercifully destroyed or overwritten during some past clutter removal. You can bet your ass, though, that I remember *why* I met her, considering that she was blond –

I was a sucker for blonds then – and she was incredibly cute, thin as a rail, about five feet five inches with an attractively round butt. Yep, that's why. She was easy to talk with, had a gentle sense of humor, where she usually smiled instead of laughed, and she liked me a lot. She was from Palatine and she told her parents everything about us, so when they came down to see her, they insisted that I have dinner with them. The item I learned from that dinner and have never forgotten was the admission from her father that their very Anglican surname was the result of a name change from generations before; his Polish ancestors had decided to adopt a more Anglican – American? – surname and had changed it. The only thought I had was, *that's cheating.* We could have done that. I could have done that. It would have saved me countless hours of spelling and pronunciation correction that I'll *never get back!* They were cheating. However, Cindy's ancestry or name change had nothing to do with our outcome.

That outcome was sealed one night as we lay on my bed in the dorm making out. We had gotten close enough to each other and comfortable enough with each other that we kissed often, and I would occasionally run my hands over her body, even her butt. This night, though, I moved my right hand over her left breast and squeezed it gently; she shifted uncomfortably but said nothing as we continued to kiss. When I tried to slide my hand under her blouse and up to her breast, she suddenly went ballistic. From the resulting tirade I captured the words, 'Why is it that boys,' and other incomplete and, in all honesty, incoherent ramblings from which I could not, no matter what I did, return her to a state of functioning reason and communication. Don't get me wrong; I really did want to fuck her, so I can't promise that I would have been understanding if she had just simply said, "I like you and I don't want to stop seeing you, but I'm not ready for that." The problem is, *she never, ever said that.* Frankly, I don't know *what* she said, because absolutely none of it made any sense at all. I walked her back to her dorm once she had returned to some calm, despite her protests. After that night, though, she was consistently busy with her studies – you understand, don't you?

so I only saw her twice, although we did get to kissing, again, but she would pull away after a short time. After I returned from spring break and the trip to Florida, I never called her and she never called me.

In February, the Alameda River Band, with Bruce, Jeff, Linda and me, had our first and last paying gig. I don't remember how we came up with that name, but we had to come up with some name, because the bar where we were to play wanted to make up flyers for our appearance. Our set was expanded from the first gig since we were expected to play longer. The most memorable moment came after my singing, which I thought was very good; I had turned the volume off the bass so that the amp would not produce an annoying hum. When we launched into *Foggy Mountain Breakdown*, I merrily plucked away with my felt pick but heard nothing from the amp. Realizing I had neglected to dial the volume knob back up, I quickly stopped playing and twisted it to the number that I had set previously, waited for the next bar and got going. Going was the key word, because I was so embarrassed at my gaffe that I picked up the tempo from the adrenaline pumping through me; the other three just followed and we all agreed that it was both the fastest and the best that we had ever played that song. Take it from me: if you ever play that song, faster is better. They paid us twenty bucks, so I can say I'm a professional musician since my cut was a five-spot. What future is there in school or work? I can make five bucks a night playing bass. At least I wouldn't starve; five bucks will buy one meal. The Alameda River Band succumbed to the growing pressures of studies – yeah, that other part of college life – and soon our practice sessions dwindled to none. Jeff and Linda had disagreements, Bruce found a lady, and I lost interest.

Fraternity recruitment and resistance continued unabated. The recruitment at the fraternity was stepping up, with several members raising the question of acceptance openly, not just with me but most of the regular gang. With me, I even had a couple tell me they thought they could get me switched into another college from liberal arts, even though I had heard that the university had a high grade point average requirement between liberal arts and business, which is where I was thinking of transferring. Some of the gang had known about the university's loophole, which was to enroll into the university under a general major, which was the equivalent of undeclared, and one would be allowed to enter any college with one's declared major at any time through the first school year. Since our high school apparently had counselors who weren't worth a crap, I was stuck. The resistance persisted because I resented the idea that fraternity members thought they could easily skirt university rules so frivolously. Perhaps, though, they were just trying to snow me, since that thought occurred to me, also. The resistance continued around our dorm, too, since we were directly across the street from one of the oldest fraternities, ATO, who always seemed to be a group of blowhard, arrogant cocksuckers, a term I use deliberately. There were an awful lot of jocks in that fraternity and they all thought they were God's gift to women, but they seemed to be a little too tight with each other. Get my drift? One night there was a loud, long shouting match between the surrounding dorms and the fraternity. I had read that one could take a standard set of headphones and connect them to an amp – like my bass amp – and they would act just like a microphone. Hmmm, I had a set of headphones and I just happened to have an amp and we had already tested it and it worked; we wheeled that huge amp to a room on the other side of the floor, lifted it onto the bed so that it faced right out the open window, plugged in the headphones, turned the amp on and dialed it to ten. With the lights in the room off and the amp solid black, we proceeded to drown out the entire block with rants and insults and incessant, meaningless chatter. It was so cool because when we stopped, there was almost total silence, until we could hear people asking each other where that amp was. I had to go down to the street and hear it. It was LOUD! People said they could hear it two blocks away, but some people figured out where it was because they had spotted the tiny, red light in the window halfway on the twelfth floor. Busted! We had forgotten about the power indicator. I ran back into the dorm, took the elevator up and we turned it off and put it up before anybody could catch us. The recruitment by the sorority sisters carried on, too. Julie had stuck to me almost like glue, so much so that everybody, dorm and frat rats alike, would talk about it. I had carefully and diplomatically reserved my decision, stating that I was open to the idea of joining the fraternity, even though I knew I wouldn't. Julie didn't seem to care what everybody thought; I was like her pet project. She kissed me several times when we were alone and even went to a bar with me the week I turned nineteen in mid-March, just the two of us. Still, she never let a moment pass to remind me that a lot of people thought I would be a good choice for membership in the fraternity, both from the fraternity *and* its sister sorority. This recruiting and resisting left me with the nagging suspicion that the final result would not be too good.

    After I moved into Mark's room, I had disassembled my little stereo unit, which was a fold-down turntable and speakers on either side. I had unscrewed the speakers from the unit and had bought extra speaker wire and wire connectors; I stripped both ends of wire and twisted them together and twisted them tight into each connector. Now, I had a real stereo with speakers that I could mount anywhere. Mark suggested we hang them in the ceiling, so we popped off one of the drop down ceiling tiles and immediately discovered that the speakers from the stereo unit fit perfectly across the rails of the drop down opening. We popped another on the other side of the room and we had stereo from heaven. The satisfaction from the clever manipulation of our environment only lasted about a week; while we were playing an album late on a week night, one of the upper class men from our floor came down to our room in his underwear, sleepy-eyed. He complained that our music was keeping him awake and we needed to turn it off. We didn't believe him, since his room was eight rooms away, and went down to his room to hear for ourselves. We could hear the music almost like it was right there in the room. Oops. I turned it off and took it down the next day, realizing that the sound carried over the drop down ceiling and could be heard in every room. We put some screws in the opposite side walls of Mark's room and hung the speakers unprofessionally from the screws. It would do.

Midterms for the spring semester appeared. We all pulled all-nighters and I noticed that the smokers, Mark, Bruce, Jeff, the guitarist and Pete, seemed to be able to stay up a lot easier than I could. For the first time since I was seven, I seriously considered smoking, but I put the thought out of my head until after midterms and spring break. I wanted to party without distractions, bodily or otherwise. I felt I did well on my midterms and that my grades for this semester would be much improved over the last, at least that's what I convinced myself to think right up to the trip. Now that it was time to go, it was time to stop thinking about school. Let's boogie! Better yet, let's party!

Around six on a Friday night, we were all to gather with our gear in the front of the dorm. Jeff, motorcycle man, was very excited and rattled off to me all the things he had checked and had prepped for the trip. I was duly impressed. I was also ready to depart. Where *is* everybody?

Pete and Barry mosied up. Mark was packing his gear when I left him; he saddled up. Benjamin, Jeff's roommate, made it down. The girls finally drifted into the picture, leaving Kevin, the sophomore, as the straggler. When he finally made his grand appearance, I announced, "It's about time! Fuckin' sophomores! We shoulda left him!" Kevin simply replied, "Fuck you!" We arranged all the gear, set the initial seating assignments, piled in and Jeff headed for Interstate 74 and Indianapolis.

Traffic was fairly heavy until we reached the sticks between Champaign and Danville. Jeff didn't set a rule for speed for any of the drivers; anyone stopped for speeding or any other infraction was on his or her own. Jeff himself drove no more than ten miles over the speed limit. In two hours we were negotiating the maze around Indianapolis, merging onto Interstate 65 and finally heading south. Jeff drove the rest of the distance to Kentucky and Mark, who had been sitting shotgun, took over after a brief rest stop. In pitch black with no star or moon light, it was eerie and cold heading up the Appalachian Mountains; we hit a short snow flurry and traffic was reacting rather crazily. Mark made it through without incident or any significant delays. When we reached the first of the tollways, the speed limit had increased and we really made good time. There were many all-night fireworks establishments scattered around, but we all agreed to stop on the way back. Let's get to FLA first.

Through Tennessee and Pete's shift, I slept most of the time without my leather flight jacket, genuine Air Force issue from the surplus store in Champaign, which I had purchased for seventy-five dollars five months before. When we were driving through the mountains, the temperature outside had dropped considerably. It was colder in the back of the van, so I asked Sandy if she wanted to wear my jacket to keep warm; she liked that jacket and immediately said she did, so she was still wearing it, sleeping peacefully.

Barry took over after a stop for stretching and relieving when we arrived in Georgia. Soon, we were back on the road on Interstate 75, the last road to FLA. I was now sitting shotgun with the maps and most of the drive was just Barry and me and neither of us talked much. By the time we reached Atlanta, it was starting to get light out, though the sun hadn't risen, yet. Even so, most were up; the anxiety was building. I asked Barry how he was doing. He replied that I could take over any time I wanted; he was getting spent since he had not been able to sleep much before his shift. I told him to pull it over at the next opportunity and I'll put us in Florida before I'm done. The traffic was light around Atlanta that early on a Saturday morning, so Barry asked Jeff it was alright to just pull into the emergency lane for a driver change. Jeff said to do it and one minute later we were back in the flow of traffic with me behind the wheel. I announced that we would stop for breakfast after we got around Atlanta, which I estimated would be about a half-hour. Some groaned but I ignored all protests; I always want to put the more challenging aspects of any journey behind me while I have the energy to do so.

I drove around Atlanta with no problems and caught the exit for Interstate 75 and FLA. A short while later we spotted an exit with quite a few restaurants and gas stations, so I pulled off to fill up and we assessed the situation. In 1975 there were few fast-food places that offered breakfast and most didn't open until ten in the morning; there was a restaurant down the street that looked open and didn't seem too busy, so we decided to drive to it after we filled up and check it out. The restaurant was more like a short order place and most agreed that it would do, so we all went inside and sat down right at the counter. After everyone had eaten and paid for their meals, we were back on the road with only a half-hour lost to breakfast. The speed limit in Georgia was very accommodating and I made good time cruising through the southern part of the state. We all noticed that it was significantly warmer and two hours after stopping for gas and eats, I crossed the state line into FLA and pulled over. My part was done and Kevin hopped up behind the wheel to drive the next shift.

Everyone was getting excited because we had made it to our destination or so we thought until Jeff reminded us that we still had five to six hours of driving ahead of us before we reached Orlando. Groans immediately replaced the excitement. Kevin announced that it would be closer to five hours since the speed limit was seventy and he fully expected to go much faster than that. Someone noticed an odd-colored vehicle with a rack of official lights on top and the words 'Florida Highway Patrol' on the side. "Now's your chance to show 'em who's boss of the highway, Kevin," Mark shouted and all laughed. Kevin just dropped the van's speed to seventy for quite a while since those odd-colored vehicles were in frequent sight. He drove to the highway intersection leading to Orlando and diverting from the interstate, where Jeff popped back behind the wheel of his van for the last leg. *Shit, I thought, we're almost there and it's not even twenty-four hours since we left our cold-ass home!*

About two and a half hours later we had reached the outskirts of Orlando, which seemed little more than an average sized city like Podunk, instead of the home for Disney's newest park, Disneyworld, which had opened only the previous year. Jeff thought he noticed that the steering was a little skewed, so he pulled into a parking lot so he could check the van and specifically the front tires. We discovered that the front tires were incredibly worn, mostly on the passenger side tire. That was our first and only setback, as it turned out. Jeff had had everything checked out for the long haul his van would be subjected to except for one thing: he neglected to have his tires balanced and the front wheels aligned. The speed of our trip combined with the considerable weight of nine people and their baggage had taken its toll; we could not go on with the front tires in that condition, so we found a service station that recommended a tire store which should be able to swap the tires, balance all of them and align the front wheels. We found it pretty easily – Orlando really was a small town in the middle of nowhere back then – and waited while the damage was switched from the vehicle's condition to our financial condition. Jeff, despite everyone's protests to the contrary, insisted that it was his expense and paid the nearly two hundred dollars for the repairs. He explained, and later proved it was true, that we would be stopping at one of his family's residences when we reached the western part of the state and they would make good on it.

The troubles with the front tires had put a crimp in our schedule, until somebody discovered that a ticket for entry into Disneyworld after a certain time would be honored for the next day. That settled it. We would delay our trip to Florida's east coast until the following afternoon and spend the night and part of the next day at the park. Sandy called her relatives in town and told them that we would all be coming to their house late and we drove off to the park.

After confirming with the ticket folks in their little boxes before the gate that today's ticket would be honored tomorrow, we bought our tickets and headed inside. Since it was a new park there was still some construction under way, but it was relatively uncrowded and we could get on rides with just a little waiting. Still, it was the usual Disney fare, with lots of walking. Despite getting to the park in the evening, we covered most of the park until it closed. Once we had all gathered back at the van, Sandy climbed up to shotgun and directed Jeff to her relatives' house in a quiet residential area of town. The man of the house came out and introduced himself and we all did the same; after chatting for a while, he offered a spot in the living room for two of us to make it a little easier for the rest of us to make room in the van. Pete and Barry took him up and they slept in the man's living room while the rest of us stretched out as best we could in the van.

The next morning, most of us were up by seven. Pete and Barry stumbled out of the house and woke the remainder stowing their stuff in the back. Sandy came out and told us that she and her friend were going to the park later with some of the relatives; she thanked Jeff for getting them to Florida in one piece, confirmed when we would be back to pick them up and if Jeff could remember how to get there – he had written the directions – and she walked to the back of the van and I followed her.

"Think you'll have fun without me," Sandy said as she stepped slightly out of view of the guys.

"Maybe not as much but I'll manage," I replied, adding, "though I might meet someone."

"That's not what I wanted to hear," she said, smiling, and threw her right arm at me with her fist doubled to softly punch my left shoulder. I grabbed her wrist with my left hand and held on until we both dropped our arms and she opened her hand. I slid my hand into hers and held it loosely as her fingers slipped around mine.

"What about you?" I asked. "Can you have any fun landlocked without me?"

"Of course," she replied wearing her teasing smirk. "Girls are different. We don't need boys to have as much fun, maybe more."

"Maybe we're obsolete," I observed, smiling.

"Could be," she said, still smirking. She stepped up to me, put her arms around me as I did the same with her and we hugged for a few seconds. As we separated, she kissed me softly on the right cheek.

Through the van, Pete yelled, "Let's go, Johnny. There's girls all over Florida."

Still smiling, Sandy said, "You better get going. Have fun. I know I will and I won't be missing you either."

Raising my eyebrows, I said, "Miss you? Never."

Sandy smiled briefly and gently pulled her hand away from mine. I watched her turn and walk toward the house before I opened the back of the van and climbed in. Jeff fired up the van and we drove slowly away as I listened to Pete critique my performance. That was the most affection we had shown each other since the concert months before, even during the drive we had just completed, when we had teased each other occasionally but never really touched. Now I missed her.

We stopped at a restaurant for breakfast, figuring, correctly, that breakfast outside the park would be cheaper than inside. Back at the park, though, it was like having it mostly to ourselves; we were beating the crowds and feeling pretty good about it until about noon when the swell started catching up. We caught the Imax show, the new surround vision technology with multiple cameras synchronized on playback, and rode a few more rides. Since we had split up, we had agreed at a rendezvous spot for lunch; when the time came, we were almost of one mind. The park was getting fuller and it would take longer to get around and longer to get into the attractions; perhaps, we should head for the exit and cruise to the east coast and around Daytona before it got too late. Besides, Daytona and Fort Lauderdale was where the spring break college action was supposed to be, right? With only half-hearted protests – are you a man or a boy? – we moved to the exit and the eventual destination of Daytona, after a stop for lunch, of course.

The trip to Daytona took more than two hours, through mostly rural areas that would make Podunk look like a metropolis. Often we would be driving on a two-lane highway right above a canal, sometimes with boats cruising, and we would wonder just how many alligators we could count before we got eaten ourselves. Once we got near Daytona, though, it all changed to urban settings and the traffic picked up considerably. It wasn't long before we encountered college students in their vehicles; they were easy to spot, mostly because they were hanging out windows, screaming at each other, or waving beers and other alcoholic beverages, all on the roadway. The sidewalks were filling up, too, and the legs and halter tops of variously tanned college age females was quickly becoming commonplace. Yeah, man.

We were all in agreement. We were not going to stop this van until we were forced to because of impending ocean water or, in its immediate absence, a parking spot on the road fronting the beach. We reached said road – the average traveling speed had decreased to about five miles per hour – and turned left so that we could park on the beach side *if we can ever find a parking spot*! Miracle of miracles, after barely five minutes cruising the beach street, there it was, our parking spot. Jeff swung the big monster of a van in that tiny spot effortlessly and instantly we were falling out of the van and onto the beach. The most disturbing distraction, by far, was the bikinis, tens, hundreds, thousands of them. There oughtta be a law about bikinis and those wearing them. Yeah, and the law should state that all bikini wearers must be detained in Jeff's van for an indeterminate period of detention. The van would be full in no time so how would we get around? Rent a tow truck to haul the van, of course. Problem solved. Now, we just have to get that law passed, preferably before sundown. Where the hell is the city council when you need them anyway? Those worthless bureaucrats.

The drinking age in Florida was 18, so Mark and Pete set off to find beer. The rest of us staked an area on the beach for central, cruised up and down the sand, chatting with anyone who would return the conversation, looking at the girls and sometimes flirting with them, and, of course, getting our feet wet in the Atlantic Ocean. I caught Mark and Pete walking across the street, Mark carrying a cheap styrofoam cooler and Pete carrying a sack. Beer break! I headed to central and waited while they negotiated through the traffic to get to the beach. Within a few minutes all the gang had congregated and we started swapping stories about what we all had heard or seen so far. The picture was clear. While the east coast of Florida was packed with college students on break, it was difficult to get around, rooms were expensive and far-flung – some students were as far as ninety minutes from the beach because that was the closest rooms they could find – and the night life was wild but packed. There were night clubs and bars that you couldn't even get inside because they were completely full. We knew at that point that we had probably made the right decision to stay on the gulf coast. Still, surveying the fine surroundings, I couldn't help thinking, *there's a lot of pussy here.*

We stayed right on the beach until after dark, drinking and carrying on, though Jeff had stopped drinking long ago; he had a long drive ahead of him. Despite some of our best efforts, we couldn't get any girls to sit with us and drink beer and talk. It may have been due to a longstanding behavior that quite a few women fall into when confronted by unfamiliar surroundings; I call it preening. One watches the behavior and cannot avoid drawing comparisons to animals bobbing and rubbing and licking themselves; when one can view males doing it, too, there's a certain comfort one can derive from evolutionary hypothesis. There are definitely traits that species share. I kept my conclusions to myself, though, and we picked up our stuff from central, loaded the van and headed west, often through desolate places where even electric lights hadn't yet invaded. Most of the time we had the road, usually two-lane, to ourselves, until we finally reached the interstate down to Tampa. Jeff diverged from the interstate, then, and went around the city, explaining that he didn't like crossing the bay on that bridge. We pulled into his relatives' neighborhood near Sarasota after midnight, but someone was still up and waiting for us. Some of the guys headed inside to spend the night in their living room, while the rest of us, myself included, stretched out in the van and prepared for sleepy time.

About seven the next morning, with most in the van still sleeping and snoring and recuperating from the drinking the day before, Jeff slapped his hand against the van several times, admonishing all inside that it was time to get up. Everyone slinked into the house to relieve themselves or whatever and when we all seemed to have our virtual shit together, Jeff proclaimed it was time to head up to the bay and drive to Clearwater to find this motel where I had reserved our rooms. The attention of everyone now shifted to me; we were all going to find out real soon just what we had gotten ourselves into.

We went the long way around again and drove through Tampa, which was something of a shock. The streets in the city were stuffed with traffic and it was quite a sight to see car after car of old people screaming at their fellow drivers, cutting each other off, and generally leaving one with the distinct impression that an accident was soon to occur. We managed to move through the city without hitting anyone or anything and vowed never to return, at least not this year. The west end of town, around the bay, quickly turned into another large island of desolation, nothing but grass and wetlands and the occasional proprietorship of various kinds, though usually gas and cigarettes. It was like that until we got to the city limits of Clearwater, which seemed extraordinarily small for a city right on the water. We found the motel just off the main drag to the beach, only three blocks from the sand. It was a three-story building, not big, surrounding a small swimming pool in the middle. It was reasonable, they had our rooms waiting and everyone was quite satisfied. The major uncertainty could now be dismissed; we had our rooms, they would suffice and we were close to the beach and any action that might take place.

As for action, "let's get to the fucking beach, right now," Kevin enthused. What about unloading and unpacking our stuff, we all asked. "Fuck that! It can wait," Kevin insisted. Secure us a central, we implored Kevin, if only to dismiss him from our immediate vicinity. It worked, since he quickly scrambled down the steps to the sidewalk, walking at an incredibly fast clip to the sand. We should get some beer and drink it before we go to the beach, just to teach him a lesson, we all agreed. Soon, we were all kicking back around the pool, sucking down beers and chatting with ourselves and others who dared to venture into our conversation corner. Eventually, Kevin came back for a towel – what an idiot – and spotted us around the pool. He wanted to know if we were gonna blow off going to the beach or what. If what meant sitting around the pool drinking beer, we might just skip the beach altogether today. "There are women on the beach in bikinis," Kevin informed us. "There are women at this pool in bikinis," I said and smiled at one of the women in bikinis, who smiled back. "Fine! You guys are wimps," Kevin admonished. "Have a beer," Pete said and flipped one to Kevin. "Alright," he said and sat down with the rest of us.

The week in Clearwater proceeded much like that. The majority of the gang would settle around the motel like nesting birds, content to just huddle together and do as little as possible. Occasionally, one or two or three would depart the nest to scour the immediate environment, to scope the vast beach and its visitors, to snare provisions of both solid and liquid variety, to break away from the nest, knowing that a return would reunite fellow nesters. Oh, there were the odd adventures and mishaps. The next day after we arrived most of us forgot that cloud cover has no effect on ultraviolet rays, so most suffered some degree of sunburn, Kevin being the worst. He was solid red for two days and completely useless for most of that time. The two sisters, Heather and April, and their friends checked in; no one was supposed to know that they were sisters but there's only so much deception that can remain successful when one discovers the weakest link, and that link was the youngest, April. She enjoyed flirting with me and that was the opening I needed; with my uncanny ability to project sincerity – which is not a trick, mind you – she confessed that they were sisters within hours after meeting them. I also received the explanation that Heather and April were and were not their real names. They were playing the game that many young women on vacation together play; they use some other name than their given first names. Men don't seem to need to do that, so it must be a gender thing. Despite all that subterfuge, they liked us and we liked them. The seven of us and the five of them even went to a nightclub together, though we didn't leave together. April enjoyed the flirting but when she got a little tipsy one night and I pushed my advantage, she actually started crying. Her mumbling explanation had something to do with what she had dreamed would happen but now it scared her; if it was meant to get me to stop, it worked, because I never pushed it again the entire time we had together. It's a position I will defend until the day I die, for reasons that you will certainly discover later if not already, and not just in this narrative but in your own life and of those you meet. No means no, jackass. Sex is not a sales prospect, to determine the reasons for all objections and overcoming them with ruthless persistence. Sex between two people can only be beautiful and meaningful when undertaken with mutual consent; if that complete consent is lacking from one partner, I can guarantee that the other partner is committing sexual abuse. There's nothing funny about sexual abuse, nor should it be anything to boast, brag or be proud of, and if you are, you're sick, jackass. Go fuck yourself, literally. When your partner says no or does something of the equivalent, such as resisting, just drop it and explode your sausage later. It might just save your sausage in the end, since I have two daughters myself, and if I find out that either was sexually abused I'll cut off the offender's cock. I'm not alone in this sentiment either, jackass, so you've been warned…Did I mention during our week in Clearwater that we drank excessive amounts of beer and other alcoholic beverages, smoked pot incessantly and caroused about without rendering anything of productive value? No? We sure as shit did.

The last day some of us did something rather stupid. We went down to the beach and swam in the ocean water with all those microscopic critters and swam in the motel pool *without* showering beforehand. The combination of microscopic critters and chlorine-treated pool water started a reaction in our ears that would catch up with us a little later; for some, especially me, it would be worse than for others. Benjamin and Kevin would both feel that reaction but it really affected me for the worse.

April and Heather stayed around the motel while we packed up for our drive back. They were from Missouri, near Saint Louis, and April asked me to leave her my address at school; she assured me that she would write and I believed her so I gave her my address and she kissed me goodbye. By then I knew she wasn't a college student but a senior in high school; the other girls were college friends with Heather, from her sorority. Like I said, April was the weak link in their chain, but she couldn't find it in her heart to blow me off. She knew if I was like all the other boys, her virginity would have ended that night she cried; I would have treated her like a sales prospect and overcome every objection and taken her to my room and fucked her. Though my rational self remained skeptical, her eyes and smile gave me a clue that she really would write to me.

Packed and ready, we left Clearwater in the afternoon for the long drive to Orlando to pick up the girls, through the desolation of rural Florida yet again. Some of it still exists but in 1975 one did not have to drive far from a city area to confront a stark absence of anything manmade. Thirty minutes from downtown Clearwater was all it took.

Long before we reached Orlando, Kevin, Benjamin and I began experiencing pain in our ears. My right ear throbbed excruciatingly and soon all I could do was lie down quietly. Kevin and Benjamin were not as bad but they each had pain in one ear, too. Jeff was a little worried about the drive rotation until Kevin volunteered to take the first shift after Jeff so he could get his out of the way while he still felt okay. That eased Jeff's mind considerably.

The girls were packed and waiting when we arrived at the house. Everyone got out to stretch and get the bags situated. I sat down on the curb, hunched over, my head down looking at the pavement. The girls were chatting about their various trips, including Daytona and the east coast and the boys they met. The guys were carrying on with bloated boasting of our exploits in Clearwater and none of it – what the girls said and what the guys said – sounded very realistic to me. Instead, I just sat on the curb silently.

"Johnny met a girl, met two girls, actually," Pete said. "One of them even asked for his address, right, Wad?"

I made no movement of acknowledgement and I could hear Sandy moving from behind me to stand in front of me as she said, "They must have wore him out. I guess girls can do that to boys, huh?"

Mark said, "He's being a pussy complaining about some throbbing pain in his ear."

"Ahhh, pooor baby," Sandy teased and everyone got a good chuckle from it.

I lifted my left arm slowly with my middle finger extended and the other fingers bent down and slowly dropped my arm back to my side. "That'll never happen, little boy," Sandy commented and everyone got an even bigger chuckle from that. I think Sandy was a prophet because that never did happen.

The alignment performed on the front wheels for the new front tires held up admirably on the drive back to Illinois. Jeff cruised out of Orlando and all the way to Interstate 75. Kevin took over, not feeling anywhere near as bad as me or Benjamin, and drove nearly to Georgia.

Barry took it through the various construction slowdowns and the confusing bypass around Atlanta without incident and yielded his shift to Pete in the early morning. We were in Tennessee by four in the morning and parked at a filling station with a large store pushing fireworks. While one filled the van everyone but me got out to buy fireworks. So far, the trip had consisted of some success at sleep but mostly gritting my teeth at the pain in my ear. I said little and moved even less from a prone position.

Pete continued his stint behind the wheel onto the first tollway until he reached a rest area and Jeff suggested a driver change. Mark hopped up behind the wheel and floored it through the rest of Tennessee and all of Kentucky, including the mountains which he had driven through the week before. There was snow on the ground but the road was clear and we made good time to Indiana. Jeff took over, then, and drove the entire distance back to Champaign, when we arrived in the middle of the afternoon. It was colder when we arrived back than when we left. Sandy was disappointed that she didn't get to wear my leather jacket at all during the trip and now complained about how cold it was. I apologized to Jeff for skipping on my driving rotation, grabbed my bag and went to my room and immediately passed out.

Early the next morning I went to the student infirmary and saw a doctor within a short time. I had an ear infection. The doctor even knew what I had done. "Let me see, you said you were in Florida," he began, "and you went into the ocean, did not take a shower when you left the beach or when you got back to the motel, and, instead, jumped into the pool at your motel, right?" He gave me a prescription for ear drops for the infection, which I filled at the student pharmacy. Six hours later it had worked wonders, reducing the pain and throbbing to a minor irritant; three days later it was gone but I was instructed to use the entire prescription, so I did.

I had to get back into the study swing of things. Florida was fun but I wanted to do better this semester than the last so I buckled down. Mark and I would hang out in the student lounge with our books and notes scattered about and he always seemed to be more alert than I was. Hey, he smokes cigarettes. I started smoking, too, and threw up from inhaling. I kept at it, though, like it was some kind of accomplishment. In reality, it was one of the worst decisions I ever made, and I keep making it about twenty-five to thirty times a day.

Mark's turn came for initiation in the shower stall and he, surprisingly, went to his watery doom without much of a fight. I knew my turn was coming and when it did, it was memorable. Six of them, including the big boys, Bruce and Mark, snagged me in the room and hauled me to the showers. Except for the initial resistance of dodging and squirming until I was firmly under their control, I let them take me to the stalls quietly and calmly. Bruce and Mark commented that I was hardly fighting at all, not like I had promised would happen. Out in the open was not where I could make my stand and I wasn't going to waste my energy fighting against the odds, but when we got to the shower stalls that would be a different story. As they started to push me through the stall, the other four had to back away, so now it was Bruce and Mark trying to get me through the stall walls. My hands and feet were everywhere, I'm sure it seemed to everyone there. Mark had to get into the stall before me just to drag me into the stall while Bruce pushed and the others tried to loosen my grip or push away my feet. Try as they might, Bruce and Mark could only get my head and shoulders into the shower about one foot inside; they even tried to turn on the shower with Mark completely inside it and getting wet but they couldn't aim the shower head to get me wet. The others held me in place and we all rested while Bruce disappeared, only to return with one of those hot pots filled with water and dumped it over my head. My 'initiation' was over, the only one on the floor that could not be put in the shower to have the water turned on him. Told ya!

My next appearance at the frat house turned out to be my last, at least while I was still at the big U. I ran into Captain Jack at the Student Union and he was all excited about his latest score. He wanted me to come over as soon as my classes were done and sample some of the wares so I said I'd drop by about three in the afternoon. After my last class of the day I walked over to the frat house with my books and papers and rang the doorbell. Instead of answering, one of the frat boys opened the door and ran out, late for class, and told me the good Cap'n was downstairs and to just go on in because I knew the way, all true. There he sat on the makeshift couch, table and refreshment stand known as party central. Captain Jack was a short guy about five feet six inches and a little squatty, like Pete, even to the hair parted on the side and the beard. He was better looking than Pete, though, and funnier, too, with a very dry, sarcastic wit and an unflappability that was almost legendary. Equally legendary was his well-known prediction that he would complete his education on a six-year plan; he was definitely on schedule for that.

Inviting me to sit down as soon as he saw me and offering me a beer, which I declined, he wielded his bong filled with supposedly one hit and passed it to me. I lit it up and sucked the smoke down deep into my lungs and felt them explode into an uncontrollable cough while there was still half the hit left in the bong. The captain laughed but took the bong as I handed it back to him with my hand covering the top and he lit up and sucked down the rest of the hit. We took turns like that for the next fifteen minutes, after which I lit up a cigarette and the captain took note of that, asking me what the fuck I was doing. I told him I was destroying any of my lung cells somehow left untouched by marijuana and that one can't help but admire my thoroughness. He asked how the trip to Florida went and other particulars about it and we chatted like that for quite a while, completely undisturbed by anyone, which was highly unusual for party central at any time of day or night. Undisturbed, that is, until one of the frat officers – whose name is forever lost in the black holes of my memory – came down to speak with me, having heard from one of the other frat boys upstairs that I was 'in the house'. The officer wanted to speak with me in private, but the captain sensed that something was uncool.

"He's my guest and anything you have to say to him you should say with me present, too," Captain Jack told him, his eyes a bit narrowed. "I know the rules, though you big boys like to think I don't care about them."

The captain's sense was keen and accurate. The officer had come down to advise me that I could not come to the frat house anymore unless I made the decision to join. It's as simple as that, he said.

The captain reached behind the couch, pulled up the bong, loaded it, and passed it to me, as he said, "It's settled. We should smoke to that." He looked up at the officer and added, "Want some?"

As the officer shook his head and slowly walked backwards to the stairs, I took the bong, lit it and sucked the smoke down and coughed again. The officer climbed up the stairs and disappeared, but we smoked for another half-hour, getting quite spanked. The captain, though, was one of those cats who got frisky the more he smoked. He suggested that I head back to the dorm and get some dinner and meet him at one of the bars on the strip at seven and get ripped. I liked the idea and that's exactly what we did. Somehow, I managed to stumble back to the dorm before midnight, vaguely remembering that most everybody else bought the beer, including several of the frat boys and some of the guys that went with me from the dorm.

Jeff, motorcycle man, stopped in my room as I read from one of my textbooks and Mark sat at the table. "Holmes," he greeted me, "that sorority sister is downstairs and asked me to tell you that she wants to talk to you."

"I swear, man," Mark opined, "that woman has got something for you."

I shook my head and looked at Mark as I got up from the bed where I sat and Jeff disappeared down the hall to his room. "I don't think I'm gonna like this, big boy," I said.

When I stepped from the elevator into the common area between the two dormitory towers, I looked through the lounge area until I saw Julie stand up from a chair, looking in my direction. I walked over to her and we each sat down in a chair next to the other. She wore a serious composure. Completely absent during the entire confrontation – no, it wasn't what I would call a conversation – was any outward expression of joviality, humor, frivolity, the warmth of her smile that I had witnessed so often, knowing that the smile, the warmth, was directly attributable to her appreciation of me and my humor, frivolity, joviality, my smile and its warmth. I can't call it a conversation because it couldn't have lasted more than two minutes and I hardly said anything, but just nodded or shook my head. Her personal world consisted of fraternities and sororities and the responsibilities and obligations to such and my personal world was one of independence and, perhaps, even an avoidance of responsibility and obligation and these two, separate worlds did not mix. There was an unmistakable sadness in her face when she insisted that the worlds were only a pretext; she was simply too old for me and that would not do. I knew when she said it that it was a lie and that may be why the confrontation didn't devastate me as much as it should have. After all, isn't it better to end an involvement with a liar than to try to prolong it and hope that the lie is just an aberration of the moment?

Finals week arrived. I was doing much better this semester than last or so I thought. Mythology was a breeze and the final was all multiple choice; I had an 'A' going in and I was confident that I had aced the final exam. Psychology was equally interesting and surprisingly stimulating and I was doing well in that class, too. The textbook was written by McConnell, a professor from Michigan University. The section of the textbook that never lost its hold on me concerned an experiment performed on rhesus monkeys in the sixties; the experiment was designed to identify what behavioral traits could be assigned to the portion of a brain called the amygdala. Half of a group of monkeys had the region of their brains where the amygdala resided surgically removed while the other half became the control group to be left unaltered. Once the monkeys subject to the surgery had recovered sufficiently they were re-introduced into the control group. Two behavior traits became immediately apparent concerning the monkeys subjected to the surgery. They could not learn, as demonstrated by the fact that no matter how many times they were presented with a bowl full of edible nuts and steel bolts, none could ever discern the difference between the two until they tried to bite each; the control group only had to bite one of each to forever determine the difference between the two and would discard the steel bolts by touch until they found an edible nut, again by touch. The second trait discovered from the monkeys subjected to surgery was that they would remain passive despite the most severe provocation by the control group of monkeys and would never display any aggression; the experimenters also determined that this passivity was, perhaps, fatal to the monkeys subjected to surgery in that the control group would escalate their aggression when that aggression was met only with continued passivity. Attendants would frequently have to separate the monkeys subjected to surgery from the control group for fear that they would be killed; this finding also required them to end the experiment since it was becoming increasingly difficult to monitor the monkeys as a whole group and they were separated permanently. How interesting! An independently functioning section of the brain which facilitates *both* learning and aggression but in its absence renders a being completely passive and forever ignorant. This apparent biological dilemma would stimulate me to develop a written paradox later. I thought I did well on the psychology final exam, which was multiple choice, true/false and short essays.

Those of us born in 1956 were born too late and too early. We were born too late to experience the struggle for freedom, the rebelliousness and experimentation of the late sixties. We were born too early to lead the personal computer revolution of the eighties. I submit, as evidence of that statement, my experience with my COBOL programming course, which required punching both code and data on eighty column cards using a keypunch machine. If you were born after 1966, say, you probably have no idea what a keypunch machine was or is or how frustrating it was to use one. If you made a typing error anywhere on the eighty columns of the card it would have to be thrown away. How's that for 'user-friendly'? I would have to stand in line to turn in my code and data cards, hopefully in the correct order and hopefully run through a card reading machine in the correct order, then stand in line to get my 'output' sheets and debug the errors, retype cards, and start the whole process over again. This is computer programming? Fuck that; you can have it! I'd rather slave for months at a time doing a thousand income tax returns, taking a respite from tax calculations only to have individual teeth pulled out without the numbing use of novocain. Still, I both understood the language and its syntax and usage and was pretty good at it and was holding up a solid 'B' going into finals week. I thought I did well in the final, which was mostly coding on paper and answering basic computer questions. If this was the state of modern computer programming, though, it was like cave men waiting for the really big invention that would make it easier to get around. "Someday, it's going to be MUCH easier to haul around Grampa other than slinging him over our shoulders, each of us taking our turn. I can see a travel device that will *roll* like rocks down a hill and we can put Grampa on the device and just *roll* him!" The other cave men, of course, would respond, "Get out of here!"

With the last final exam behind me it was time to vacate the big U and get the flock out, as they say. The Oldsmobile chariot awaited and all the items were packed and stored and ready for the trip back to Podunk. I donned my helmet and mounted my trusty Honda steed and prepared for the trip through the outback. The motorcycle had seen some strange moments but had undergone a design change, the result of an encounter with a telephone pole while my brother, Jeff, was riding it and attempting to escape the Reservoir police. They had towed the offending motorcycle and had required a payment for the towing and stowing charge to a civilian businessman before releasing the offending motorcycle; my father was really steamed about that and a later, and similar, event would extract his vengeance upon both the Reservoir police and the civilian businessman. The design change was a slightly bent handlebar. The strange events were being 'chased' and eventually stopped by the campus police for 'running a stop sign'; okay, I did, but there was no traffic or pedestrians, just a freaking campus police officer a hundred yards away. "Were you trying to run from me, boy?" the officer asked. Oh, no, officer, I enjoy being stopped for trivial shit and chit-chatting with the campus' finest. How's the wife and kids, by the way? I did find this school on the northeast part of town that was always devoid of humans in the late afternoon but had a really cool 'platform' in the back, which was a huge grass covered mound that rose up from the rest of the yard about eight feet and leveled for about an area of twenty-five yards by twenty-five yards. It was fantastic for jumping and I would go there often to do nothing but race to the lift and be propelled in the air for twenty, thirty or more yards, which was definitely cool, to jump completely past the platform and land on the ground beyond it and stop just before the fence would decapitate me. Jumping motorcycles was an addiction that I could easily identify with, but today the idea was riding back to the home front of Podunk and starting an early summer, coming a full month prior to its solstice. Hey, ya gotta love college timing.

Act Fourteen
Gravity

True to her word I received a letter from Saint Louis while still on campus from 'April'. The statement that 'April' was and was not her name became clear in the letter, although the return name and address tipped me off. April was her middle name and her given first name was Janet; her sister's middle name was Heather but her given first name was Juliet, usually just Julie. Professing her undying love for me and promising a night of unbridled passion if I would only drive to Saint Louis, actually Crestwood, and visit her, Janet also confessed that she was totally smitten by me. Well, uh, not really. She didn't write any of that. The message that she did convey was to call her and arrange to come and see her, if I really wanted to. I really wanted to, so I called her and had a nice conversation. She still liked to flirt from long distance but when it got too close – shit, you'd think I'd learn from some of this, doncha think?

We arranged a rendezvous the weekend after she finished school during the first week of June. For some reason, possibly motivated more from a safety perspective than anything else, Janet told me that Julie was interested in seeing me, too, and, for an equally strange reason, possibly motivated by a strong attraction to Julie, I liked that idea.

I drove down to Saint Louis and found her house easily by following her directions and consulting a map of the city. I parked on the street in front of the house but I never got to the front door before she walked out the door and came up to me and hugged me. She took me inside to meet the parents, who were quite nice, but when her father said that Janet had told them everything about me I couldn't help thinking, *I bet there's a couple things she left out.* Julie was there, too, and said 'Hi.' She was cool and I somehow expected that.

We all went to Busch Farms and Stables, where they keep the Clydesdales, and we drank free beer as long as we wanted. You can imagine why we all went there, except, of course, the parents, who did not go. When Janet and I had a moment alone, we made out a little, enough that I wanted to come back and see her again, and I did, two weekends later.

This time Janet, Julie and her sorority friends and her fraternity boyfriend and his fraternity friends and I went to a farm about two hours southwest of Saint Louis. We stayed there that day and night and drove back the next day. In my memory, it was a complete disaster, with more greek shit accompanied by seclusion and ignoring; Julie's fraternity boyfriend and his frat pals were pure assholes disguised as human beings; they really didn't want me around and excluded me from any and everything that they could. I think they thought they were better than me. Funny how everybody thinks they're better than you and how it all goes around like that; eventually, with everyone being better than everyone else, it becomes an exercise in sheer delusion. The two facts of which I am *dead* certain is: I am no better or worse than anyone else and we're all in this together. When one considers that no one has gotten out of here alive yet, with everyone thinking they're better than everyone else - that their 'tribe' is better than your 'tribe' - wouldn't it be the ultimate irony that the only time every one of us was finally united was at the simultaneous moment of our deaths?

Janet was even excluding me. I could sense that she was their greek recruit; she was going into that sorority thing and they were starting on her early. I sweated it and took it and drove back to my car and kissed her goodbye forever. Don't ask me where her letters are because I'm not completely sure, except that they must be in a landfill somewhere in the Midwest.

One other unexpected event occurred before the summer officially started; my brother, Jeff's appearance changed dramatically. I hadn't seen him in months, since I had only come back home once to get my damaged motorcycle and he was not around then. Out with his friends, Mom said. When I finally saw him at the end of April, he was considerably taller than me and his chubby little body had been replaced by a lean, muscular stature with a concave stomach. When I first saw him like that I wondered what happened to my *real* brother. Who is this guy? It was a legitimate question. This new guy *was* different. He was certainly more confident and had an even greater disposition toward anger and temper.

We sat in the den, the room we converted from the porch, just me and my brother. One of us said something and the verbal jousting was on. That quickly escalated to threats and challenges and 'let's take this outside,' so we did. *Okay, let's see what this new guy's got. I know the old guy was mostly talk.* We circled each other with our fists clenched and our arms in various defensive positions; I threw a punch that missed and the new guy countered with a right cross that caught me flush on the left cheek. Suddenly, I was standing before him with 'stars' in my eyes, but I quickly knew that the new guy would cream me like this, since I couldn't really see all that clearly and he could punch; instead, I rushed him and tackled him and we wrestled for five minutes until we both declared a draw. At least I could still outwrestle him, but that wouldn't cut it. I would have to make peace with the new brother and I did. Once, we had calmed down and were back inside, I complemented him on his punch and admitted that it stunned me. That seemed to please him and I also said I probably deserved more for all the stuff I had done to him in the past.

"That's all in the past," the new bro said. "Just remember, you can't do that stuff to me any more. I'll give you even more than that, if you do."

"I can see that," I said.

The dramatic change in his appearance came mostly from drugs, speed in particular. We also called it meth or methadrine or amphetamines. They were little white pills, not quite as big as aspirin. We used it at school for all-nighters. Jeff used it for the high, the energy boost, and its ability to suppress appetite. Thus, the weight loss occurred. Speed was not like crank today, although they're related, and people could get just as crazy and dependent on speed as they are with crank. It just took longer and required more of those little white pills. Speed definitely had its advantages; it sure made you feel energized and confident.

I needed a job. Dad had friends and those friends told me through Dad to go over to the Court of Claims; they were looking for some summer temporary help. I went over and talked to the office manager and he asked me when I could start. How about tomorrow? Be here at eight thirty. Will do. I had a job.

I spent the first half-day filling out employment forms, reading about policies and procedures as a state employee and a Court of Claims employee, in particular, and learning about the Court of Claims. What is the Court of Claims, one may ask? It's the judicial body where citizens can file for relief of grievances against almost any state agency or employee acting officially as a state employee; however, it's mostly for smaller redresses and a considerable number of claims filed with the Court of Claims come from prisoners seeking relief or redress. I spent the rest of the day completing small tasks, shuffling around stuff, re-organizing, mostly busy work.

Since the previous summer, the four of us, Kent, Kerry, Jeff – when available – and I, had changed quite a bit. We could get into any bar we wanted, well, everybody but Kerry. The other three all had full-time jobs, but I didn't. Okay, so I hadn't changed, but Kerry had some connections in the state job pool and Kent had landed at the Secretary of State's mailroom under the state complex. He worked across the street from where I worked but we didn't get to see each other very often during work hours; I was the office gofer in the Court of Claims, so I just did what they told me, including when to take a break and lunch. It was fun when I could get out of the office and hook up with Kent; he'd go on his rounds all through the underground complex connecting the state buildings in the blocks surrounding the Capitol building. You could start by entering the Centennial building from the street and come out of the State Office building two blocks away and never hit the ground floor until then. Until Kent started working there, I didn't even know the underground tunnels existed and I had lived in Podunk all my life.

The night life was heating up. Kent still had no steady girl, but he did alright, unless I was with him. Ya gotta figure that, right? He would go out almost every night and I wouldn't do that; hell, I couldn't afford to go out as often as I did, but I went anyway. When you're a young man, nightclubs and bars tend to attract women, too. For live music, we would go to a bar near where we both worked called the State Bar; I saw Cheryl from high school there once – her boyfriend was leading a band that played a cover of *I Just Wanna Make Love to You* from Foghat. That was the first time I could remember hearing that song and I would buy several Foghat albums later. Cheryl looked good, especially without her glasses – ah, the changes to someone's appearance through the magic of contact lenses, a relatively new development. She didn't pay any attention to me, however, didn't even say 'hi'. Kent and I pulled a stunt there one night, too. It was a contest to see how many women's butts one could pinch. I won the contest by pinching about forty butts; and that was forty *different* butts. Yeah, man, that place could be hopping. Only one caught me and I watched her walk through the opening all around the crowd to the other side, turn around when she looked at me and walk all the way back to tell me, "I know you did that." She was looking at me with mock severity. I said, "Me? No way." I smiled as I said it and she smiled back and walked back from where she had just come. I guess I had added a condition to the contest which Kent did not approve, because he came up to me and said, "You call that pinching? You're hardly doing anything." He waited a few moments for a particularly beautiful woman to walk by – oh, did I mention we were staked out in front of the women's restroom? – and, instead of pinching her ass, he literally grabbed her ass with his right hand and squeezed it so hard, she jumped off the floor. After her initial surprise, though, she looked at him smiling that little boy's devilish smile that Kent turned on at will and she smiled back briefly; still, modesty got the better of her after a moment and she slapped his arm. "Now, *that's* how you pinch a chick's ass," he informed me.

Jeff was there that night as he was most of the times we went to the State Bar or any of the other haunts we would frequent. We established a routine very quickly for monetary reasons more than any other; we would gather at Kent's house or some place, most likely out at Center Park on the reservoir, and split two six packs between the three of us before we went to any bar. It was better, and cheaper, to drink – and get drunk – at the price of store-bought beer than the prices they would charge at the bar. It also gave us the opportunity to smoke a little lieutenant before hitting the pussy trail. The rule was to *never* enter a bar before ten at night; if we managed to down the beer we had bought before then, we would buy some more and drink it in the car, quite often on the way to the bar. We were so religious about it, we would even sit in the parking lot of the bar and finish the beer while it was still cold. We drank fearlessly.

Our cast of characters was slowly expanding, including Fez and Ollie. Fez was a true character, a real African from Sierre Leone, but of Persian ancestry. I had no idea if he was Muslim, but if he was, he had certainly fallen away from its typical routines and strictures. He was our age and loved to drink and play with the ladies when he could. Fez was generous with his money even though he rarely had much of it but he also wasn't averse to asking strange requests, such as the night when Kent, Jeff and I decided we weren't going to the General Assembly, the disco open until 3 in the morning, but Fez really wanted to go there, by himself if he had to, which was exactly the case. His problem was his shirt, a tank top with no sleeves. You couldn't get in the General Assembly in a sleeveless shirt. I was wearing a shirt with sleeves, Fez deduced, and we were both about the same size, so let's swap shirts. Ah, what the hell, who can refuse a crazed, drunken Persian with wild hair? It was around that time, the middle of summer seventy-five, that Fez just kind of disappeared. Hey, Fez, if you're reading this, I still have your tank top. Got my shirt?

Ollie, on the other hand, was a regular, good ole white boy who liked to smoke cigarettes, pot, drink beer and alcohol and occasionally shoot heroin. Okay, so maybe that's not so regular or good, but he was an old white boy, considering he was nearly thirty and we were still in our teens. Oliver was his given name but no one ever called him that. He worked with Kent in the mailroom under the Centennial building. He was extremely laid back until some woman was unfortunate enough to stoke his interest, after which he would become boisterous, loud, and would laugh at anything he said, most of which wasn't very funny. About my height with blond hair to his shoulders but balding on top and a bit of a paunch, he was a likable bloke, easy going, although he really did think of himself as a ladies' man. We got a good laugh at that, because we knew the kind of ladies that he usually ended up with, although when we would remind him of that skank from last week he would often remind us about who we went home with, as if one skank is better than no skank. I dunno, you tell me. The one night that he shot heroin while he was out with us, he spent most of the time sitting at the table, his head bent back, his eyes usually closed or rolling slowly, his body slowly swaying from side to side. Sounds like fun, huh?

The General Assembly was the local disco bar. Yep, 1975 was the year disco took off and we could be found there most weekends, often both Friday and Saturday nights until three in the morning. Do that regularly and you're gonna pay some price for it. I paid for it by usually leaving rip-roaring drunk and it was a definite good thing that I almost never drove there. Kent always drove, first in his big, blue bomber, that Impala, or the new car he bought that summer, a compact tan Chysler. I always suspected that I might be getting rip-roaring drunk because of the constant strobe light activity, which is a misnomer since strobe lights are not constant by definition but you get the drift. It was probably due more to the fact that I was drinking from about eight at night until I couldn't keep my head off the table, whenever that was. Three in the morning? Shit, I rarely remember leaving the disco at any time I went there. At least I stood out, so that everybody could remember the short, skinny, white drunk. When one goes to a place with blacklights, one will usually wear some clothes that are solid white, since it turns a pleasing shade of violet, but not me. I found a solid red shirt – no pocket for my cigarettes, though – that I wore exclusively to the GA as we abbreviated it. Solid red in blacklight instantly stands out from everything else and I was exceedingly cool when I wore it. It even attracted the chicks, of whom I would dispatch with amazing consistency through my lack of 'pussy skills'. Of course, I had my own meeting with skankville at the GA one night when I took my Mom's car and parked next door in the heavy machinery business. I put the car right next to a yellow earth mover. I remember that much. Kent had to tell me about the skank part, which, as a blessing this time, I cannot remember, the memory having descended into the black hole of my brain and flushed for all time. Kent spared me certain details except to explain how embarrassing it was to sit at the same table with the two of us and watch me kissing a face full of pimples on top of a rather squatty body. Apparently, I came to my senses in a brief moment of lucidity when she went to the bathroom as I immediately got up, said goodbye and left. She was wandering around the disco looking for me at the same time that I was scraping the car along the yellow earth mover to leave a long yellow stripe on the car as a reminder of my stupidity from the night before. Yes, somehow I made it home without smashing into anything and I removed the stripe with car wax, leaving no visible scratches at all. There was the night when Jeff, Kent and I sat with three of the most beautiful girls in the building, which was a signal to get so drunk I couldn't keep my head off the table and Kent had to take me home while Jeff went home with all three girls; I should mention that they wanted to fuck us so bad that all three settled for Jeff and fucked him all night and the next morning. Sometimes it pays to have a third friend to attract three girls so that the third friend can't hold his liquor even though he knows he's gonna get fucked if he can just stay sober. What a loser! To say that Kent had a hard time forgiving me for that travesty is putting it mildly. On the other hand I provided Kent with a huge amount of humorous and unbelievable incidents, like the morning I woke up with blood smeared all over my pillow and my left thumb throbbing and torn. Another night at the GA with the usual outcome, Kent driving me home, though I was a bit belligerent. After pulling into our driveway, Kent watched me get out of his car and slam the door again and again without success. Following several attempts and noticing that the door was failing to close because I was holding myself up with my left hand inside the door rim, he calmly got out of his car, walked around his car, and pushed me away from the door, saying, "I'll get it. Go inside and get some sleep, little man." He closed the door and watched me stumble inside before he got back behind the wheel and drove home himself. To say that Kent had an easy time forgiving my belligerence and laughing outrageously every time he reminded me of that night is also putting it mildly. Honestly, I cannot say whether I had fun at the GA or not but I sure went there a shitload of times trying to have some.

  Kenny and Dave from the defunct Joint Session had moved into a house on Walnut Street together, living with Kenny's dad. Kenny called me one day, wondering what I was up to and inviting me over for beers and chat. I met his father as soon as I got there, a crusty old guy, muscular and just a tad taller than me, wearing a sleeveless white T-shirt, olive green work pants, a face badly in need of a shave, but a friendly old guy, nevertheless, with little to say but easy to smile. I had an idea about retrieving a notebook with poems or lyrics, since I always wrote them with music playing in my head, that I had loaned Kenny. When I mentioned the notebook, Kenny got it for me while I sat down and drank a beer. He set the notebook on a table and told me about the work he and Dave were producing for an album and how much my lyrics had taught him about rhyme and structure. After we had downed several more beers, we were standing a few feet from each other in the living room when Kenny lunged for me, kissing me on the lips and trying to hold my head steady against his face. After a few moments of struggling to free myself, I pushed him away, but had to hold him away as he came back at me again. Once I convinced him that I wasn't attracted to him or any other male like that, he finally calmed down and looked at me with genuine remorse. Kenny sensed, rightly so, that his sexual aggressiveness had just broken any bond we may have had; I looked at him with true contempt because I now could not trust him. I didn't care whether he was 'in love' with me or not; his actions were out of line. I grabbed the beer I had been drinking, gulped the remainder, set the can down on the table and left. I completely forgot about the notebook, which was fateful. Though I saw Kenny once more, he didn't have the notebook with him at the time. That notebook had some good stuff in it but its location is still a mystery to me.

  The first part of my adventures with the Court of Claims lasted but two or three weeks, consisting mostly of busy work and harmless flirting and gazing with the secretary, who, of course, was beautiful and married. My boss now developed the last part of my adventures. I was to work at the Archives building, less than a block away, and scour the closed cases in their vault and pitch all duplicate documents, of which I was assured would be considerable. I was to replace the files back in their original location as someone else would come over later and rearrange them to reclaim the space. We'll check up on you occasionally to see how you're progressing, he further assured me. Obviously, that was meant to convince me that, despite my further work being unsupervised and unobserved, I had better be showing up at the Archives building and doing it or else. After the first three days of no appearance by anyone, even the guards, into the bowels of the state archives where I was now consigned, I realized that no one was ever going to appear. I had merely to sign in and log the date but no time and sign out in the afternoon. I was literally on my own after that, free to wander around the underground tunnels of the Capitol complex with Kent running his mail rounds for hours at a time, free to hop in my car and drive around, once going out to the reservoir with a quart of beer and drinking it while watching the waves lap up to the shore of the park, free to just hold my head, hung over from the night before, unable to eat the eggs Mom made me that tasted like rubber.

I was also free to read the cases which I was opening to discover and toss the duplicate documents. I can recall two of the cases quite clearly, both involving prisoners. The first concerned a prisoner's claim for monetary reparations due to an injury he suffered while operating one of the huge items of equipment in the prison laundry. The court had ruled that the prisoner suffered his injury due to his own negligence. "Face it, ya poor white trash, ya just weren't payin' attention." It wasn't the case or the arguments or the outcome that caught my eye; it was the accompanying black and white photograph which I can still see as though I'm looking at it right now. Standing before the huge piece of equipment which caused the injury are two men. On the left is a guard holding a shotgun in his right hand and holding the prisoner's right hand up, bent at the elbow. On the right is the prisoner wearing a dark, short-sleeved shirt, his right arm held up by the guard, and halfway between the right elbow and shoulder is a semi-circle of flesh missing, thick globs of dark blood dripping from what used to be part of his arm. Both men wear expressions that are so matter-of-fact that it's almost chilling. I don't know if the prisoner was in shock but he looks like he's simply at a doctor's office undergoing a routine examination. "Don't fret about that three-inch chunk of my arm missing, doc. It'll grow back in a week. Happens all the time." The second was the story of the Tennessee Stick Man. His given name was in there, but I don't remember it and the case rarely used it to refer to him, even the man called himself the Tennessee Stick Man. The Tennessee Stick Man had served fifteen years in prison for armed robbery, only to be released when authorities finally arrested the real perpetrator, who, under questioning about his various crimes, confessed to this one. The court ruled that the black former prisoner, the Tennessee Stick Man, who was really from Tennessee and only in Illinois for a short time visiting family and friends, was wrongfully incarcerated and should be paid $75,000 for the inconvenience. Performing a quick calculation, that's five thousand dollars for every year that he sat his black ass in prison for a crime he did not commit. Apparently, according to the Court of Claims, the stick business is not a very lucrative endeavor.

My Court of Claims career came to a merciful end in mid-August. The boss left a message with the guards that I was to call the office when I got in. He said that I should wrap up what I was working on in the cage that day, clean up the cage and finish the rest of the week at the office. I managed to clear out three quarters of the archives space in the Claims cage and threw out about six barrels of duplicate legal documents. The boss was happy, the secretary was looking as good as ever, and I spent the last three days doing the occasional busy work and chatting. They sent my last paycheck to my house.

Terry, our baseball and football buddy, got married that summer. It was the first real wedding of a friend that I attended and I had no real idea what to wear. For some reason I was thinking this should be like the prom and I actually rented a sky blue tux and wore it. Of course I felt like an idiot in a tuxedo that didn't match the wedding party and all the other men were wearing a dress shirt, pants, a tie and jacket, though some weren't even wearing a jacket. The affair was unspectacular, although I'm sure Terry and his new wife would have a differing opinion, but I mean that in a good way; there were no altercations between the two families, no one got stumbling, bumbling drunk, either during the wedding or at the reception, as I have since seen all of that and more. Through Kent and Kerry, the newlyweds wanted me to know that they thought it was a very nice touch wearing a tuxedo to their wedding and they appreciated it and thought I looked very good. That made me feel better, because I got an enormous amount of ribbing from the guys, so much so that I almost ended up the stumbling, bumbling drunk at the reception. It helped that I was the only one that had smoke that day.

I saw an ad on the TV for a Kawasaki motorcycle, a 400 cc for less than a thousand bucks. I had to have it, so I went to the local Kawasaki dealer, newly opened on Stevenson Drive, and rode home on my new Cow after a half hour of 'negotiating'. I rode it everywhere, to work, to the park to drink and smoke, to softball practice with the guys' softball team, even when it rained and the water felt like BB pellets shot from a gun. The scene at the park had changed somewhat, since all of us were of drinking age, at least the ones with birthdays in the first half of the year with the others enjoying the lifting of this age restriction by virtue of being former classmates. The two Ricks, both attending ISU, were out there frequently and we would drink and smoke and throw the frisbee; Steve, who still worked at the grocery store, would show up and drink but not smoke and throw the frisbee or play softball; Kent and Jeff would be there frequently and Kerry occasionally. Kerry was seriously in the midst of wedding plans and preparations. That wedding was going to happen pretty darn quickly in the early fall; can you guess what might precipitate such a hasty nuptial?

Still, it was virtually impossible to bring the various camps together for sustained periods. The only thing that could actually bring them all together was inviting the lieutenant for a sit-down. For marijuana, everyone would put aside their considerable psychological and lifestyle differences, smoke a little and talk with each other civilly. Maybe that's what we need for every meeting between two or more hostile camps at all levels; imagine what might happen if the Palestinians, Jews and the other regional Arabs and interested parties all sat down together and passed around huge spliffs provided by the meeting's hosts, the Jamaican intermediary team. The Arabs might demand hashish but the Jamaican team would simply produce spliff after spliff in a never-ending spirit of ganja consumption. So many of these 'meetings' over the years have been called 'historical', yet have so little to show for it; you know a meeting hosted by spliff spinning Jamaicans will have no equal.

Charlie's move to Wichita allowed him to drive with a friend to Podunk for a few days and he taught me some new frisbee throws, so I got to practice them out at the park. My favorite was the 'thumb' toss, where I place my right thumb under and against the edge of the frisbee and flick my wrist with the disk tilted down on the far side, pushing my thumb against the edge as it leaves my grip. The thumb toss, when thrown properly, can be the most accurate and produce the fastest rotation of any throw that I've tried. It's fun to watch the recipient of my thumb toss try to grab it nonchalantly, only to have it spin and bounce off their hands; they'll shake their hand in slight pain because that disk came in fast and spinning hard. One of my coolest moves was to catch the frisbee between my legs, pull it up behind me, toss it in the air, grab it with my thumb under and against the edge of the disk, and flick it back to my frisbee partner, all in one fluid motion. I know there are people out there who can throw the thumb toss as well or better than me, but I haven't met them, yet; not even Charlie can throw it better than me.

With another state fair just a memory, it was time to get back to higher education, in all the connotations which 'higher' brings. Mark and I had discovered an exception to the university policy – if you look hard enough, there's damn near an exception to everything – requiring freshmen and sophomores to reside in a dormitory. I can't remember what it was, but we invoked it and found an apartment on the near west side of the campus, barely a block from the quad; that was definitely an improvement from Oglesby Hall, which was a good twenty minute walk and only if you moved fast; we were five minutes from most classes, certainly a procrastinator's dream location. The only negative aspect of the apartment was its location in the building, since our apartment was on the bottom floor of a three-floor dwelling; that wouldn't have been so negative if it wasn't for Thunderthighs, the woman who lived above us. Of course, it's true that Thunderthighs is not a very original term and probably used too frequently, but in her case it was deserved. She would have her boyfriend over quite often and neither Mark nor I could ever hear him move in that apartment above us, but as soon as she got up from anywhere, it was thump, thump, thump. I can only thank the unknown, hidden conservators of the universe for their nurturing of hard rock and stereo equipment improvements, because cranking music as loud as we could stand it was our only recourse to a Thunderthighs movement.

One of my first acts after I had registered for classes was to make my one and only visit to my college counselor. Maybe I should have recognized the probable outcome of my visit just by the strong resemblance of the counselor to my sociology professor, the aged sage who advised that her college degree would always be worth three times more than ours. Frankly, what did that have to do with sociology? I suppose it had something to do with a fragile perception of place in the world, some older woman at the age where contemplation of legacy - what one leaves to the world - is beginning to squeeze its grip on her. The question I have always formed when I think of her statement is this: will she always be worth three times more to the world than any of us, meaning me and all my peers? I can't answer it without exaggerating my true worth to the world, a defense mechanism to bolster self-esteem, which is exactly the motivation which prompted her to make her statement in the first place. Only the individuals, collectively and as a whole, scattered all over the world can vote on that question.

The outcome with the counselor was short and succinct. I wanted to transfer from the college of liberal arts to the college of business. What did I need to do? She pulled out her chart of minimum grade point averages needed to transfer from one college to another.

"Let's see," she began, scouring the chart. "To transfer from liberal arts to business you'll need a GPA of 4.4."

I felt my jaw drop but caught it before it hit the floor. "Four point four?" I asked in disbelief. I added, "If I had a four point four GPA in liberal arts I wouldn't *want* to transfer, since that's a solid A, not even an A minus!"

She pursed her lips as she said, "Sorry." Of course, she wasn't.

I left the counselor's office knowing one thing, if I wanted to stay at the University of Illinois I would be stuck in liberal arts. I also had three thoughts; I should have enrolled in general studies so I could transfer to a college I really wanted once I figured out what the hell I wanted to do, but I didn't know about that little loophole thanks to the whiz-bang counseling services provided by my high school; it was easier to get into the college you wanted if you were just enrolling at the university than it was to transfer, meaning they valued more and more bodies than the ones they already had, which was stupid, in my opinion; and I was stung, once again, by the bite of my peers, the absolutely enormous numbers of baby boomers. Yes, friends, I was born too early and too late, and my ass was beginning to hurt from all the bites.

At this point in my life I was losing any sensitivity I had developed and should have held on to about college studies, instead concluding that this was simply a clever descent into Dante's Inferno. It must be mere coincidence, then, that the number of colleges at the big U were the same as the 'rooms' enumerated in the Inferno. I would believe that if I didn't know that there is no such thing as a coincidence, only that it lacks a reason yet discovered or fully understood. Thus, I found myself in Purgatory with a diminishing capacity to remember what I was supposed to be learning and a similar lack of caring about it, too. I enrolled in courses that I could take based on my major and meeting or exceeding the minimum number of 'hours' to remain a full-time student, but I can only recall calculus and the accounting introductory courses. The others have been mercifully flushed down my memory's toilet in a curious exercise of personal waste.

Mark and I were getting along as best we could. We had some difficulty in keeping the apartment from resembling a toxic waste dump from time to time – especially keeping the dirty dishes from overtaking the sink – but we managed, that is, as long as Steve was away. Unfortunately, he couldn't stay away and Mark slowly spent more time with him as the semester progressed. Steve was a friend of Mark's brother, originally, and the two had hooked up a few times when we were at Oglesby Hall, but Steve started showing up at our door, first on a weekly basis, meaning every weekend, followed by visits more often. Steve was the type of person who liked what he liked, even if he couldn't explain why, which was the usual result, and he liked Mark and didn't like me. He would rarely, if ever, invite both of us out; it would just be the two of them. Steve was what I call an 'exclusive' person; if he didn't like you, you were excluded. There was nothing you could do about it; he was never going to like you because you were going to constantly be excluded from any activities where your 'inclusion' would lead him to like you. This is why I claim that 'exclusive' people live lives of self-reinforcement; if they are constantly challenged, their self-important tiny world crumbles around them. They tend to cluster with like-minded 'exclusive' people; that way they can all reinforce each other while they collectively stagnate. He was the embodiment of contradiction, too. Here was a guy who was a reasonably successful ladies' man, because he was quite attractive with his medium length blond hair, rugged good looks and stout, muscular frame combined with above average height. The girls were attracted to him, though he treated most like crap. Yet, he rarely engaged in any sports activities for a very good reason. You would go out to an open field and watch this hunk of a man throw the football like a girl and catch it like a klutz. I shit you not.

For most of the semester, the Cow faithfully stood just outside the apartment, viewable from the large window in the kitchen/living room where eye level was level with the grounds. I bought a cover for the motorcycle to protect against the elements, but I rarely rode it anywhere, and I never let Mark ride it either, except for one time. We were invited by my father for a weekend in early October to come down to Podunk and play golf on Sunday with him and another member friend. Mark had heard about the country club's golf course and was pretty excited to go, so we drove down in separate vehicles; Mark drove his big bomber of a car and I rode the Cow. Mark did pretty well on the course that Sunday and I performed my usual inconsistent hacking. Mark wanted to ride the Cow back to Champaign so I let him and watched him tool off as fast as he could go; he was back in the apartment a half-hour before I arrived. It kind of pissed me off that he speeded on my bike and without a motorcycle license. No more riding my bike for you, big fella.

Living in the apartment made me develop a growing sense of isolation. Mark and I did less and less together, even though we both could go to bars and drink whenever we wanted; that option required money and we had less and less of that, too. Occasionally, we would get bored or pull all-nighters and need an outlet to reduce the effects of the speeders – those little white pills, remember? – and go across the street to one of the scattered all-night study buildings with vending machines, pinball machines and plenty of seating. We would play one of the pinball machines, which I think was called *Royal Flush*, with thirteen targets scattered around it, one for every card denomination, bumpers and tilt-capability galore. Mark was especially good at it but I had my moments, too; once we drove it up to twenty free games while playing for about two hours early in the morning – meaning sometime after midnight – and we sold the games to a guy for a buck, doubling our fifty-cent investment; we needed to actually do some studying at some point during the night. The isolation grew from seeing people from the previous year very infrequently coupled with meeting no one of any real interest; after I would walk to Oglesby Hall and none of the dorm rats from the year before were there, I just didn't bother going there unless I was invited, which was just as infrequent. Some of the guys had already joined the frat, but since I was virtually persona non grata in the greek world, I never went there. I didn't meet any girls of interest; maybe it was me, but it just seemed that all the attractive ones had dropped out, transferred or died. It was a real chore going to school now – looks like it's time to spin a doobie. Excuse me.

Thanksgiving came and went and with it my trip back to Podunk came and went. Certainly, during one of those nights home I went out with the boys and ripped it. Ho-hum. I would get excited at the prospect only to have it dissipate during the event. Drinking should have been getting old, but it was increasingly the best method for pushing away, briefly, the sense of isolation slowly overtaking me. Marijuana was just making me think more – that was not what I needed. I was thinking too much, I think. Fortunately, I was never doing the driving; I was being shepherded around like a privileged drunk, except I was rapidly depleting what monetary resources I had saved.

Back at school I buckled down as best I could to finish with a flare. The flare had practically died out for calculus; I had skipped classes too often in a course which was totally unforgiving. I was lost in that class with no hope of grasping much of anything. I sacrificed it to concentrate on the other courses, crammed through the finals, packed up my necessities and left the collegiate environs for the few weeks of holiday and a new year.

Mom and Dad had a surprise for Jeff and me. There was some type of convention or function taking place for a few days before Christmas in New Orleans – accounting, shrine, united way? We had no idea and didn't care – so we could go with them and spend a week in New Orleans through Christmas. Let's go to the birthplace of jazz, the French quarter, Bourbon Street, great food, and naked women on display as you pass by or conveniently when a door opens just as you get to it. Wait! Let me check my schedule as I may have more important things to do like think and drink too much. Oh, well, looky here, I just happen to have a big hole in my schedule during that very week. Jeff says he's going? Cool! He said he just scored some really fine weed. Just kidding, Mom. You know I don't smoke that stuff; I only smoke this stuff, these Merit cigarettes, because I deserve them, so long as I pay for them in advance.

We arranged our luggage in the huge trunk of the Buick Electra, took our places in the vast interior, turned on the cruise control as we left early in the morning four days before Christmas and arrived in New Orleans before the day was over. It was after nine at night so we had room service for dinner and prepared to wake up the next morning in the big city smack in the heart of Cajun country.

We stayed at a motel right in the French quarter, where most of the jazz nightclubs and strip joints were located. It was a good thing that I didn't really mind jazz or women stripping, although one had to be twenty-one years of age to actually enter most of these fine establishments. That was little deterrent, however. Jeff and I would cruise up and down the streets, side streets, everywhere, and hear plenty of jazz and other forms of music and see plenty of female flesh and never have to pay a dime. In 1975, there were still some things that were free. It just depended on how drunk, friendly, desperate, or benevolent the doorman at the strip joint was. As for the music, walls were simply ineffective. They wailed, man!

Despite the eye-opening and ear-splitting experience New Orleans was at that time, there truly is very little remembrance to be conveyed. There was the breakfast at a five-star restaurant which served eggs benedict that one could die for. There was the twenty-fifth day of December, much like the twenty-fourth before and the twenty-sixth which followed. There was the night Jeff and I ventured to a small square in the quarter, met some guys, one of whom had a reefer ready for consumption. It wasn't that good, so Jeff proceeded to roll one of our own, which duly impressed all in attendance; until a local constable wandered into the vicinity and completely freaked our smoking buddies, who scattered immediately, and even spooked Jeff, to be honest. We both fired up a cigarette and I calmly greeted the approaching representative of New Orleans' finest, who greeted me just as calmly. He asked our ages and we accommodated him, while I added that we were down from Illinois with our parents staying at the Holiday Inn on vacation and had decided to take a stroll. He advised us to be careful, looked us up and down one more time, and, failing to spot the bag of lieutenant in my pocket due to an inability to conjure x-ray vision, he walked away just as he had arrived. A couple days later we were back on the road, taking our time and resting for the night in Memphis. We were up the next morning early and Dad drove only a short while to breakfast. After filling our stomachs, he gave me the keys and I drove the rest of the distance to our driveway in Podunk, arriving about one in the afternoon.

Barely a half-hour later I sat with Kent in his house, a beer in our hands. No one else was home at his house and we made good use of it, smoking and telling tall tales and drinking beer after beer. The day before a storm had dropped a significant layer of freezing rain until the temperature had dropped sufficiently to turn the rain to snow and keep the layer underneath frozen. That storm was the most pressing reason why we stopped in Memphis instead of driving all the way through, but I joked with Kent that a few days before we were cruising around the French Quarter of New Orleans gazing at naked pussy in short sleeves. Shit, who would want to come back to this? Kent always had a way of dispelling such talk from me. Lookin' is one thing and fuckin' is another, little man, he said. That would put me in my place.

We drank all afternoon, not really pounding them down, just sucking on them at a slow and steady pace. I called home to see when Mom had dinner planned and left Kent to fend for himself about six thirty. Staying just long enough to eat, answer questions as to where I might be that night, receive the greater than usual admonishment to be careful because of the road conditions, I was back in Mom's relatively new Opel Manta, a silver beauty with black leather interior and a stick with considerable power. It was fun to drive but I didn't abuse it or try to come up with excuses so that I could drive it as often as possible; I had two vehicles of my own, though both were the two-wheeled variety. Still, that was my decision to buy them and I didn't feel comfortable asking to drive the Opel too much. However, tonight was different. We'd been out of town for a week and I hadn't seen any of my buds since then and Mom wasn't going anywhere. Besides, they knew that Kent always drove when we went out to bars and I didn't lie about our aim; we were going to hit a joint or two and party and try to meet some babes. Well, I left out the babes part but I think they knew anyway.

Back at Kent's house, we cracked open two more beers and got started. We were both a little shy money-wise so we dismissed the GA completely. I think we were both in need of just chilling out, wearing regular clothes and listening to rock music, not disco. We thought of and also dismissed some other places, but finally decided to check out Romie's, a fairly small, comfortable place with plenty of seating, no dance floor but a decent sound system that played strictly rock n roll. It had been a while since we'd been there, mostly because it wasn't really known as a place to score chicks, but we thought it would be a good change of pace. Hell, we'd been there before when it was cooking; maybe two days before New Years Eve the babes might accidentally stumble into the place.

The magic hour arrived, which was always ten at night, and we grabbed our gear, another beer for the drive, and walked out, carefully since it was quite slippery, to Kent's car. As he backed down the steep but short drive to the road, he couldn't slow the car and it crossed the street, smacking the car that was usually parked directly across from his drive. We both got out and surveyed the damage, which was non-existent to Kent's car but a good sized dent was evident on the neighbor's car. Kent hadn't been out in two days and he suggested that we should take my Mom's car; his reasoning was that, if the neighbor thought he hadn't driven his car at all over that time, it wasn't Kent that had hit that car. I decided that was okay, Kent asked if I was okay to drive, and I replied with a bit of anger that I was. He pulled back up his drive, parked the car, and hopped in the Opel, commenting that it was a really nice ride. We drank our beers with an eye out for the police and pulled into Romie's parking lot without incident.

There seemed to be more of a college crowd, the appearance being the tip-off, since most college boys and girls were a little less scruffy than the rest. It felt pretty good to me, though Kent wasn't too thrilled but we grabbed an open table and signaled the waitress. Soon, we were downing beer from the pitcher she brought and Kent paid for. The pussy looked good and I was feeling unusually talkative, much less introverted. After a while some girls came in and grabbed the table next to us. Kent tried to make small talk but they didn't pay him much mind; however, one of them was this full-bodied babe about five feet four inches with long, straight blond hair and a very attractive face. She smiled at me. I smiled back, introduced myself and asked what school she went to. She said that maybe she didn't go to school so how could I be so certain? I said that I read minds and bet her that she went to Illinois State. Granted, I was just guessing, but I was going to run with it either way. Her eyes suddenly got wide as she asked me how I knew that. I reminded her that I read minds and added that she should be careful what she thinks about me or I'll take advantage of it. She let out a little laugh but a much bigger smile filled her attractive face and I was on and could not be stopped. Kent just sat next to me in stunned amazement, which soon became outright disbelief when I suggested to her and her friends, since we were all talking to each other anyway, to come join us at our table and they did.

The three girls were all attractive, but I really liked the blond and talked to her more than the others, though I didn't ignore any of them. Her name was Carolyn and she had a great laugh, too, because I had everyone laughing and having a good time almost until closing time. Kent was even in a good mood, despite his dislike of college women. When the girls said they had to leave, Kent and I decided it was time to go, too. We finished our beers and Kent asked me if I was okay to drive as I slipped on my leather flight jacket; smugly, and with a slight slur, I brushed his question aside. Of course, I'm okay to drive. Let's go. We walked out to the Opel and climbed in. I pulled out of the parking lot and turned in the opposite direction than Kent expected. When he asked what I was doing, I told him I was going to head out to the interstate, which was under construction and intersected with Chatham Road at a stoplight. He thought that was stupid but I said we could get home faster than going through the city streets and all the stoplights. I made the left turn at Chatham Road and started to speed up, since this section was more rural and the speed limit was higher. When the road converged from well-marked lanes to a standard two-lane road and grew narrower, I had already passed out. The Opel, though, faithfully kept on at forty-five miles per hour, into the ditch where the road had narrowed and right on to the first drive across the ditch to a business. When the Opel hit the drive, the force buckled the doors open; neither Kent nor I wore a seat belt so we were immediately ejected from the car. Kent headed toward the rocks and snow on the side of the road and I went flying in the opposite direction. Gravity eventually reclaimed its hold and, just like any tumble one takes in life, there were consequences to pay.

Act Fifteen
The Great Depression

I came crashing down on the road, twisting slightly from left to right. There was no tuck and roll this time. I was airborne with my eyes closed, the absolute worst kind of pilot. I *was* prepared, however, since I was sensibly wearing my flight jacket. How could I have known, barely a year before, that I would be taking an unscheduled flight sometime in the near future and I must have maximum protection should my flight prove faulty, so I bought this flight jacket from the local armed forces surplus store? I *couldn't* know, it's that simple. I just looked cool wearing it.

Now I wore it crumpled and twisted and bleeding and torn in the middle of a tar and gravel road, dark and barren from the revolting elements, with the many resting for the revelry they hoped to enjoy two nights later on New Years Eve. Lying there with little sign of life, my body oozed the only sign I could give, the warmth of the red liquid slowly flowing through the lacerated openings of my exposed body; and there could have been more openings, but that leather flight jacket had performed its admirable job well. For all its reaches, not a single injury would be discovered. It would forever display the scrapes where it had collided with the road behind the right shoulder–the force of that collision snapping my collar bone–but it nevertheless had protected my fragile body. All my other injuries lay outside its scope. And the sign of life dripped irrepressibly, staining the tar that had already tattooed my right hip.

Some weary traveler, some poor soul, happened upon the gruesome scene later, how much later I don't know. Kent was still unconscious lying in the ditch, his fall somewhat cushioned by the snow still covering the ground and rocks. The traveler may have checked our condition, may have run to a house close by, may have jumped into the car and driven hurriedly to the only open establishment back toward town.

The poor soul may have been someone from the area who, miraculously, had heard a noise out on the main road and ventured into the freezing cold to investigate. I may never know, but that weary traveler, that poor soul, began the series of dispatches and calls that resulted, over an interminable time frame, in my pointless rescue. Since so much time had elapsed, due to the weather, the time of the accident, the distance for the police to cover, the distance to the scene and to the hospital for the ambulance to cover, it did seem pointless. The sign of life was weak at best and it was dripping incessantly.

Kent awoke, groggy and still quite drunk, with the wailing sirens of the State Police cruisers as they approached in a frenzy. The first troopers arrived to secure the scene and to check the conditions of the hapless victims. Kent ventured into the road and toward the troopers, and the biggest, all six feet and seven inches of authority, restrained him. He looked at my crumpled, twisted, bleeding body on the road and totally freaked, screaming at the trooper that they need to do something, anything. The trooper warned him several times to calm down but Kent would have none of that, so the trooper laid him out with one punch against the Opel Manta, resting comfortably on its side against a telephone pole. Kent slid down along the car to settle on his butt and quietly sat there uncomplaining until the ambulance arrived, a time period he believed seemed forever. It could have been just ten minutes, or twenty minutes, or a half-hour, or even an hour. How would Kent know without a watch and no real desire to mark time? He was still inebriated and now he was hurting from a straight right delivered by a man bigger than he was who obviously knew what he was doing. All he could think about was the apparently lifeless body of his friend scattered on a lonely road and surrounded by uniformed men who would do nothing but watch.

The live version of Commander Cody and the Lost Planet Airmen's tune called *Hot Rod Lincoln* ends with the hero wrecking his car and being investigated by the po-lice; they missed the six tons of hash in the back seat and the ten illegal Mexican immigrants he was smuggling into the country, among other assorted sundry, typical seventies items any self-respecting stoner would carry. In my case, the po-lice did *not* miss the half-bag of leaf now scattered all over the interior of the totaled Manta and they reasonably assumed that I was drunk since they could easily smell the alcohol on Kent's breath with little effort. As the ambulance whisked me away in its futile attempt to save my worthless existence, they had to charge me with something, because one has to have fractured *some* law to end up with a totaled vehicle in a ditch and the driver's body laid out in the road. The state trooper responsible for filing charges wrote me a ticket for illegal lane usage, an infraction with the uncontested outcome of a twenty dollar fine. They also presented my father with a bill of eighty dollars to replace the sign the Manta destroyed on its path toward the telephone pole. If the po-lice *hadn't* missed all that, why didn't they charge me with it? As Kent so aptly put it later, "They were reluctant to charge you with anything, because it meant paperwork and follow-up, so what was the point? We all thought you were dead."

I suppose that everyone worked frantically. "He has a pulse! His breathing is slowed but he's still alive!" I'm sure you've seen all the paramedics shows and movies and they probably did that and maybe more. The ambulance rushed me to the hospital–the unCatholic one, by the way–and the emergency personnel were at the ready and I was whisked into the operating room and prepped and a miraculous thing occurred. Normally, they just cut away your clothes; they neither have the time nor the inclination to save your designer wardrobe. Yet, they delicately, fastidiously and gently removed my leather jacket. Perhaps it was a gesture of respect, though I assume that I'll never know. In any event, they set that leather jacket aside as though it were the blessed robe of King Solomon and let no further harm come to it.

I was prepped, stabilized, sewn back together and pumped full of morphine. Within hours my condition was so improved that they moved me out of the intensive care unit and into a private room where I could recuperate solo. The morphine was great. It's little wonder that opium derivatives are considered narcotics. Troubles? Shit, I had none. Just keep dripping that morphine into me, okay?

There was one bit of trouble brewing, however. The brain bashing coupled with the heavy morphine dosage I had just endured were beginning to scramble my memories. Names to faces, even some faces, events, they were all vacating the gray matter between my ears as though to say, "You know, Non, you're bent on such a thorough self-destruction, we're gonna find a new home while we still have time." Some memories remained, though. Ah, loyalty is instilled in some of the most unexpected places, so why do I remember *him* and not *her*? I liked her. I could do without him.

I awoke some time in the late afternoon the following day, plastic tubes descending from a portable arm above me and slowly, drip, drip, dripping into a vein of my left arm. Everything was white and bright, I was alone, and I thought, *Great! Now I'm on an alien spacecraft where they're going to perform probing experiments, only to discover how horrid an example of humanity I truly am and sail me above Lake Michigan where they will hover and slowly lower me into the water without even the benefit of a raft. I'll bet the water will be freezing. Hello hypothermia.*

  A woman in a simple white dress down to her knees soon entered and if she was an alien this next part might not be so bad after all. "You're awake," she said. "Good. We were all worried about you when they brought you in last night."

  Ah! So she's a nurse, I'm in a hospital lying in a hospital bed and Kent and I must have had some terrible accident. I wonder how Kent is faring. I dared not ask, though. I didn't want to hear bad news. "What's on TV?" I inquired. "Anything worth watching?"

  "Aren't you hungry?" she asked. "Do you have an appetite?"

  "Sure," I replied, "but it's on vacation. I think it's in Texas, today."

  She laughed. What a relief! At least the mental meltdown currently taking place in random areas of my brain was skirting around the various pockets of humor I had stored over the years. I needed that humor. If you've paid attention so far, you're in complete agreement. That's about all I had.

  She checked the liquid in the bottle and the tubes and my arm. She tucked up the sheets under my neck and smiled. "So, you're not hungry?" she asked again. "It's no trouble. I can get you something from lunch right now." She proceeded to tell me what was on the lunch menu, which did not convince my appetite to return from Texas any time soon.

  "Orange juice would be nice," I replied, politely. "Thank you."

  She reached for the TV remote on the stand next to the bed. Looking sweetly down on me, she said, "What do you like to watch?"

  "Anything but doctor shows," I replied, looking back at her sweetly, and sensing that my appearance was ghastly. "I don't think I'm in the mood."

  "It's still early in the afternoon," she advised, still looking sweetly down on me, and I was thinking, *man, she has got to have one hell of a stomach to look at me like that*. She added, "I know there's soap operas on." She raised her eyebrows in anticipation.

  "Yeah," I agreed, now suddenly feeling uncomfortable about my expected appearance, "backstabbing, lying and cheating will make me feel better."

  "Which ones do you like?"

  "Pick one," I told her. "They've all got it in abundance."

  She turned on the TV and tuned it to a soap opera, asked if the sound was alright and I replied that it was, she said she would be back soon with orange juice, and, mercifully like a nurse should be, she left and I was alone again. If I wasn't in such excruciating pain, I would have gotten up to view my horrid appearance, but I couldn't even sit up without tremendous effort combined with a constant throbbing sensation from the various parts of my torn and bruised body. I wondered how Kent was doing. I didn't want to hear that he was dead.

Some minutes later, the nurse opened the door and I heard her talking to someone outside the room. After a few moments of back and forth between the nurse and voices that I thought I recognized, my parents stepped into the room, slowly, apprehensively. They stood in the room for a few seconds taking in the scene, looking at me and trying to avoid an obvious expression of shock which I would be able to ascertain. Mr. DeScript moved to the chair at the end of the bed, sat down and smiled at his battered son magnanimously. Mrs. DeScript moved past the bed to the window, smiling once very weakly at her son, and gazed out the window, ignoring the other chair between the window and the bed.

"So," Dad began, wearing that smile that tells you this isn't all that funny, "I hear you had quite an adventure."

"I had morphine for breakfast," I said, smiling back. "Bet you can't get that at a five-star hotel."

"No," he replied, "and if you could it wouldn't be printed on the menu."

I smiled again. At least dear old Dad could still follow my twisted imagination. Mom could only look out the window.

There was a long pause when no one said anything. We all glanced about, focusing on some inanimate object, gathering the resolve to take the conversation in a new direction. Mom slowly turned around, looking at me and forcing a prolonged smile, and asked, "Are they taking good care of you?"

Immediately, we all heard a knock on the door and Dad responded, "Come in."

Instantly, the door opened and the nurse carried my glass of orange juice to the table next to the bed and set it down. "Can I get you anything else?" the nurse asked, looking down at me sweetly.

"Not right now," I replied, smiling sweetly, "but you'll be back to check on me regularly, won't you?"

"Of course," she replied, her smile widening.

In my best pick-up voice, I said, "See you then."

She turned to glance at Mr. and Mrs. DeScript and asked, "Would you like anything?"

"No thank you," was Dad's quick response.

The nurse stepped to the door, stating that she would leave us alone, opened the door and exited hurriedly. I looked at Dad, then Mom, smiling, and each returned my smile.

Still looking at Mom, I said, "I get room service." I looked over at the door leading into the room, where the closet was located on one side and the bathroom was located on the other. "I haven't checked to see if the room has a jacuzzi, but I think I can get a sponge bath if I ask." I glanced back at Mom and she forced a slight chuckle.

If you think the rest of the conversation followed the same lines as above, you'd be wrong. Sure, it's virtually impossible for me to turn off the jester, so there was more of that, but there was talk about my health, how concerned they were and how much they hated getting the call every parent dreads late at night. There was even talk about the vehicle, but I let it go because I couldn't fathom why they would care about Kent's car. In fact, I didn't completely understand why they had seen or wanted to see the condition of his car. It was Kent's car; we went out in Kent's car, like we always did, right? That's what I thought and what I thought they thought. I was beginning to experience the cruelest injury from the accident; parts of my memory, and the brain cells used to hold it, were destroyed. That was never coming back. The worst thing about it was that I didn't even know it, yet.

The end of the conversation was signaled by a comment that I should get some more rest. They said some more platitudes, displayed their concern and courage, and left. Almost immediately, I went back to sleep, which was difficult to do with the constant throbbing in my right shoulder. You experience that throbbing when you break your clavicle on the right side. That's your collar bone, for the medical-terminolgy-challenged among you.

When I awoke later that night, I had a lot more energy and a lot less pain. I managed to get out of the bed, unhook the cable from the stand dripping into my left arm, and make it to the bathroom to relieve myself. Yep, I took a long, hard look at the face staring back in the mirror. Non DeScript's hair was wild, stringy, unkempt and particularly unattractive; his face was patched, sewn, clipped together, bruised and blue. Hardly non-descript. As I looked at the image in the glass, I didn't seem to have any feeling at all about it. Another day, another obstacle, another ugly truth revealed. It didn't even matter to me whether my fellow cousins anywhere else on the planet had similar experiences or whether this was uniquely mine. I just didn't care at the moment, and when I was done with my bathroom exercise, I trudged back to the bed, hooked up my drip cable and slept through the night and into New Year's Eve day.

When a different nurse came to check on me in the morning, I was already awake, though I was hardly active. I was just daydreaming about nothing significant and becoming more self-conscious about my appearance. She tried to cheer me up, so I nodded and glanced in the opposite direction. She asked if I wanted breakfast and I wondered if I already had consumed my morning morphine allotment, but I was hungry now, so I said I would try and eat some eggs, toast, and whatever else. She didn't return for quite some time, but I ate most of what she brought me. There wasn't any point in starving to death now.

A doctor came in later that morning to check on my recovery and filled me in on all my injuries, all of which I had deduced, anyway. He asked me if I remembered what happened. For some reason, the jester remained in hiding and I told him that I couldn't remember anything.

"Well, apparently," the doctor began, "you were thrown out of your car and landed on the road and took a pretty good beating. You had lost a lot of blood and when they brought you in, your initial assessment was less than fifty-fifty. You're lucky. What do you think kept you alive?"

I had already checked the closet and the only item in it was the leather jacket dangling from a hanger. I pointed to the closet and replied, "That leather jacket in the closet."

The doctor glanced over at the closet knowingly and nodded. "Normally," he said, dryly, "we cut off clothes from accident victims, but leather's tough to cut, and based on your injuries, everyone thought it was worth saving." He paused and looked down at me from the foot of the bed. "Why were you wearing it?" he asked.

"It was cold that night," I replied, nonchalantly. He asked a few more medical questions and left, so the moral of this exchange is: if you're considering being thrown out of a moving vehicle at forty-five miles per hour, and you want to survive, invest in a thick leather jacket.

That afternoon I had two sets of visitors drop in to my recovery room. The family made an appearance right after lunch and stayed for about an hour. A couple hours later Kent and Kerry walked in to see how I was doing, how I looked, how I felt. Kerry seemed to be his usual smiling, optimistic, easy-going self, but Kent's expressions and demeanor revealed to me a sense of apprehension, even dread, that went unexplained. His display was something I had rarely witnessed and I was silently concerned when they left.

Before they left, I asked Kent what happened to his car. Both looked at each other conspiratorially and neither answered the question. I was still so wasted that I didn't insist on an answer and just let it go.

I spent New Years' Eve in a hospital bed sound asleep. Happy

New Year! Welcome to 1976.

One of the first acts performed for me in 1976 was the removal of my IV butler. The nurse left the connector in my left arm "as a precaution, in case you need it later." That case would be, for example, if I should take a turn for the worse and be, once again, tossed into the grip of deathly throes. Ye of little faith. C'mon! Go for it!

The family stopped by, providing some company and chit-chat. I could manage to clean myself by then, so I got the usual compliments about how good I was looking. Skipping a couple days of showers or baths has a tendency to reflect poorly on one's appearance. Once you take that plunge, everyone notices how good you look.

I also possessed a bit more mental clarity. The morphine was wearing off. However, the morphine had succeeded in conquering my nicotine addiction. I had lost my normal desire to get out of my bed, snag my pack of cigarettes and step outside to light up. I wasn't even searching with safe regularity for them.

Kent dropped in that afternoon, alone, squeezing in a little time in his typical holiday revelries to try to cheer me up and clear me up at the same time. I asked again about his car and he knew at this point that I possessed most of my mental faculties and my analytical abilities had been reasonably restored. He firmly advised me that his car had only left his driveway to smack into the car parked across the street, so we had taken Mom's car and that I was driving.

I recall that my response was something like, "Why in the fuck did we do that?"

Kent's response was to spend the next half-hour revealing to me the whole sordid story of that night, sometimes beginning with, "Do you remember...?" Of course, I never did remember and still don't to this day.

When he was done, I asked, "So, that blonde babe was really sweet on me?"

"Gave you her phone number at college and wanted you to call her if you came to town," was Kent's reply.

"Well, then," I replied, "that explains the piece of paper in my jacket with the name 'Carloyn' and a phone number."

"You're pretty sharp, there, Einstein," Kent said. "Figured that out all by yourself."

"I was going to call that number, anyway," I insisted. "I would say something like, 'I'm conducting a survey to piece together my shattered existence and was wondering if you could tell me why I have a sliver of paper with your name and phone number in my jacket?"

"And she might answer," Kent followed the logic, "'Is that how you meet girls? Get so drunk that you total your car driving home and visit the hospital's emergency room?'"

"Only the special ones," I countered.

"Good luck, slick," Kent said, looking away.

Over the next three days I was visited daily by the physician in residence, checking my progress and the wounds which needed mending. Nurses changed the dressing on my right hip, the only exposed area of my body below my waist which sustained any damage, where my leather jacket stopped. It was tinged blue and would eventually leave two faint blue stripes about an inch and a half in length, a tattoo of Chatham Road tar. I also got up and out of my room on occasion, wandering around the hospital to just limber up. Closer and closer to the end of those three days, the prognosis of hospital discharge grew, until finally the nurses all agreed that once the physician in residence checked me, they would allow me to leave. My parents waited, the physician arrived, checked my chart, asked some basic questions and signed off on my discharge. Out I went, back into the real world with the hospital's personal parting gift, my very own sling. "It will keep your right arm from moving around too much while your collarbone fuses back together," was the advice I was given by several medical persons. I had to wear it before they would roll me out of the hospital, so I put on my parting gift to heal the only bone I had ever broken, the one that snapped after my right shoulder slammed into the pavement, milliseconds after my face did so.

While I convalesced at the homestead for the next couple weeks, I occasionally ventured to Kent's house for a bit of smoke and drink. Usually, he would drive to my house and pick me up; sometimes, Kerry and Jeff would make it, sometimes not. The one consistent act was that I would never go out with any of them, partly to honor my parents' concerns, but mostly because I myself was concerned. Had I learned any lesson at all? I wasn't too certain.

When the sealed envelope from the big U arrived, I opened it and read the news that I had already been expecting. My grade point average was getting better and I had settled into a consistent B average, though outside my own major and college at the big U. I knew I had to keep my grades up for my transfer to complete to State and I wasn't going to jeopardize that. It was what I expected, nothing more, nothing less. I felt no sense of relief. I had bigger issues to deal with. It was just one less issue.

With Dad hot and heavy into the accounting season, he did take some time off during one day on a weekend to drive me behind the local Buick-Opel dealership to show me the battered and beaten remains of the silver and black Opel Manta I had driven that fateful night. It was destroyed beyond any hope of repair, that's for sure. The doors were crumpled and the top and sides were smashed and twisted. It was a wreck. I couldn't say anything. I could only think that the fine automobile sitting there in a mangled heap was no comparison to the replacement the parents had since purchased. A red and white Manta with automatic transmission – some 'slightly used' model – was no substitute. I tried not to think about any of it. I'm not really sure what Dad wanted to accomplish. It was done, over; there was no undo button. Sorry, this is life; that other stuff is called delusion. You can live in whichever house you want, but if your house eventually falls down on top of you, which house do you think you were living in? Unless, of course, you don't keep it up. Then, you're just plain stupid. You should live on the street under a cardboard box. That requires little, if any, upkeep, with one extra bonus: cardboard boxes are easily replaceable. Stick houses are not.

With the old man lost in the profit/loss world of others' business endeavors and my sole means of transportation locked – so to speak – outside my apartment in Champaign, it fell to little bro to run me up to the big U for the start of spring semester, which, of course, starts in the dead of winter. Jeff dutifully drove me up in my still battered condition, helped haul my shit into the apartment and said a quick goodbye. He wasn't staying. It was just a responsibility, now completed. Later!

Mark had not arrived so I could do what I wanted. What I wanted to do was rest, so I did just that. I didn't even worry about meals, just rest. I was tired, body and mind.

The following day, Mark, with his best bud, Steve, pulled in and unpacked and immediately left. Mark asked if I wanted to go party with them, but I declined. The scars on my face, which were fairly imperceptible to begin with, didn't register with either, so I didn't have to explain what I did on my vacation. I didn't want to explain it anyway.

Manic-depression is an elegant and descriptive term. Bi-polar disorder possesses a poetic resonance, but it lacks the former's descriptive power. I don't know what it's meant to explain. Does it mean that mania originates from the North Pole and that depression originates from the South Pole? Does it, instead, mean that mania races around a pole clockwise and depression races in the opposite direction or vice-versa? Hand it to the medical establishment to muck up what was a perfectly fine, descriptive diagnosis to make it more antiseptic, clinical and devoid of any human connection. That's what we pay them big bucks for, right?

I should have been reading myself and recognizing the symptoms by now but I didn't. The mania should have been easy to spot and the depression, with its dark and ugly components, should have been easily distinguishable, but I thought I was just moody. And everyone else thought so, too. "Are you in one of those moods?" was a question I heard directed toward me frequently. I must be moody, then, but I wasn't. Instead, I was riding the soaring flippancy of a 'natural' high interspersed with fighting the dark and ugly 'truth' of those around me. They were responsible, I would think, and wouldn't they be sorry when I'm gone. The plunge would last for hours or, during particularly bad episodes, days at a time, with the ugly thoughts repeating over and over and over. To see anyone, to hear anyone, to speak to anyone was dreadful and avoided. Just let me lie in bed interminably. Leave me alone.

As slowly as I would descend into my private mental hell, I would pull myself out just as quickly. Help was never available except in the gray matter between my ears. No one understood and I could not explain nor did I ever really try. I'm just moody.

The mania was not as soaring as I began one more semester at the big U, but the depression was deepening and lengthening and spreading like a three dimensional form growing exponentially. Freezing rain carpeted the twin towns a week after classes started and I fell on my sling-borne right arm. Searing pain shot through my upper body and I cursed my fate and those around me, silently, of course. Hours later I was deep in my hole with escape foreboding and even light dimmed to specks, but it's just a mood swing, nothing more. I'll swing out of it. I always have. Unless I move to the exit before I can climb out again. I managed to avoid the exit, though, and Eddie helped me. You remember Eddie, don't you? The one everybody had forgotten, who had rendered himself insignificant. *I'm not insignificant*, I thought, *and you're gonna fucking remember me. I'll never let you forget me like Eddie,* I would think as I climbed out of the hole once again.

Barely three weeks into the spring semester and it was time for football, Super Bowl football. This year, the Pittsburgh Steelers would represent the AFC and some hapless team would represent the NFC. No, I can't remember who represented the NFC, but just like the other three Super Bowl appearances by the Steelers throughout the seventies, the Steel Curtain would vanquish the pretenders to the crown. The Steelers were good when they made the Super Bowl and their opponents were not.

For some reason lost forever in my mind, Steve disappeared Super Bowl weekend and Mark wanted to go to the Ground Round, get a table early, eat peanuts and popcorn, drink Sangria and watch the game. Nobody else was around that weekend to meet us, so it was just Mark and I at the restaurant, drinking sweet-tasting, Spanish-doctored fruit wine and cheering the black and gold. Good game. What was the final score? Don't ask me, I have no clue. All I know is that Pittsburgh scored at least one more point than the other team. That qualifies them as the Super Bowl champion.

  I didn't wear the sling to the restaurant as I had taken to wearing it less and less. My right arm was not painful and I only wore it as a precaution from class to class and back to the apartment. I was going to class more frequently and my grades reflected that but meeting women of any interest at the big U was a dwindling prospect. I was locked in the apartment in the twin cities of the big U every weekend and only occasionally did I venture forth from its confines. Besides, I had no effective means of transportation except the Kawasaki motorcycle and I was not in any shape to maneuver that. It was also too damn cold.

  There were times, though, when I awoke from my self-induced fog to go forth. One weekend in February was especially warm so I set out for Podunk, my thumb being my only guide and my legs being my first means of propulsion. I hooked up with a couple going to Clinton and sat in the back seat, passing on the smoke they offered but mostly enjoying the company. They even dropped me off out of town to avoid being hassled by the police. That was followed about fifteen minutes later by a guy who actually knew my family by name and drove me straight to my parents' driveway, which was some five miles out of his way. He was quite the chauffeur, but these adventures in hitchhiking might be unusual and it was the only time I ever did it other than when I had car trouble.

  I called Kent when I got home but I had to leave a message with his sister because he was already out for the evening. He called me the next morning and we got together at the bowling alley in Reservoirtown to play shuffleboard and drink beer. I drove the red replacement Opel Manta with automatic transmission and rack and pinion steering, which tends to respond quickly at any slight movement of the steering wheel. Jeff was there, too, and we all drank a lot of beer and played quite a few games of shuffleboard until it was late in the afternoon. Despite all that, I drove home without incident. Whatever lesson I had learned a few months before I had put on hiatus, though I stayed home that night. I would have hitched back but Dad made Jeff take me back to Urbana. Jeff only stopped long enough to see me get out of the car with my pack on the street. When my foot hit the ground above the pavement, Jeff was already turning onto the next street and making his way quickly out of town.

  Spring break loomed and Florida again beckoned, but this time I would be going with some friends other than from school. Kent and Jeff had secured that week for their paid vacations from full-time work and we were getting ready as much as we ever would, which is to say, not much. There would be no motel reservations, no extensive trip planning, no special time to leave or be anywhere, just have plenty of beer and smoke for the ride and clothes to last a week. We were gonna wing it and Kent and Jeff were going to show those college geeks how to party.

I had plenty of warm weather clothes at home, which was mostly what I intended to pack, and a suitcase was at home, too, so there was no need to bring any clothes from school. When the Friday before the spring break weekend came around, I dutifully attended classes, walked hurriedly back to the apartment, grabbed what essentials were essential, unlocked and fired up the motorcycle and took the long way home, burning rubber whenever feasible, however. I rode right to Kent's house and knew things were going as planned – did we plan this? - when I saw the tan Duster sitting in the driveway. Parking the bike on the street, I flipped the kickstand down, turned off the motor and walked up calmly to the door. Before I could reach it, Kent opened it and shouted, "What the hell took you so long, college boy?"

"Shut up and get me a beer," I greeted him.

"Get it yourself," he replied, "or are you college kids too good to open a refrigerator?"

I had reached the door and Kent shoved his right arm forward, I curled my hand around his, and he yanked me hard, smiling heartily. As he pulled me inside, I commented, "And you better have some smoke ready for fire, too."

As he slapped me hard on my back, Kent asked with mock surprise, "What? You didn't bring any?" Following me into the kitchen as I opened the refrigerator door and withdrew a can of Bud and popped it open, he added, "You know you have to pull your own weight in the smoke department or Jeff and me will be smokin' without ya."

"Got plenty under my seat outside," I said, nodding out the window.

Kent reached for a box on the counter and handed it to me. "I was just waitin' for you," he advised, "so you could spin a small, straight one instead of the big bombers I usually roll." I took the box and sat down at the table. Kent reached for the phone and said, "I'll see if I can get ahold of Jeff to find out when he's headed this way."

It was true that I could roll a better joint than Kent, although I usually had to spin against a surface. Kerry could spin a smooth, straight one in the air, just like the old-time cowboys, although I had never seen anyone spin a joint with one hand. I dropped a handful at the top of the box and used the paper case to roll out the seeds and stems. With that completed, I pulled out a paper and scooped enough of the pile onto the paper, smoothed it along the width of the paper, set it against the table and spun it. After licking it once it was tight, I displayed it for Kent as he continued chatting with Jeff about nothing in particular, which usually meant pussy.

Hanging up the phone, Kent opened the door to the back yard and I followed with the joint in one hand and a lighter in the other. Once outside, I stuck the joint between my lips and flicked the lighter and sucked on the end of the joint as I lit the other. Pulling the smoke deep into my lungs and soon trying to suppress a cough, I passed the joint to Kent. Back and forth we passed it and in a few minutes, there was a small stub left. I pulled out my alligator clip, attached it to the joint and we smoked it right to the end. The tiny piece left was stubbed out by Kent, who immediately swallowed it. Waste not, want not.

Jeff arrived before we could finish our second beer together, shocking us both with his punctuality, though we didn't let on. He brought some really good smoke and we were testing that minutes after he arrived. We drank and smoked cigarettes and lieutenant and had a good time, right up to our usual departure time. Were we leaving for Florida after all that? Shit, no. We were going out to bars to try to score one more time before leaving for FLA.

I didn't want to leave the bike parked on the street, so I rode it back to the parents' house while Kent and Jeff followed me in Kent's car. Rolling it into the garage along the side where I could find the space, I opened the house door and announced I was going out. Closing the door before receiving an answer, I jogged to Kent's car, flung open the back door, plopped down in the seat and closed the door just as Kent steamed out of the driveway backwards. Seconds later, Jeff handed me a beer and we were off.

We drank a round at Romie's. It was dead. We drank a round at the music bar near the Capitol complex. There was no music that night and it was dead. We tried another tavern downtown and ran into some friends of Jeff that Kent knew, too, though I had no idea who they were. There were a few women in attendance so we took root there and drank and drank with nothing but talk to pass the time. There was a pool table and both Kent and Jeff played some games, but a girl eventually sat with us and we engaged in frequent conversation, although she wasn't that hot. She had a nice smile and was spirited, to say the least, so she was fun to banter with.

When we closed the bar, Kent and Jeff were disappointed and

frustrated and pissed off and ready to call it a night. I felt pretty good and could have gone a while longer but we had a long trip ahead of us and we should be catching some winks. Kent drove me home and I went to bed almost as soon as I walked in the door.

I was up early and drove to the bank so I could withdraw close to a thousand dollars from my savings account. It was still early when I returned, but Kent said he would call when he was ready. When most of the morning was behind me, I couldn't wait any more, so I called Kent. That I roused him from slumber would state the obvious. Kent and Jeff had stayed up for hours after they dropped me off, drinking beer and smoking, and Kent was feeling the very nasty effects of a hangover more severe than he had felt in some time. He suspected Jeff would be experiencing the same.

"Let me call him to get his ass outta bed," Kent explained, "and I'll take a shower and be ready to go."

One hour later, the phone rang. Kent called to tell me that he's leaving to pick up Jeff and he'll be at the hacienda in a half-hour. It's after noon and we're not making very good time.

Forty-five minutes later there was a honk out in the driveway. I told Mom that I'm leaving and she wished me a good time and be careful. Out in the Duster Jeff and Kent are laughing and both tipped an open beer in my direction. "Hurry up, slick," Kent yelled out the car window.

"Open the trunk, dick," I yelled, swinging my suitcase.

"Oops," Kent muttered, and he turned off the car, opened his door and stepped back to the trunk, laughing constantly. He inserted the key into the trunk lock and twisted it. Lifting the trunk lid I spied the remnants of two cases of beer along with their two suitcases. I was impressed with how much room the trunk held from such a little car. I also knew the laughing probably stemmed from a little smoke both had on the way over to my house. Without shifting anything, I tossed my suitcase in the trunk, slammed the lid closed and moved to the passenger side of the car. After I opened the back door, I flopped onto the seat as Kent fired up the car, shoved it in reverse and spun the tires in the driveway.

"Hey," I admonished him.

"Sorry," Kent replied, unapologetically, as he joined Jeff in snickering.

"It's about fucking time," I said. "You guys are pathetic."

"We're fuckin' hung over, little man," Jeff stated, a bit peeved, "so fuckin' chill."

We headed to the interstate, the first leg of our journey, and we'll leave it at Litchfield and start moving east. We hadn't even reached Sixth

Street and the smell filled the entire car.

"Jesus, man," I asked in astonishment as I rolled down the window to my right, "which one of you farted? I need fresh air *bad*!"

Kent started snickering, as he gulped his beer. "This is definitely helping the hangover, but I think we're gonna be ridin' with constant farts for a while!" He laughed heartily as I slid over to the left side and rolled that window down too.

Jeff laughed a little too merrily. "Think I'll join you," he said, between laughs and beer gulps.

"Holy shit, that's rank!" Kent exclaimed as he rolled down his window and stuck his head out.

"Great!" I shouted. "I'm locked in a car for the next twenty-two hours between dueling fart boys." Kent and Jeff laughed uproariously and tipped their beer cans together. Having snagged my own beer from the cooler in back, I sucked a draft and asked, "Well, who's gonna spin one? At least, let's add a little sweet smell to cover the foulness coming from your asses."

Jeff opened the glove box, pulled out a baggie with about a dozen joints, withdrew one, and handed it to me as we merged onto the interstate. "Fire it up, little boy," he said. "You can take a couple of drags to catch up, if you want."

I pulled my lighter out of my shirt pocket and fired up the joint, taking one long drag and coughing a bit. Passing it up to Jeff, who took a big suck, he passed it to Kent and around it went until we extinguished it. Finally, we were on our way, with the occasional fart smell permeating the rolling vehicle, followed by uncontrollable laughter from the perpetrator.

What should have been barely three hours in Illinois seemed to take forever. We stopped to piss. We stopped to eat. We stopped for gas. We stopped for minor groceries. We stopped for cigarettes. We rolled into Indiana around five in the afternoon and I wondered if we would just have to turn around and come home once we got to Florida, assuming we actually made it. Once we could find a place to stop in Indiana, Kent announced it was my turn to drive. *Good,* I thought, *now we'll make up some time.*

The going was slow on the two-lane highway to Louisville, but it opened to four-lane before we reached town and continued that way to Lexington, where we would catch Interstate 75. It seemed to take a long time to get there and I was beginning to think we made a mistake, but once I hit the interstate, we started flying. Of course, we had to stop to piss, or stop to eat, or stop for gas, or stop for more minor groceries, or stop for cigarettes. I suggested we combine some of the activities during a stop and they bought it. Shit! Glad we're not going around the world. I could hear it now as we fly halfway across the Atlantic Ocean. "Put 'er down between those waves. I gotta pee!"

All the stopping and starting and the plodding along took a lot out of me. Kent could sense it and he decided to take the wheel. Have at it. I'm whipped. He drove on into the night, almost to Atlanta, and we made good time with fewer stops.

Jeff took the wheel for his turn. He wanted to drive late at night and he planned to drive all the way to Florida before he turned over his shift. Damn if he didn't! Kent and I woke up barely an hour from Florida and Jeff was going great guns. When we crossed the state border, I advised him to watch his speed as there would be a considerable number of Florida state troopers along the way to greet us. I knew he had been steaming along but this was Florida. Five minutes later there was the first state trooper laying in wait. Jeff knew I wasn't bullshitting then.

Before he could get to the turnpike east, Jeff finally petered out and pulled off at an exit. We all thought it was a good idea to get some gas and eats, so we found the appropriate exit and took a break. Satiated an hour later, Kent sat behind the wheel, ready for the last leg to Daytona. Everybody wanted to stay in Daytona and fuck beautiful college, spring-break pussy. Ah, dreams!

We made really good time across the state and were at the outskirts of Daytona before noon. Amazing! We all agreed that we had to get right to the beach. Just keep going east and follow the signs to the beach. And, soon, there it was. We could only go left or right or straight onto the beach and into the ocean. The latter choice was unpaved and illegal so we turned left to park on the beach side of the street. To me, it had a feeling of deja vu, I have been here before and done the very same thing. Out we stumbled, our cooler in hand, towels for the beach in tow, and we were poppin' beers on the Atlantic coast. Fuckin'-A!

Perhaps one may sense the outcome which awaited us. Well, it wasn't that we couldn't find a motel. That was easy, maybe too easy, since it turned out to be the very first one we tried, it wasn't far from all the action, it was well-kept and not a run-down hole, and there was lots of pussy running around it. We were thinking that this was right, we were going to show these college kids how to party. That was for sure.

Until the night fell and we went out to find some action. We found some alright and couldn't get in. It seems you had to get there early and get a stamp. It was packed and the bouncers wouldn't let anyone in without a stamp. Everywhere else we went was more of the same. We had kept to our typical schedule by drinking until ten before leaving to party, but by that time everything was already packed. The places that weren't packed were that way for a very good reason. They sucked. We slunk back to our motel room to drink and smoke and ran into a group of college kids, so we opened up our room and invited them to party. When it was all over and everyone had separated, we were bushed and ready for bed, thrown a no-hitter. Figuratively, we didn't even put the ball in play, we just watched the 'Ks' mount.

The next afternoon was more of the same, and Jeff and Kent were constantly bitching about college girls and how fucked up they were. They could be, there was no doubt about that, as you might recall Cindy. What my two companions were really lamenting was how these girls could talk rings around them, making them feel like country bumpkins, which, of course, pissed them off even more. I could hold my end of a conversation with any of them but it would invariably lead to the questions, "Who are your friends and why are you with *them*?" Both were legitimate questions and hard to answer, but I had a lot of history with them. I was loyal, but I was questioning in my own mind just why I was with them, too. A history which includes a six-day detour through the hospital can do that.

That night produced the same result and, by then, Kent and Jeff had enough of Daytona. We checked out the next morning, and I convinced them to hang around until sundown before taking the long trip across the state to Clearwater. Still, Kent, especially, was tired of the east coast of Florida. "Anything's *gotta* be better than this shithole!" he exclaimed. No more spending any of our money here, not even for dinner. Let's ride. We took off for the west coast before five that afternoon.

I have been here before, I thought, as the sun went down and we were cruising through the desolation of central Florida. At least we could drink beer with little apprehension. Skirting around the bay late at night, we could see the lights of the peninsula and our destination. We rolled into Clearwater before 10 and found a room at the very same motel where I had stayed the year before. Two blocks from the beach. Excellent! Maybe this was the turning point. *I have been here before.*

Unfortunately for Jeff and Kent, it was more of the same, except that we were in Clearwater, which meant less pussy than Daytona and more families, including families with great looking mamas and little tikes. It was almost hilarious to see them strike up a conversation with Mama. Where were you going to put the little one? Under the bed? Out in the hall? Lock them in the bathroom, making them sit in the tub until they sparkle, or wrinkle, irreversibly? Wait a minute! Look out!

Heeeeeeeerrrrrrrre's Papa! Ooh, that's awkward. Somehow, though, I imagined that both had already experienced something like that anyway so it was no big deal to them. One thing was certain each and every time–they would still be held scoreless. As for me, well, that was the story of my life so far.

I suspected more than once that, if it were just Kent and me, we would have found it a much more enjoyable excursion. We might have been able to do better with the ladies, too, being just two instead of a threesome. I don't mean to place the fault on Jeff for the disaster that would be the Florida vacation which we would soon vacate, but his nagging and ragging seemed to be constant, loud and irritating, not just to the two of us either. Nothing was good enough for Jeff. There was fault with everything. The scenery wasn't that great. So what's the big deal about Florida? The beer is too high. The gas is too high. The food is too high. The cigarettes are too high. The women are too high (on themselves). After all, they're just pussy and they like to fuck as much as I do, they're just too high and mighty to admit it, the cunts.

When Jeff would start up, which seemed to be about two minutes after he awoke, Kent would fall right in with him. It's a fucking tourist mecca, I would try to explain. And it's high tourist season. The people who live here depend on it and the prices reflect that. Typically, the response would be focused on 'mecca', like it's some type of hidden college phrase. After awhile, one surrenders. I still wish it had just been Kent and me. It was his car, at least. Jeff's car would have been lucky to reach Indiana. Jeff might have liked it. Hoosier girls, woo!

The night scene in Clearwater was better. It was less crowded, there was good music and dancing, and we all had a god time when we went out, but the whole endeavor had already been poisoned and there would be no antidote unless Jeff and Kent and – me???!!! - got laid. That was not to happen.

We didn't venture from Clearwater the rest of the week and we stuck it out for the entire time planned. We explored the beach and enjoyed the scenery–girls–and we enjoyed the weather, which was quite good the entire time we were in Florida. It wasn't enough. When the following Saturday after we left Illinois rolled around, both of my companions were ready to leave. Jeff got up and was spouting off about leaving from the moment his feet hit the floor of his room. We packed, stowed the bags in the trunk and drove away, not even making a pass through the town or along the beach, just straight out to the highway leading out of town. We bought enough beer to last us to the border, because Jeff was so pissed off at Florida he didn't want to spend any more money in the state than necessary. He was even willing to drive us clean out of there and he did, as fast as he could make that Duster go without risking the attention of the Highway Patrol.

Maybe it was the negativity of both Kent and Jeff. Experience with those who normally display negativity has convinced me that it almost always encourages disaster to befall. That's another story, but it seemed to hold true on our way back.

Before we could exit Florida, Jeff was complaining about feeling sick. He even pulled into a rest area to throw up, but he was bound and determined to drive us out of there. As soon as he could find a place to pull over in Georgia, he did. After Kent took the wheel and I sat shotgun, Jeff laid down in the back seat all to himself and slept, fighting whatever bug, or self-induced 'infection,' had taken up residence. He had driven a good seven hours and now it was Kent and me. Jeff's shift was over and maybe he would be quiet.

Kent was doing fine, although he was bitching frequently about the construction and the detours and how slow the going was. I didn't notice anything, but it might have been that he had too many beers during the drive out of Florida and he was a little tired and the construction delays and detours and jogs around pylons and gates and lack of shoulders was wearing on him. We were still quite a ways from Atlanta, crawling along yet another construction area with no shoulder, when Kent lost his concentration with the tight lane, drifted to the right and off the pavement and slammed into a series of potholes which were so jarring they woke Jeff up. Kent heard an earful from both of us and blew off the steam back at us, but twenty minutes later and still twenty miles from the Atlanta bypass, the right rear tire blew. Kent and I were pissed, but the only one who wasn't pissed was the sickly Jeff. Instead, he jumped out of the back seat, yanked all the gear out of the trunk once Kent had opened it, set everything up next to the stricken tire, whipped off the bolts, pumped up the rear of the car, pulled the stricken tire off, slapped the spare on, whipped the bolts on, pumped the rear down, and tightened the bolts in fifteen minutes, tops. If Kent or I tried to help, we just got in the way. Kent simply carried the stricken tire to the trunk and I cleared the area so he could lay it down. We put away all the gear, set everything back in the trunk, and Jeff announced that it was my turn to drive. Kent's eyelids were droopy and he offered no resistance. He tossed me the keys and I took my place behind the wheel, signaled to get back into the driving lanes and on to Atlanta.

It was easy then, and it still is now, to drive around Atlanta and find one's self at any time in the wrong lane going in a direction one didn't intend. It didn't help that it was already dark as I started around Atlanta from the southern end. Eventually, as we progressed around the western edge of the town, I found myself in the wrong lane going in a direction I didn't intend. I knew it pretty quickly when I noticed a sign for a town not on the route and the traffic moving with me had significantly dwindled. I heard from my companions a few choice words of ridicule, but I turned around, re-connected with the bypass and we were soon free from the clutches of Georgia's largest metropolis.

Since my car mates slept most of the time I drove, there was little stopping, except for gas and a rest room foray, which I would combine since I can hold it for a pretty long time. We entered Tennessee and the first toll road and my attitude became "drive fast. You're paying for the privilege." There were no police vehicles anywhere in sight except at toll booths, nor were there many vehicles in either direction. At times I was cruising upwards of ninety miles per hour with a complete sense of calm and justice.

While in Tennessee, we stopped for gas and when the car slowed so I could exit the interstate, both Jeff and Kent awoke. Looking around, they immediately spotted the fireworks signs, and they were suddenly lively and talkative. While I pumped gas they went into the store and bought as many fireworks as they could carry in a brown paper sack. I bought a little but I wasn't into it. I was into driving as fast as I could without incident so I could get back home and put an end to the trip that had lost its fun aspect about a week before.

I made good time to Nashville. Only one car passed me the entire time. Since I had never been to Nashville or driven around it before, it was one hell of a sight. I woke up my companions and we looked at the town with awe, since the bypass around town wasn't very far from the heart of the city and it wasn't as big as it is today. If we hadn't been on a schedule we would have checked it out. It looked pretty cool.

Out of Tennessee and off the first toll road and into Kentucky and on to the next toll road we drove. No cops, a handful of cars, and speed considerably above the limit over a hundred miles, we moved closer to Indiana. I would soon have to exit the interstate system and travel two-lane highways for the most part into the southwestern slice of Indiana, cut west around Evansville and move into Illinois.

Ten miles from the border with the daylight sparkling, having driven all night from below Atlanta, Kent announced that he would drive the rest of the way. Although I wasn't tired and I really wanted to drive into Illinois, I pulled over and yielded the wheel to him. Jeff hopped in to the shotgun seat and I sprawled in the back seat, struggling to sleep and having it elude me mostly.

A scant three hours later we were back in familiar territory. Kent pulled into the parents' driveway and I exited, pulled out my suitcase, shook hands and went inside straight to my bedroom and crashed for hours. When I woke up late that night I fixed something to eat, drank some beers watching TV and went back to bed a few hours later. I didn't call Kent and he didn't call me, but I roared by his house on my bike the next day when I was leaving to go back to school. The Duster was gone so I rode by all the way to Urbana.

The effects of the accident had diminished, at least the physical aspects. Up and down was my mental state. Class was easy except for tax accounting, which was tricky. Fucking legislators. Well, that's what you get for electing attorneys.

A couple weeks after I returned from Florida, Dad called. He wanted to come up to Urbana and take a ride with me to Decatur. He wouldn't tell me why. He just said he wanted to talk and show me something.

When he knocked on the door and I opened it, he didn't want to come in. He just said, "Come on! Let's go."

I locked the door and followed him out to his car and we took off for Decatur. He said he had been thinking that I should have a car to get around. He didn't tie it to my grades or school progress, just that I should have a car. His old friend and long-time accounting client, Paul, who owned an Oldsmobile dealership in Decatur, was talking to him and Dad had brought up the subject of me having a car. He said he had a couple used models I might like and he should bring me over and take a look at them and drive them around.

When we got to Paul's dealership, he came out and shook both our hands, made small talk with Dad for a while, then introduced his sales manager and excused himself. I didn't take that as a good sign, until the sales manager took me over to the red Torino I had noticed right away. Yeah, it looked just like the Starsky and Hutch car except for the white stripe, which was missing on this one, but it looked good, daunting, intimidating, a muscle car. He asked me what I thought of it and it looked in good shape. He went into a spiel about its history since it only had 20,000 miles on it, but I didn't really care about that. I wanted to drive it. He went inside for the keys, fumbled with the notion that he should ride with us until Dad's scowl convinced him of the error of his suggestion, and I got behind the wheel, pumped the gas twice and fired it up. Oh, man, did that car have an excellent low growl. Depress the gas pedal and it roared. I drove it off the lot and around town and spun the tires and that was it. Yeah, I'll take it.

Dad paid for it right there, tax, title, license, granny's butt wipe, everything. I followed him back to Podunk so we could show Mom. It was an excellent car, for a while at least. It would do.

I still had that phone number of the blonde, full-bodied beauty, Carolyn. What the hell? Now that I had a ride, I could swing over to Normal, stop in on the Podunk boys going to school there, and, hey, I was transferring there anyway. Let's boogie!

I called her to make sure she was going to be around and not out of town. She remembered me, for sure, but it was somewhat awkward. She was still interested in seeing me, though, and told me where she was living and that I could come over to her dorm any time. That was enough for me. Road trip.

I had no real place to crash, so I left early Saturday morning and was there in an hour. I drove as close to Watterson Towers as I could get and went inside where the local phones were that you could use to call a resident. I buzzed Rick and got him out of bed. "Let's have breakfast, dude," I told him over the phone. "Get your ass outta bed. You gonna sleep your life away?"

I waited for what seemed like hours but was only 30 minutes and he finally came down with a friend with long, brown hair. He introduced us and Steve seemed like a pretty cool guy. I drove to their recommended breakfast hole and we had some eats. They asked what I was gonna do the rest of the day and I told them I was going over to one of the other dorms and check up on Carolyn. They gave me some shit about not even being a student there and already having a girlfriend but I ignored them.

I dropped them off and asked if they were going to be around their dorm for a couple hours. I suspected my trip over to see Carolyn wouldn't take long. They said they would and I drove away to the west side of campus.

I found Carolyn's dorm easy, since it was one of only two big dorms on that side of town. I walked in and up to the elevators. When the door opened I stepped in and punched the sixth floor and was dutifully lifted to that floor. Exiting, I looked at the dorm room numbers and headed left. When I found her number, I knocked on the door and felt the tenseness rise. I could hear noise on the other side of the door and it opened slowly.

"Hi," Carloyn said, with a practiced smile. "Non, right?"

"Yeah," I said, nervously. "How are you?"

She stepped into the hallway and closed her door, leaving just a small crack. "I'm fine. You?"

"I'm doing well," I replied, glancing at the floor.

We spoke for about a half-hour, mostly forced and awkward small talk. She never mentioned the accident and I didn't either. She informed me, though, that she wasn't attending State in the fall semester. She had received a scholarship that she had applied for to attend school in England for at least a year. I tried, as best I could, to continue the conversation so that it wouldn't seem obvious that all I really wanted to do was continue a relationship with her which I would add to when I transferred to State, but now there was no need to do that. Still, maybe it was the way the conversation went, the difficulty I had making her smile and laugh, the tension I felt about the whole thing, that I was left with the impression that it wasn't going to work with Carolyn anyway. Good thing she *was* going to England. Imagine seeing her frequently on campus, only to have her ignore me or avoid me. That would be fanfuckingtastic!

I caught up with the boys after leaving Carolyn. We talked a little and they told me about a place they had a line on for renting next year. They expected to have it set in a week or two and would keep me in the loop. There would be enough room for me but I didn't have to commit until I was ready. We ventured to a park and threw the frisbee for a while and drank beer and smoked a little cannabis. I stayed through dinner, when we went into Bloomington. I was feeling pretty good about transferring and staying with the boys, and the female population, especially their collective appearances, was a highlight. I thought I was going to like it here. I drove back to Urbana in a good frame of mind.

I hadn't been over to Oglesby Hall in quite a while to see the old gang, so one day the following week I drove my new ride over there, parked in the lot across the street from the dorm and went up to the twelfth floor like I still lived there. As soon as I started walking down the south hall, I heard, "Johnny! Johnny the Wad!" Some things never die.

I showed Pete and Jeff, the motorcycle man, the new ride from the window. Soon, everyone wanted to take a ride, so we did, though just to the store to get beer. When we got to the parking lot, which was usually quite open, I spun the tires a few times to leave my mark and we went back upstairs to drink, smoke and shoot the shit. All the main gang had committed to the fraternity and they would all be living there the following year. Since they didn't know because I hardly ran into any of them, I told them about my transfer to State, explaining that it was to get into Business with a major in Accounting, which I couldn't accomplish at the Big U. I hid the equally important reason that I wanted a change away from the Big U, I wanted to party with people who weren't interested in fraternities and sororities, and I wanted to be at a school where the girls were numerous and appealing in appearance. The Big U was sorely lacking in all of that. Goodbye and good riddance is what I had been thinking for some time but I never said so.

Jeff remarked that there was a motocross event scheduled near St. Louis that weekend and he was planning on going. He was looking for people to go along and help split the expenses. I had never personally seen the real professionals in international motocross compete except on TV and that sounded like fun. I told Jeff to count me in and he went over the details and I promised that I would meet them at the dorm at the appointed hour.

That Friday night after dinner we all gathered at the dorm. I drove the muscle car and parked it in the big lot across the street and carried the little gear I was bringing to the meeting area out front. There, Jeff, Pete and Barry waited patiently since I wasn't really late. They were anxious to get going. They asked where Mark was. I had to be honest and tell them I didn't know where he was. When I saw him that morning before we split for classes, he had told me that he decided not to go. He and Steve had made other plans and I didn't see him the rest of the day before I drove over. In further honesty, I could have waited, since he usually came back to the apartment for dinner, but I took him at his word and left without him.

It only took a few minutes to load up and we were off, Jeff in the driver's seat, Pete and Barry sitting on the back seat and me riding shotgun. I was most familiar with getting to St. Louis so I would navigate, which was a good thing right away. Jeff wanted to drive down I-57, connect with I-70 and take the 270 bypass to get to the motocross site, but I talked him out of that right away. "Sure, it's all interstate until you get to Missouri, but it's about 50 extra miles, and that's about an extra hour," I advised him.

"How would you get there, then?" Jeff asked.

We took the new and unfinished interstate 72 out of town, exited onto route 10 to Clinton, turned on route 54 all the way to Podunk. Once in Podunk, we hooked up on interstate 55 to the bypass 270 around the north end of St. Louis. We got to the motocross parking area by ten that night, in time to get some fast food dinners to go. Jeff had checked it out and all we had to do was pay for parking and we could sleep in his van, use the portable potties scattered all over the grounds, but we had to skip showers. We could live without that for one day. We'd be driving back after the race was over the next day.

We rose early the next day, partly due to the lack of comfort sleeping on the floor of a van. We could walk down the staging area of the race where the riders and their contingent were roped off from the onlookers. The bikes were impressive. This was going to be good.

In 1976 the premier motocross rider in the world was a guy named Roger DeKoster from Europe, and to be more precise if memory serves, the Netherlands. He was there as were other top riders from around the wold. The top rider from America was a guy named Brad, though his last name escapes me. He would probably be DeKoster's main competition. Brad would be riding a Husqvarna and DeKoster rode Suzuki. Early in the afternoon, the race began and we found some good positions around the course to watch the action, though we could move all around the course at any time.

The course was laid out on the side of a hill that rose some 200 feet above the bottom with lots of turns and burms scattered all over. The longest straightaway, the length of the course, was at the bottom of the hill, negotiated from the top of the hill, straight down, to a ninety-degree turn to the right followed by a quick 180-degree turn to the left. There were four burms along the straightaway, a left turn leading up the hill, with more turns, then twists down into the middle of the course, back up to the top and over to the turn leading straight down. We stood, for most of the race, in line with the course leading down to the bottom and the two turns before the straightaway. One could see all of the course from there except parts of it out of view at the very top.

Once the race was underway, the styles of the two main competitors who we followed could not have been more dissimilar. DeKoster attacked the course with such smoothness that it seemed like he, his bike and the course were all one and the same. While all the other riders would slow or stop and bump through the turns, DeKoster sailed through each and every one so slickly that it seemed the course controlled his deceleration and acceleration itself. There was no herky-jerky motion from him during the entire race. The American on the Husky, Brad, was a different story. He made his way to the head of the pack, well behind DeKoster, through sheer brute force, willing his motorcycle through ruts and slams and burms and turns by muscle only. DeKoster was so smooth, I watched him come down the hill toward me with three riders in front, the farthest rider closer to the turn than from the top of the hill. DeKoster flew down the hill and spun through the 90-degree turn having passed all three riders with such effortless motion that I was stunned and awed. He lapped everyone in the race. No one could even finish the race on the same lap as DeKoster and watching how smooth and consistent his riding style was, none of us were surprised. He had no real competition that day.

The Great Depression

We were in no big hurry to leave and we chatted with some fans along the way back to the van, including a few girls with halter tops. I love halter tops, especially from behind. We stood around the van and drank beer as surreptitiously as possible, waiting for the initial surge of the crowd to dissipate. When we finally got on the road back to the Big U, we were all in agreement that it was one of the best spectacles we had ever witnessed. I almost wanted to get my old Honda and jump it again, but my motorcycle days were coming to a close.

Jeff had liked the Kawasaki I had bought and I was realizing how much trouble it was to keep up a motorcycle. I wasn't as mechanically oriented and inclined as one should be to own a motorcycle. Jeff and I talked about that and he offered me $400 for it, since I hadn't ridden it in months and knew it needed an oil and filter change and maybe more.

The weekend before finals concluded, Jeff decided to run up to his parents' house for some get together and wanted to take my bike with him. He came over to my apartment that Friday night with $400 in cash and I helped him put the bike in the back of his van. I waved to him as he drove off with the only street bike I ever owned.

Finals were easy. There were no surprises. It was time to get out of town, this time permanently. It was depressing in some respects, and the darkness and ugliness would accompany me. I couldn't leave it behind. It followed me everywhere.

I had seen my twentieth birthday come and go that spring. No fan fare, no big celebration had occurred. It was just another day. I was now entering my third decade on this planet and I had yet to enter the wonderful world of pussy. Change could be good, bad, or indifferent, but change was definitely headed my way. I just wanted to get fucked once before I was forced to make some unexpected exit out of this world. Are there gods of fuckdom? If so, are you listening? Exploding my sausage in a solitary manner is getting old! I could use a little help here. It would be nice to have change be a good thing for once. Hey, I'll even slow down on the masturbation, as long as you hold up your end.

Act Sixteen
Variable(s) Plus Constant Equals Change

The middle of May in a college town means there's a crush of people trying to get out. Don't let the locals tell you different. Once finals week concludes a college town is transformed into a ghost town, because the vast majority of students don't live there, nor do they have any desire to do so. May not only brings an end to a semester, it also brings an end to a school year. Some students will never return—having given up—or graduating, happy to have a diploma. "Call me in fifteen years after I have established myself in corporate America. Maybe I'll donate some money. Right now, I have to earn a living. Thank you."

  I was one of those who had given up on the Big U, but I wasn't uncaring. I knew I'd be back. For all of its faults in my eyes, it was more a lack of planning than anything else. Honestly, was any part of American education prepared for the crush of millions upon millions of students straining every imaginable resource for not quite twenty years, only to have that crush reduced to a mere and immediate trickle? If your answer is 'yes', let me deliver to you the award you have justly earned, the Deluded Idiot Award. Of course, American education was unprepared for that crush. Fuck, *all of American society was unprepared for that crush.* And our 'leaders,' along with our descendants, are unprepared for that crush when it retires from active working lives. The strain on Medicare and Medicaid, *alone*, will break the national bank. Because, here, at the onset of the third millennium, is a relative world peace only occasionally disrupted by fanatical "religious fundamentalists" who want nothing less than to order you to live your life the way they say you should. And, rightly so, we should all be telling them to fuck themselves, three, four, or infinite times. Actually, since they claim we love life too much and they love death, we really should give them what they want, because they are a threat to human existence anyway, due to the *More For Me Syn-*

drome that Adolf Hitler and company made infamous, also appropriately captured in George Orwell's *Animal Farm*. Sooner or later, you will have to kill all of them or be destroyed yourselves. Sorry, that's part of your future, kids.

This world peace is an aberration. There have always been baby booms. The natural consequence throughout all of our collective, fucked-up human history, is to generate wars every forty or fifty years. This has a tendency to kill excess human beings, which you may or may not have deduced on your own. Yet, the baby boom from 1946 to 1966, *more or less and world-wide,* is an exercise for the human species to explore uncharted territory. We have *never* been here before. Do you really think our 'leaders' and our descendants, most not exactly the sharpest on the block, are prepared for our retirements? I think Aerosmith recorded a song on their debut album which was called *Dream On.* Dreams, unfortunately, won't put food on the table. Where do you think we're headed, keeping in mind our fucked-up history?

However, I digress, and jump, undeservedly so, ahead in history. This tome, after all, is squarely placed in 1976, the year of the American bicentennial. I only mention that for you kids who did not experience the *onslaught* of bicentennial propaganda. It was everywhere, every day, or so it seemed. Of course, the bicentennial only marks the date when a number of radical, but relatively well-to-do, white guys signed a document calling for independence from England. There were no persons of color who signed that document. There, also, were no persons of female persuasion who signed that document, either. I wonder if there will be as big a bicentennial onslaught in 2063, two hundred years after the Emancipation Proclamation, or 2124, two hundred years after women were finally given the 'right' to vote for their 'representatives?' *Waddayuthink?*

Believe it or not, I actually had thought of all of this back then as I was renting a truck to haul my stuff out of Urbana. Well, honestly, I hadn't thought of the baby boom stuff. Shit! Even I was unprepared for that crush. And, I hadn't conceived of 'religious fundamentalists' directing planes into skyscrapers and suicide and roadside bombings on a seemingly hourly scale, but, Shit! Again! Please excuse me when I state the fucking obvious. *I can't think of everything!* If I could, I'd be perfect, and, thus, be rendered a non-candidate for existence on this planet. I keep trying, though. And, you know it, I keep failing. I may descend into the depths of disgusting darkness and ugliness–you only have a limited clue so far–but I keep climbing out. I'm in shit up to my singed eyebrows and there is *nobody* that can help me. This is not a recent understanding, though.

The local truck rental dealership rented me a pretty big truck for a reasonable price, cutting a check for deposit. I also rented what I call a two-wheeler, for stacking boxes on its bottom lip and rolling up the ramp into the truck. I had already boxed most of my stuff, so when I rolled up to the street in the truck, Jeff and Roger with me to help, I knew it wasn't going to take very long to stow it in the truck. Hell, I had far more truck than I needed, but I wanted that ramp to make it easy.

Moving day in the seventies, for me, was setting up tunes. Nobody back then cared about TV on moving day and I didn't even have one. Tunes were necessary, though, because moving is boring, whether coming or leaving. If one is leaving, the tunes equipment was the last thing packed and stowed. If one is coming, the tunes equipment is the first thing removed and immediately unpacked. Tunes were the way to go and I had them, though I had to borrow Mark's receiver. I had a tuner given to me by Steve, Mark's friend. I suppose I shouldn't be cynical, since it was an excellent tuner when one connected a long antenna, but I don't know why he gave it to me. Maybe it was stolen? Especially since it came with a green cloth bag. Who buys audio equipment in a green cloth bag? At least he gave it to me. He never wanted money for it.

Off came the mattress, which never touched the floor or ground until it was in the truck. Next went the box spring right into the truck. We tore down the frame and put that in next with the headboard, which was the old bed from Grampa DeScript. The dresser, a couple of chairs, miscellaneous furniture and boxes were next into the truck. Whatever else was left got thrown into a box and hauled out. I secured everything in the truck and we took apart the tunes and put them in the truck, threw up the ramp and two-wheeler and locked the truck. In less than two hours we were done packing up everything I had at the Big U.

We had some beer in the frij and the three of us had brought various quantities and levels of lieutenant, and Mark wanted to smoke one before we left. Jeff spun one, we fired it up, drank some beer and chatted about what we would do this summer.

"So, you're joining the frat for next school year?" I asked Mark.

"Yeah, those guys are okay," Mark said. "You know, they really wanted you, too."

I shook my head. "I couldn't get in the school I wanted, Mark," I complained.

Mark shook his head with disappointment. "They always said they could get you in there," he reminded me. "You know, they always said that and they could have."

I nodded and remarked, "For frat guys, most of 'em were alright.

I just don't want to join a fraternity. I just don't."

A few minutes later, we were shaking hands and vowing to keep in touch. Jeff, Roger and I stepped out of the apartment after I gave the key to Mark, I unlocked the truck, the three of us climbed in and I drove out of Urbana, never to live there again.

The drive to Podunk was uneventful, until I stopped for gas. That's when I realized–too late–that some canopies over the gas dispenser islands are too low. I swung the truck in close and scraped the truck against the canopy. Damn! If they notice that dent about 18 inches long, it's gonna cost me. Don't let on and maybe they won't notice.

Unpacking was even quicker. We were done in an hour. Okay, boys, here's your reward. Beer for all and I'll even share some of the good stuff, not that ragweed you've been carrying. Jeff followed me to the truck rental dealership the next morning and the owner walked out, took a brief glance at the truck, asked how it handled, I replied that it handled well, and I cut another check for the balance. Apparently, truck renters bang those low-hanging canopies at gas stations regularly, since I thought that dent couldn't be overlooked. Hey, if the owner's satisfied, so am I.

The weekend passed slowly, boringly, depressingly. Kent, Kerry and Jeff were already deep into their softball season, with practice scheduled for Saturday and a modest tournament scheduled Sunday. Kent warned me that I should be at the practices if I wanted to play on their team, but I didn't go to the practice Saturday and I watched the game Sunday as more of a spectator, although one who could drink beer at any time. All the team members had their uniforms, which I would never get since they would start their season long before school was out, some time in March. I didn't even bring my glove to the game Sunday. Even so, the leaders on the team remembered me from the year before, when I would ride my bike to their practice but rarely played. Maybe they might have a place for me later in the summer, but I didn't think that was likely so I didn't place much emphasis on softball.

When the work week rolled around, I got on what I really wanted that summer, a job and the pay that would come from it. I had heard that the Department of Motor Vehicles often hired college students for the summer to help process drivers license applications sent through the mail. I had to make some calls to find out where to apply, but when I discovered that fact, I went down and applied that day. I had to take a test for coding aptitude, which was a breeze. The evaluator took the test and my application, totaled my score and asked if I could start first thing Monday at the DMV office on Dirksen. That was funny. I didn't have anything planned that day, that week, that summer. I think I can be there since they would pay me.

Later that week I was in the basement going through some of my stuff that we had rushed down there to get it out of the rental truck, and I noticed the old dumbbells and weights Dad had bought for Mike years before. Suddenly, I had this notion: what if I lifted weights for the summer? What would happen? Would I notice any difference in my strength or my body composition after just three months of weightlifting? I didn't know the answers, but I had never lifted weights before and I wanted to see if I could change my scrawny appearance. Next, I had to decide what lifts I would do, since there were a lot to choose from. I finally decided to do the easiest, the simplest, since this was all a test and I wasn't certain anything would come from it. This would just be recreational weightlifting, like Chuck, my neighbor, used to do to build up his stamina for motorcycle riding competition. The easiest was curls, so I took the bar and placed two 10 pound weights on either end, tightened the screws holding them in place, and curled 35 pounds as many times as I could in one effort. I could do twenty, pulling the bar up to my chest and slowly, deliberately lowering it for the maximum effect. The following day, determined to do better, I curled twenty-two, and the next day, I curled twenty-two, again. I remembered hearing exercise advocates saying one should rest the day after a workout to let one's muscles develop, so I skipped the next day. When I curled the day after my rest day, I did twenty-five and it seemed easier and more productive. That sold me. I decided to curl four times a week, preferably Tuesday, Thursday and Saturday and Sunday, but I also decided that it didn't matter if I stayed on that schedule as much as I didn't skip two consecutive days. I kept that promise and before the end of the following week, I was curling 35 pounds more than thirty times. That's when I made the next crucial change. It was taking too much time with the same weight, but if I added five more pounds, could I curl at least twenty? When I bested twenty the next time, that was my routine. Once I could curl thirty times with the current weight, it was time to add five more pounds. And I stuck with it, because I could see the difference and, perhaps more importantly, I could feel the difference. With this change, came a change in my attitude, too. I was confident and I didn't put up with any shit from the guys, Jeff especially. Even they were seeing the difference.

Jeff had a friend who needed help moving furniture into a new apartment, which was the upstairs portion of a house. Kent and I agreed to help for beer and smoke. I deliberately took some of the more difficult tasks, like the bottom end of a couch. When anyone said that they should help me with that, I just advised them to get that top end moving. The owner of the apartment stopped by and he turned out to be Mister D, my gym teacher from high school who was a casual acquaintance of my dad. When he saw me move furniture in my scrawny appearance with as little effort as I seemed to show, even he was impressed. This was a guy with pretty damn solid biceps and calf muscles himself. He was no physical slouch and he was praising me and giving the bigger guys, Jeff and Kent, shit about their physical prowess. But it was true. Lifting weights in just that short of time, about a month, had made me physically stronger in my upper body while my legs were always strong and I didn't get winded like my companions.

Work at the DMV was sometimes tedious, but, since my supervisor loved me because of my magical ability to code licenses without consulting the cheat sheets, I had it made. Coding a drivers license in the state of Illinois was easy for me, once I understood the rules. Every drivers license in Illinois starts with a letter, followed by eleven numbers, or eleven numbers, a dash, and one or two extra numbers, though those dashes and extra numbers were extremely rare and usually occurred with fraternal twins with similar given names and middle initials. That, in and of itself, is rare.

Here are the rules. The letter is the first initial of the driver's surname. The next three numbers are code numbers assigned to consonant groups, those being similar in sound or usage. For example, the consonants b and d were in the same group, assigned the number 1. The consonants s and c were in the same group, assigned the number 2. Some consonants, such as h, were not assigned to any group, so they had no value as far as coding a drivers license. The consonants were counted after the first letter of the surname only, to a maximum of three numbers, and the next consonant was included ONLY if it was separated by the previous consonant by a vowel or was from a different consonant group. As a further example, the name Abdignale, would start with A, followed by 1, the numeric value assigned to the consonant group which includes b, but, since d is in the same consonant group as b, it is skipped, and the next consonant to be included would be g, since it is separated by the last consonant group by a vowel. The next three numbers are combinations of the driver's given name and middle initial. Each given name would comprise a number from 000 to 980, by increments of twenty. Some specific given names, usually the more popular, had their own values, such as Harold and Mary. Adding a value from 0 to 19 would be the numeric equivalent, from a chart, for each letter, with some combined, of the middle initial. The next two numbers were the year of birth, minus the two century values. The last three numbers were specially modified julian dates, as they were typically described for computer applications, for the day of birth from the first day of the calendar year. They were specially modified in that every month consumed at least thirty-one calendar days for this code, regardless of leap year or the real number of days in the month, with one final trick; a female driver's julian date code would have the constant value of 600 added. Thus, a male born March 15 would have the last three numbers of the driver's license be 077, while a female would have 677. The dash followed by a number (or numbers) would refer to those rarities where all the coding for multiple drivers yielded the exact same driver's license, so they would be distinguished by a dash and a number for the first driver assigned that code. The second driver would be issued a '-2' and so on. With the code rules, though, you can see why it would be so rare to have similar drivers licenses and why it would most often involve fraternal twins, since twins of each gender could never have the same license number.

It was fun. You would get a pile of letters and some would have money in them, despite being advised to send only a check or money order, and others would actually have expired drivers licenses, and some others not so expired. I was instructed, of course, to turn over any of these occurrences, but sometimes I slipped an unexpired Illinois driver's license in my desk drawer and smuggled it outside the building at the end of the day. Mostly, it was just to see if I could do it, and I could. I eventually destroyed them, though I had thought about selling them. In my corner of the world, there wasn't much call for it, since one could still legally buy beer and wine at nineteen years of age.

Wouldn't you know it, though? One of those college students hired and working in my group would be a petite and cute little blonde named Candy, from Havana. When we finally all had a break together and introduced ourselves, I listened intently as she said she was from Havana.

"That's where my dad's family is from," I said.

"I know," she replied, almost too nonchalantly. "When I saw your last name, I thought you might be related to that teacher whose name is all over the schools there."

I must tell you. That smile that came from her lips was a little more than just a welcome. It was more than a sign that she liked me. It was a signal that if I played my cards right, she'd be in bed with me some time that summer. I liked the prospect, except for two nagging thoughts. She knew my family and its history and, as a reasonable extension, so did the rest of her family, and she didn't go to State, so there was *no way*

I was going to make a long distance deal out of a one-time fucking experience, no matter how many times she fucked me. *That never works*, was my overriding thought. Why didn't I listen to that thought all of my life??? Shit, that sure would have made things more palatable.

We went out for lunch several times, usually with other members of the group, but sometimes just the two of us. I once asked her if someone would like to go out for dinner or a movie or something with her, would that mean she would have to stay in town and find someone she could crash with that night. She said that she would have to since she lived at home in Havana and drove into work every day and drove back after work every day. I simply could not bring myself to ask her to do that and she couldn't bring herself to say that it didn't matter if she liked someone. I liked her smile and her laugh and how easily she talked to me. I could not take advantage of her, and I knew I could. Besides, no matter what you think, exploding my sausage, even *thousands of times*, never hurt anybody, not even me.

Little bro finished high school and was actually accepted at Southern Illinois University. How did that happen? Dad had been checking houses for sale. The neighborhood was changing in ways he didn't appreciate. The subdivision was growing with houses now directly across the street. Houses in the neighborhood now had new owners and new fences, a condition he and the other older owners were prohibited from building. He felt isolated from most of his friends who lived more in the town.

When he discovered that an older businessman was retiring and moving to his second home in Florida and preparing to put his house on South Grand Avenue, less than a block from the country club, up for sale, Dad contacted him and the two reached an agreement. In July, we prepared to move from the second house I had lived in and the only one I remembered. Boxes were everywhere and Mom was very good about packing her stuff and the essentials and labeling every box. There was eighteen years of accumulated possessions, along with eighteen years of worthless crap that got thrown out. Of course, during one period of relative inactivity, I managed to slip the canvas bag full of magazines into the trunk of the Torino. I couldn't leave that behind.

Soon, a moving company with its huge semi pulled up and they packed all the items as Mom and Dad directed. Even with a crew of three, it took two days to fill it, but when it was full, they closed up the truck and drove away. I had to go to work, but when my work day was over, I drove home to a different address, heading *into* town, instead of away from it. The driveway was all blacktopped and there was a section at the front for two cars to park. I pulled around the moving truck and parked next to Mike's little Opel GT and walked inside.

Through the front door, one was met with a living room about twenty-five feet by fifteen feet in size to the left and an open area with a closet door at the end of a four foot enclosure to the right, a wall opposite the closet door of about six feet in length. On the other side of the wall was a storage area and a corner which ran to a single step and a utility room about five feet by fifteen feet with a washer and dryer hookup, the water heater and the furnace, with a door leading outside to a four foot square landing and four steps to the driveway. Opposite the storage area from the front door was a door leading to the garage and a second door leading to the garage was next to the washer and dryer hookups. On the other side of the utility room was the kitchen.

There was a second living room on the opposing side of the first, roughly the same size as the first, and a separating wall about three feet in width between both living rooms. That living room wall contained a gas fireplace on either side and was open at both ends at a length of roughly fifteen feet.

Offset slightly towards the first living room was a platform of two steps about twelve feet long. In the middle of the platform was a corner to a fork, the beginning of two halls about six feet in length, each hall leading to a bedroom. The left hall led to the parents' bedroom, the right to the bedroom I would be sharing with my brother, Jeff. That bedroom was about twenty feet square with an ample closet in the opposite corner from the doorway. Turning left and walking through the room one would enter a large bathroom with a full-size shower but no bath. The stool was stuck next to the front wall of the shower and a large sink was opposite the shower. The bathroom alone was the size of a small bedroom, easily ten feet by twelve feet. In the left corner of the bedroom was a sliding door. On the other side of the sliding door was the parents' bathroom, which led to their bedroom, slightly larger than our bedroom.

The last room in the house, off of the second living room though a sliding glass door–the entire side of the living room was thick glass– was what I called the party room. It was huge, though the roof was just colored panels like you would find over a shed. The width of the party room was nearly the length of the living room, just shy of twenty-five feet, but it extended through most of the back yard at almost thirty feet. On the far end was a smaller sliding glass door which led to a porch about six feet by ten feet and enclosed with screen. Opposite the porch and close to the living room was a single door leading to the tiny backyard, landscaped with rock and plants and paver steps leading to the fence gate and driveway.

    With only two bedrooms and no basement, where did that leave Mike? For the immediate answer, he moved all his stuff into the party room, bed and all. At almost thirty, I thought it was time Mike got out on his own. He was working, he could afford his own place, most of his troubles were behind him, so I began a not-so-subtle campaign to get him out. We couldn't enjoy the porch if we had to walk through Mike's bedroom. Heck, we didn't have a party room. It was Mike's bedroom. There was quite a bit of tension, most of which I managed to stir up, but in a matter of weeks, Mike announced that he was moving out and he did. Then, he did one better. He had been dating a woman named Olga, who had four children. They announced their engagement and planned their wedding for just a few weeks away.

    Damn, my campaign worked better than even I thought it would. I felt such a sense of triumph and largess, I decided to give Olga's troubled oldest daughter, at that time about sixteen, my bass and amplifier. She had expressed an interest in playing and I hadn't played it in over a year, so I just gave it to her, though her mother insisted she pay for it so I took twenty dollars for both. Did it help? I doubt it. She was a brat who could be virtually uncontrollable when she went into her vicious temper tantrums. The other kids were a little shy, maybe overwhelmed at everything, but Olga was, well, different. A heavy-duty redhead, she could be sweet one moment and bitter and attacking the next. I can't say I knew her well. I certainly did not nor did I want to. There was something about her that reminded me of Cindy, the woman I had dated who went partially psycho when I rubbed her breasts. Who wants to get closer to that? Not me.

    In late July the blessed day came. The wedding was held outdoors at a friend's house with just a few guests and a man picked by both to perform the simple ceremony and who was recognized by the state with the authority to perform weddings. Once the wedding was complete, everyone was invited to the parents' new house for the reception, where we all drank plenty of champagne and other liquor-based beverages and ate. It was short and to the point, and the newly-married couple retired to their residence, where those who had come out of town also went. That was it. Not much to it, huh? I hardly saw either one for the rest of the summer. At least they got something out of it: the boat. Since Mom had traded in her car, which had the towing attachment, Dad had installed the towing attachment on his Mercedes, but had grown weary of lending his car so we could take the boat out. We never took it out and it had sat for almost two years unused. Dad gave the boat to Mike as his parting gift, so to speak, and he had it towed out to a friend's house on the lake. Mike was cordial enough to extend an open invitation to call him and he would meet us at Steve's house, but neither Jeff nor I were inclined to take him up on it. I hadn't ridden in the boat since I left for college and I never would again.

Late one morning during this summer, I woke up and Mom offered to fix me breakfast. Immediately after that offer came this observation. "I noticed there was a yellow stripe on the right side of your car this morning when I went out to get the paper," she said, a little too casually. She asked, "How did that get there?"

"I don't know," I responded, with equal casualness. "I better take a look."

I threw on my clothes and walked out to the car, and, sure as shit, there was a thin yellow stripe down most of the right side of my red Torino. It looked like paint, vehicular-style paint, like the paint on earth movers and other construction vehicles that would be parked in the construction company parking lot next door to the General Assembly disco, which is one of the few details I *did* remember about the previous night. It was also coming back to me that I had parked next to one of those construction vehicles on the *right* side of my car. *Perfect,* I thought, *as smashed as I was last night I had backed right into that construction vehicle and scratched my car permanently.*

I didn't panic, though. I went into the garage and dug up some car wax that you rub in, because I knew that sometimes when the paint came off of the *other* vehicle, that friction wasn't enough to scratch *your* paint, and the *other* paint could be removed with a reasonably good car wax product. As soon as I applied the wax and rubbed it around with a cloth, the yellow paint came right off, leaving no scratches or any other tell-tale signs. I was done in twenty minutes and the car looked just like it did the day before. The previous night was the last time I went to that disco for a long time and I only went out to a bar with the boys once more that summer. I could have been learning my lesson, but it seems that's a fair subject for debate.

Jeff and I had a dilemma. Having finally moved to a house with cable access and having it rigged in three rooms including the bedroom we shared, we had no TV but we didn't want one. Cable could pick up radio stations far away and 'broadcast' them through the wire, but you needed a tuner and an adapter which connected to the cable on one end and split into left and right channels for connecting to the tuner. We had all that after the cable guy installed the rooms. He just gave us the adapter when we asked. Jeff had a pair of jerry-rigged speakers that worked pretty well. What we didn't have was a receiver/amplifier and we couldn't use Mike's. I scoured the paper over the next week or two and finally saw what I liked, a Harman Kardon receiver with excellent specs and wattage output at a more excellent price, less than four hundred dollars. As a bonus the same audio gear company was offering a very reasonable Dual turntable for ninety-nine dollars. Since I had saved a little more than that just from working that summer, I skipped on down there and landed both. I took them home, carefully opened the boxes, removed the gear and all the accessories and hooked them up. I had grabbed some extra RCA audio jacks, what are called composite cables now, and connected the tuner to the receiver. I turned on the tuner and the receiver, tuned it to KSHE in St. Louis and was listening to decent live FM rock for the first time in a long time. It was Jeff's idea about the cable and radio, but he was definitely impressed with the setup. Not only could he listen to decent music from radio stations, he could even play his albums. Now, all he had to do was get a tape recorder, preferably one that could record his superior medium of choice: eight track. That's where he and I disagreed. The future of enthusiasts' tape recordings would be cassette, I predicted, and the only proper 'superior' recording mechanism would always be reel-to-reel. One of us was right. Got a clue which one?

    The summer of 76 seemed to fly by at a time, for me, when summers were especially fun. I had played a little softball with the boys, but quite often I would call Rick and meet him and some of the guys from State and other friends and we would throw the frisbee, drink beer, and smoke cigarettes and cannabis for hours and hours out at the park on the lake. Charlie, still in Massachusetts, had flown into town for a week and had taught me quite a few frisbee throws that I was still learning, but my favorite, and the one I can still throw better than anybody except a real frisbee pro, was what I call the thumb toss. With my hand palm side up, I put my thumb under the frisbee and hold the edge pinched between my thumb and index finger. With just a flick of my wrist, I can spin the frisbee with such rapid RPM that the recipient has to concentrate on squeezing it hard or it will just bounce off the hands. And it hurts, too. There are tricks to controlling it when you throw it like that, such as keeping the outer edge of the frisbee dipped slightly to the ground so that it cuts through the air with its quicker rotation instead of the air catching it and sending it sailing far away from the intended target. With more practice, I could launch the thumb toss fifty or more yards high in the air and have it seemingly drop from its heights right to the recipient. Whenever anybody sees me throw a frisbee with the thumb toss, they always want to know how I do it. Even Rick and his friends wanted to know, but when I show people, they try it, it goes badly and they quit and never try it again. Still, they are always impressed when I snap one that sails in a virtual straight line right to them, while they have to loop their tosses and they never have the same velocity or rotation. Even Charlie can't throw the thumb toss like I can.

The allure of the State Fair, beginning the second week of August, had waned for me and I skipped attending it. Instead, it signaled the rapidly approaching end of the summer for college students. Our supervisor at DMV took the time to check with all the summer help for our expected last day of work and the address where DMV should send our last paycheck. I intended to work right up to the day before I would leave for Normal, which is exactly what I did. Barely a week after the fair closed down until next summer, I worked my last day at DMV. I said goodbye to cute little Candy and all the others that afternoon. Candy wanted me to look her up at Western Illinois if I ever got over there and I said I would, but I knew that I probably wouldn't make it.

All of the stuff that needed to be packed was already in boxes and ready to move. The next day I got up and drove down to one of the national rental shops and rented a small trailer. I had a hitch installed on the Torino, so I hooked it up and drove back to the homestead. Jeff helped me load up the furniture and I carried all the rest of the boxes and set them in the trailer, kissed Mom goodbye, said goodbye to Dad and Jeff, fired up the muscle car and drove off to Normal.

For those of you too young to know or were somewhere else experiencing nirvana outside the realm of the real world, there was no interstate between Chicago and St. Louis in 1976. Sure, maps showed it existed, until you looked real close and saw the designations between 'controlled interchanges' and 'four-or-more-lane highways' flip back and forth on the map. Lincoln was one of those places where the designations would flip, because Interstate 55 disappeared at Lincoln and merged onto US 66 at the outskirts of town, with speed limits of thirty miler per hour and traffic lights. They were building the bypass around town that would eventually be Interstate 55 but it wasn't completed then. Hell, there were still places south of Podunk toward St. Louis where the local road still intersected with the 'interstate;' they hadn't built those bridges, yet, or cut off the intersection with a frontage road. The Eisenhower Interstate System was still a work in progress, and going through Lincoln was a major pain in the ass with its many railroad tracks, traffic lights, stop signs, and grandmothers traveling to the grocery store on the highway at thirty-five miles per hour in a fifty-five miles per hour zone. Ahhhh! I hated it.

After what seemed like an eternity towing a trailer behind my muscle car, but what was really less than an hour and a half, I pulled into the driveway of 405 Normal Avenue in Normal. Yeah, that's right! I was going to live on Normal in Normal. That's a lot of normal, maybe too normal. If I was truly *ab*normal, would I be able to exist and function under and in conditions *too* normal? Only time would tell. I had unpacking to do and I didn't think about it too much, especially when I walked in the door and was greeted by the sweet pungency of cannabis smoke.

"You just missed it," Rick said, looking up from the couch already set up in the living room. Two other guys shared the couch with him and the other Rick was sitting in a chair next to the couch but at the corner of the room. You'll easily get confused if I call both by the same name and even more confused when I write that both were about the same height, both had blonde hair parted in the middle and both wore glasses. That's the end of the similarity, because the other Rick didn't party as much as we did and he had been dating Kris since high school and would marry her soon after college, while the rest in attendance at that moment had never really dated any girl steady. Because he was more serious, I'll call the other Rick 'Richard' from here on.

I just smiled and pulled out a joint I had rolled for the end of the trip. "It's times like these," I replied, as I displayed the joint, "when it pays to be prepared." I whipped out my lighter and lit up the joint and passed it to the guy sitting at the end of the couch next to me, a good looking guy who would soon be introduced to me as Brad, or Brad the ladies' man.

I stood while we smoked the joint to a sliver and Steve, who I had met with Rick last semester and was sitting in the middle of the couch, asked for the roach so we gave it to him. Everyone but Brad the ladies' man offered to help unload the trailer, but I told them I could handle everything but a few of the items of furniture and I wouldn't get to those for a while. Steve offered to show me the room I would be sharing with the other Brad, so we went to the front hall and up the stairs. The hall ran along the outer wall of the upstairs section and there were four bedrooms, each to the left. My room was the room at the end of the hall in the back of the house. There was also a back stairs right off my bedroom which led to the back door, though you could turn left at the bottom of the stairs and enter the dining room. That stairs seemed to be the easiest to get items up to my room, so I propped open the back door and started moving my stuff into the room. Rick and Steve had setup their tunes and were cranking them all over the house so I just set my gear in the room and left it boxed while I moved the rest.

Once I recruited some help for the bed, mattress, desk and chair and got those upstairs, it was time to take the trailer to the closest location in Normal, which was about a mile away, along the route out of town north to El Paso and Chenoa. With that done, I drove to a liquor store to grab a couple of six packs of beer and spend the rest of the day and weekend partying, or, maybe, getting unpacked.

Over the course of the next two days, the rest of the house mates made their entrances. Eric, with his fashionable mustache and John Lennon glasses, pulled in from Quincy before I had finished unloading. He had met Brad the ladies' man first but was closer to Rick and Steve and he was the first cool person I had ever met from Quincy, not slighting Kerry's relatives, since I had only met them once and had only spent part of a day with them. Eric was just a laid-back cat. Nothing seemed to rattle him and he was always smiling. He was rooming with Richard.

My roommate, the other Brad, wandered in from up north somewhere. He had curly, red hair, and a laid-back, low key demeanor. His tone was usually very low so that sometimes you couldn't hear him. Immediately, he became Brad the Red, though I never called him that. We discussed the room arrangement and we moved my bed into a corner and I helped him move his stuff into the room. One of the first things he told me about himself was that he was a homosexual and would that bother me? I said that it wouldn't and it didn't. Then, he said that if I had somebody stay overnight, just tell him and he'd make arrangements to sleep in one of the other rooms, probably with Brad the ladies' man downstairs, since they were old friends and he didn't share his room with anyone. I told him the reverse holds, too. I'll find a place to crash. I liked Brad the Red. He was quiet and accommodating.

Drifting in the following morning, Saturday, from the nether regions of the northern Illinois tundra came David and his little brother, Lance. That this should bode for the typical expectations one would have of both, I'll save one the time which only experience can yield. Yes, they would both be fashionably late and often. We would wait for them, usually, though there would be times when we simply would not wait. Getting seats at a concert which is strictly general admission would be one such instance where we would not wait. In that context, it's 'you snooze, you lose.'

David and Lance were likable blokes, though they could display a little temper, too. David had the added burden of having to take his little brother under his wing and skirt around the requirement for freshmen to live in a dorm. Lance, to his credit, understood that and made just about every effort to be out with people he would meet that his brother didn't know, to take care of his grades on his own, to fix his own meals and generally take care of himself. Lance was a little looser than David, but I think a lot of that was his age and desire to belong. Other than that, they were eerily similar in approach, demeanor, reaction and temperament. They were almost identical in height, though David's hair was already receding. Lance liked to remind him, too. Hell, we all did.

Bringing up the rear after the sun had already set, Fu Manchu Steve pulled in, carried all his belongings from his car, with the generous and unsolicited help of some of the others, into his room downstairs while the rest of us watched in the living room, and introduced his fiance, Susan, and left. *Nice meeting you, Steve. Hey, bring that fiance of yours back any time. She's a looker.* I call him Fu Manchu Steve for fairly obvious reasons, since he had a very thick fu manchu. Come to think of it, he had very thick hair just about everywhere. Everywhere, that is, except for where he shaved so he could have his fu manchu. Steve was easy going, too, though you would have had a hard time being able to tell. He was almost never around.

Assuming you were counting and assuming you counted correctly, that's ten of us sharing one house with six bedrooms, one and a half baths, living room, dining room, tiny coat closet and a basement. With about seven cars and a drive that would park three deep from the garage–which we never used–to the road, we had to figure out a way to get cars in and out of the drive. The initial solution, which we changed later after a severe setback to the Torino, was to leave a set of keys in the dining room so that one's car could be moved at any time. It worked for a while.

The boys figured there was no action at the bars Sunday, so we just hung out at the house, drinking and smoking and settling in. Classes wouldn't start until Tuesday, since Monday was the reschedule day, when last minute changes and additions were allowed. That night we walked to tavern row in Normal and drank a few and got used to a packed joint as everybody, it seemed, was out walking around headed to bars, restaurants, etc. Last chance to party while it was still summer. Tomorrow, school is in session. Don't be late. Hangovers permitted.

Tuesday rolled around and I attended my two classes for that day with diligence. Since it was just introduction of the teacher and the students and passing out the course schedule, it didn't take all that much diligence. Thursday, though, we were promised, we'd start getting into it hot and heavy. Who can wait for that?

I stored my weights downstairs and I pumped the weights after classes when I returned to the homestead. Everybody had some homework, but most of us completed it before dinner, myself included. Nothing much was going on, but there was already a party that the boys were planning to attend that Saturday. Rick was telling me that was what it would be like most of the time. That's a shame. I only wanted to study, read my textbooks and go to the library. Why am I expected to party every weekend? I have educational goals to meet, gray matter to fill eagerly. I am *not* a party animal!

I haven't convinced you, have I? Well, alright then, let's party.

Wednesday I would attend my other three classes, along with Business Organization and Management, which was a four hour class with an hour every Monday through Thursday. My first class was at nine in the morning, so I was up reasonably early and ready to walk to campus and my class on time. I had my materials for the next class, too, scheduled at ten. I got to the building for my nine o'clock class and found the room easily.

The room had a foyer from the door about six feet in length where many students were standing as they decided where they would sit. From the foyer I could only see the last two rows at the back of the room, but immediately I spied a beautiful little blond, her hair falling over her shoulders and ending just above the mounds of her ample breasts. I squeezed past students until I could survey the entire classroom. There were three or four other attractive females, but my gaze soon returned to that cute little blond wearing a soft pink blouse with thin straps over her shoulders and loose white shorts failing to cover her thick, smooth and shapely thighs. As I watched her setting her materials on her desk, I noted that she sat in the back row. *Oh, that's a good sign*. It means she's not a goody-goody who's compelled to sit in the front row craving the constant attention of the instructor. The seat next to her and closest to me was unoccupied. *Oh, that's a good sign*. She was clearly the most attractive woman in the class and I thought I should get to that seat. That's where I want to sit. I stepped deftly around the students already sitting in the back row and the next row of seats until I stood before the empty seat next to her and calmly asked, as I looked down at her face, "Is this seat taken?"

She glanced up at me with her round face practically glowing, and her mouth opened with an inviting smile as she replied, "No." *Oh, that's a good sign*.

I smiled awkwardly and asked, "Mind if I sit here?"

With no break in that infectious smile, she said, "Not at all." *Oh, that's a good sign*. Immediately, she glanced down at her desk and reached into her purse on the floor to retrieve a pen and set it on her desk.

I slid into the seat next to her and set my books on the desk. I pulled out the notebook and text book for the next class and slid them under the seat on the tray. Pulling the pen from the ring binder of the notebook, I opened it and set the pen on the first blank page and tried to avoid staring at the physical features of the fine-looking woman now sitting next to me. It was hard. The top of her blouse came down below her breasts and I could see the soft white curves at the top. Her thighs were smooth and succulent and the skin of her visible body was tanned and fit. As the instructor strolled in and sat down at the desk at the front of the room, I wondered how I was going to be able to sit next to this beauty for the next class period Friday.

"Okay, for the next five minutes," the male professor commanded as he began to organize his desk, "look around the room and if you're not happy with where you're sitting, get up and find a better seat because after five minutes I'll call the roll and make my seating chart here," and he lifted a sheet of graph paper, "and that's where you'll be sitting for the rest of the semester."

Nervously, I glanced around the room and watched a few of my fellow students get up and change their seat, but with my peripheral vision I waited for that beauty next to me to get up and move. After five minutes of five separate eternities, the professor barked, "Okay, settle down for roll call." The cute little blonde sat calm and poised next to me as I glanced at her and she flashed a confident smile. *Oh, that's a good sign.* I smiled back at her as calmly as I could, knowing that I was going to be sitting next to her not just the next class period but the whole semester. *Oh, that's a good sign, too.*

A few names into the roll call and I heard an intriguing name, Desiree. Instantly, in a strong lilting soprano next to me, I heard, "Here!" I glanced over at her desk top and lifted my gaze into her face and was greeted by another inviting smile as her gorgeous hazel eyes looked into my brown ones. *Now, that's not a name you hear every day,* I thought. It was becoming easier to smile back at her, too.

The professor finished the roll call and handed stacks of the course schedule to one of the students seated in the front row and the stacks were passed around and back until everyone had a copy. He went over his class rules, expectations, went through the schedule and announced our first assignment for homework. He opened up the rest of the time for questions and once those were exhausted, class was dismissed with fifteen minutes left.

As I sorted my materials slowly, expecting the blonde next to me to be slow, she suddenly stood up from her desk, packed and ready to leave. I swung my legs out of her way as I reached for the books under my desk, grabbed them and set them atop my others and stood up to follow her. As I struggled to stay directly behind her, I glanced at her rear and admired, for the first time, one of the most outstanding bubble butts I had ever seen. I almost couldn't lift my eyes from it as I watched it tighten and sway with each step she took.

When she reached the hall she walked slowly, as though she were waiting for me. I stepped up to walk beside her and when she looked in my direction innocently, I asked, "Desiree, right?"

"Yes," she said and smiled. "You can call me Dezzy," she added. "All my friends do, but *never* Dizzy."

"Never," I assured her. "You know, we have one thing in common."

"What's that?" she asked.

"We both go to school here."

"And we both have the same Marketing class," she countered. "That's two things."

I thought for a moment if I should say it, but I decided to plow straight ahead, damn the torpedoes. "But there's one thing we don't share in common."

"And that would be?" she asked, dangling her question, awaiting my response.

"We don't share the same gender," I replied, calmly, "so your female friends would probably frown if I followed you into the women's restroom to continue our conversation."

She laughed briefly and I heard her giggle for the first time. It was wonderful and I knew I wanted to hear it again. Quickly changing her expression into a stern countenance, she said, "Why would you want to do that?"

As I glanced down to make my way down the stairs and stay next to her, I asked, "You wouldn't invite me into the women's restroom?"

She glanced behind her and some of the people around us heard me ask her that. With eyes all around us narrowed and looking at us like we were strange, she lowered her voice and said, "No, I wouldn't invite you into the women's restroom."

"Got it," I quickly shot back, rescuing the moment. "Dezzy will never invite me into the women's restroom so don't ask." She smiled and suddenly those looks around us changed to smiles.

We had reached the outdoors and she announced, "I have to go back to my dorm before the next class." She turned left and started to walk away.

"Which dorm is that?" I asked, raising my voice.

"Watterson," she said, stopping to turn around and face me.

"Ah, the windy twin towers," I said.

"That's the one."

"See you Friday," I said and she turned and walked away. I stood there and watched her beautiful bubble butt tighten and sway until it disappeared from view behind a building.

I wanted to get out and be more active in this new college community, so, combining my experience as a referee for intramural football games during my freshmen year, I had applied for the same position at State. They were fairly picky about the referees they would hire, requiring applicants complete a test unless they had worked previously, but it was easy and my previous experience convinced the department to hire me. Most of the games were uneventful and none of the house boys were really into playing football, so I didn't advertise my position much. It was fun, though, and there were never any moments that I couldn't handle. I even got to referee some games on the university's football field, which was pretty cool. During halftime of one game on the school's football field, my supervisor, who was a physical education major about six feet tall and built like a linebacker, asked if I wanted to throw the ball with him. After a few warm-up tosses from both of us, he wanted to see how far I could throw it. Standing at the opposite forty yard line, I sent him across the fifty yard line toward the goal line. He kept slowing down and telling me to throw it as he crossed the thirty, the twenty, but when I finally heaved it, he caught it on the fly in the end zone, more than sixty yards from where I stood. He was only kidding when he told me to see if I could throw it in the end zone. When he threw it back and his release slipped so that the ball bounced and bounced, never reaching me, he was mightily impressed. Not bad for a short, skinny slacker.

David and Fu Manchu Steve knew some guys trying to form a softball team to play that fall semester in a shortened intramural season and they asked if anybody else wanted to play because they needed a few more to meet the minimum number of players for the team. Lance was going to play and I brought my glove, so what the heck. Play ball.

We never practiced with each other at all and our first game was Thursday. Maybe some of the guys didn't get the memo, because we only had nine players show up, which meant that every time we went through the batting order, once the ninth batter was through, we would be assessed an 'out' for the missing tenth batter. The odds were against us.

Maybe because of that, the other team took us lightly. We were the home team, so they batted first, managing to put a runner on second but failing to plate him. In our half of the first, the guys were hitting it around pretty good and the other team's defense was less than sparkling. Still, having filled the bases with two outs, we could only score two runs, having sent eight batters to the plate, so they must have felt like they dodged a big bullet. I could hear their talk as we switched positions on the field, but they couldn't score a run after two innings, not particularly impressive in slow-pitch softball.

I batted last so it was my turn up first. I saw why the guys were hitting the opposing pitcher pretty well when he grooved one right down the middle for me. I waited patiently, trying to time it so I could place it between the outfielders and was a little disappointed when it took off straight to dead center field. I ran hard to first base, watching the ball and the center fielder, realizing, as everyone else did, that the ball was not coming down soon. As my foot touched second base I saw the ball bounce off the dirt behind center field a good ten yards past the fielder. Running as fast as I could as I rounded third base, I heard the coach say, "You can slow down. He just got the ball." I slowed to a leisurely trot and stepped on home plate before the shortstop even touched the ball, having hit our team's first home run, a towering shot way over the center fielder's head. So, if you're wondering, simple curls with weights at the end of a bar can make a difference. Even though the home plate umpire immediately called us out for the missing tenth batter, the other team was stunned, as were some of my own teammates. Our opponents never could recover from that and we walloped them nine to three and it wasn't even that close.

Friday morning came and I was anticipating my next encounter with that little blond girl in Marketing and not having to attend another business organization and management class. Jeez, was that class boring and the instructor, a middle-aged woman from the old country, didn't exactly inspire gushing enthusiasm. I was going to like Fridays. It was the last day of classes for the week. I'd probably be glancing frequently at that fine, full-bodied female frame sitting next to me in Marketing and enjoying that view, and I didn't have a BOM class. Nothing wrong with that.

I walked into my nine A.M. class earlier than I usually did because I had been up and ready to go and couldn't wait. My book, notebook and pen were already on my desk when Desiree squeezed by and said, "Hi."

"Good morning," I said, smiling up at her infectious smile.

As she settled into her chair, she asked, "Are you ready for the weekend?"

I looked at her, letting my eyes move up and down her luscious body covered by her loose white cotton blouse, which failed to hide her brassiere underneath, and her white shorts that barely reached her thick, smooth thighs. I enjoyed how her choice of color contrasted with her deep tan. "Just get me though these classes today so I can party," I replied.

"Got any plans?" she asked, smiling as she opened her notebook, looking at me sweetly.

I smiled as I looked in her eyes. "There's a party tomorrow that I'm going to," I said.

She frowned briefly. "Oh," she remarked, "I'm going to Heyworth for the weekend to be with my family."

My face reflected my lack of familiarity as I asked, "Where's Heyworth?"

The instructor strolled into the room and announced, "Alright! Let's get to it." Immediately, the background chatter filling the room came to an abrupt end and all eyes followed the instructor to his desk at the front.

"Tell you later," Desiree whispered, looking at the instructor.

Once the instructor dismissed class, as I printed the last of my notes, having abandoned long hand due to my sloppy use of it, Desiree squeezed past me, but stopped and turned to wait for me as I gathered my materials. As I stood up from the desk she sauntered toward the door and out to the hall while I followed right behind her.

As she slowed to let me reach her right side, she asked, "You asked about Heyworth?"

"Yeah," I said, smiling easily, "where's that?"

She smiled back as she replied, "It's south of Bloomington, about fifteen miles."

"Do you like it there?"

She frowned a bit when she replied, "There's not much to do, it's so small." She brightened, though, as she added, "It's quiet, though, and I like that."

"Do you go home a lot of weekends?"

She shook her head and looked away. "Not a lot," she said.

"Driving your car?"

She chuckled as she looked back at me with a warm smile. "No, I don't have a car," she said. "A boy I know is coming to pick me up."

"Oh," was all I could manage to blurt.

With sudden and unexpected concern on her face and in her

voice, she stated, "He's a friend I've known since high school." She smiled and quickly added, "Have fun at your party." She turned to her left and I instinctively gazed at that beautiful bubble butt bounce slightly as it moved away from me. Turning to walk to my next class, I wondered about a boy from Heyworth and what that meant. I suppose I couldn't expect a fine babe like Desiree to have no boys in her life, but it was encouraging that we talked like we did and that she seemed to show genuine interest in me, the man, the boy, with no description.

On a positive note–granted, 'positive' is relative when it concerns my twisted mind–I could picture the cleavage from those full breasts struggling to get out from the vee of Desiree's blouse all day. I was thinking that I probably wouldn't even have to open the canvas bag stashed under my bed tonight. My mind is definitely twisted but not at the expense of a vivid imagination. Up goes the blouse over her lifted arms, snap and off the shoulders slides the bra straps, lying down and my hands hook under her shorts and panties and down they go over her feet, and, my, my, there's a full-figured naked female waiting patiently underneath me, legs conveniently spread wide. Imagine that.

The rest of the day's visit to classrooms scurried past with a merciful rapidity. Back at the boys home, the crew with whom I most felt comfortable and accepted–Rick, Steve, Richard and Eric–were all hard at work on their respective class assignments for Monday. This was going to be a friendly competition to determine the best brain in the house. I wasn't going to let anyone get ahead of me so easily, so I read all my assigned chapters, completed all my quizzes, questions, and compositions and was ready for a relaxing evening following dinner, a meager and uncomplicated affair as dinners seem to be when prepared by college students.

Brad the Red was out late on this Friday night, thus leaving me to my own devices come bed time. Since I didn't need any devices that night, I had a lovely dream about a little blond girl, about five feet four inches in height, who had managed to wander into the boys home, up the stairs and into my room and bed. At the tail end of this dream sequence, I had a certain physical reaction. I think I have previously described it as 'exploding the sausage.' It's certainly a more pleasingly intense sensation than watching explosions on the Fourth of July.

Saturday. A day to get up late, drink coffee late, eat breakfast late (if at all), smoke pot late, go to the grocery store early, buy beer. No. Scratch beer. I had learned my lesson in less than a week. In a house full of college boys, beer purchased for long-term consumption and left in a shared refrigerator will disappear in record time. Of course, no one knows exactly how. With ten boys it's three times worse than the kids in Family Circus, with the ghosts of I Don't Know, Not Me, and It Wasn't Me. I would no longer buy beer for any period greater than one day, or else the remainder would certainly be confiscated by Not Me and company. At least everyone respected a new stash of beer that would suddenly appear that day in the frij. Once daybreak arrived, though, it was every beer for itself.

After the trip to the store, we took a stroll out to the quadrangle for a little frisbee tossing, smoke breaks and beer guzzling, the last two being performed as surreptitiously as possible. That was good enough for a couple hours. After that, it was back to the boys home to listen to music or watch television or sit out on the porch or in lawn chairs on the front lawn and watch the world pass by, and comment about how excellent that 'young tail' looked, should some 'young tail' pass by. Inevitably, they would, being the college town with the still valid reputation as a decent party school.

Fend for yourself for dinner was the order that evening. Charcoal grills were set ablaze and soon cheeseburgers, hot dogs and steaks–steak on a college student wage, something which exists only in fairy tales–were cooked and on their way to the kitchen, dining room and down the esophageal tubes toward some of the boys' stomachs. Ah! Don't forget the after-dinner smokes and the impromptu planning meetings for the upcoming festivities. I heard Rick and Steve say that we never go to a party before ten at night because that's when the most activity takes place and the girls are sufficiently under the influence. I smiled at Rick, thinking that I had heard the same advice from Kent and Jeff back in Podunk. So, as little as they trusted each other and avoided crossing paths, Rick and Kent weren't as different as they liked to think they were.

We all had some hours to kill until party time, so what should we do? Wouldn't you know it? It's 1976 and somebody has a tiny bag of cocaine and is willing to share a few snort lines. Out comes a tiny rectangular mirror, coke chunks are chopped up, lines are laid out and twenty dollar bills are rolled up like straws. Not everybody gets to indulge, though. Some of the boys are gone for the night already and some had never set foot in the house all day. Others were indulging in their own way, so it was just a select few, but coke being coke and the tremendous stigma still attached to it, I'll just write that I indulged in it, snorting some other unnamed person's cocaine stash and always leave it at that.

With the witching hour upon us, we climbed into the muscle car and drove to our appointed rounds. Of course, once we descended upon the party, we were asked to donate for the beer we were about to consume. Grudgingly, all of us, Rick, Steve, Eric, Brad the ladies' man, and I, gave a few bucks each, grabbed a plastic cup and hovered about the tap, ensuring that we at least got our fill. Since no one else was tending the tap and keeping it pumped and primed, I volunteered. Oh, yeah, it was a small price to pay so that I could watch the babes stagger and sway to the beer tap for a refill. Usually, I would hold the tap and fill their cups, looking them over with a sly smile plastered on my face. Sometimes, the girl would mention that she hadn't seen me before and we would exchange a few lines, but mostly it was just scoping each other out. If it was a guy, I usually let him fill his own cup, but I drank enough to cover my donation.

There wasn't much introducing, but I did meet some of the regular girls, the girls who would eventually hang out and party with the boys regularly. Most had fucked Brad the ladies' man at one time or another but had no inclination to do it again. I only call him a ladies' man. I never said any of them were steadies and that was probably mutual.

All in all it was like going to a bar with lots of pussy, something I had a bit of experience doing, but it was a whole lot cheaper and the women were a little more educated. There were a lot of girls in attendance and I was quite pleased that I had transferred. In two years at the big U I had never been to a party as packed with fine pussy like this very first party. I thought things were surely going to change here.

Some time after two in the morning, though I certainly wasn't keeping track of time, since more than one girl was falling into me over the course of the night, we climbed back into the muscle car and I drove us quite ably to the boys' home. Believe it or not, we didn't go right to bed, either. I had beers left from a previous purchase that day and I offered and we smoked a little, too. To be honest, it was no big deal. None of us were going to be up in time to go to church, and, if we were, we weren't going anyway.

Sunday was a day of rest and we absolutely rested. Some of us watched football, the last week of exhibition. Next week, the games counted. I had no interest in going anywhere so I didn't. I just hung out and helped clean up a little bit when somebody ragged about how bad the house was looking and did as little as possible. Maybe it was because I felt a little out of it from the night before. Still, I didn't have a hangover nor was I ralphing–that's vomiting for those of you less slang-educated–so I wasn't complaining. In any event, just being 'out of it' was enough incentive to drink a beer or some other alcoholic beverage or two to, *perhaps*, get over the 'out of it' feeling. I drank three to be safe.

Back to class the following day, as it would be after *every* weekend, I would eventually be sitting next to that fine little blond girl with the oval face, big eyes, and full-sized, adult features. What a chore to be forced to face that at the beginning of every week?

There she would sit in the desk next to me, always seemingly wearing just enough to cover her sensitive, secret areas and avoid arrest for 'public indecency.' Who came up with that term has some buried issue with determining what's decent and what is not. I had an unshakable sense that, should I be confronted with an unobstructed view of Desiree's sensitive, secret areas, I was *not* going to consider that view 'indecent' in any possible application of the word.

When class dismissed, I was up first but I didn't have to wait for her since she was right behind me out the door and next to me almost immediately in the hall. She asked about the party and I told her where I thought it was and that I enjoyed it and that we were all there pretty late. She claimed that she knew the people at the house where the party had been and asked how I knew them and who did I go there with. I told her their names and she seemed to recognize them. She asked where I was staying and I told her about the house on Normal Avenue with the nine other boys.

"Does Rick and Steve and Eric live there?" she asked, now greatly interested.

"Yeah, they do," I replied, starting to think how small this world really is.

"I was wondering where those guys were staying," she remarked, "since they said they weren't going to be in the dormitory this year." She paused and looked in my eyes warmly, smiled, and asked, "So how do *you* know Rick and Steve and Eric?"

I smiled back as I told her that I had gone to high school with Rick and we were the same age and I had transferred from the Big U. Rick had discussed with the other boys about whether they would have room for me and they all agreed that I could stay with them, so that's how I ended up on Normal in Normal. She remarked that I must have a good sense for friends because she had known those guys for quite a while, and she knew they liked to party, but they took care of their business, and were decent people. So I could depend on them to not be 'publicly indecent,' I thought, and smiled briefly at the inside joke. She made a comment about how she'd like to see them again and I ought to let her know when we planned having our own party at the boys home. I promised I would let her know and I left thinking that this was a really good development. She knew some of the boys staying at the house and they could certainly vouch for me. I liked that idea.

Back at the boys home after classes, I got the chance to talk to Rick and Steve, who shared the room upstairs nearest the front of the house, about Desiree and what she had said. When I described her, both knew instantly who she was, although her name helped, too. They had seen her around campus for quite a while but really got to know her the year before, when she lived in a room at Watterson and they would run into her at parties. "She liked to talk a lot and laugh a lot, but she could be weird at times," they cautioned me. When I asked them to explain what they meant by weird, they both stated, in different terms, that she didn't want to be close to any guy, it seemed. She didn't date anybody she met on campus and really resented anybody trying to make a move on her. "Well, we're just telling what other guys have told us. We like her because she's fun, she likes to party, and we were never interested in her like that. Anyway, good luck, bro." Great, now I would have to rely on luck to somehow get close enough to Desiree to have a chance to make sweet love to her and that wonderfully fine, full body. If it involves luck, I'm fucked now, and not how I want to be fucked.

My educational portion at State was going well. I stayed on top of the assignments and went to class regularly. None of it was too difficult and even Desiree noticed that. We would compare our results for quizzes and tests and I would frequently know the answers to questions the instructor asked during class. Quite often she would ask before class about some things she didn't particularly understand and I would help her as much as I could. I did it truly because I wanted to help her and she instinctively knew that. The boys would compare their scores in various classes and it was clear that I was holding my own, perhaps even leading everyone.

The softball team did well during this shortened season. We finished with a winning record and we were never blown out. We had some pretty good players, even though we almost never practiced. We won our first playoff game after a bit of a struggle, coming back in the last two innings to take the lead and holding them to none. Our next playoff game in the first week of October was shaping up to be the same, although we were cutting it close, waiting until our final inning. Down two runs we had runners on second and third with two outs and I was waiting on deck, knowing that I was going to come up and at least tie this game if not win it outright. *I just need this batter to get on somehow and I'll win this game for us. Cumon!* The next batter had been on base twice before, but maybe the pressure got to him. He tagged it weakly down to second base and was thrown out at first. No more softball for us.

I decided to take a break from parties and festivities the weekend after our playoff loss and drove home to relax and visit with the parents. They were interested in how I was doing and I felt really good about my transfer, even though it meant leaving Dad's school. I got home in plenty of time for dinner and ate watching television in the TV living room. Dad had some beer for me and I drank some beer, watched TV and chatted with Mom and Dad. It had been a while since I had done that during a school year.

The next morning Dad got a phone call from Mike. The night before Mike had been out at his friend Steve's place on the lake, where the boat was being kept, and the two of them had tried to get the boat out of the water. When Dad told me about that, I thought that was simple enough. *What do they need our help with?* As it turned out they literally had the boat *under* water, so getting it *out* of the water would entail *lifting* it out of the water and bailing the water still in the boat out until it could be set on the water without fear of sinking again.

Out to the lake Dad and I drove in his car under completely overcast, gray skies, a blah type of day, though it was still warm for autumn. Once we arrived we declined to enter the house and walked around it out to the dock in the back. As soon as I saw the front tip of the boat lurching above the water facing the shore, I knew what had happened. The last time one or both of them had taken out the boat, when they returned and tied it to the dock, they failed to turn the bow out to the lake, instead leaving the stern of the speed boat, with its aft lower than the front and even cut lower in the middle for the outboard engine, exposed to the elements which might kick up from the lake. A day of strong winds had churned up the waves, which came over the aft and swamped the boat completely so that it set on the mud at the bottom of the lake, though fortunately close to shore that it wasn't a total loss. I could only shake my head at the friggin' bonehead who managed to break that simple rule of boating: never expose the lowest part of a boat to the water side. *Fuckin' idiots,* was all I could think.

Into the cool water we jumped, except for Dad, and cut-out plastic jugs for bailing were scattered on the dock. Mike, Steve and I lifted the aft of the boat out of the water, but there weren't enough bailers to get the water in the boat out fast enough. Eventually, their side sank and down to the bottom went the boat. We tried this arrangement a few more times with the same results. Disgusted, I told both of them to get on the dock with bailing scoops ready and everybody needs to bail furiously or we'll never get this boat out of the water. Dad looked at me and asked, "Do you think you can lift that boat all by yourself?" I think he was actually considering getting in the water to help, even though he was just as disgusted about how this took place as I was. "Watch me," was all I replied. I stepped around in the mud to prepare myself mentally, went to the far end of the engine and felt around for sharp edges and to decide where I would place my hands to get a good grip. I bent down into a full squat with my head under water, slipped my forearms under the boat and lifted the aft completely out of the water. As soon as it broke the surface, everybody on the dock laid down and scooped water out of the boat, not even caring if they smacked into each other. Straining under the weight of hundreds of gallons of water, I still held that boat above the surface for several minutes, just enough time to watch the water drop about two feet from the top of the boat. As everyone continued bailing furiously, I tested if the boat would ride on top of the water a couple times. The last time I tested it, it held safely and I relaxed my grip and told everyone not to stop now. I stepped away from the activity and hopped onto the dock, walked around the bodies lying on the dock bailing, and grabbed a towel and dried myself off. After ten minutes of watching, I put a foot on the side of the boat, felt it rock a little, and slowly climbed into the boat and into the water still inside. Taking a bailer I scooped out enough water so that I could actually see the bottom of the boat. That was enough. "Okay, now let's turn the boat in the right direction, and you guys can finish bailing," I announced. We turned the bow out to the lake, tied it securely to the dock, Mike and Steve and their friends climbed in and continued bailing. Dad and I turned to the house, walked off the dock and around the house to his car and drove home. I took a shower almost as soon as I walked in the door. Mom couldn't believe I lifted the boat out of the water by myself, even after both Dad and I told her together. "I guess lifting weights has some advantages, huh?" I told her. She called Mike later and when he told her the same thing, then she believed it. Go figure.

There was something about that little blond girl in my Marketing class that wouldn't let go of me. I loved her appearance. Her body was everything I wanted in a woman. Her breasts were full and round in proportion to her size, which was also attractive. She wasn't real short but she wasn't challenging me height-wise, either. Her waist was thin and her thighs were just fantastic, smooth, clear, thick and muscular. Her arms were strong, too. She said she used to work horses, even traveled frequently to Kentucky for the stables and races. Her long, straight, blond hair was sexy, and framed in that hair was an oval, clear, smooth face and complexion and a smile which was warm and inviting. Her eyes were big and hazel, though they seemed to change color sometimes, and I thought I could see green one time, or light blue the next, or gray another time. Then, of course, there was that round and conspicuous bubble butt that was hard not to look at when she walked away. Actually, I could follow that butt anywhere. No way was I getting lost or distracted. It was in perfect proportion to her body, meaning it wasn't wide, it just stuck out prominently from the side. Her only blemish, if you could call it that, was one of her top front teeth was discolored, the result of a car accident and having it knocked out. They saved it, but the tooth had lost some of its nerve connections and the enamel had turned a bit yellow. She wasn't outwardly self-conscious about it, until you pointed it out to her. It was obvious to me that it was a sensitive subject to her and I avoided staring at it and never talked about it again.

Desiree was hard to figure out. We had a party the second weekend of school and I told her about it, but she was evasive. Finally, after Friday's class, she said she was going home for the weekend, again. Something pushed me and I asked if that boy who was only a long-time friend from high school was coming to pick her up, again. She said that he was and asked me if it mattered to me. I scoffed. Why would it matter to me? Isn't he just a long-time friend from high school, who only enjoys driving you back and forth from school to your family's home like a dutiful chauffeur and nothing more? He just drives away out of your driveway until duty calls, right?

If looks could kill, I wouldn't be writing this since I would have died at that very moment. Undeterred and quicker than she could come back with anything, I displayed even more bravado, when I casually said, "Anyway, you have fun in Heyworth this weekend, okay?" Immediately, I turned away from her to walk to my next class, already regretting that I was losing another opportunity to watch that beautiful bubble butt in motion. However, I didn't think this long-time friend from high school was *just* a friend.

The following week when we would see each other in the only class we shared, we were civil with each other, but we both showed the other the cold shoulder. Monday and Wednesday, I fiddled around after class was dismissed so that she would leave before me and I made no effort to catch up with her and she made no effort to slow down. Doing it that way, though, I got to watch that butt.

Friday, I walked into class and she was already sitting at her desk. I said, "Hi," as I sat down and she suddenly smiled and wouldn't look away. She watched me sit down and get situated and wouldn't look at anything else.

"Goin' home this weekend?" I asked as sweetly and innocently as I could muster.

"No," she said, smiling. "I don't know what I'm going to do this weekend. I might go to a party or two. I might stay in my room. I might go to a bar. I haven't decided."

"I'm going to a party tonight and another party tomorrow," I said. "Maybe you'd like to go?"

Desiree smiled convincingly as she replied, "Oh, I probably know which parties they are. Maybe I'll see you there."

When we left class, she waited for me. She said I should know about her long-time friend from high school. Yes, he was more than a friend. He had been her boyfriend in high school and occasionally they would still go out together. She insisted that it was more what he wanted, that she didn't feel very close to him but she had such a long history with him and it was hard for her to just forget about that. He was, after all, a decent boy and treated her well. Suddenly, she asked what time I was planning on going to the party tonight. I told her we wouldn't leave the house until sometime after ten at night and I asked her why she wanted to know. She smiled and said she just might surprise me.

Abruptly, she turned and walked away and I stood there unmoving, watching that butt bounce, my eyebrows furrowed, wondering what that all meant. She turned her head back and I raised my gaze to her face a little sheepishly. Certain that she had caught me staring at her butt, she flashed me a wickedly beautiful smile, turned her head forward, and kept on walking toward her dorm. Now I really was confused.

Back at the boys home for lunch, I stood before the stove browning a grilled cheese sandwich when Rick stepped into the kitchen. "What's happenin', bro?" I asked in our usual friendly manner.

Reaching the refrigerator, he opened it to grab a carton of milk, and replied, "Couldn't be better for classes, but, say, man, I don't think I'm going to that party tonight." He opened a cabinet door, pulled down a glass, inspected it for cleanliness, set the glass on the counter and poured the milk into it.

Watching the progress of my sandwich, I asked nonchalantly, "Why not?"

"Brad asked me for five dollars for beer for his friends' party," Rick replied, incredulity in his tone.

"He wanted it now?" I asked, turning to see the expression of disbelief on Rick's face.

"Yeah," he replied, shaking his head. "Can you believe that?"

We heard the front door open and close and feet step through the living room, then the dining room, and Steve appeared at the kitchen door. When he spotted Rick leaning against the counter behind the refrigerator, Steve's face contorted into anger as he asked, "Did Brad ask you for five dollars for beer for that party?"

Rick looked at Steve and laughed as he said, "Yeah."

"You didn't give him any money, did you?" Steve asked.

"No way, man," Rick said, shaking his head. "I just told him I didn't have any money with me."

"Good!" Steve exclaimed, starting to turn away.

I lifted the sandwich from the pan, placed it on a plate and turned the burner off. As I grabbed the plate and my glass of milk and turned to walk to the dining room, I said, "So, let me get this straight."

"Don't bother," Steve advised me.

"No, I like to go over these things, so I can remember how ridiculous this has turned out," I said.

Rick just laughed and said, "That's Brad for ya."

"First, the friend's having the party," I began as I sat down at the table. "Then, he's leaving town for an emergency. Then, he *is* having the party, but his car's broke down and that's why he's *not* leaving for an emergency. Then, he's not going to be able to get any beer so everyone has to bring their own because he needs to get his car fixed. Then, he's *not* having the party because nobody wants to go to this party and have to bring their own beer or whatever. Then, he *is* having the party, because some other friends loaned him money to fix his car, so he *does* have money for beer. And, *now*, Brad's asking for money for beer for this party, pay in advance. That about sum it up?"

Rick laughed and Steve commented, "You forgot about the girls from out of town coming to rescue the party and then backing out."

"Yep," I said, taking a bite from my sandwich, "forgot that."

Rick rinsed his finished glass of milk and returned the carton to the refrigerator. "So, are you going to the party?" he asked me.

"Not if I have to pay in advance," I advised them, my introduction to Brad the ladies' man's schemes that never stop changing now complete. "I don't know Brad like you two do, but I have a gut feeling that when I give him money for beer, I'll neither see that money again nor will I get any beer for it."

"Well," Steve began, "if the party folds and you don't get any beer, Brad will eventually pay you back."

Rick laughed. "Yeah, after you hound him for days and weeks," he stated.

"So, what do you want to do tonight?" Steve asked Rick.

"We can just hang out here, or walk across campus to the bars, whatever," Rick replied. "What are you going to do?" he asked me.

"Well, since the party's out," I answered, "I don't know, yet. I'll finish up my classes this afternoon and decide then."

In our minds, though, we had already decided what we would do. We didn't want to spend the money, nor could we reasonably afford, to go to the bars. There were no other parties of interest, so we were just going to hang out at the boys home for the evening. We made a beer run, some other folks came by, we combined some money and food we already had in the house and organized a cookout, ate and listened to music with the television on but its sound off. Many took turns spinning doobies and we smoked and were having a good time.

About eight in the evening, the phone rang and Richard answered it as several of us sat in the living room joking around and listening to the music. Richard could barely hear the person on the other end except that they wanted to talk to me, so he yelled my name, even though he was only sitting five feet away from me, and held the phone toward me. I asked him who it was and he just shook his head and shrugged his shoulders, but he said it was some girl. While all the boys were going on about that, I stood up from the sofa and stepped past Richard's chair and took the phone from his hand. Yelling into the phone that it was me while shaking my head to Rick's offer to turn down the music, I heard the girl say her name: Desiree. I asked her to hold on and she said she would. Handing the phone to Richard, I ran upstairs and lifted the receiver off that phone. When I heard her say she was still on the phone waiting, I asked her to hold on again. Leaving the upstairs phone off the hook, I ran downstairs and took the phone from Richard's hand and set it on the receiver. To the general disappointment of everyone in the living room, I ran back upstairs, picked up the phone and said, "Hi."

"That's better," Desiree said. "Are you surprised?"

"A little," I confirmed. "How'd you get this number?"

"Would it surprise you if I said I know how to spell your name and I looked you up in the campus phone book?" she asked, and I could see her smiling on the other end.

"Yeah, it would," I said, laughing, "since nobody can spell it right."

"So, how do you think I did it?"

I laughed again. "Don't know," I said. "Enlighten me."

She laughed. "I glanced at your homework and the quizzes and wrote your name in my notebook when you weren't looking," she said. When I didn't respond right away, she added, "So, I'm not a dumb blond like everyone thinks I am."

"I never said that," I remarked.

"But I'm not so dumb, am I?" she insisted.

"I don't think you're dumb at all," I replied. "I think you're pretty smart, though you may not show it outwardly, and I enjoy talking with you."

"So, did I surprise you by calling you?"

"Well, I wasn't expecting your call," I replied calmly. For some reason, I was finding it very easy to talk with Desiree. Normally, I would be nervous and anxious and my speech would be slow and stammering and self-conscious, but not with this girl. With her, *I* was different.

We talked for about a half-hour, about the party that never happened, about what it was like at the Big U, about her 'boyfriend,' Mark, about the boys at the boys home, and just anything that came up. She wasn't leaving town for the weekend, and she asked what we were doing the rest of the night. When I replied that we were going to sit around and listen to tunes and drink and smoke with some friends, both boys and girls, she asked if it was all right for her to come over and party, too. Sure.

Before we hung up, she wouldn't say she would or wouldn't come over. I was learning that about Desiree. It wasn't so much that she was noncommittal as it was her way of interaction with boys, or men. She liked suspense, the idea that she was unpredictable. She could be both forward and direct, while shy and reserved. I wanted her and I hoped she would come over.

Just before ten that night, we heard a loud knock at the front door, and Lance got up to see who it was. When he yelled my name and said there was somebody asking about me, I got up to go to the front door while the rest of the boys just looked at me with that natural male curiosity. That cute little blond girl stood on the porch and smiled, big and bright, when she saw me in the hall.

"I think we should let her in, bro," Lance advised.

"You better have a beer for me," she advised, still smiling comfortably.

As I stepped around Lance to hold the door open and motioned for her to come in, I said, "We've got beer and smoke and entertainment." I paused a moment and added, "And Lance. What else could anyone want?"

As she stepped in and passed me, she said, "And Lance is nice and polite, but I did come to see you."

I peeked at Lance with my eyebrows raised and he shook his head and mouthed, "Mmm." I didn't reply at all but just followed her into the living room and introduced everyone. Once that was done, I gently nudged her waist toward the kitchen to get us both beers. She admired the house and when we returned to the living room, some of the boys and she renewed old acquaintances. As we sat on the sofa close to each other, she whispered, "See, I told you I knew them and they knew me." When I turned to look in her eyes, she was already looking in mine and she wrapped her left arm around my right arm and leaned against me.

Except for trips to the kitchen for more beer or to the bathroom to drain it, we sat on that sofa close to each other for hours. It had turned a bit cooler that late September night, and she had worn a light jacket, which she immediately removed. Wearing jeans and a long sleeve blouse open to the top of those luscious mounds of her breasts, she was soft and sensual leaning against me. During a brief time when everyone left the living room and we were alone, her left hand, casually laying on my right leg, starting rubbing my thigh. I lifted my right arm over her head and placed it gently over her shoulders and pulled her closer, looking in her eyes and down to her mouth and admiring the fullness of her lips. When I looked up into her eyes again, her eyes were cast down, but she lifted her gaze and stared into my eyes unblinking. I leaned my head toward hers and pushed my lips against hers and she pushed back. I could feel her hand squeeze my thigh, and she lifted her arms and slipped them around my arms as we shifted our positions to be more directly opposite. As we moved our lips and mouths against each other, I could feel her mouth open slightly. I pushed my tongue between her lips and felt her tongue greet mine and, immediately, we moved our lips and mouths and tongues with more energy and passion and I could hear her soft sighing. Two of the boys returned to the living room and we separated and looked at each other. Unashamed and lacking of apology, our separation was the only acknowledgment of the others returning. Instead we just stared in the others' eyes, smiling and squeezing each other.

There were more moments like that until it was after midnight and she said it was getting late and she should go back to her dorm. I offered to have her stay for the night and she smiled, squeezed me, and said she couldn't do that tonight but maybe some other time soon. I believed her.

As I escorted her to the door and opened it and stepped onto the porch with her, she turned to me and slipped her arms onto my shoulders and I wrapped my arms around her waist and pulled her against me so hard I could feel her soft breasts flattening against my chest. Again, our mouths met and our tongues invaded the others' mouth and our heads twisted and turned and pushed for minutes. When we separated slightly, I offered to escort her back to the dorm. It was late and a woman shouldn't be out by herself that late. She would have none of that and soon she stepped off the porch and I watched her walk down the block, across the street to the campus and disappear behind the clutter of buildings in the distance.

The next two weeks, though, brought the return of the mysterious, unpredictable Desiree. She was civil, sometimes even sweet and bubbly, but usually she was detached, aloof, a little bit more than uncaring. Perhaps, that's a bit harsh, but that's how it seemed to me. I had no real clue what she was experiencing, feeling, and undergoing when she thought about me. We weren't really talking that much to each other and I only saw her before, during and immediately after our Marketing class.

I asked her out for dinner but she said no. The weekend after our make-out party, she went home, but her face contained a level of pain—when she told me she went home—that I hadn't seen before. The next weekend, she called again on Friday and we talked for a long time. She didn't want to come over that night but she said I'd probably see her that weekend.

The boys and I went to a party near the center of town. It was hard finding a parking spot, but we managed to land one a block away and walked to the house. There were kegs galore, lots of smoke, a private room where coke was lined up, plenty of tunes. What more could college kids ask for? Pussy, maybe?

Just when you think it can't get any better than this, what with all the attention I was receiving from some of the regular babes we all knew, in walks Desiree, and she's never more than a few feet away from me until we finally left the party close to three in the morning. A few times I would go outside for some air, to smoke a cigarette in peace, and she followed me outside and smoked a cigarette with me. She would wrap her arm around mine and squeeze me and look so innocently at me, waiting for me, wanting me. I would kiss her and she would kiss me back and we couldn't stop. I even went so far as to wrap my arms around her and slide them down her back, her waist, and over her blue-jeaned ass, when I would pull her tight against me. She didn't bother to stop me. Instead, she kissed me even more passionately.

She left before we did and that's when I considered the party over. I didn't lobby with effort to leave. I just asked if the hosts thought the party should be wrapped up. Soon, we all agreed that the hosts didn't, but that's because they were all going to bed soon with company and they couldn't care less if the party went on or not. Let's go and we went.

With school work moving toward midterms and my grades vastly improved from previous semesters, it was looking like a very good choice I had made to transfer. I liked the boys I lived with, there was plenty of excellent feminine sights to behold, and a cute little blond girl was playing cat and mouse with me and I liked it. I had a thing for blonds back then and she sure had the body to go with that long, straight blond hair. I was actually wondering what color her pubic hair would be. I sure wanted to know.

The weekend before midterms arrived and I had talked to Desiree after Friday's class, wondering what she was planning for the weekend. She was planning to go with Mark–she always called him 'a friend'–out of town, maybe to Kentucky. She loved that part of the country with all the horse farms, and woods, and small mountains. It was relaxing to be there. She asked what I was going to do and I told her that we were planning our pre-midterm party for Saturday and I was sorry that she would miss it. I really was hoping you'd come, I told her.

Friday night we started preparing for the party, ensuring that everybody knew what their piece was and could get it done the next morning and afternoon. Once we finished our planning meeting, it was time to party and we did, of course.

I thought about calling Desiree since I knew she wasn't leaving for Kentucky until the morning but I decided against it. I didn't want to appear desperate.

The next morning I was up and ready, well, ready after a couple cups of coffee and several cigarettes. After breakfast we all cleaned the first floor of the house and set up the entertainment, which was stored in Fu Manchu Steve's room. He and Susan had spent the night in his room, but they were already gone and he wasn't certain that they would even come to the party. As a gesture of solidarity, he offered his room to store the music gear so that we could keep the party guests from messing with it.

With the house now designated as 'clean'–we waited for General Steve to give it his blessing since he was the pickiest of us all about cleanliness–we broke into packs. Each pack was assigned a specific duty or duties: pick up the kegs, secure more smoke and prepare it, get some coke for us and 'special' friends, grab some food for a late afternoon cookout for us and a few invited guests. Rick, Eric and I were the members of the beer keg pack. We had already reserved three kegs, a tub, a tap and we were going to need ice and cups. We agreed that we get everything late in the afternoon and set up the first keg when we got back and store the other two kegs in the tub in the bathroom just off the dining room and next to Fu Manchu Steve's room. When it came time, while others were performing their duties and starting up the grill for our early dinner, we drove down in the muscle car to the liquor store in Bloomington and executed our plan to perfection. Upon our return, we had fresh keg beer for all in ten minutes. Rick and I took off for cups and ice and we were back in no time. We left the bags unopened on and around the kegs in the tub and covered them with towels. Our pack was done and it was time to eat, drink and be merry. Piece o' cake.

We had the tunes going early. We had to test it, the test was successful, so let's just leave it on. We stacked up the albums and that part was ready.

Some of the regular gang arrived early, some had dinner with us, some came for early beer, some even left with the promise that they would return, some brought smoke and coke, but the party was getting in gear. As it got into the evening, some of the boys were wondering if we overdid it. It was about eight and there were hardly any people who had come by yet. The first keg was going strong and some worried that we bought too many. Eric reminded everyone that if we didn't tap a keg we could return it for a full refund. That eased some people's minds. I thought, as did Rick, that too much beer in too many kegs was better than running out. That would hurt the attendance for our next party.

The worry was premature and unnecessary. Less than an hour later both sides of the street at the boys home were filled with cars and all the people who had ridden in those cars were packed in our house, though some people in our house had walked across campus. We were enjoying the obvious success of the party, which normally didn't hit this stride until after ten, when I heard somebody say something to me about a blond girl, and I turned to the hall leading to the front door and saw her. That cute little, full-bodied, blond girl with the fantastic bubble butt, Desiree, was standing at the end of the hall smashed on all sides by wall to wall people, looking around. I squeezed around people and she saw me and smiled. Shouting above the din of music, I asked her why she wasn't in Kentucky. She asked me if I was disappointed that she wasn't in Kentucky. I looked in her eyes and put my arms around her waist, leaned to her right ear and told her I was glad she was here and let's not talk about Kentucky any more. When I leaned back, she smiled, put her arms around my neck and gently pulled my head to hers and kissed me, long and hard.

I was by her side all night and it seemed that we were in constant contact the entire time. Because I had set my car closest to the road, when we were in need of more ice, I was the logical choice to go. Rick and Eric, going stag that night, discussed with me about working out some kind of arrangement using some guest's car, since Eric's car was blocked. With Desiree right beside me, her arm around mine, I asked her if she wanted to get ice with me and she said she would love to. All four of us piled into the muscle car and I weaved it out to the street, and we were back with plenty of ice in twenty minutes. Desiree liked the muscle car, even though I didn't show off its power.

With the night giving way to early Sunday morning, I could feel a longing for Desiree. I thought that she was feeling it, too. I could look in her eyes and see a calm appreciation and I could hear in her voice an expression of acceptance and satisfaction. I could listen to her giggle when I said or did something humorous, which was often. She had a great sense of humor and I loved her giggle. I loved that almost lilting tone in her voice and the way she moved her arms and hands around and over my body, whether we were standing or sitting. We were touching each other frequently, kissing each other passionately when the opportunity arose.

As the party was winding down and it was well after two in the morning I was beginning to feel a little fatigued. I had drunk a lot of beer, smoked a lot of cannabis, but I wasn't out of it. I was just tired. I knew why I wasn't out of it, though. That cute little blond girl by my side the entire night kept my spirit up, my senses tuned, my attitude crisp and clear. I knew that the die-hards would go on partying until possibly daylight, but I was not about to do that. I gazed into those big hazel eyes and asked Desiree if she was as tired as I was.

"I'll walk you back to your dorm," I said, "or even drive you back if you want."

"Are you ready to go to bed?" she asked, staring back, her eyes moving all over my face.

"Yes, I'm kind of tired," I replied. "Of course, you can stay with me. I'd love to have you stay with me."

Her expression was calm and she smiled a bit as she said, "I don't want to go back to the dorm. I want to stay here with you." Her arm slipped out from my arm and around my back and she nudged my back. I put my arms around her waist and pulled her to me and kissed her passionately and she kissed me back with equal passion. Soon, I had slipped my hands over that fantastic butt and squeezed her hips hard against mine. She broke away, looking up into my eyes, and whispered, "Let's go up to your room now."

Knowing the rules, I had to break from Desiree and find Brad the Red. When I located him outside, I quickly came up to his side and said, "I need the room, Brad."

"Okay," he replied, calmly. "I'll go up and get some stuff right now and it's yours."

I walked with him back into the house but told him I would wait for him downstairs. He went up to the room and grabbed a sleeping bag and articles like toothpaste, toothbrush, shampoo, etc. He took all of that down the hall and the stairs at the front of the house and set it in Brad the ladies' man's room. When he came into the living room, while Desiree and I were embraced, he announced that he had everything he needed and the room was mine. We waited for him to leave the room, and we kissed for a long time. We were alone in the house and time didn't seem to matter. I felt no anxiety, no sense that I must hurry. That time did not matter and I felt absolutely no anxiety were both due to one continuing aspect of the entire evening: Desiree was constantly and continuously at my side, in unbroken contact. When our bodies finally leaned apart, with our hands still touching the other, and I looked into her beautiful, big eyes, her eyelids narrowed seriously. I heard her whisper, "Let's go upstairs."